VALKYRIE'S DAUGHTER

BOOK THREE OF THE LUNAR FREE STATE

John E. Siers

Theogony Books
Coinjock, NC

Copyright © 2021 by John E. Siers.

All rights reserved. No part of this publication may be reproduced, distributed or transmitted in any form or by any means, including photocopying, recording, or other electronic or mechanical methods, without the prior written permission of the publisher, except in the case of brief quotations embodied in critical reviews and certain other noncommercial uses permitted by copyright law. For permission requests, write to the publisher, addressed "Attention: Permissions Coordinator," at the address below.

Chris Kennedy/Theogony Books
1097 Waterlily Rd.
Coinjock, NC 27923
https://chriskennedypublishing.com/

Publisher's Note: This is a work of fiction. Names, characters, places, and incidents are a product of the author's imagination. Locales and public names are sometimes used for atmospheric purposes. Any resemblance to actual people, living or dead, or to businesses, companies, events, institutions, or locales is completely coincidental.

Cover Design by Shezaad Sudar.

Ordering Information:
Quantity sales. Special discounts are available on quantity purchases by corporations, associations, and others. For details, contact the "Special Sales Department" at the address above.

Valkyrie's Daughter/John E. Siers -- 1st ed.
ISBN: 978-1648552311

To physicist Lisa Randall, whose well-written books got me really thinking about the nature of that mysterious force we know as gravity and inspired me to name a starship after her.

Prologue

"The first years of the Lunar Free State were a wild ride for all of us 'original' citizens. One day, I was just an engineer, happy to be working on the design and construction of experimental spacecraft for the Deep Space Research Institute, and the next day—or so it seemed—I was a project manager building a city on the Moon. One day, I was just 'Hey, Mick' to everyone who knew me, and the next I was the commander, and those same people were saluting as they passed me in the corridors.

"The idea of a paramilitary society was the brainchild of Ian Stevens, though I suspect he got some help refining the concept from the two military veterans on his staff, Charlie Bender and Lorna Greenwood. It seemed—even to me—to be a crazy idea at the time, but I was willing to live with it and try to make it work. After all, a lot of other crazy ideas such as gravity-powered spacecraft and cities on the Moon had worked for us. I've never thought of myself as a social engineer, but I figured that if anyone could pull it off, Ian was the man. So, I put on the uniform, returned the salutes, and tried my best to act military.

"It wasn't difficult because my basic job hadn't changed. I was still an engineer, and my military mission included the same tasks I'd always done—identify needs, come up with engineering solutions, build them, test them, and put them to use. After a while, the salutes and military courtesies became automatic, and the uniform started to feel comfortable, like an old pair of jeans.

"There were some tough times, when supplies were running short, everybody on Earth wanted our heads on a platter, and people were throwing nuclear weapons at us. That's when I really started to appreciate the advantages of living in a structured society. We all had a common mission—to survive and to continue to build a nation—and we all shared equally in the benefits and the adversity. More importantly, we all had our orders, we knew what was expected of us, and we buckled down and did our jobs. There was never a question about who oversaw what, who worked for whom, or what needed to be done. We were brothers in arms, and we trusted each other with our lives. We were proud of who we were—the underdogs, a few hundred people standing firm against a few billion enemies. I guess it was sometime during that period that I finally came to understand the meaning of *esprit de corps*.

"Through all of that and the years that followed, I was still an engineer. I don't think I've ever stopped being an engineer, but somewhere along the line, things started happening that forced me out of my quiet little engineering world and onto the center stage, a place I never expected to be.

"It didn't happen overnight. I gradually shifted from being the guy who was expected to come up with clever solutions to new problems to being the guy who was expected to keep everything we'd already built running smoothly. That was OK, because we'd built well, and running smoothly was the norm. I still had time to get involved in new projects, but mostly, my involvement was limited to looking over the shoulder of some bright, young—younger than me, at least—engineer I had assigned to the project.

"I noticed those funny little uniform accessories on my collar and shoulders were getting heavier. People weren't calling me commander anymore, they were now calling me admiral, but my command was still the Corps of Engineers, and I expected that would always be the case.

"And then, overnight, everything changed with the arrival of the alien Mekota and the untimely death of Ian Stevens. Ian had not only been our leader for as long as the Lunar Free State had been in existence, but he was also my friend and my immediate superior officer. The shock of his death was followed by another shock—the realization that some people wanted me to take his place. I can't describe the relief I felt when various constitutional issues were sorted out, leaving Lorna Greenwood as our acting CEO. I supported Lorna and led the charge in the Directorate to confirm her in the position permanently.

"It wasn't just my desire to avoid the job that made me support her. We had made First Contact with a hostile alien race. They had killed our beloved leader and seemed bent on conquest, perhaps even on our destruction. We were involved in an interstellar war, and I believed we needed a warrior to lead us. Lorna Greenwood was a warrior, perhaps the finest warrior the LFS has ever produced.

"I think she did a fine job as CEO, despite criticism from various sectors and her own misgivings about her performance. I only found one occasion to fault her—when she decided to resign as CEO. She had her reasons, and I agreed with those reasons, but I thought she exercised terrible judgment in choosing me to succeed her.

"After her graceful exit from the CEO's position, Lorna went back to what she did best—commanding the Lunar Fleet. I relied heavily on her and Charlie Bender, who served as our foreign minister for many years. Despite his insistence that he was not a diplomat, Charlie put together the alliance with the alien Akara which endures to this day. Once that alliance was forged, Lorna combined the forces of Luna with those of the Akara Copper Hills Clan and gave the Mekota a thrashing that got the attention of just about everyone in this corner of the galaxy.

"There are, as we found out later, a lot of nasty characters out there, but everyone was afraid of the Mekota until we, with the help of our newfound Lizard friends, turned their fleet into scrap metal and sent them running back to their homeworld. As it turns out, that got us respect from people we didn't even know existed and made the whole neighborhood a lot more peaceful. It was Theodore Roosevelt who coined the phrase, 'Speak softly and carry a big stick,' and I guess that pretty much defined our interstellar policy from that point forward."

Excerpt from *The Reluctant Admiral:*
The Memoirs of Michael O'Hara
Third CEO of the Lunar Free State

* * * * *

Chapter One

Valhalla—Lorna Greenwood's Estate

White Peaks Province—Planet Copper Hills Prime

"Calling Doctor Carla...hello..."

Dr. Carla Greenwood, Ph.D., Fellow of the Lunar Research Institute, Nobel Laureate, and Director of the LRI's Astrophysics Division looked up from the screen in front of her and said the most intelligent thing she could think of.

"Huh?"

"You've had your nose against that screen almost constantly since you got here," Lorna told her. "You're supposed to be on vacation."

"Look who's talking!" Carla snorted. "You've had three solid days of meetings with the Akara High Command. You're supposed to be on vacation, too, Mom."

"I am, and thanks to those meetings, my precious leave time didn't start until today. If I'm not mistaken, you are scheduled to lecture before colleagues at the Copper Hills Astrophysical Institute next week—which gives you the same sort of excuse for extra time away from the LRI. Meanwhile, you're here to relax. So, kick back, take a deep breath, and enjoy the sunset. You won't see one like this back in the Sol System."

"Of course, you won't," Carla admitted. "Alpha Akara has a totally different spectrum than Sol—much more in the blue range, which tints everything a lovely shade of violet. OK, it's beautiful. I've seen it, but I really need to stay with this stuff. It could be the most important piece of research in my field that's been done in the last century."

"You mean, the most important piece of research that's been done by someone other than my daughter?"

Carla glanced sharply at her mother, but Lorna's obvious glow of pride made it impossible to take offense. Instead, she found herself smiling in return.

"There are other people doing meaningful research out there," she replied. "Not everyone in the known universe thinks I'm the most brilliant scientist alive. You may be a bit biased."

"Hey, the Nobel Prize Committee agreed with me." Lorna shrugged. "But OK, tell me, what's so special about this piece of research?"

"If Takahashi is correct—and so far, I can't find a flaw in his work—we are stuck in this universe." Carla gestured at the screen. "There may be a thousand, or a million, or a billion other universes out there, but we'll never see them."

"I should be concerned about this because…"

"Well, at this point, it's only of interest to theoretical physicists," Carla conceded. "Bubble theory predicted other universes existed over half a century ago, but we've never been able to figure out how to prove their existence. If this work is correct, we never will. We thought hyperspace was the key. Twenty years ago, everybody knew you couldn't exceed the speed of light. Einstein told us that, and, except for a few cases involving weird subatomic particles, he was right—in normal space. It wasn't until we figured out that normal space wasn't the only space available that we managed to find the way into hyperspace and discovered that general and special relativity don't work the same way there. That gave us a lot of new avenues to explore, but now, Takahashi is telling us that hyperspace—our hyperspace—is part of our universe. It's not a gateway to anywhere else and, in fact, according to the work he's done, no such gateway between universes can possibly exist."

"I'm devastated…" Lorna looked at her in mock horror. "We're stuck here! In another few million years, we will have explored the whole galaxy and then we'll only have a few billion galaxies left. I feel claustrophobic already, like Alexander the Great, who went to the sea and wept because he had no more lands to conquer."

She hung her head and wiped an imaginary tear from her eye.

"There's no evidence Alexander actually said that," Carla protested. "It's a twentieth-century myth."

"Well, if he didn't, he should have," Lorna retorted. "And I'm sure he would have, if he had ever met this Takahashi person."

Despite herself, Carla began to giggle—she hated when she did that because it sounded so immature—but she couldn't help herself. Once again, her mother had proven to her the folly of taking oneself too seriously.

"You win, Mom," she said. "I guess it can wait. It took us nearly a century to figure out how to get around Einstein. It's probably arrogant of me to think I can get around Takahashi in a few days." She touched an icon to save her notes, closed the interface, and pushed back from the desk.

"If anyone can do it, you can, honey," Lorna assured her, "but the brain works better if you relax occasionally. Neither you nor I get a chance like this very often." She waved a hand toward the windows and the stunning view of the mountains, the valley below, and the strange and beautiful colors of the sunset.

"You're right," Carla admitted. "And it's even less often we get a chance to do it together. I'm sorry I haven't made more time to see you lately, Mom. I guess I'm not much of a daughter."

"Oh no, honey, you're not the one who needs to be sorry. I'm the one who's been off playing space ranger all these years. I should have spent more time with you when you were growing up."

"Stop it, Mom! I am proud of you and everything you did. You were my role model," Carla insisted.

"Right..." Lorna gave her a wry grin. "That's why you became a scientist instead of joining the Fleet. Some role model."

"You were the best at what you did, and since I couldn't hope to be as good as you, I decided to be the best at something else...and here I am." She flashed a charming smile that took Lorna back more than a decade to the image of the brash, but already brilliant, girl Carla had been in her teenage years.

"You turned out fine, honey." Lorna regarded her daughter with pride. "And now, as you say, here we are. We've got an evening together to catch up on things. Tomorrow, Heart of the Warriors is coming here; I know he's one of your favorite people, 'Egg of the Queen.'"

Carla grimaced as she remembered the nickname the Akaran Fleet Admiral had bestowed upon her. But her mother was right. Heart was one of her favorite people—a reptilian uncle of sorts when she was growing up.

"And the following day," her mother continued, "we're going hunting for near-dragons along the western range. Heart says he knows an area where there are some real trophy-class giants. Want to come along?"

Carla shook her head. "The only hunting I like to do is with a holocam, and I prefer to do that with creatures that aren't likely to eat me if I get too close. Bring back some near-dragon steaks, and I'll enjoy them, but stalking something that close to the top of this planet's food chain is not my idea of relaxation."

"Actually, that's part of the reason we're going," Lorna told her. "Since the Akara imported Terran beef cattle ten years ago, the near-dragons have discovered a new food source. They've been raiding the ranchlands in the valley and doing a lot of damage to the herds. In the past year, they've even taken a couple of Akara ranch hands who got careless. The ranchers petitioned the ruling council, so Heart of the Clan declared an extended hunting season in this province. I don't think it will do much to thin out the near-dragon population, but it might teach them to stay away from the Akara and their livestock. Sure you don't want to come along?"

"No, thanks; I'd rather not be remembered as an off-world tourist with a camera who got careless like one of those ranch hands." Carla gave her mother a wry grin. "Not that any near-dragon would dare to mess with my mom, but you won't enjoy it as much if you have to watch out for me. I'll stay here and play with Takahashi's theory."

"Suit yourself, but you don't know what you're missing," Lorna told her.

"You really love it here, don't you?" Carla observed. "All this..." She waved her hand around to take in the lodge with its luxurious accommodations, the beautiful mountain scenery around it, and the hundred-thousand-hectare estate the grateful Akara had given Lorna after the Lunar Fleet, under her command, had saved their homeworld in the Battle of Copper Hills Prime. Most of the estate was high in the mountains, which meant its climate was far more pleasant for humans than the hot, humid lowlands below. The Akara, on the other hand, with their reptilian metabolism, liked hot, humid places. They regarded those of their kind who lived up here as strange, eccentric, and a little bit crazy. Lorna likened them to humans on Earth who chose to live in Alaska.

"Yes, I do love it, honey. For the last few decades, I've spent most of my time in a sealed environment on Luna or aboard ships of the Fleet, but, unlike you—and most of your generation in the LFS—I was born on Earth and grew up there. I love being under the open sky. I could spend all day watching thunderstorms move across the valley, hiking the mountain trails, or hunting near-dragons. I think about retirement all the time, and how much I'll enjoy it here after that.

"Don't get me wrong," she continued. "I love Luna, and I love the Fleet, but I've been there and done that long enough. It's time for the younger generation—your generation—to step up and take over."

"You're not that old," Carla snorted. "With the longevity treatments, you'll be in your prime for many more years. Besides, Uncle Mick is older than you, and he's not talking about retirement yet."

"Mick O'Hara would go crazy if he didn't have interstellar problems to solve and titanic projects to work on every day. The LFS is his drawing board, his laboratory, his proving ground, and he's done more to advance us as a nation than anyone could have expected in such a short time. Lord knows, he's been a far better chief executive than I ever was. My most significant achievement as CEO was to arrange for him to take over as my successor, and you are right—fortunately for the Lunar Free State and its citizens—he's not thinking of retiring any time soon.

"And neither am I, for that matter," she admitted, "at least not for a few more years. I have this occasional daydream about it, mostly when I take some leave time and come out here. I have pretty much decided this is where I want to spend my retirement. I just haven't figured out when that will happen, yet.

"As for the longevity treatments, your generation will benefit from them a lot more than mine. I may live to be 150, but you may live two centuries or more because you started the treatments so much younger."

"Well, there you go." Carla grinned at her. "You've still got what...110 years to go?"

"Flattery will not score points with your mother, young lady, especially since you know better than that. I was fifty-five when I gave birth to you, and that was about three decades ago, in case you haven't been counting birthdays."

"You still look more like forty-five, Mom, and a very good-looking forty-five at that. Back on Luna, everyone knows you, but I'll bet if you went to one of those Caribbean resorts on Earth, you'd have to fend off the young men with a spear."

"I have little or no interest in young men, my dear, except when they show an interest in my daughter...especially if that interest appears to be reciprocal. Care to tell me about this young physicist from North American University in Arizona I've been hearing about?"

Carla looked stunned.

"Mom! How did you…" She shook her head in disgust. "Oh, never mind. I should have guessed. You've got half the LFS Intelligence Service keeping an eye on me."

"No, only a couple of agents—" Lorna gave her a wicked grin, "—plus some people from the Diplomatic Corps. You have been spending a good bit of time on Earth lately, and, to a lot of people—especially Charlie Bender—you are a precious natural resource of the LFS."

"Arrrrgghhh…not Uncle Charlie! By now, he probably knows what brand of toothpaste Bjorn uses. He probably knows more about him than I do, and that's not fair! Did you have to drag him into this?"

"No," Lorna replied, "I didn't. In fact, it was Charlie who brought it to *my* attention, which left me at a loss since you'd never mentioned your boyfriend to me. Carla, please understand, from Charlie's point of view, you are a national resource. You have knowledge in your head that is top secret—refinements of our understanding of gravity that have led to major enhancements in our warship drive systems, to name just one item. I know you're sworn to secrecy, and you wouldn't violate your oath, but you should have realized Lunar Intelligence and SID would get a little concerned when you started getting intimate with someone who isn't an LFS citizen."

"Intimate? *Intimate?*" Carla screamed. "Exactly how much interest has Admiral Bender shown in me? Are there cameras in the bedroom in my condo in Phoenix? Does he have a log of Bjorn's comings and goings?"

"No, Carla, he doesn't," Lorna insisted. "At least not that he's shown me. Camera surveillance would be an unconstitutional violation of your privacy as a Lunar citizen, and Charlie respects the law. As much as you may revile him for it, he cares about you and has your best interests at heart.

"I know what you're feeling," she added. "I felt the same way, with all of the security he wanted to put around me after those bastards tried to kill me during my term as CEO. That was before you were born, but Charlie's always been there to watch my back when I needed it, and he'll do the same for you. Besides, he approves of this Bjorn of yours—says he's a nice young man and not much of a security risk. For Charlie, that's as close to high praise as you'll get. More importantly, it's all I have to go on since you haven't told me anything. If you're serious about the guy, I'd really like to know more, but I'd like to hear it from you, not from Charlie."

"I'm not that serious about him," Carla insisted, her anger softening in the face of Lorna's calm, reasonable tone. "He's just a nice guy, and we seem to get along really well. We enjoy each other's company, and, just for the record, we rarely talk about our work. Truth is, we're as far apart in our work as we can be, considering we both call ourselves physicists. I'm an astrophysicist, a cosmologist, way out there on the macro end of things. If it's smaller than a planet, I'm not interested. I spend my time studying anomalies in gravity wells around supergiant stars. Bjorn's a particle physicist, at the opposite end of the scale. If it's bigger than a nanometer in size, he's not interested. He deals in quantum energy transfers at subatomic levels.

"I mean, we can understand each other." She shrugged. "I know the basics of his field, and he knows the basics of mine, but our views of the universe are quite different. On the other hand, we share a common love of pizza and a dislike of pretentious sushi restaurants, and we both like a quiet evening with a glass of wine and soft music. Oh yeah, and since he's never been off Earth, he seems fascinated by my tales of what it's really like out here. I know he would have loved watching this sunset."

As she spoke, Carla's voice grew wistful. Watching and listening to her, Lorna felt a pang of regret. *My little girl's grown up,* she thought, then she realized Carla had grown up over a decade ago, when she'd first gotten her advanced degrees and set out to make her mark in the world of science. *And now, it looks like she'll be sharing her life with someone else. But you knew that would happen someday.* Carla might have said her relationship was not that serious, but Lorna knew the signs. Her daughter was in love.

"Well, honey—" she forced herself to smile, "—why don't you invite him out here the next time both of you can squeeze in an extended vacation? You can certainly afford passage to Copper Hills Prime, and this place is as nice as any resort on the planet. Great food, romantic views..."

"I'd like to, Mom, but you're not here very often."

"I don't need to be, honey. Let the staff know you're coming, and they'll have everything ready. They keep the place in shape all year round. It's their full-time occupation, whether I'm here or not."

Carla knew it was true. The staff her mother mentioned consisted of the entire village of Akara, which was located on the estate. The villagers cared for the property and worked the land for their own benefit. Under Akara social structure, they formed a sub-clan that owed their allegiance to Lorna, as their feudal lord—or lady, in her case. Nonetheless, Lorna paid them well for whatever work they did around the lodge, including grounds maintenance, cooking, cleaning, and such.

They, in turn, provided her with anything she required in the way of farm produce. The reptilian Akara were pure carnivores, so most of the crops they grew were intended as feed for the meat animals they raised, including Terran cattle, but they also grew spices and tended a small garden of Terran and local vegetables specifically for Lorna's table. They also gathered wild fruits and berries and hunted an assortment of wild game.

In exchange for keeping her pantry stocked and performing whatever other services she required, Lorna allowed them to live rent-free on her land and keep whatever profits their labors brought them, without tax or tribute. They were fiercely loyal to her and considered themselves well-off compared to the subjects of other Akaran nobles, who would have taxed them for such privileges. It was understood that anyone among them who didn't love and respect the Great Warrior Queen of the Humans was welcome to go live somewhere else.

"Look, honey," Lorna continued. "I really would like to meet this Bjorn of yours, but you're an adult. You stopped needing my permission for anything a long time ago, and I want you to be happy. If bringing him up here will do that, don't wait until you can work it into my schedule because you may be waiting a long time.

"Or you might consider something shorter," she suggested. "It's less than an hour's flight from Phoenix to Lunaport, and a couple of hours from there to TerraNova—especially for an important member of the Lunar Research Institute who's entitled to hitch a ride on an express courier ship. If your guy has never been off Earth, you might want to show him Luna first. Since he is a physicist, you could introduce him to some people at the LRI, and you could time it for a period when I'm at home in TerraNova—which is a lot more often than I'm here. You can manage that kind of trip over a weekend, though a few extra days on Luna wouldn't hurt."

"Mom!" Carla looked at her in amazement. "That's a wonderful idea. I'm sure Bjorn will love it! I don't know why I never thought of it."

"Love and war have a lot in common, daughter," Lorna replied with a conspiratorial smile, "and I'm the best military strategist in this corner of the galaxy."

* * *

"Most people who hunt near-dragons do so with a more potent weapon," Heart of the Warriors remarked, "usually something that can blast one out of the sky at, say, two hundred meters or more."

As he spoke, the old Lizard war leader gave Lorna a chop-licking flicker of the tongue she had learned to interpret as an amused grin.

She regarded him with a raised eyebrow. "I notice you are not one of those people." She looked pointedly at the long assegai spear he was toting, along with the quiver of sling-launched javelins he wore over his shoulder.

"Ah, yes, but then I've been doing this for a long time, whereas this is your first. When I saw what you brought to the hunt, I feared you had seriously underestimated the beasts, but it appears I was wrong." He bent down and grasped one of the spiral horns of the fallen near-dragon. With an effort, he lifted its head, revealing the rows of wickedly curved teeth that filled its mouth.

"It may be my first near-dragon," Lorna told him, "but it's not my first hunt, nor is it the first time I've put an arrow into a dangerous game animal.

"I'll admit," she conceded, "the idea of hunting a predator that can fly did give me pause, but when I looked at the video you provided, I realized these creatures don't fly so much as glide. They need a running start or a high cliff to take off from. They gain altitude slowly and spend most of their time riding wind currents, looking for prey on the ground. They brake almost to a hover when landing. Flight allows them to locate and get close to their prey, but they usually stalk and attack on the ground."

"Very observant." The old Akara nodded, a gesture he had learned from his many dealings with humans. "But sometimes, a wounded near-dragon will charge its attacker. That's the reason for this." He brandished the assegai. "In case the javelin doesn't do the job, and the near-dragon decides to make a meal of you."

"I considered that," Lorna replied, "so I brought a backup weapon." She showed him the antique pistol holstered on her hip—a Desert Eagle chambered in .50 Action Express. She had used it once back on Earth to take down a rogue male lion that had attacked her hunting party without warning.

"Fortunately," she observed, "neither your spear nor my gun was necessary this time."

"Indeed." He favored her with another chop-licking grin. "I was impressed when I saw your arrow fly true, Warrior Queen, but even more so when I saw it go completely through the beast. I am compelled to inquire further about this unusual weapon of yours. The People developed the concept of a bow and arrow centuries ago, but when we developed firearms, bows fell out of use. I don't think ours were ever as sophisticated as yours, and no Akara bow could propel an arrow with such speed and accuracy."

"We call it a compound bow," she told him, "because the wheels around which the string runs multiply the mechanical advantage, like pulleys. This bow requires about twenty-seven kilos of force to draw back, but when the upper and lower cams roll over at the end of the draw, it only requires about five kilos to hold it in place. That makes it much easier to hold at full draw while I take aim.

"Of course, the arrow is still subject to the force of gravity. The sight has a built-in laser rangefinder that determines the distance to the target and adjusts the aiming reticle to allow for arrow drop. When I first brought the bow from the Sol System, it was calibrated for Earth's gravity. I had to make a small adjustment for the slightly lighter gravity here. Accuracy isn't hard to achieve with a sighting system like this and a bit of practice.

"The arrows are woven carbon fiber and fly true to about eighty meters. These broadhead points are razor sharp, and the arrow passes easily through most game animals. Near-dragons have tough skin, but it's no tougher than that of some Earth animals I've hunted. Some arrowheads have expanding points that cause more internal injury, but these give better penetration."

The old Akara lowered the near-dragon's head to the ground and stepped back to look at the whole beast—nearly four meters from snout to tail tip, with a nearly six-meter wingspan.

"A fine kill," he told her. "You've introduced something entirely new to the hunting sports of this world, Warrior Queen. I imagine someone could make a lucrative business of selling such bows to Akara hunters. That presumes, of course, they could be sized down to Akara dimensions, without losing significant power."

"I'm sure they can." She looked thoughtful. "Akara are shorter than humans, which means you'd need a bow with a short riser and flat limb angle. Your people have long arms for their height, so draw length wouldn't be an issue. You also have sufficient strength to pull the draw weights required for effective hunting—twenty to thirty kilos. It's possible there are bows already available on Earth that would work quite well here. They'd have to be left-handed models, but those are available as well, since a significant number of human hunters are left-handed, like your people."

She shook herself out of her reverie. "Anyway, that's something I need to mention to Carla. She's the businesswoman in the family and is already worth a lot more money than I am, largely thanks to this device." She pointed at the little electronic package clipped to the front of her hunting vest.

"Ah, yes." Heart nodded again. "The Gadget—without which we wouldn't be having this conversation. I had forgotten my dear little Egg of the Queen was its inventor."

The Gadget, Carla's original name for her creation, was officially known as the AHSI device, the Akara-Human Speech Interface device, and had started out as a project Carla—then just 15 years old—had built for a Lunar science competition. Prior to that, the only way the Akara and their human allies could converse was by using special sound equipment controlled by an artificial intelligence—or AI—to translate. It was assumed any other method of audio communication was impossible, since human vocal cords could not reproduce Akara speech, much of which was beyond the high frequency end of human hearing. In addition, the Akara could not speak or hear most of the low frequency sounds of human speech, though they could taste such sounds through their vibration sensitive tongues.

For more than a dozen years after the Akara of the Copper Hills and the Lunar Free State joined forces, the LFS Fleet contingent at

Copper Hills Prime had included a battlecruiser equipped with an AI that served as a communication hub for any humans on the planet who needed to talk directly to the Akara.

Akara who visited Luna could avail themselves of Mike, the Lunar AI-in-residence, but those who wanted to go to Earth for business or diplomatic reasons had to equip themselves with a computer interface with a translation program that could convert the written Akara language into written English, and vice versa, and spend time writing notes to their human counterparts. Since the Akara written language was phonetic, such notes were easily translated into electronic format, but the process was still somewhat cumbersome. The best alternative was a sign language that heavily limited what could be conveyed. The same limitations applied to humans who ventured out of the Copper Hills capital, away from the communications network served by the battlecruiser's AI.

Over the years, attempts were made to create computer-based translation programs, but it was generally agreed that none of them did justice to either language. To communicate complex concepts or abstract thoughts and feelings accurately and efficiently, an AI was required.

That was the accepted thinking until precocious, teenage Carla dared to question the basic premise that humans and Akara could not speak each other's languages. With the help of Mike, the only native speaker of the Akara language she could find, Carla determined the problem was simply a matter of sound frequency and range. She put together a simple electronic device that shifted the sounds of Akara speech down to a lower range that humans could hear and compressed them into a smaller range of frequencies that humans could reproduce. She dubbed the resulting output Low

Akara and, with Mike's help, taught herself how to understand and speak it.

Then she added additional electronics that would shift Low Akara back up to the frequency and range of normal Akara speech. Based on Mike's judgment that the results should be understandable to a native Akara speaker, she entered The Gadget into the science competition. There, she demonstrated to the judges that not only could a human learn to speak Low Akara, but that the Akara could also learn a high frequency form of English, which The Gadget could convert into understandable human speech.

She won top honors in the competition, and the marketing people from Terra Corporation, the commercial arm of the Lunar Free State, immediately contacted her, wanting the rights to manufacture and sell the device. With advice from Uncle Mick O'Hara, CEO of the LFS, Carla formed a Lunar-chartered corporation to handle the business implications of her invention. She cut a deal that guaranteed she would not have to work for the rest of her life, but that was OK, because she intended to devote herself to scientific research anyway. Now, fifteen years later, she was doing just that, but her corporation was still in business, and royalties from The Gadget were still coming in.

Thanks to her own study of Low Akara, Lorna was able to communicate easily with the Akara on her estate, and occasionally, as she was doing now, converse in English with an Akara who knew the high version of the official language of the Lunar Free State. Heart spoke it fluently, to the point where his words came out of the Gadget with hardly a trace of accent.

Lorna made a mental note to pass Heart's remarks on to Carla. Bow-and-arrow technology was a little out of the corporation's usual line, but she was pretty sure Carla's marketing department would jump at the opportunity to bring more Earth products to Copper Hills Prime and other Akara worlds.

She looked down at the near-dragon at her feet. It was an impressive and beautiful creature, and she thought about how its head would look mounted on a wall in the main lodge. That, however, would require careful preparation and shipment back to Earth since taxidermy was another art the Akara hadn't pursued.

* * *

Heart of the Warriors sliced off a shred of the steak on his platter and held it out to Dusty, Lorna's tan tabby cat. Dusty reared up on his hind legs and snatched the morsel, which he devoured in an instant.

Cats were the most common pet among Lunar citizens, as they were more adaptable to life in a sealed environment than dogs. Dusty had been born on Luna but was still a kitten when Lorna brought him to Copper Hills Prime. He was now a permanent resident on the estate, where the house staff spoiled him at every opportunity. Most Akara took an instant liking to Terran cats, and Heart was no exception.

Lorna had been watching Heart feed the appreciative feline, but now she paused with the wine glass halfway to her lips as the impact of his last remark, delivered in a perfectly matter-of-fact tone, sunk in.

"I must have misheard you. Would you say that again, please?"

Carla had also stopped what she was doing—slicing a bit of the excellent sirloin on her own plate—and looked at the Akara. She wasn't as attuned to interstellar politics as her mother, but she understood the significance of Heart's remark.

Heart seemed unaware of their reaction. He sliced off another large chunk of his steak and bit into it with obvious relish. He swallowed the nearly raw mouthful quickly. Akara teeth, like cat's teeth, were suitable for seizing, holding, and tearing prey, not for chewing.

"Delicious!" he declared. "Terran beef is one of the better products you have brought to our world, and it's perfectly prepared. My compliments to your chef."

"Heart..." Lorna said carefully.

"I said, Warrior Queen," he replied, "that we have recently discovered another human civilization, albeit a primitive one. I thought you might be interested to know of this."

"Of course I'm interested, but I'm even more interested to know why you mentioned it. In the years since we've met, that's been a taboo subject between our people and yours. We've asked you many times about these other humans you alluded to when we first met, but all we get are vague and evasive answers. You usually tell us it's a legend or something you've heard from other spacefaring races and then you change the subject. What's different?"

"Officially," he told her, "it's still a taboo subject, as you say. And that is why you are hearing about it here, at a private dinner on your own estate, rather than in an official meeting in the Capital. It's also why you, a well-respected person in our eyes, with no official diplomatic standing, are hearing it from me, a retired old warrior who also has no official standing.

"You must understand, Warrior Queen, the Mekota are not the only race that is fearful of humans. There is a tacit agreement among spacefaring races—including all the clans of The People—that we do not give or trade advanced technology to humans. Further, we do not tell humans about the existence of other humans on other worlds.

"In your case, the first rule is moot since your technology is superior to ours in many ways. We did violate the second rule when we needed your help against the Mekota—it was what you might call a teaser to get your interest. But we were fighting for survival and needed every bit of persuasion at our disposal to secure an alliance with you. Since then, the Hearts of the Combined Clans have prevailed upon the Heart of the Copper Hills to revert to the original policy of non-disclosure."

Lorna nodded in understanding. The People, as the Akara called themselves, were a loose collection of clans, scattered over many star systems that ran like a string of beads along the Akara frontier. Humans of Earth had made contact with several of these clans for commercial purposes, but the Copper Hills Clan was the only one with whom the nations of Earth had full diplomatic relations and, in the case of the Lunar Free State, a mutual defense treaty. Its homeworld, where Lorna's estate was located, was just under sixty light-years from the Sol system.

"There is concern that, if ever the clans of humans unite," Heart continued, "they will dominate the galaxy, and that concern was reinforced by the apparent ease with which you smashed the Mekota and sent them reeling back to their homeworlds. You reduced a vast empire to a fraction of its former size in an incredibly short time."

"*We* smashed the Mekota," she insisted. "Your people and mine. It is doubtful either of us could have done so without the other."

"True enough, and we of the Copper Hills are grateful for your help on that occasion. Personally, I think the concerns about humans are unfounded. I've found you to be an honorable people and the best comrades one could hope for in time of war, but I don't make policy for the Combined Clans, nor for any of our allies."

He lapsed into a brooding silence, which Lorna allowed to continue for a moment. Then she spoke up again.

"I repeat, what's changed?"

"There is mutual interest," he replied. "The human civilization in question lies in the domain of the Otuka, a race you haven't met, but one that has proven troublesome for us. They're not invaders, not conquerors like the Mekota. They're simply a lawless rabble whose concept of civilization involves piracy and other predatory acts committed on those weaker than themselves. They don't dare engage our military forces in a stand-up battle; barring extreme numerical advantage on their side, we could easily wipe them out. But they prey on commercial shipping and have been known to pillage trade outposts and frontier settlements. They've been getting bolder of late, and, sooner or later, your people will encounter them. They've been moving closer to your shipping lanes, and it's only a matter of time before some of your commercial ships will fall victim to them.

"In truth, the Combined Clans would prefer that we not discuss the Otuka with you. Some of The People practice appeasement, paying tribute to the creatures to allow safe passage of trading ships. Others, like my clan, send warships to escort shipping vessels through their space but do not actively seek confrontation. Many believe we should leave that situation as it is, lest the Otuka become even more troublesome than they already are. We have no desire to see them united against us any more than we want to see humans unite. In any case, you will most likely find out about the Otuka when you start losing ships to their piracy, but if you then act against them, they will not hold The People responsible."

"I see." Lorna looked a bit puzzled. "But obviously, Heart of the Copper Hills does not agree. What you've just told me would be sufficient to get our attention and our help in dealing with these Otuka creatures, but what does that have to do with the human civilization you mentioned?"

"There is a moral issue involved," Heart told her, choosing his words carefully. "The Otuka are not like either of our races. They are warm-blooded mammals like you, but oviparous—egg layers—like us. They have six limbs, like the Ay'uskanar—another race you haven't met—but the Ay'uskanar are...well, the closest analog you have would be insects, and the Otuka are not an insectoid species. They have an internal skeletal structure and a hair-covered outer skin. They use four limbs for locomotion and the other two for manipulation. You might think of a creature from your Earth mythology, something called a centaur. That description fits the Otuka closely enough to make me wonder if they did not visit your Earth at some time in your distant past.

"Like The People—and humans, for that matter—the Otuka are carnivorous, but unlike us, they lack the moral restraints of civilized carnivores."

"Meaning?" Lorna was beginning to see where this was going.

"Meaning we don't eat other intelligent, tool-using, rational, civilized creatures, not even primitives. They do."

"And the primitive humans you mentioned?"

"Are a food source for the Otuka. The planet is a sort of game preserve for them. We believe humans lived there long before the Otuka discovered them, another mysterious seeding of the Progenitors. They roam freely, in a basic hunter-gatherer society, but periodically, the Otuka come to harvest them. They take thousands at a time but leave enough behind to breed and replenish the herd. The Otuka are the reason this particular human society never progressed beyond the hunter-gatherer stage."

Carla had turned pale as a ghost, and the rest of her dinner sat untouched in front of her. Lorna, however, had a different reaction. Her meal was also untouched, but there was cold steel in her eyes. In an instant, she had become the Lorna Heart knew well—the Warrior Queen, the Valkyrie.

"Of course," she said, quietly. "Progression to the next step in civilization would require them to build farms, villages, and fixed installations. That would make it easier for the Otuka to find them, to harvest them, as you say. They retain a nomadic lifestyle for survival. I would imagine they rarely form tribes of more than a few dozen individuals."

"That is correct," Heart agreed. "One of our exploratory ships discovered the planet three years ago. We tried to make contact with the inhabitants, but they fled from us in fear. We made several additional trips to their world to study them, and during one of those expeditions, the Otuka came to collect their harvest. Our exploratory team evaded detection and returned with evidence of the events that took place. Since then, the debate has raged as to what action we should take, and the issue was not resolved until the last meeting of the Council of the Combined Clans.

"The Council decided to take no action at all. Heart of the Copper Hills protested the decision but was overruled. At that point, he resolved to bring the matter to the attention of your people. And that, Warrior Queen—near-dragon hunts and excellent dinners notwithstanding—is the real reason I am here tonight."

He slid a data card across the table. "This will tell you where to find the planet in question. It will also give you our best information about the rather vague boundaries of what can be called Otuka space and background material on the Otuka themselves. Use it for whatever purpose you see fit."

Lorna picked up the data card and looked at it, turning it slowly in her hands. There was silence for a moment, then Carla spoke.

"What are you going to do, Mom?"

"I no longer make policy decisions for the Lunar Free State," she replied, still looking at the data card, "but as the one who often has to carry out that policy, I think I know what the people back home will decide. I suspect we'll be paying a visit to this primitive human planet, and we'll establish a presence there. Hopefully, we'll have better luck contacting them. They may be willing to trust us because we're human. If the Otuka come to collect their harvest, their first contact with us will likely be extremely unpleasant for them. As for piracy and such, I don't have to ask what our policy will be. It's already established through dealings with pirates in our own system. Piracy is what we call a capital offense, meaning if you do it, you die for it."

She looked sharply across the table at Heart. "What? Something amuses you, old War Lizard?"

Heart had gathered Dusty up onto his lap and was scratching the cat's ears with his partly extended talons. Dusty, in turn, was purring loudly in appreciation, and Heart favored Lorna with another chop-licking Akara grin.

"I am amused by the thought of your first encounter with the Otuka," he replied. "I expect they will not find it to their liking—if any of them survive it. I am reminded of a bit of wisdom that goes back to our earliest days of dealing with other races, an old proverb that says, 'Walk softly when dealing with creatures who keep predators as pets.'"

* * *

"So much for the mother-daughter vacation." Carla watched Lorna pack her travel bag shortly after Heart departed. "How soon are you leaving?"

"In about an hour. I'll leave *Javelin* at the orbital facility to take you back. You can't leave until you've finished your lectures at the Institute, and the crew is doing some overhaul work on her drive anyway. There's a frigate, LFS *Cygnus,* about to depart for Luna. I've ordered them to hold for me."

"That's my Mom…off to save the galaxy again." Carla smiled gently. "But like I said, it's what you do best."

"I probably won't go out on this one," Lorna replied. "I doubt we'll need an entire fleet to take care of these Otuka creatures, but I've got to get word back to Luna, and I will hand-pick the force that goes to deal with them, including a commander with absolutely no sense of humor. The phrase 'kick ass and take names' pretty well describes the mission parameters I have in mind."

Her expression softened as she turned to embrace her daughter.

"Enjoy your two weeks, Honey, and when you get back, bring your young man to Luna. I'd really like to meet him."

* * * * *

Chapter Two

TerraNova City, Luna

"Actually," Bjorn Hansen remarked, "it's been a rather…intimidating experience."

"What has?" Carla looked at him, puzzled.

"Meeting your family."

After returning to Earth, Carla had taken her mother's advice and persuaded Bjorn to come with her to Luna for an entire week. It hadn't required much persuasion, and now, four days into the trip, they were having dinner at one of Luna's better restaurants on a balcony overlooking TerraNova Park.

"Intimidating? My family?" She looked skeptical. "The only real family I have are Mom and Grandpa Tom Perry. Surely you didn't find him intimidating?"

"Oh, no," Bjorn agreed. "He's quite an interesting man and amazingly spry for…how old did you say?"

"A hundred and eight. Or is it nine? I forget, but you're right, he's amazing. He's supposed to be retired, but he still serves in the Directorate, and he's on the board of Luna University. He was over eighty when the anti-aging treatments became available—too old to get the full effect from them—but he just keeps on going; hopefully, for another decade or two."

"I'd really like to get to know him better. Your mother, on the other hand…" Hansen continued with a grin. "I'm sure you'll agree she's a little intimidating—former CEO of the Lunar Free State and current admiral in command of the Lunar Fleet, where I understand they call her the 'Iron Maiden.'"

"Well, the Navy calls her that, but she's the 'Babe on the Horse' as far as the Marines are concerned," Carla replied with a grin.

"The what?"

"It's a long story, and for you to really understand it, we need to visit the LFS Space Museum or return to TransLuna to see the Fleet anchorage. All LFS warships have big, bold, vividly colored artwork on their hulls that depicts the ship's namesake, which is usually some creature from mythology, some person or group, or some event in history."

"I've seen that in pictures. I think it's pretty cool, though I can't imagine how difficult it must be to create a work of art that big on a curved surface while working in zero-gee in a vacuum."

"Mostly, it's done with programmed robots, working from a master pattern unique to each warship. No two are alike," she said. "Anyway, Mom's flagship has always been LFS *Valkyrie*—a big, front-line battlecruiser named from the mythology of your Scandinavian ancestors. The ship's hull artwork depicts a fierce, beautiful warrior maiden, in armor, with streaming blond hair. Her sword is raised high, and she sits astride a winged horse—the Valkyrie, or in Marine-speak, the 'Babe on the Horse.' The Marines claim she looks like Mom, but you probably don't want to mention that to her. It's something she gets embarrassed about. I've used it to irritate her over the years, but that's just because I have a low, evil sense of humor."

"And you can get away with it," he said with a grin. "I'm not tempted to try. If I recall my Norse mythology, the Valkyries were the handmaidens of Odin, and they were the ones who chose the warriors to be slain in battle. Like I said, an intimidating woman."

"Well, maybe a little," she admitted.

"But then there's your extended family—maybe not blood relatives, but just as protective," he continued. "That includes your Uncle Mick who is the current CEO of the LFS. When he speaks, kings and presidents on Earth take notice."

"Right," she agreed, "and then they go running to the news media and revile him for his policies. Not that any of us up here care what they think."

"And then, there's your Aunt Annie," Bjorn went on, "the Commandant of the LFS Marines, and Aunt Ronnie, another Marine, who has more medals on her uniform than anyone I've ever seen and who looks like she could kick the stuffing out of a grizzly bear. And let's not forget Uncle Charlie, Foreign Minister of the LFS and Director of LFS Intelligence Services. I get the feeling if he doesn't like me, I might disappear, without a trace, with no record I ever existed."

"You would mention that." Carla grimaced. "Actually, though I didn't know this until Mom told me, he's been keeping an eye on us for some time, but, apparently, he likes you." She flashed a quick smile.

"Uh huh," he replied, with a grimace. "If he didn't, I would probably already have disappeared. Like I said, intimidating. If I didn't love you so much, I'd be running for the hills by now."

"I know…you're my prince," she told him, reaching out to touch his cheek. "You're going to rescue me from all those dragons. But really, they're wonderful people. They just need to get used to the idea that I'm not a little girl anymore. Give them time.

"Honestly, I hadn't intended for you to meet them all at once. The big dinner party was Mom's idea. That's surprising because she's never been a party person. Thankfully, she kept the guest list to a minimum. With her connections, she could have included half the Lunar fleet and everyone currently serving on the Directorate."

"Carla..." Bjorn's voice was hesitant. "You've got all these people that are family to you, but I'm just wondering...you've never mentioned your father."

"And I never will," she said, with finality.

"Sorry. Taboo subject, I guess."

"No, silly—" she gave him a warm smile, "—there are no taboo subjects between us. It's just that I don't have a father."

"You don't know who your father is?"

"No, I meant exactly what I said—I don't have a father. I'm a double-egg baby. I had two mothers instead."

"Huh?"

"It's an obscure, high-tech procedure that involves joining two egg cells that mutually fertilize each other—no sperm cells required. I don't fully understand the mechanism but then bioengineering is a little out of my line. It's an *in vitro* procedure which requires the resulting embryo to be implanted in a host mother—in this case, my mom, who also contributed one of the egg cells, so she really is my biological mother—one of them—as well as my birth mother. It's an advanced biotech process that can't be done just anywhere, so it's not very common. And I really don't have a father."

"I've heard of the process." Bjorn was looking at her as if she had suddenly become a stranger. "But it's illegal most everywhere on Earth, even in countries that have the technology. I understand it's outlawed, like other forms of cloning, because of issues involving genetic deterioration, particularly in the immune system."

"Well," Carla said, with a sudden hint of anger in her voice, "I guess that's what happens when politicians pass laws to regulate science they don't understand. I am not a clone. A clone has only one parent—it's a genetic copy of another person. And, yes, there are issues involving genetic deterioration with clones, but they don't show up until you get to the fourth or fifth generation—clones of clones of clones of clones and so on."

Her anger had grown as she spoke. Bjorn dropped his gaze to the table, so she reached out and grabbed him by the chin.

"Look at me!" she demanded. "I repeat, *I am not a clone.* I had two parents. The double-egg procedure is rare, but not because there is anything morally wrong with it, and it does not produce any of the biological issues associated with cloning. It is, however, expensive—much more so than a normal male-female *in vitro* procedure. It's readily available on Luna, but rarely used, because it appeals primarily to lesbian couples who want a baby that is biologically related to both—lesbian couples like my mother, and her beloved, long-dead life-partner Carla Perry, my other mother, after whom I am named. Is there any part of that you do not understand?"

Bjorn looked at her and decided Carla had inherited some of her birth mother's intimidation factor. It was an intense, angry side of her he had not seen before but, if anything, it made her more attractive.

"No, darling," he said quietly. "I understand perfectly. I'm sorry if I seemed...insensitive. I love you, and I hate to see you upset."

"Yeah, well, I should have told you." Carla calmed down immediately, and Bjorn marveled at the amazing power of the words 'I love you,' but he realized the effect was possible only because he truly meant what he said.

"Anyway," she continued, "the procedure is legal in Geneva—about the only place in Europe where it is—and in Singapore or Tokyo. It isn't common, it's expensive, and it only appeals to people who have special circumstances. I find it ironic that abortion is legal in the United States while conceiving a baby by the double-egg method is not. Politicians! Idiots!"

"Is abortion not legal on Luna?" Bjorn was learning to phrase his questions very carefully. The wariness must have been noticeable in his voice because Carla suddenly smiled.

"No, it is not," she told him, "except in cases of rape or child abuse, and even then, if there are no health issues for the mother, it's not encouraged. I guess the people who founded this nation thought that, with all the modern, effective, and non-harmful methods of contraception available, there was no excuse for an accidental baby—that any such baby deserved a chance at life, and that consenting adults needed to take responsibility for it."

Her tone suddenly became more serious. "By the way, that brings us to another topic we've never discussed. I've had my annual contraceptive shot, so we can continue to enjoy each other's company to the fullest, but I'm not planning on taking them forever. I guess I need to know how you feel about children—*our* children—as in Bjorn and Carla make a baby."

"I can't imagine anything that would make me happier." He gave her a brilliant smile that faded to a more serious look. "Does that mean you've thought about it—that you're willing to become Mrs. Carla Hansen?"

"Yes, I've thought about it…and no, I'm not," she told him, but there was a twinkle in her eye.

"But…"

"I may be willing to marry you. It's not absolutely necessary by Lunar custom, but it is common practice for those who want to have children."

"But you just said..." Bjorn looked confused.

"I said I wasn't willing to become Carla Hansen. I'm a Moonie, my love, a Moon person, and under our custom, women don't take the surnames of their husbands when they marry. Also—again, according to Moonie custom—any kids we might have will get the surname of their biological parent of the same sex. If they're boys, they'll be Hansens. If they're girls, they'll be Greenwoods. And that brings me to the real issue, the only thing that's making me say I may marry you, instead of I will marry you..."

"And that is?" Bjorn Hansen was very nervous, not knowing whether he wanted to hear the next part.

"I want to share my life with you. I want us to be together, I want us to have children together, but..."

"But...?"

"But I'm a Moonie and, right now, there are about 385,000 kilometers between us—or there will be when you go back to Earth. I don't belong there, and I don't want to live there permanently. I have...well...to call it a career would be a masterpiece of understatement. I am a highly respected Fellow of the Lunar Research Institute, head of the Astrophysics department, in charge of pretty much all the research that goes on up here in that field, and for obvious reasons, it's considered a more important field here than it would be at any research institution on Earth.

"Some people also say I'm very good at it—actual research that is, not running a research department. Maybe the Nobel Prize has something to do with that, but I think that prize is based on politics more than scientific ability. I'm convinced I got it because somebody on Earth wanted to curry favor with the Lunar Free State. And maybe they love me up here on Luna because I'm not shy about funding my own research.

"All the same, I love my work and the people I do it with. I'm not about to give that up and go to Earth, not even for you. I love you, but if I must make that kind of sacrifice, it will destroy our relationship. I wouldn't be human if I didn't feel a lot of resentment over something like that.

"By the same token, you are a respected physicist with some serious work under your belt. Other physicists line up to hear you lecture, and half the research journals on Earth—and even here on Luna—beg you to publish an article or two. You've got position and tenure in Arizona, and you are pretty much beyond the point of having to beg for grants.

"I can't ask you to give that up." A note of misery had come into her voice, and Bjorn felt a lump in his throat. "And you'd be perfectly right to resent it if I did. With your credentials, you could get a position at the LRI, even without my help. I think you'd like it here, and I noticed you got along well with Dr. Harrington who would most likely be your boss. But you'd practically be starting over, with no seniority, working with people you don't know, on projects not of your own choosing. Anything you want to do on your own would have to be sold to the Research Board along with any need for funding your projects might require. I might be able to help you with that part—I am disgustingly rich—but the Board still rules when it comes to committing research resources.

"You'd have to work for seven years as a Provisional Citizen, because that's how long you have to be here before you can be considered for full citizenship, except under extraordinary circumstances, and being married to me isn't one of them. After that, you'd have to be judged worthy to be granted citizenship. It's not something you automatically get after a set length of time.

"People on Earth say we're bigots and anti-social and all sorts of uncivilized because we don't welcome just anyone who wants to come up here and set up camp, but that's the way we are, and I wouldn't want it to change, not even for you. I don't think you would have any problem—we love scientists here—but you can't take it for granted. And that, of course, assumes you want to become a Lunar citizen in the first place. There's no such thing as dual citizenship here—if you want to be one of us, you'll have to formally renounce your U.S. citizenship.

"So..." she said with a sigh, "where does that leave us, other than several hundred thousand kilometers apart? I've heard of long-distance relationships, but I really don't think they work that well. It's hard enough for Moonie couples who have separate careers, especially if one of them is with the Fleet and has to be gone for months at a time, but they have a common place both of them call home, and they are citizens of the same nation.

"My project in Arizona is almost complete. I've already spent more time on it than I can really justify, and people are starting to ask questions. It's time to wrap it up and then I'm going to sell the condo. We need to decide what we're going to do quickly."

She looked thoroughly miserable, but Bjorn felt relieved. He didn't need to worry anymore about how to broach a delicate subject, because she had done it for him. In fact, he thought with an amused chuckle, she pretty well beat it to death.

She gave him a sharp glance, and he decided he'd better explain the reason for his amusement, lest she take it the wrong way and get angry again.

"You're never going to solve the problem, darling, because one of your basic assumptions is flawed. I've been guilty of a little flawed thinking myself, but you've just straightened me out, and the solution is perfectly clear. God! We'd make a great research team!"

"Only half of that team is going to be sitting at this table in a few seconds, unless you explain yourself," she said with a growl, but then her tone softened. "C'mon, love, this is too important. If you've got the answer, share it with me."

"Sweetheart, you've painted a rosy picture of my career on Earth," he told her. "Obviously, you're looking at it from the viewpoint of a Lunar scientist—one who's never had a research project turned down because it didn't fit the world view of some politician or some member of the Board of Regents who still thinks the Earth is flat and that splitting atoms is The Devil's Work. One of my colleagues in Arizona had funding pulled from his project because some half-baked, pseudo-scientific nut case told the news media he was trying to create a Black Hole, and the Earth would be destroyed if he succeeded. The media never checked the nut case's credentials because he was a member of one of those Save the Earth environmental groups, but they sure went after my colleague and the university, who decided it was easier to shut the project down than to try to defend it to people who couldn't possibly understand the science involved.

"Yes, the journals have published a lot of my work, but I've had two papers rejected because they showed flaws in the favorite theories of the illustrious Dr. Hajerian of Oxford, at a time when the rest of the world was fawning at his feet. You mentioned the Nobel Prize. Hajerian was nominated for it the year I tried to publish those papers, and nobody wanted to spoil it for him. After he got the prize, for his flawed work, he suddenly decided his theory needed revision. He then published papers that looked suspiciously like mine. I think I know who sent him copies of my rejected papers, but I can't prove it.

"Yes, I generally get funding for my projects because I scale them to fit available resources—usually far less than what is available at the LRI. You people got tired of asking CERN if you could use their facilities, so you built your own supercollider on the Moon, and it is twice the size of the one in Europe.

"Seriously, a lot of scientists on Earth would willingly sacrifice a significant body part—an arm or a leg, or maybe even one of each—for the opportunity to work at the Lunar Research Institute. Given the choice between being the Director of All Things Scientific at Nowhere University on Earth and being a research assistant at the LRI, many would pack their bags for the Moon in a heartbeat. Granted, North American University at Tucson is not exactly Nowhere U. It's one of the top ten venues on Earth for my field, but it's far short of the LRI. The Lunar Free State is the only nation in history that has 'The advancement of scientific knowledge and understanding of the Universe' listed in its Constitution as a national goal.

"I would love to have the chance to come and work for the LRI, in whatever capacity my not-so-spectacular credentials merit. The only reason I haven't discussed it with you is...well...I didn't want you to think I was using our relationship to get my foot in the door. If we do get married, there are going to be a lot of green with envy people back in Arizona who will say I only married you so I could get a job with the LRI, or maybe so that my rich wife could fund all those projects that NAU at Tucson couldn't afford.

"Seven years to become a Lunar citizen? Lady, I want to spend a couple of centuries with you. Seven years is nothing; it'll be over before we know it. As far as I'm concerned, we'll still be on our honeymoon. And I would be honored to become a citizen of the LFS.

"So, I'm sitting here, with my hand out, saying, 'Please take me home with you to the Moon,' like a shameless beggar. If you still want me despite that..."

"Of course, I do, you foolish man," she told him, turning her head so he wouldn't see the sudden tears in her eyes. "I just wish you'd told me earlier...would have saved me a lot of needless worry."

"Me too," he said, taking her hands in his. "I'm glad you finally brought it up, but it still makes me uncomfortable. I wish there was some way I could get here without your influence, and I really don't want any help funding my research. I just want to be sure that—"

"Bjorn," she cut off his protests.

"Huh?"

"Shut up, take me back to my place, put your gentlemanly scruples away, and let's have a night of wanton passion. OK?"

"Yes, dear," he said, meekly.

* * *

Fleet Command HQ—TransLuna Station

"Attention on deck!"

Lieutenant Commander Robert O'Hara jumped to his feet, as did the other officers in the briefing room. The two women who had just come through the door needed no introduction, at least not to anyone who had spent more than a day or two in LFS military service. Vice Admiral Robin Torrey commanded Second Fleet—Luna's Expeditionary Force. Admiral Lorna Greenwood commanded everything—the combined fleets of the Lunar Free State.

O'Hara felt a bit nervous, not because he was the lowest ranking officer in the room, which he was, but because this mission represented a couple of firsts for him. This would be his first in command of a real warship—LFS *Timberwolf*—a brand new *Predator*-class destroyer that, in his humble opinion, was the most beautiful ship ever to come off the ways of the Lunar shipyards. His previous command, the corvette LFS *Coyote*, was hyper-capable but was of a class usually relegated to escort and patrol duty, not to serious space warfare.

More importantly, this would be O'Hara's first combat mission. He'd been in action before—had, in fact, distinguished himself in that action—but this was his first assignment where space combat was the expected outcome, where he and his ship would be out looking for trouble, not just on guard in case trouble found them. What's more, they would be looking for it in another star system, a long way from Luna.

This would be his first mission of any length outside the Sol system, away from his wife and infant son. He'd known that would happen when he took command of *Timberwolf* and was assigned to Second Fleet. He'd just hoped it wouldn't happen quite so soon.

The roomful of brass didn't bother him because he'd been there and done that many times. O'Hara was the son of Fleet Admiral Michael O'Hara, CEO of the LFS, and had grown up knowing Admiral Greenwood as Aunt Lorna for as long as he could remember.

Like Lorna's daughter Carla, he had chosen not to follow in the footsteps of his famous parent.

His father had come up through the ranks of the Lunar Corps of Engineers, but when the time came for higher education, Robert O'Hara had chosen the Fleet Academy instead of the Lunar Engineering College. At the age of twenty-two, with a brand-new ensign's commission in the LFS Navy, he had reported for his first assignment as the nominal executive officer of LFS *Coyote,* a corvette assigned to the Outer System Guard. He was called executive officer—effectively second-in-command—only because he was the junior of just two officers assigned to the ship, which had a total crew complement of thirty people. The other officer, Senior Lieutenant Mary Jane "M.J." Weathers, was *Coyote's* captain. Most of the slots that would normally be filled by officers on larger ships were assigned to NCOs, and that meant O'Hara had to wear many hats. He was assigned every task aboard ship that needed officer supervision but wasn't worthy of the captain's personal attention.

O'Hara didn't mind; it gave him an opportunity to learn every aspect of the ship's operations. He remembered one bit of wisdom passed along by most of the instructors at Fleet Academy: *Listen to your senior NCOs…they usually know more about their area of operations than you do.* He listened, and he learned.

He served aboard *Coyote* for almost two years, passed his advancement exams, and with a favorable rating from Weathers, was promoted to lieutenant. Not long after that, his knowledge was put to the test.

* * *

With a typical OSG mission profile, the corvette was doing patrol duty beyond Neptune's orbit but inside Sol's hyper limit. A tiny speck in a vast volume of space, *Coyote* had seen nothing for weeks except a few outbound LFS freighters on their way to Alpha Akara. When tactical reported a new inbound hyper signature, it was assumed to be another freighter, but *Coyote* changed course and headed for an intercept to confirm its identity. Then four more ships—smaller, with warship drive profiles—popped out of hyper behind the first ship, obviously in pursuit.

Captain Weathers ordered a challenge and got an immediate—allowing for communications lag—response from the first ship, an Akara freighter squawking for assistance and claiming to be pursued by ships of unknown origin, presumably pirates. The four pursuers did not respond. *Coyote* sent an alert to Lunar Command, a message that wouldn't be received for several hours, and altered course once again to get between the freighter and the unknowns.

The LFS had had plenty of experience dealing with pirates of Earth origin, a problem that had existed since the earliest days of mining in the asteroid belt. No interstellar pirates had ever been encountered, but the Akara reported that piracy was a problem in some regions.

There were Rules of Engagement for dealing with pirates, and the first rule was to determine that they were pirates. These unknowns were acting like pirates, but it was possible the freighter and its crew were guilty of some malfeasance, and the pursuers were chasing them for legitimate reasons. *Coyote* could do nothing unless the unknowns committed a hostile act. In other words, pirates always got the first shot.

Rob O'Hara had gone aft to Engineering when the ship went to battle stations. *Coyote* was too small to have an Auxiliary Control compartment—a secondary bridge from which command could be exercised if the primary bridge took battle damage—but basic combat protocols still applied. Under combat conditions, the exec and captain were not supposed to be on the bridge together. O'Hara's primary responsibility was to direct damage control and stand by to take command if something should happen to the captain. Unfortunately, something did.

The corvette had succeeded in getting between the pursuers and their target and had challenged the unknowns repeatedly, to no avail. Soon, they were within missile range, but they gave no indication they were aware of the LFS corvette. They were close enough for *Coyote* to get good readings, but those only told Weathers they were of an unrecognized type, not previously cataloged, and a little smaller than an LFS destroyer, but significantly larger than a corvette. *Coyote* continued to close. Soon, they were in beam range, and without warning, the bogies opened fire.

Their x-ray lasers were typical of weapons used by the Akara, several other alien species, and several Earth nations. They were not as powerful as the gamma-ray lasers, or grasers, preferred by the LFS, but they were powerful enough against an unarmored, lightly shielded patrol vessel.

O'Hara heard Weathers issue a course change order that was cut off in mid-sentence as *Coyote* shuddered from stem to stern.

"We're hit!" the engineering tech at the damage control console exclaimed. "Looks like the bridge. My God, I've got CEF!!!"

O'Hara was shocked. Catastrophic Environment Failure meant *Coyote*'s hull had been opened to space, with explosive decompression occurring immediately. The captain and her three-person bridge crew would have been wearing shipsuits—helmeted, airtight coveralls that would allow survival in vacuum—but the sheer violence implied by the CEF might have killed them anyway.

"Bridge comm is down, helm is down, tactical is down, secondary bridge systems not responding..." The litany of damage chilled O'Hara to the core, but even more frightening was the knowledge that, even if Weathers had survived, she could no longer function as Captain, which meant Rob O'Hara had to take command.

"Damage control party to the bridge," he ordered. "Switch helm control and tactical to Engineering. Come to course three four zero plus forty-five and go to two four zero gravities—evasive action, Plan Delta." *Coyote* might be lightly armed and armored, but she was quick, and O'Hara was not about to give the enemy an easy target. "Have we got long-range communications?"

"No, sir. Communications are down. Helm control shifted to my station. Course three four zero plus forty-five, two forty gravs, Plan Delta, acknowledged. Harris! See if you can get long-range comm functions restored." The calm voice of Master Chief Petty Officer Wilson, *Coyote's* senior engineer, was music to O'Hara's ears. He tried to keep his own voice calm.

"Tactical?"

"Coming up on your console now, sir..." the master chief replied. "I have targeting and fire control coming up on my station. I show all four birds still hot and graser batteries still online. Bravo battery still tracking Bogey One, per last orders."

O'Hara realized the NCO was reminding him they ought to be shooting back. Despite needing to give the pirates the first shot, Weathers had been maintaining firing solutions for her weapons.

Coyote's two sets of twin 120mm grasers, mounted in turrets on the top and bottom of her hull, would have maintained their lock as long as their independent fire-control systems didn't go down, and the ship's violent course change still left the enemy in the lower turret's field of fire.

"Grasers open fire as you bear, target Bogey One. Do we have missile lock?"

"Lost it when we changed course, sir."

O'Hara gritted his teeth. The corvette was too small to carry the broadside armament and independent targeting systems of larger warships. All four of her missile tubes were forward firing, meaning the ship had to be pointed within about thirty degrees of the enemy for the missile seeker heads to lock on target. He could launch the missiles under manual control, steer them toward the enemy, and hope they locked on as they approached, but that was far less certain than a lock before firing. What he should have done was fire the missiles first and then order the course change.

"Base course to one seven zero, minus forty," he ordered. "Go to evasion Plan Echo. Advise when missiles lock on."

Coyote shuddered again, and more red lights appeared on the damage control board, but this time the damage was less severe.

"Point Defense One out of action, sir."

It wasn't much of an issue since the enemy didn't appear to be using missiles—point defense was useless against beam weapons. A moment later, there was some good news.

"Graser hits on Bogey One, sir. Alpha turret, locking on. Missile Three locked. Missiles One, Two, and Four locked—all missiles locked, sir—targeting Bogey One."

"Fire at will, Master Chief!" O'Hara realized he was leaving three of the four bogeys untargeted, but he was not going to make the rookie mistake of splitting his limited firepower. He might not be able to take them all, but at least one of the enemy was going to know he'd been in a fight.

"Missiles away!" *Coyote* shuddered again, this time in reaction to her own fire, as mass drivers hurled four missiles out of their tubes. "Alpha turret firing, grasers recycling, sir."

Then more bad news.

"Hit on the starboard side, sir," the technician on the damage control console reported. "We are losing atmosphere in compartment S-3. Starboard loading rack is jammed, possible battle damage. Can't reload tubes three and four."

"Sir," the tech looked up at O'Hara, "damage control team reports the bridge is totaled, no survivors. The captain's gone. What are we gonna do, Mr. O'Hara?"

"That's *Captain* O'Hara, Biggs," the master chief growled. "And we are gonna man our stations and listen for orders. Clear?"

"Aye, Master Chief."

O'Hara paid little attention to the exchange, concentrating instead on his tactical display. The small screen was nowhere near as good as the tactical plot on the bridge, but it was all he had.

The range to the bogey was relatively short for missile engagement, which was good since it allowed very little time for the enemy's point defense to deal with *Coyote's* meager four-missile salvo. O'Hara watched in dismay as one of his missiles was picked off short, but the other three reached attack range and detonated, sending X-ray lasers lancing into the enemy ship. The bomb-pumped lasers were more powerful than *Coyote*'s small-bore grasers, and

O'Hara felt grim satisfaction as he noted a small cloud of debris and atmospheric gases streaming behind the bogey. Then Bravo turret fired again, and the displays registered yet another hit on the enemy ship.

"Target aspect change!" the master chief sang out. "Major course change…looks like they're going for disengagement, sir."

O'Hara couldn't believe his eyes. He hadn't inflicted that much damage on the lead bogey and none on the other three, but the display confirmed what the senior NCO was telling him. The enemy had executed a radical course change and was cutting the chord—the shortest way back to the hyper limit. It would take them some time to get there, but they would be out of beam-weapon range in very short order.

"Come to one one zero minus three," he ordered.

"Aye, sir," the Master Chief acknowledged. "One ten minus three. Range still opening."

Quick as she was, the enemy's maneuver had been calculated to make it difficult for *Coyote* to stay with them. O'Hara was giving chase anyway, to make sure they weren't trying to go around him to get back on the freighter's tail. He noticed they had shifted formation, putting their damaged lead ship as far away from the LFS vessel as possible.

"Retarget for Bogey Three, Master Chief," he ordered, naming the enemy vessel nearest to them.

"Aye, sir, but we are out of the graser envelope. I have tubes one and two reloaded, locked on to Bogey Three now."

"Fire one and two, master chief. Let's see if we can't take a nip out of their tail feathers, just to let them know we're still here."

He realized that, despite her battle damage, *Coyote*'s drive and maneuvering ability was unimpaired. That meant the enemy didn't know how much damage the corvette had taken, and his aggressive charge, coupled with the damage he'd inflicted on one of them, had convinced them they were dealing with a much more formidable opponent.

He watched as one of his two missiles was picked off, but the other detonated, spearing the trailing bogey with its powerful energy beam. The enemy ships seemed to have little in the way of point defense and had to use their offensive armament to stop missiles, with less than effective results. The enemy ship wavered a bit but then got back in formation and continued to open the range. O'Hara chased them for another twenty minutes and fired two more missiles before they got out of range, scoring two more hits on the trailing ship. With her superior acceleration, *Coyote* was just beginning to gain on them when they reached the hyper limit and jumped out of normal space.

The battle was over. He'd bluffed, and they had folded, and he had no idea who they were.

* * *

The post-action review board had commended O'Hara, promoted him to senior lieutenant, and made his command of *Coyote* permanent. Of course, they'd reviewed the ship's logs and automatic recordings, but they'd also interviewed Master Chief Wilson—the only crewmember besides O'Hara who'd been called to testify. The master chief had been the first to congratulate him on his promotion to the captain's chair. *Listen to your senior NCOs...*

O'Hara was proud of his beautiful new destroyer, but he would never forget *Coyote*. Now, almost five years after the battle, he realized he might finally have an idea about who the attackers had been. If he was right, this mission could bring an opportunity for a little payback...for Mary Jane Weathers and six others of *Coyote*'s crew who had died in that battle.

* * *

"You've all seen the mission brief," Lorna Greenwood began, "and everything in it is alpha-level classified. We are going into the territory of an alien race we've never met, with the deliberate intention of picking a fight with them. You can imagine what Earth's news media will make of that. We must also consider the interstellar implications for some of our allies. Be advised that the information about the target star system, its planetary inhabitants, and the Otuka who exploit them comes from a highly trusted source who prefers to remain anonymous.

"This mission has two parts. The first is to make contact with and study the human inhabitants of the planet. The mission parameters are intended to cause minimum disruption to the primitive culture that exists there.

"The second part is to prevent the Otuka from using those humans as slaves, as a food source, or for any other purpose. Because you will be operating deep in previously unexplored territory, we have allowed for a great deal of commander's discretion. That being said, it seems likely you will need to keep your force hidden, allow the Otuka to begin an incursion such as the one you saw documented in the mission brief, then terminate that incursion with extreme prejudice, using whatever force is required.

"It might be useful to let a few survivors escape, to spread word of our displeasure with them, but that's one of the matters we have left to the discretion of the force commander. The complete disappearance of their incursion force will likely get their attention as well.

"Are there any questions?" She looked around the room.

There were no questions, nor any hint of an objection. They had all seen the observational data, including the rather graphic video from the cameras the Akara researchers had placed to observe one small tribal group of humans—one of the first such groups to fall victim to the alien harvest. When they placed those cameras, the Lizard scientists had intended only to observe the primitive humans. They had not expected to see the horrors the cameras recorded.

"Our intention is to make them lose all interest in this star system. Based on the data we have on the Otuka," Lorna continued, "we may need to repeat the lesson several times before they get the message. That may require an escalation of forces over time, but that decision can't be made until after the first encounter.

"If there are no questions about the objectives, I will turn the podium over to Admiral Torrey. This mission falls under the command of Second Fleet, and all of you have been drawn from Second Fleet's T.O. except for the scientific team." She nodded to the mission's scientific director, Dr. Mercedes Warren.

Anthropology—likely to be the primary focus of the scientific mission—was not Dr. Warren's specialty. She was an exobiologist who had been involved in both significant "First Contact" events in Lunar history, the first meeting with the Mekota, and later, with the

Akara. Her team included anthropologists as well as exobiologists and other scientists whose input might prove useful.

"Because of the second part of this mission, the scientific team will report through the chain of command to the overall mission commander. That's the big picture, people…now for the details." Lorna stepped back from the podium. "Admiral Torrey."

Like Lorna, Robin Torrey was an "original" LFS citizen, one of the first group of settlers to come to the Moon more than forty years ago. She'd commanded just about every class of ship the LFS had ever built before reaching flag rank. As the commander of Second Fleet, she now flew her colors aboard the battlecruiser LFS *Amazon*.

"As you will no doubt have noticed," Torrey began, "the order of battle for this mission includes all of Second Battle Group, specifically battlecruiser *Sorceress*, heavy cruisers *Arapahoe* and *Spartan*, and the full BG-2 complement of light cruisers and destroyers. I presume all of the captains involved are present in this room?"

"They are, ma'am," Rear Admiral Amy Ling advised.

"You, Admiral Ling, are the overall mission commander," Torrey continued.

Ling nodded, her delicate Asian features a study in calm, unquestioning attention to orders.

Seated in the rear with the other destroyer captains, Rob O'Hara had a good view of the briefing room, and he noted with interest that, while most of the warship captains were men, the three top-ranking people in the room were women. Not surprising, he decided. When Lorna Greenwood needed someone to go out and kick ass, she most often called on Robin Torrey. From the Chinese War to the First Mekota campaign to the Battle of Copper Hills Prime, Torrey had taken part in just about every fleet action—had, in fact, taken over fleet command at Copper Hills Prime, when Greenwood's flagship was disabled.

Torrey, in turn, often called on Amy Ling when she needed a job done in an orderly and proficient manner. Ling, another original citizen and combat veteran, had been Greenwood's flag captain, commanding LFS *Valkyrie* for many years before getting her own flag, which she now flew aboard *Sorceress.*

The LFS Bad Girls Club, O'Hara mused, *and woe unto any enemy who mistakes them for the weaker sex.*

"You've seen the basic mission plan," Torrey told them. "You will note there is no end-of-mission date specified. This mission will continue until the objectives are met. If the Otuka haven't shown up in six months, we will send a relief force to take over your station, but don't plan on coming home before then. If you engage them earlier, you'll remain on station in case they return. We're in this for the long haul, people.

"Six months means at least three resupply cycles, so we will be sending heavily-escorted colliers every sixty days. We'll expect a picket to meet the convoy out near the hyper limit, to advise whether the system is secure so they can proceed.

"We're assigning two *Cheetah*-class express boats to your group. You'll be able to send regular status reports back with the supply train, but if anything of consequence occurs, the E-boats will allow you to send word back quickly. In addition, since they are capable of planetary landing, you can use them to get the scientific team out of harm's way in a hurry if the Otuka show up. The safety of the scientific team is a top priority.

"You have the data on the star system, as well as everything we have on the inhabited planet. It's Earth-like to within 90%, and gravity, atmosphere, and topography are within comfortable limits. It has slightly more axial tilt than Earth, which means more seasonal variations, and its distance from the primary gives it a longer year. Most of the native human population will be found on three land masses within twenty degrees of the equator. Seasonal variations make for extreme winters north or south of those latitudes, while the equatorial belt has a temperate climate by Earth standards. We have limited data on native flora and fauna, but there appears to be nothing detrimental to human development—except for the Otuka, who aren't native to the planet.

"As Admiral Greenwood advised, most of the operational parameters have been left to commander's discretion—meaning you, Admiral Ling. No one from Fleet HQ has been there and seen the situation, nor have we had any encounters with the Otuka. You'll be writing the book as you go. Are there any questions?"

"Ma'am," Amy Ling spoke up, with a nod toward the Marine officer sitting next to her. "Colonel Bartley has brought something to my attention—an area in the Op Plan that needs further discussion."

"Meaning," Lorna Greenwood interrupted, with a hint of humor in her voice, "that you've discovered something really important those fools at HQ have completely overlooked. Does that about sum it up, Rock?"

"No, ma'am," Lieutenant Colonel Veronica 'Rock' Bartley replied. "I'm sure it's one of those things Fleet HQ, in its infinite wisdom, has simply left to our discretion, but we think we need a little guidance from above."

Another bad girl of the LFS, Rob O'Hara thought. Rock Bartley was a combat veteran and had the medals to prove it, including the Lunar

Medal of Honor, earned during a boarding action on a Mekota warship.

"Nice save, Rock," Torrey conceded with a wry smile. "OK, tell us about it."

"Well, ma'am, if we have to let these Otuka start their dirty work before we act, there may be major mayhem on the planet by the time we get involved. We may need some boots on the ground to, as Admiral Greenwood says, terminate them with extreme prejudice. I don't think we'll need a carrier to get the job done, but an AT would come in handy. It would give us a couple of gunships and three assault landers, not to mention an extra three hundred Marines."

Torrey looked at Greenwood.

"She's right." Lorna shrugged. "We fools at HQ overlooked something important." A quickly suppressed chuckle ran through the crowd.

"But that's within my discretion," she continued. "I don't think we have a suitable unit online, so I, or my hardworking staff, will have to find an Assault Transport and a battalion of Marines to fill it. As for you, Rock, you'll have to take command of that battalion as punishment for pointing out our shortcomings."

"Yes, ma'am," Bartley responded with suitable humility and no hint of the smug satisfaction she had to be feeling.

Her regular assignment, as BG-2's Marine commander, was primarily one of oversight. Marines assigned to a regular warship—a full company to a battlecruiser such as *Sorceress* and lesser numbers on smaller ships—reported up the chain to the warship's captain. Bartley didn't take direct command of them unless an operation required coordinated action by Marine units from several of the group's ships.

As commander of a battalion aboard an AT, however, her authority would exceed that of the ship's captain in all matters except the actual operation of the ship. Assault transports had one mission—deliver Marines wherever they were needed at the direction of the Marine commander of the battalion they carried. The same command protocols applied aboard the big assault carriers, except the commander was usually a general officer—brigadier or above—and the Marine units aboard consisted of a full division, plus several specialized battalions.

"Anything else?" Torrey looked around the room. The assembled officers looked serious and attentive, but no one spoke.

"Very well," she told them. "You will return to your ships and prepare for extended deployment, departing in thirty days. There will be additional briefings prior to departure, but your time starts now. That will be all." The attendees jumped to attention as Torrey and Greenwood departed.

Thirty days to prepare for extended deployment, Rob O'Hara thought. *Including getting personal affairs in order, saying goodbye to family, and wondering if your son will recognize you when you get back, assuming you do get back. Well, don't blame anyone but yourself. You could have gone into engineering instead.*

But Fleet was in his blood now; he was really where he wanted to be—commanding his own ship in the service of the Lunar Free State. He was proud of himself, and he knew his family shared that pride. This was the pain that sometimes went with that pride—the pain of separation and uncertainty that military families had been going through for a couple thousand years. He imagined the centurions of Caesar's legions felt the same way as they marched off to fight the Gallic Wars.

But that doesn't make it any easier, does it?

* * *

TerraNova City, Luna

"That's wonderful, honey! I'm so happy for you," Lorna said, softly. The fleet might know her as the 'Iron Maiden,' but now she looked rather misty-eyed.

"That's it? You're happy for me?" Carla looked stunned.

"Did you expect I wouldn't be?" Lorna was genuinely puzzled.

"Well, I expected at least an argument or two, like maybe 'He's not worthy of you, honey,' or 'He's an Earthworm, have you considered the consequences?' or 'Don't you think you're rushing things?' or..."

"Would any of those arguments change your mind?" Lorna inquired with a smile.

"Well, no," Carla admitted, "but at least they would have given me a chance to use all my carefully prepared counterarguments to convince you I have thought everything through and that I'm serious about it."

"I never doubted it, honey, and besides, I like him. He may actually be worthy of you. So, where is he?"

"Wandering around TerraNova on his own," Carla replied with chagrin. "I expected to need at least a couple of hours to convince you, so I told him not to show up here until 1930 hours, assuming the great physicist can figure out how to read a 24-hour clock. Do you know they still use that silly A.M. and P.M. system back on Earth, as if the Sun is going to be at the meridian everywhere in a time zone when the clock says noon? Then again, most of the United

States still measures things in feet and miles and quarts and gallons. What an unscientific, confusing system."

"I know, honey. I grew up there, remember?"

* * *

Bjorn Hansen wasn't having any trouble reading the clock. Rather, he was having trouble extricating himself from a group of newfound comrades who insisted he remain and drink with them.

Bjorn had spent the afternoon strolling around the gardens and shops in the broad concourse that connected the two major sections of TerraNova City, Luna's underground capital. He'd realized early on that his Earth-style clothing screamed tourist to everyone in sight, but he found the Moonies he encountered to be cheerfully helpful and courteous.

Then he had wandered into Corporal J's Place. The crowded bar seemed a bit rowdier than most places in TerraNova, but it wasn't until he'd ordered a drink at the bar that he began to wonder why that was. It didn't take long to figure it out. The décor, as well as the uniforms and off-duty clothing worn by most of the patrons, made it clear he had wandered into a place claimed by the Lunar Marine Corps as its own special watering hole. He was just pondering what to do with that information when a huge, burly Marine walked up, clapped him on the shoulder, and inquired in a cheerful tone whether he was new in town.

"Yeah, I guess that's obvious," Hansen had replied with a smile, hoping honesty was the best policy. "I'm an Earthworm."

"Buy the Earthworm a drink, courtesy of the LFS Marines," the Marine announced, loudly.

The bartender, a cheerful grey-haired man with one arm, looked up with a grin.

"A drink for the Earthworm, coming up." The requested drink appeared in front of Bjorn in an instant. "It's on the house, Corporal Bronski. I wouldn't want to ruin your reputation by letting you buy somebody a drink."

"You are a prince among men, Mr. DaSilva," the Marine pronounced.

Bjorn felt an arm drape over his shoulder, and a warm, curvaceous, feminine body pressed against his side.

"An Earthworm!" The female Marine's contralto voice carried an unmistakable Spanish accent. "I haven't been with an Earthworm since I left Nogales."

Bjorn turned toward the speaker, who was a good-looking young woman—honey-skinned, petite, perhaps a few inches over five feet tall, dark hair done up in a tight braid, and deep brown eyes above a seductive smile. Well, maybe petite wasn't quite the right word. The arm draped over his shoulder had some hard muscle on it, as did the shoulder that supported it, and he could feel more muscle in the hip that pressed against him.

"Nogales?" he stammered, trying to think of something polite to say. "You're from Mexico?"

"Not anymore, *mi cariño*," she told him. "I'm a Moonie now—provisional citizen. Three more years in the Corps, and I get full citizenship."

"Hey, Vasquez," another Marine called out. "Why wait? You can be a citizen tomorrow if you do something stupid and heroic, and they pin a medal on you."

"Or you could be dead," Bronski chimed in. "Screw that hero stuff."

Bjorn relaxed a bit, as the banter among the Marines shifted away from him, but before he could breathe a sigh of relief, Vasquez shifted it back.

"Doesn't matter," she said. "If you die, they make you a citizen, but forget about that. We're being deployed soon, so I gotta think about tonight. How 'bout it, Mr. Earthworm, you up for a party?"

"Uh…actually," Bjorn stammered, "I'd love to, but…I mean, you're really very attractive, but I just got engaged today. I'm supposed to be meeting my fiancée later, and—"

"Well, congratulations." She beamed at him. "But hey, later's later, and you ain't married yet. How about an early bachelor party?"

"I don't think you want to do that, *chica*," the one-armed bartender advised. "Not unless you want to tangle with the Babe on the Horse…at least, if this fellow is the Earthworm I think he is."

Vasquez looked sharply at the bartender, who was grinning from ear to ear. Then, obviously confused, she looked back at Bjorn.

"No way," she declared. "The admiral's got a boy toy? I heard she was into girls."

DaSilva leaned across the bar and gave her a conspiratorial whisper that was clearly audible to all nearby.

"No, the admiral's not into boys," he told her, "but the admiral has a daughter. Word has it, the admiral's daughter has an Earthworm boyfriend she's been showing off all around town."

He turned to Bjorn. "Would that be you? Dr. Hansen, is it?"

"Guilty!" Bjorn admitted readily. He would have pled guilty to just about anything to fend off Vasquez and her seductive attentions.

"No shit!" Bronski looked stunned. "Man, you got balls. Imagine, walking up to Old Lady Greenwood—the Iron Maiden, her bad self—and telling her you're gonna marry her daughter. Not me, man."

"Actually…" Bjorn grimaced. "That's what I'm supposed to do later tonight. I mean, Carla's already said yes, but we haven't told her mother yet."

"Oh, man!" Bronski exclaimed. "You need another drink!"

"Wait!" Bjorn demanded. He looked around the bar, which wasn't crowded yet. The Marines were boisterous, but not too numerous.

"This round's on me. A drink for everybody, to celebrate my engagement!" he announced, and the Marines responded with a raucous cheer.

"And one more on the house, in honor of the occasion," DaSilva boomed, producing another boisterous explosion of cheering.

Bjorn looked around with a grin, soaking up the good will the Marines were offering. For a moment, he forgot about Vasquez, but the woman wasn't done with him yet.

"And this is from me, in honor of the occasion," Vasquez proclaimed. She encircled Bjorn in an iron-grip hug and gave him a hot, wet kiss whose intensity and duration left his head spinning. For a moment, he regretted not having accepted her earlier offer…but only for a moment. When she finally pulled back, to the tune of more cheering and catcalls from the Marines, he looked at her in awe.

"Wow! You better watch that, lady. You could kill somebody with a kiss like that," he told her. "What is it you do in the Marines, anyway?"

"I fly a Raptor," she told him with pride. "I'm Death from Above. When the bad guys give these dirt eaters too much trouble, they call me in and I tear 'em up. Then they go in and clean up the mess."

Her pronouncement brought more catcalls from the rest of the Marines, but nobody challenged her description. She turned back to Bjorn, and her expression softened a bit.

"Who would have guessed it?" she mused. "A raggedy-ass girl like me, from a rundown *barrio* in a border town…when I got the chance to join the LFS Marines, I figured I was just gonna be another grunt. But somebody looked at my tests and figured I could be a pilot, so here I am. Gotta love the LFS."

By this point, she was almost misty-eyed. Bjorn was amazed, but he also realized they had something in common.

"I'm a scientist," he told her. "It looks like I'm going to be a provisional citizen, just like you, and I think I'm going to love the LFS, too."

"That calls for another drink!" Bronski declared.

* * *

"Bjorn?"

Carla looked at her fiancé, who appeared to be somewhat disheveled and unsteady on his feet. He was smiling sheepishly and at a loss for words.

She raised an eyebrow toward the Marine, wearing a town patrol armband, standing behind Bjorn.

"No problem, ma'am," the Marine assured her. "He just got a little lost and told me where he needed to go, so I brought him here."

"Thank you, Sergeant. I'll take it from here. C'mon, love." She escorted Bjorn through the door and closed it behind him.

An hour later, after two cups of coffee and a couple of trips to the bathroom, Bjorn was a little steadier and very apologetic.

"I can't believe Carla didn't warn you about that place," Lorna remarked. She obviously found the situation highly amusing, much to her daughter's distress.

"They were really nice to me," Bjorn protested. "They treated me just fine, right from the beginning."

"Of course, they did." Carla rolled her eyes in dismay. "They welcome everyone, as long as they understand the LFS Marines own that place, and they will use any excuse whatsoever to prove they can drink any Navy rating, engineer, scientist, or naïve Earthworm tourist under the table. And, unlike their male counterparts, who are usually perfect gentlemen, female Marines will use any excuse to seduce said tourists, leaving them passed out drunk with silly grins on their faces!"

"Actually, one of them tried," Bjorn replied, "but she backed off when she found out I was engaged."

"When she found out you were engaged, or when she found out who you were engaged to?" Lorna inquired, with a knowing smile.

"Well, the latter, I think," Bjorn admitted, "but I didn't tell them. It was the bartender, the one-armed guy. I don't know how he knew, but he did."

"Mike DaSilva." Lorna nodded. "He owns the place, and he's always piped into the latest gossip."

"Gossip? *Gossip!*" Carla was furious. "You mean, our engagement is now a matter of public gossip? Arrrrrrggghhh!"

"Relax, daughter. It just means everyone on Luna will be happy for you, including the Marines. It'll probably be a wild night at Corporal J's tonight, especially since a lot of them are shipping out on an extended deployment soon, and they just found out about it today."

"Oh, right, Maya mentioned something about that," Bjorn remembered.

"Maya?" Carla glared at him.

"Look, love, she came on to me." Bjorn met her glare with simple honesty. "I turned her down, but it wasn't easy. She's a damned good-looking woman, and she was awfully aggressive. But I turned her down because I love you, and that's not something I'd throw away for a quick fling with a sexy Marine."

Carla melted.

"Naïve Earthworm tourist," she mumbled as she put her arms around him and pressed her head against his, cheek to cheek.

"Now you look, love." She pulled back and looked him in the eye. "Moonies are sexually liberated, as some Earthworms like to call it. If you get an opportunity to hop in bed with a hot Marine babe in the future, I won't mind if you take her up on it as long as you tell me about it as soon as you get a chance. Just don't do it behind my back, and don't lead the other woman along with promises you don't intend to keep. As long as I know—and she knows—you're coming home to me in the morning, I'm fine with that."

"Fine with it?" Lorna inquired with a crooked grin. "Hell, daughter, I'd think you might want to join them. Marine women are wild, girl. At the very least, I'd think you'd want to watch."

"Mother!" Carla sounded exasperated—exasperated but not shocked.

"Just speaking from experience, dear," Lorna replied calmly. "Your other mother died over thirty years ago. Surely you don't think I've done without female companionship all that time?"

Bjorn Hansen was no longer in an alcohol-induced fog, but he still felt a pleasant glow, and he still remembered the excitement he'd felt in the presence of Marine Sergeant Maya Vasquez. Resisting had been the right thing, he was sure, but his wife's and his future mother-in-law's commentary on the subject certainly gave him food for thought.

Yup, I think I'm gonna love the LFS, he mused.

* * *

LFS *Sorceress*, Lunar Fleet Anchorage

"I've never seen anything quite like this." Amy Ling studied the holographic representation of the planet they were now calling New Eden, paying particular attention to what the scientists had dubbed the Shattered Moon, a jumble of small asteroids clustered at the L5 point of the star-planet system. The asteroids were orbiting the common center of the La-Grange point, but Ling was certain it would take some heavy duty mathematics to figure out how the whole system stayed in balance. It was a perfect place to hide a battle group tasked to keep an eye on the planet.

"With all those rocks moving around, we'll need to keep the docking buffers up or suffer a few dents in the hulls." Commodore Jake Roundtree was captain of LFS *Sorceress* and Ling's flag captain. He shook his head as he looked at the display. With her heavy armor, *Sorceress* could withstand a low-velocity collision with an occasional rock, but destroyers and other light ships could suffer damage.

"I don't want to keep the buffers online," Ling told him. "That's an emission signature we don't need. Anyway, the scientists tell me if we tether the ships—we'll use docking buoys—to one of the larger rocks out there, it won't be a problem. This system's been stable long enough that the smaller debris has been swept up and collected by the larger bodies. Stay close enough to one of the big rocks, and we won't have any small ones bouncing off our hulls. We may need an occasional station-keeping tweak, but thrusters should be adequate for that.

"If it doesn't work out," she continued, "we'll have to go to full stealth and pretend to be a hole in space."

She didn't like that option. Maintaining the tight emissions control required for full stealth meant shutting down or reducing power to a lot of systems, even lighting and environmental control, which would make life aboard a warship less than pleasant, especially on a long deployment. It also meant, if things got tense, bringing the ships to combat readiness would take longer. The upside was that they would see the enemy coming long before the enemy saw them. Probably…

Unfortunately, the Akara hadn't collected much technical data on the Otuka ships, as they were more concerned with avoiding the marauders than studying them. The information they got didn't show any advanced stealth, weaponry, or defensive capabilities, but the Akara had not engaged the Otuka in battle, so there was no evidence they did not have those capabilities. Ling knew the Otuka didn't attack escorted Akara merchant convoys, or so the briefing indicated, and that was good news. If the Otuka were afraid to attack Akara warships, LFS warships would be a nasty surprise for them.

Of course, it was all theoretical. Ling's task force was still being assembled and shaken down via simulation exercises. She had her warships in order but was still waiting for the assault transport LFS *Okinawa* to get its Marine battalion and gear aboard. The scientists were still preparing and begging her for space aboard the warships to stow gear they couldn't fit into the research ship, LFS *Edwin Hubble.* For all that, the mission was on schedule. Barring last minute changes, they would deploy in just four days.

* * *

TerraNova City

Maya Vasquez was two rounds into happy hour at Corporal J's and just beginning to feel a pleasant glow on her last night before deployment. She would be reporting to LFS *Okinawa* in the morning and might not see TerraNova again for a long time.

She didn't know where she was going or for how long, but there were a few clues in the orders she'd gotten. *Okinawa* was listed as being attached to the Double Deuce—the Second Battle Group of Second Fleet. Second Fleet was Luna's interstellar expeditionary force, so wherever they were going was probably a lot of light-years from Luna.

As far as she knew, there were no major conflicts going on. The Double Deuce might be going out for a show-the-flag mission along the Akara frontier, but missions like that didn't require an AT full of Marines. Besides, the orders called for HD pay for the duration, and for Marines, Hazardous Duty pay usually meant combat. Vasquez was pretty happy about the extra money, which would accumulate in her account, because it was unlikely she'd have much chance to spend it out there.

That's OK, girl, that's what you signed up for. Oorah! She felt a little adrenaline rush as she imagined herself rolling her Raptor in on a target, weapons hot.

"Excuse me, are you Maya Vasquez?" The cheerful feminine voice interrupted her musings, and she looked up to find a tall woman with light brown hair and blue eyes, wearing an outfit Vasquez characterized as civilian casual. The logo on her tunic was that of the Lunar Research Institute, and Maya guessed she was a scientific type.

"Yes, ma'am, that's me," she replied. "What can I do for you?"

"I had to come down here and see what you look like." The other woman was smiling, but her eyes studied Vasquez carefully. "I'm Carla Greenwood."

Nobody had ever accused Vasquez of being slow. Her grin vanished, and the fog in her brain cleared instantly. She brought up her hands, as if to ward off an attack. "Hey, *chica*, I was just having a little fun. Nothing happened. Your boyfriend turned me down cold. I'm not looking to follow up or anything."

"Relax, Marine," Carla told her, still smiling as she pulled up a chair and sat down. "I'm not looking for a fight. I just wanted to see what you look like, and I'm impressed. I can't believe he passed you up for little old me."

Vasquez relaxed, her own smile returning. "You ain't so bad looking yourself, lady. But hey, he's in love. I guess that's all there is to it."

"He's a lovable teddy bear," Carla acknowledged, "but mostly he's a naïve, inhibited Earthworm. A Moonie guy would have taken you up on your offer, then come home to tell me about it."

"Yeah, maybe." Maya nodded. "So, where'd you stash Prince Charming, anyway, or did he go back to Earth?"

"He's over there by the bar, trying to be invisible, wondering whether you and I are gonna go at each other. Hey, Bjorn!" Carla stood up and waved at her fiancé, motioning for him to join them. She turned back to Vasquez.

"Can we buy you a drink, Marine?"

* * *

"It'll be OK, honey. Six months, and I'll be back. I wanted you to enjoy tonight, to give you something to remember while I'm out there."

Rob O'Hara was distressed by his wife's lack of appetite. The food was excellent, as it should have been, considering what it was costing him. Earthlight was the best restaurant in TerraNova, not the sort of place one visited frequently on a lieutenant commander's pay. His wife was on half-pay maternity leave from her job as a med tech at the Lunar capital's primary hospital. With his deployment, her leave could be extended six more months if she chose to exercise the option.

She probably wouldn't. Baby John was six months old, they had relatives available for daycare, and work would help ease her loneliness. Besides, full pay would fend off any financial concerns. She would also have his pay, so she wouldn't lack for necessities and even a few luxuries, but he was sure she was fretting over the cost of tonight's farewell dinner.

"I know," she told him, "but I was thinking maybe we should have stayed home tonight, just the three of us."

"He's only six months old…too young to understand. He's happy with his grandmother tonight, and I'll see him before I leave in the morning."

"He'll be a year old before you get home." She shook her head sadly. "He'll need to get to know his daddy all over again."

"We knew this was coming," he reminded her. "It goes with the territory."

"Yes, and I thought I could handle it," she replied. "It just feels a lot different when it's here and now. I'm sorry, honey, I don't want to spoil your last evening before you go." She gave him a little smile. "So, let's eat, drink, and be merry."

"Well, let's not drink too much," he told her. "We might think of other things to do once we get back home and put Johnny down for the night."

* * *

"I'm sorry I'm gonna miss your wedding." Vasquez was getting a little fuzzy around the edges, and it showed in her voice. "I don't know where they're sending me, but word is we won't be back for at least six months."

"It's OK." Carla was equally fuzzy, but a pang of concern registered through the warm glow. She was pretty sure she knew where the Marines were going, but she couldn't talk about it. "We'll get together and party after you get back. Just take care of yourself, girl."

"High on my priority list, ma'am. I gotta hang around for a couple of years and become a citizen." She gave a parody of a salute.

Carla and the Marine noncom had taken an instant liking to each other. Bjorn hadn't known what was going to happen when his fiancé came face-to-face with his would-be seductress, but now, having had a couple of drinks himself, he was feeling much better about the whole situation. He even got a chuckle out of some of the off-color Earthworm jokes the two women tossed back and forth.

Now, however, it was time to go. Mike DaSilva had rung the last call bell an hour earlier and had just turned up the lights as a signal that the few remaining diehards needed to be moving out. The three of them got up from the table, and Maya came around toward Bjorn.

"One more time…call it a wedding present," she said and proceeded to wrap herself around Bjorn and give him a hot, passionate kiss.

"Wow!" Carla exclaimed, as the Marine finally disentangled herself, leaving Bjorn looking stunned. "That's what I call a kiss! Do you give lessons on how to do that?"

"Sure do," Vasquez replied. She stepped up and wrapped herself around Carla and delivered an equally passionate kiss to the other woman.

"That's how we do that," she proclaimed as she disengaged once again. "I do other girls, too, just for variety."

Carla's head was spinning. She was completely straight in her sexual orientation, but *Damn*, she thought, *that woman can kiss!*

"I think my mom needs to meet you, lady," she told Maya.

"Don't do admirals…chain of command problems, ya know." The Marine winked at her.

"Call it a Section 136," Carla advised, with a wink of her own.

Realizing the rigid, paramilitary structure of LFS society could hamper social interaction, the powers-that-be had added Section 136 to the Code of Military Protocols. That section specified that occasional, temporary, and infrequent sexual liaisons between military members in the same chain of command were OK, provided neither member was coerced, that they were sufficiently far apart in the chain of command to have no regular duty relationship, that they were discreet about it, and that it did not affect the performance of their duties.

Vasquez remembered an old, grizzled gunnery sergeant in basic training explaining that Section 136 had been written so that the top brass could get laid. Otherwise, the gunny advised, flag officers had nowhere to go since just about everybody they knew was either someone at their level, with whom they had to work, or someone in their chain of command. The lower ranks, according to the gunny's wisdom, had much more in the way of options.

Seeing the thoughtful look on Maya's face, Carla leaned in and whispered, "I'll introduce you to her when you get back."

* * *

LFS *Sorceress*, Lunar Fleet Anchorage

The Bad Girls Club was meeting in Amy Ling's spacious quarters aboard *Sorceress*—a final meeting before Ling took the Double Deuce out to deal with the Otuka.

"Do you have everything you need, Amy?" Lorna Greenwood asked.

Ling shrugged. "I've got everything the T.O. calls for, including Rock Bartley's AT full of Marines. I don't think we'll need more than that, but if we run into something we can't handle, we know the drill."

Lorna nodded. Ling was commanding a powerful force, but they were dealing with an unknown enemy. If the Otuka showed up with a force sufficient to overwhelm the Double Deuce, the drill was simple. It had been defined decades ago in Luna's earliest contacts with alien races. Ling's first duty would be to dispatch one of the E-boats to report what had happened. Her main force would cover the courier's retreat, making sure the enemy did not follow. After that, Ling would try to disengage, but under no circumstances would she return to Luna unless she could be certain the enemy could not follow, which was difficult when dealing with aliens whose technical abilities were unknown. More likely, she would make a stand and fight to the end. Better that her force be wiped out than to lead a powerful enemy back to the home system.

The final determination would be Amy Ling's, but Lorna had confidence in her judgment and her courage. Ling would do what was necessary. If it came to a final stand, the enemy would be given a hell of a fight.

"Your ops plan looks good," Robin Torrey remarked. "Assuming the Otuka don't have the system under surveillance, and they aren't already there when you arrive, you should be able to hide pretty well in the Shattered Moon cluster. Even an Otuka scout that manages to get in close should only see *Hubble* in orbit, which should entice them to come back in force to protect their hunting grounds." Torrey hesitated a bit, then shrugged. "Of course, we have no idea how they think, so…"

"So, as far as predicting how they'll react or what to expect, I might as well cast runes or examine the entrails of a chicken," Ling remarked.

"Right," Torrey acknowledged, "though I might suggest a deck of Tarot cards instead."

*****

Chapter Three

TerraNova City, Luna

"It's been a wonderful day...and night," Carla whispered.

The only response was a gentle snore behind her head. The arm around her shoulders didn't move, despite the soft stroke her fingers gave it.

Just a typical guy, she thought, *sound asleep on his wedding night.*

In fairness, Bjorn had done all that was necessary to make the marriage complete before falling asleep. Besides, the last few days had been as stressful for him as it had been exciting for her. Although he was a big hunk of a man, over a hundred well-toned kilos of blond haired, Scandinavian good looks, he was mostly quiet and shy. He wasn't one for fancy ceremonies and high-profile parties, and he'd certainly had enough of those to last him for a while.

For that matter, the last three months—their entire engagement—had been stressfully busy for both. First, Bjorn had applied for a position with the LRI. Carla had, at his insistence, stayed clear of that process. He was overqualified for the available research post, certainly more qualified than other applicants, and he succeeded without a word of recommendation from her. He listed only Earthworm colleagues as references and submitted his own published work for documentation.

On the other hand, Carla mused, Dr. Basil Harrington, Ph.D., F.L.R.I., Director of the LRI's Sub-Atomic Physics Division—Bjorn's new boss—must have known Bjorn was Carla's husband-to-be. That may have accounted for the speedy response and the generous terms of the offer he extended. Harrington was known to be slow and methodical and a notorious penny-pincher. He might have been impressed with Bjorn's credentials, but all the same, Carla figured she should probably write off a couple of the favors Harrington owed her.

* * *

Once past that hurdle, Bjorn had gone back to Earth to tender his resignation at NAU and wrap up his projects there. Carla needed to wrap up her own NAU project, clean up a few loose ends on Earth, and return to Luna to plan their wedding. Her mother had not been very helpful.

"I'm a military strategist," Lorna had told her. "I plan wars, campaigns, and battles. I don't know how to plan victory celebrations. This is one of those times when I wish your other mother were still alive—not just because she'd be happy for you, but because she was much better than I am at planning social events."

Carla had plenty of help though. Scarlett MacRae, wife of CEO, Uncle Mick O'Hara, had plenty of experience planning and coordinating social events. She was Terra Corporation's Director of Marketing and would also have been Luna's first lady if the LFS had put any stock in such designations. She once remarked to Carla that she might not have married Michael O'Hara if not for the Lunar custom of women keeping their own surnames after marriage.

"It was bad enough, having married an Irishman," she'd proclaimed in her noteworthy Scottish accent, "but I don't think I could have gone the rest of my life with the name Scarlett O'Hara. Who would ever take a woman with that name seriously?"

In any case, people did take Scarlett MacRae seriously as she smoothly arranged for pre-wedding events, the ceremony, the reception, and a thousand little details Carla would never have considered.

If anyone involved was inclined to give MacRae trouble, she could turn to Carla's other volunteer wedding planner, her dear Aunt Annie.

Lieutenant General Anne McGraw, Commandant of the LFS Marine Corps, had never married and had no children of her own. She'd always been close to Lorna Greenwood and had treated Carla like the daughter she'd always wanted. She vowed to get Carla's wedding accomplished in what the Marines called an orderly and proficient manner.

MacRae, for her part, was not at all reluctant to use the Marine Commandant for her intimidation factor. When a caterer appeared about to renege on his commitments, MacRae turned to McGraw.

"Lassie, he says he can't possibly deliver the food on time in the quantity specified. He has scheduling problems."

"Hmmm..." McGraw turned to the caterer. "Do I need to send some Marines over here to help you?"

"Help me with what?" The caterer looked bewildered.

"Help you get your head out of your ass," she told him, without a trace of humor in her voice. "If you don't need their help now, you'll certainly need it later, unless you get those scheduling problems worked out to our satisfaction."

MacRae could only marvel at the way the problems in question seemed to evaporate and were never mentioned again.

* * *

Carla had wanted a simple, private ceremony with a few close friends and her extended family in attendance, but she'd quickly realized that wasn't going to work. There were too many people who would be hurt or disappointed if they weren't invited. She understood the celebrations and ceremonies weren't just for her and Bjorn. They were a way for others who cared about them to share the joy. With that in mind, she asked Bjorn how many people he wanted to invite from the groom's side of the event. He had looked at her in surprise.

"Ah…anybody I might invite would be an Earthworm, love. I don't think many of them could afford—"

"Nonsense." She'd cut him off. "I'm rich, remember? We can charter a shuttle, round-trip, with a couple of days on Luna, accommodations at the TerraNova Hilton. You'd be surprised how cheap a package like that can be. So come on, darlin', contribute your share to the guest list."

As it turned out, Bjorn had a brother in Sweden who ended up being his best man and a small gaggle of friends, male and female, mostly former colleagues at NAU, who were delighted to get an invitation to the wedding, especially since it included an all-expense-paid three days on Luna. Most of them had never been off Earth before.

Everything had come together today, with a Catholic wedding in the TerraNova Cathedral. It wasn't the largest church on Luna, but it was large enough to accommodate the two hundred friends and family members they had invited.

Carla had been raised Catholic, which was a bit surprising since her birth mother had no religion of her own. Lorna claimed to believe in God, but her faith was a personal thing she chose not to display in public. Carla's other mother, Carla Perry, had been a Catholic, and both women had shared a common friendship with Luna's first Catholic Bishop, the Reverend Daniel DeForrest. Lorna had seen to it that her daughter was baptized a Catholic at birth and had steered Carla to Father DeForrest for a proper education in the teachings of that faith. DeForrest, a Jesuit who had been sent to Luna by the Vatican as both a scientist and a priest, was a man of deep faith but with a pragmatic view of organized religion in general. Lorna trusted him to give her daughter both an anchoring in faith and a healthy dose of skepticism about religious zealotry, Christian and otherwise. He'd succeeded, in part due to Carla's powerful intellect and questioning nature.

DeForrest, now in his 90s, still enjoyed a good debate on matters of faith, morality, ethics, and such. Lorna and Carla were participants in such debates whenever DeForrest was their dinner guest at home in TerraNova. He had been more than willing to come out of retirement to perform the marriage ceremony.

Carla was painfully aware of a few people who couldn't attend the wedding. She knew Veronica Bartley and Amy Ling wanted to be there, as well as one of her favorite cousins, Rob O'Hara, Mick and Scarlett's oldest son. And of course, she reminded herself, her newly acquired friend Maya Vasquez was also among the missing. True to her faith, Carla murmured a little prayer for those people. She wasn't officially connected with the LFS military, but she'd been with her mother at that dinner on Copper Hills Prime. She knew where those people had gone, and her prayer was for their safety, their Deliverance from Evil.

Remembering the Copper Hills dinner brought a smile to her face as she thought about an uninvited, or so she thought, guest who had shown up for the reception. Heart of the Warriors had not come to the church for fear his presence might somehow disrupt the ceremony, but he had appeared at the reception, accompanied by the Akara Ambassador. The guests, and the ambassador, had been shocked when Carla, with a gasp of surprised delight, had rushed over to embrace the old war lizard.

Bjorn—who had never met an Akara before—was stunned, but he recovered quickly and held out his hand when introduced. Shaking hands was not an Akara custom, but they had learned it from the humans. Heart gave him a firm handshake, expressing his fervent hope that Bjorn would prove a worthy mate for the Egg of the

Queen. Carla was thrilled by Heart's presence. How many brides, she wondered, could say a guest had journeyed sixty light-years just to attend their wedding?

The wedding was over, but Carla hadn't been quite ready to settle down. There was, after all, the honeymoon to enjoy first.

* * *

LFS *Sorceress*—New Eden L5 Point

"How the hell did the bastards get so close without our seeing them?" Jake Roundtree snarled.

"We let them do it," Amy Ling told her flag captain. "We knew this could happen, remember?"

Ling wore her usual, unemotional, oriental mask, but inside she was seething. I *let them do it, not we,* she told herself. *It was my choice not to put pickets on the far side of the primary. Of course, we didn't expect them to be so stealthy in their approach…*

The Otuka horde—a disorganized, unruly formation of over a hundred ships—had come out of hyperspace on the far side of the star system with the star between them and New Eden. Ling had chosen not to put pickets on that side to watch for a hyper signature because of the time it would take those pickets to rejoin her formation if the enemy approached from the near side instead. She'd figured the Otuka would follow a normal in-system approach, accelerating halfway to the target, then flipping over and decelerating the rest of the way. It was the fastest way to get to the inner system, and fusion-powered gravity-drive ships didn't need to worry about the energy expended to achieve that quick transit.

If the Otuka had done that, Ling's forces would have seen them coming. The Otuka, however, were not in any hurry. Or maybe they always cautiously approached a target, being, in Ling's view, the marauding, uncivilized, and paranoid creatures they were. They'd accelerated about a third of the way into the system, still on the other side of the primary, where Ling's force couldn't see them. Then they'd gone ballistic, coasting in with no emission signature by which to detect their presence. They'd let the star's gravity pull them around in a sweeping curve toward New Eden, then fired up their drives when they absolutely had to so they would not overshoot the planet. Then, they lit up in Ling's tactical displays like a sudden burst of fireworks.

It had taken them at least five times as long to come in that way—a couple of weeks instead of a few days—but by doing so, they had stayed off the Double Deuce's detection grid until they were almost there. The horde would arrive in planetary orbit in twelve hours, but worse, if any of Amy's warships tried to move out of concealment—even under low power—the Otuka would see them. She had no choice now but to sit and wait for the enemy to arrive.

She'd ordered *Hubble* to break orbit and rejoin the battle group in its hiding place as soon as the Otuka had been detected. Moving with as much stealth as possible, the scientific ship had complied, and the approaching aliens gave no indication they had seen the maneuver.

The problem was that *Hubble's* scientists were scattered over at least twelve different sites on New Eden's surface. Ling couldn't use the E-boats to retrieve them because the express couriers had powerful gravity drives whose signature the aliens would detect, if not on approach, then later when the Otuka were closer, and the E-boats were trying to rejoin the fleet. Only three of Ling's warships—*Sorceress* and the two heavy cruisers—carried landing craft suitable for planetary retrieval of the scientists, but those didn't have much in the way of stealth capabilities. Again, she might get them down to the planet, but they'd probably be detected on the return.

That left the four heavy assault landers aboard *Okinawa,* and again, Ling found herself thanking whatever gods or fates there were for Colonel Bartley's foresight. Intended to be dropped into a hostile planetary environment, the Marine craft did have stealth capabilities, including scatter fields and fully shielded drives. They could get onto the planet, make a pickup, and get back without the enemy seeing them…once, anyway. After that, if the Otuka detection gear was any good, they might be spotted on the return, somewhere between the planet and the Shattered Moon, where even the slightest emission signature might be detected in open space.

Any one of the HALs could have taken all the scientists off the planet, but four HALs couldn't be in twelve places at once. Paradoxically, the landing craft could drop in like meteors and land just about anywhere, but once down, they were much slower moving from place to place in atmospheric flight. If all went well, they could get about half of the scientists off the planet before the enemy got there. The rest would have to lay low and avoid the Otuka the best they could until the aliens made their intentions clear enough to justify an engagement. After that…

One hundred twelve of them, against twenty of us. The numbers were meaningless without knowing the capabilities of the enemy warships. For that matter, Ling didn't know how many of them were warships. *For all I know, these could be cruise ships, bringing their version of tourists here for a safari. If so*, she decided grimly, *they are about to get a lesson that will elevate the term 'dangerous game' to a whole new level.*

* * *

Planet New Eden—Research Team Alpha

"They're not going to be able to pick us up, are they?"

"Not yet, Dr. Phillips," Mercedes Warren replied, "but don't worry. Admiral Ling is not going to abandon us."

Phillips, despite his doctorate, was the youngest and least experienced member of the team, but he had proven his worth, if not with his knowledge, then with his simple, bold approach to the mission.

After landing on New Eden, the scientific team had established a base camp and spent a month there, learning the basics of New Eden's ecology. They'd seen no sign of human habitation, but they had expected none. The site had been deliberately selected because it was far from any concentration of the indigenous population.

After the first month, they had established five remote camps to give them a feel for the diversity of the ecosystem. It wasn't until the third month that they had set out to find the native humans. Warren had personally taken charge of one of several teams—the one for which Phillips was the resident anthropologist—and started a thirty-kilometer hike toward an area where orbital imagery had shown a tribe of Edies, as the scientists called New Eden's aboriginal humans, camped on the forested slopes of a broad river valley.

As they approached the area, Warren had gotten the feeling they were being watched—tracked by Edie scouts, perhaps—but they hadn't seen anyone until they crossed an open meadow and looked up to find two of the aborigines at the forest edge less than a hundred meters away. Though the Edies were obviously watching them, Warren's first instinct had been to freeze. She had motioned to her team to do the same, but Phillips was in front of her and hadn't see the signal. Instead, he had forged ahead, raising his arm to wave at the natives.

"Hallooooo," he had called out to them.

The Edies, both males, armed with spears, had looked at each other, then back at Phillips. They had said nothing, but one of them had shifted his spear nervously into a guard position. They had exchanged glances once again, then melted back into the forest, gone in an instant.

Phillips had looked disappointed. He had thrown up his hands, as if seeking enlightenment as to why the Edies didn't want to meet him. Then he had turned back to the rest of the team, who were looking at him in dismay. When Warren questioned him, he had defended his approach logically.

"Look," he had told her, "it's obvious they know we are here. We can't pretend we don't see them, so why not make a direct attempt to communicate?"

"We don't want to frighten them," she had protested. "We're obviously different. They might think we're supernatural spirits or something."

"Right!" He had snorted. "Supernatural beings who stumble over rocks, have to help each other climb slopes, and spend half their time swatting at those annoying insects they have here. Lady, we're just human, and they know it. The only thing they don't know is whether our intentions are friendly, and the best way to settle that is to approach them openly.

"These are simple hunter-gatherers. Their population density isn't high enough to make crime profitable or warfare necessary to defend their territory. The only problem they have with us is that they don't know us."

Warren had thought it over and decided the young scientist was probably right.

"Arachnids," she told him.

"Beg your pardon?"

"Those insects you've been complaining about aren't really insects. Eight legs, more like arachnids."

"Ugh! Flying spiders!" He grimaced.

"Also, in case you haven't noticed, they don't bite or sting. They seem to be attracted to our perspiration, perhaps for the salt content.

In other words, they want to drink your sweat. Maybe that's why the natives don't seem to be bothered by them."

Exobiology was Warren's specialty, and she was finding lots of interesting life-forms to study. She had advised Phillips she was willing to try it his way. They had moved a short way into the woods and set up camp in a little clearing. It hadn't been long before they realized they were being watched again.

Other than short forays to examine native flora and fauna, they had stayed close to camp. Over the next few days, they had caught brief glimpses of the Edies, and on the fourth day, they had seen their first female.

"That's encouraging." Phillips had been bubbling with enthusiasm. "In a society like this, simple human physiology dictates that men are hunters and warriors, and women are gatherers and artisans. If we are seeing women, that means they don't consider us dangerous, even if they don't want to meet us yet."

The Edies were a handsome race. They were tall and muscular and appeared to be in good health. New Eden was a bountiful provider for their sparse population, and the climate in the area was warm and pleasant at this time of year. The natives wore garments that were sparse and simple, yet modest, compared to Warren's expectations. She had expected naked savages, and she had expressed that opinion to Phillips.

"You only find that in tropical climates, where clothing is unnecessary any time of the year," he had told her. "This climate is temperate, and though it's warm now, they get some pretty cold winters. Once people discover clothing as protection from weather, they soon realize it also protects tender parts of the body from scratches and other injuries. After that, they tend to wear at least some clothing all year 'round, though these people don't seem to have much in the way of body modesty."

Warren had chuckled. Phillips had obviously been captivated by the young female Edie who was watching them from the forest about forty meters away. The girl had auburn hair that fell well below her shoulders. It was streaked with green and grey to match the body paint that decorated her golden-tan skin. She was showing a lot of skin, wearing little more than a short kilt-like skirt and a halter that restrained, but didn't really cover, her well-developed breasts. The skirt and halter appeared to be made from some sort of animal skin, as did the pair of simple, laced boots that covered her feet. The garments were streaked with the same colors, and Warren realized the intent was to provide camouflage. *It works,* she reflected. A couple of steps into the woods, and the natives became nearly invisible.

Phillips had raised his hand almost timidly and waved at the girl, who promptly vanished into the forest.

"Careful, Doctor," Warren had cautioned, with a grin. "Don't let your male hormones get in the way of scientific objectivity."

* * *

That observation had been made three days earlier, and they hadn't seen the girl since. Now, the Otuka were coming, and any discussions of Edie dress codes had been put aside in favor of more important considerations, like survival.

"We need to emulate the natives," Warren told her team. "They tend to stay back in the forest and spend very little time in the open. Any of them who appear under open sky seem nervous, and they always bolt for tree cover when startled. These people don't seem to fear local predators, so any agoraphobia they have is probably due to the Otuka.

"If the Edies think it's a good idea to stay out of open spaces, we should do the same. The cover here is good." She gestured to indicate the dense top canopy provided by the strange, broad-leafed alien trees, towering nearly fifty meters into the sky.

"Let's keep under it but stay alert and don't assume the trees alone will keep you safe. Our orbital gear was good enough to spot this Edie settlement despite the tree cover. Let's assume the Otuka gear is just as good. Be prepared to move quickly and to defend yourselves if necessary."

To illustrate the point, she drew her sidearm and checked its magazine. Phillips swallowed hard. He had a sidearm and had been trained in its use—had even been required to go to a firing range and prove he had learned something from the training—but he wasn't a gun person. He never expected he'd have to use the damned thing. After all, that was why they brought the Marines, wasn't it?

* * *

LFS *Okinawa*—New Eden L5 Point

"Colonel, they're going in."

"I know." Rock Bartley's reply was curt.

"But they're deploying all over the planet!"

"I know." Her reply was a bit stronger this time, as she tried to convince the young Marine lieutenant to quit stating the obvious.

Bartley sensed the man's frustration, which was echoed by the rest of her staff. Swarms of Otuka small craft were deploying from their ships, heading down toward New Eden, while the Lunar forces waited in hiding and did nothing. She felt she owed her people an explanation, though they already knew what was going on, as they had been briefed long before the aliens arrived.

"We have to be sure," she told them. "We are almost certain they are the Otuka. We almost certainly know what they are going to do. There's maybe one tiny chance in a billion we're wrong, that they're just a bunch of interstellar tourists with cameras who want to take videos of the colorful natives, but because of that tiny chance, we need to sit and wait for them to do something, otherwise…"

Otherwise, what? She knew waiting was going to cost lives, certainly native lives, and possibly those of some of the scientists and her Marines as well.

"Otherwise, we are no better than they are, killing intelligent beings without justification," she finished. "We have to be better than that, even if it costs us in the end."

She turned back to her displays. The Otuka were strung out in low equatorial orbit, a string of over a hundred bright beads that encircled the planet, unaware they were being watched by the satellites Amy Ling had deployed in higher orbit when the Double Deuce first arrived. The relatively tiny devices had been mostly passive until now and had been shut down completely during the Otuka's approach. Now, they were back online, tight-beaming their signals directly to the hidden Lunar battle group. Those on the other side of the planet had to relay their imagery through a repeater satellite, but the lag was no more than a few seconds. If something of significance happened down there, Bartley and her team would know, but until then, all they could do was wait.

The waiting proved mercifully brief. One of the first groups of Otuka craft touched down near a large native encampment under surveillance by the satellites. In the enhanced imagery, Bartley and her staff could see dozens of aliens leaving each craft, spreading out, and moving line-abreast toward the encampment. The native humans tried to flee, only to be intercepted by groups of hunters coming in from the other side. The imagery wasn't good enough to show weapons firing, but humans who crossed the path of the approaching aliens abruptly stopped moving. Then, the hunters and their prey—who were now fleeing back into the encampment—came within range of the hidden cameras the scientists had set up in the trees to watch the encampment. The imagery, like that provided by the Akara in the mission brief, left no doubt as to what was happening. Bloody slaughter. Men, women, and children—the Otuka did not discriminate.

The scientists who had been studying the encampment had been retrieved before the aliens arrived, but it was hard to watch the natives dying, knowing there was no way to save them. Bartley was about to query the flagship when Ling's voice came over the command channel.

"All units, Attack Plan Alpha, execute on my mark. Three, two, one, mark!"

Plan Alpha was the simplest and most straightforward of the plans they had developed, and Bartley knew Ling considered simplicity to be a virtue beyond all others in battle. They had contingency plans if the Otuka presented them with any surprises, but Ling's order relegated those contingency plans to the scrap heap.

The plan called for the Double Deuce to execute a straight-in, all-up attack designed to blow a large hole in the Otuka's low-orbit formation. The hole was then to be occupied by *Okinawa* and her escort of four destroyers. Since her Marine assault craft were designed for planet-side action, not space combat, the AT needed to get in close to deploy and support them. The destroyers were tasked with keeping the enemy away from her while she did that. Meanwhile, the rest of the battle group would deal with the Otuka ships. If the enemy was foolish enough to remain in orbit, Ling would split her force and roll them up in both directions.

As soon as the Double Deuce closed within range of the orbiting enemy, a lot of missiles were going to be launched before the Otuka had time to figure out what was happening. Surprise was right up there with simplicity in Amy Ling's playbook.

Bartley had her own mission. First priority, rescue the scientists. Second priority, protect the natives. Third priority, wipe out any of the enemy who didn't surrender. After the imagery she had just seen, Bartley was hoping none of them did.

"We're moving out now, Colonel," Captain Josh Herzfeld advised from *Okinawa's* bridge. "Estimated time to drop point: 47 minutes."

Bartley acknowledged. She had decided—with Herzfeld's concurrence—that even if the enemy wasn't completely cleared from their path, *Okinawa* and her escorting destroyers would go to low-orbit levels, drop their Marines, and then, if necessary, withdraw. Regardless of the outcome of Ling's first thrust, it was 47 minutes to drop point. The only question was whether they would be making the drop under fire.

She keyed her command channel. "Launch bay, all units, this is ComCon. Assault Teams and Raptors to Ready One. Prepare for launch in 47 minutes."

* * *

Planet New Eden—Research Team Alpha

"I can see a whole bunch of them, about three hundred meters away! They really do look like centaurs—half horse, half…well, more simian than human, with curled horns, like mountain sheep."

"Dr. Phillips!" the voice crackled in his earbud. "Will you please get your ass back into the woods! Those centaurs are coming to kill you and anyone else on two legs." Mercedes Warren sounded thoroughly exasperated, but Owen Phillips was too busy to notice. The Otuka—about thirty of them—were moving slowly in his direction.

He scanned the group with his binoculars and was shocked to see one of the aliens raise what appeared to be binoculars as well. The centaur looked directly at him, then lowered the instrument and pointed in his direction.

Phillips had just decided that did not bode well when something hit him from behind and knocked him to the ground. An instant later, he heard a sharp crackling sound, as a bright-as-lightning rod of energy flashed through the space where he'd been standing.

A noise beside him caused him to turn, and he found himself face-to-face with an Edie female. He was sure it was the same girl he'd watched a few days before, and it was obvious she had knocked him down. Now, she favored him with a string of whispered, but strangely musical, words. It was the first time an Edie had spoken to an off-world human. He guessed from her expression that the words were not very complimentary. *Probably calling me an idiot, telling me to keep my stupid head down,* he imagined. For want of a better response, he nodded vigorously. *You're right, I'm an idiot.*

The Edie motioned for him to follow and began crawling rapidly through the tall grass toward the tree line fifty meters away. Her retreating derriere was an enticing sight he was more than happy to follow, but after crawling the first few meters, he decided to risk a glance at the approaching enemy. He raised his head for a quick look, and his heart sank.

The resemblance between the lower half of an Otuka and a horse was more than cosmetic. The creatures were built to run fast. The aliens were galloping in his direction and rapidly covering the distance between them. Phillips realized with despair that he and the girl were not going to make it to the tree line. He redoubled his efforts. The girl was slightly faster but slowed to wave him on. *No, don't stop.* He willed her to keep going. *I'm toast, but you might still make it!*

He thought about the sidearm at his hip. *Can't stop them all, but maybe I can delay them so my little guardian angel can get away.* He raised the pistol unsteadily, trying to aim at the leading centaur, now less than

100 meters away. He started to squeeze the trigger, then stared in amazement as the alien went down in an explosion of gore. Then he heard the growl of the autocannon, lagging the impact of its supersonic projectiles, and watched in awe as the Marine gunship screamed across the field.

* * *

As she pulled up out of her strafing run, Maya Vasquez thumbed the countermeasures button on her control yoke, leaving a cloud of EMP dazzlers, hot flares, and radar-confusing chaff in her wake. She didn't think any of the donkey-boys down there had a surface-to-air missile in his pocket, but she was taking no chances.

"ComCon, Cobra Two, I have scientists—at least one of them—at Grid Echo Seven, coordinates zero one four by two three seven. Area is not, repeat not, secure, so bring the cavalry along with the pickup."

"Cobra Two, ComCon, roger that. Echo Seven at zero one four by two three seven. Understood, area not secure."

At the top of her climb, Vasquez pulled the Raptor all the way over on its back, then rolled into a dive for a return pass. As she reacquired the target area, she noted the aliens had done the smart thing—they'd scattered. She'd managed to knock down about five of them on her first pass, but they weren't going to oblige her by lining up again. No problem, she decided. They'd scattered, but they hadn't scattered widely enough. She punched in new settings on her weapons-select panel.

* * *

On the ground, Phillips felt like cheering as the gunship came around for another pass, but this time, the attack craft seemed to be holding well away from his position, and its guns were silent as it came in. The centaurs had organized themselves, and several of them raised their weapons and shot at their attacker. Phillips was sure at least one of them hit the ship, and he saw the energy bolt reflect off the armored side of the Raptor, doing little or no damage.

He looked around and, to his surprise, found the Edie girl half-crouching less than two meters away, watching the scene unfold. He turned back, just in time to see a stream of small, black objects spreading out from dispensers hung under the gunship's stubby wings. The objects arced lazily toward the ground.

"Uh-oh, that can't be good," Phillips muttered. He whirled around and, this time, it was his turn to tackle the Edie girl and pull her to the ground, just as all hell broke loose among the centaurs.

* * *

Vasquez had deliberately piloted her run away from the scientist and his native companion, because she knew anything near the strings of cluster bomblets she dropped would be shredded.

The bomblets used technology that dated back to the mid-twentieth century. Made to fall nose down when they were dropped, they didn't require a fancy proximity fuse. They were intended to hit the ground, and the impact triggered a small charge that kicked the bomblet back into the air—about two meters up—where it detonated, sending a spray of deadly steel 10mm balls in all directions. Anything standing within fifty meters of the detonation would most likely not be standing afterward.

The gunship's dispensers laid down a path of destruction over 100 meters wide. Vasquez had planned her run carefully, and both Phillips and his companion were well outside the kill zone. The centaurs were not so fortunate, but they were big, tough creatures. A few inside the zone were only wounded. A few who managed to get down behind rocks or fallen trees were uninjured. Survivors that were still on their feet bolted for cover.

Vasquez made one more pass, ripping up the field between the centaurs and the scientist with 30mm cannon fire to discourage the aliens from moving in that direction. When she looked back, the field was empty except for the two humans but then three other scientists emerged from the tree line. Dr. Warren had come to try to rescue her prodigal team member and had arrived just in time to see the show.

"Cobra Two, Rescue Two, inbound to your area with a heavy weapons squad on board. What is your status, over?"

"Rescue Two, Cobra Two, area secure," Vasquez advised. "Have five, repeat five, people in sight awaiting rescue."

Vasquez came around for another pass, scanning the area for any sign of the donkey-boys. She was starting to pull up again when threat warning indicators in her helmet display started screaming at her. She pulled the Raptor into a sharp roll to the left, just as a powerful energy beam from above narrowly missed her and blasted into the forest below. She switched the helmet display from ground attack to wide area tactical and found the source of the enemy fire—no less than six Otuka aircraft were diving on her from above.

"Rescue Two! Wave Off! Wave Off! I've got six bogies in the air over the LZ. Engaging now."

She snapped her ship into a hard, climbing turn to meet the enemy. The Raptor was designed for ground support, not air combat, but it was far from helpless, and right now, it was the only attack craft available for the job.

* * *

LFS *Okinawa*—New Eden Orbit

Colonel Bartley was not a happy camper. She knew as well as Vasquez that the Raptor was not designed for air-to-air missions, especially at six-to-one odds.

"Where are they?" she demanded.

"Planetary grid Echo Seven," her TACOPS controller responded. "Orbital progression will bring us over that area in forty-one minutes."

"Not soon enough," Bartley snapped. She keyed her console, putting herself on *Okinawa's* ship-to-ship channel. Under the current command structure, the four screening destroyers were hers to command.

"*Timberwolf*, this is Marine ComCon."

"*Timberwolf* Prime, go ahead ComCon."

Bartley smiled. The Prime suffix told her the destroyer's captain had decided to take the call personally, and she recognized the face that appeared on her screen.

"Captain O'Hara, how's your gunnery?" she enquired.

"As good as any in the fleet, Colonel," Rob O'Hara responded without hesitation. *Timberwolf* had earned high marks for gunnery in her workup trials.

"Good! I need you to break formation and park yourself over planetary grid Echo Seven ASAP. Six enemy aircraft are disputing our claim to air superiority. I need you to explain it to them, with appropriate application of directed graser fire. Can you do that?"

O'Hara blinked. Warship grasers were not normally considered suitable for attacks against planetary targets. Conventional thinking called for such attacks to be conducted with bombs, missiles, or kinetic weapons—massive objects moving at meteoric speeds. Grasers lost some of their effectiveness in the atmosphere due to absorption and scatter.

On the other hand, in space, they were good to 10,000 kilometers or more. They wouldn't lose much energy firing straight down through a hundred kilometers of atmosphere, all but the last ten kilometers being fairly thin. Targeting systems that could hit a warship at space battle ranges should certainly be able to hit an aircraft at a fraction of the distance.

O'Hara glanced at his displays. Lieutenant Raczak, his navigation officer, had been paying attention and already had the course laid in.

"Roger that, Colonel. *Timberwolf* is en route to target area," he advised.

* * *

Planet New Eden—Research Team Alpha

Close, Maya Vasquez reflected, *but not close enough. If I coulda got one more of the bastards, I bet the last one would have run away.*

She had gotten four of the six Otuka ships, three with 30mm cannon fire, the fourth—with the cannon's magazine finally empty—with a swarm of air-to-ground rockets ripple-fired from her starboard pod. Like her Raptor, the alien craft were not intended for air combat, but in the end, their superior numbers carried the engagement. She'd taken some damage from energy beam hits in the initial furball, but nothing critical. Then, when she'd gone after her fourth kill, one of them had hit the rocket pod under her left wing pylon. The exploding rockets had riddled her ship with fragments, taking out several critical systems.

Got me, too, she thought, clamping her left hand over the bleeding wound in her side. Her helmet displays were no longer working. She looked at the ruined instrument panel in front of her. Any readouts that weren't completely smashed were conveying only bad news. *Half my PFCs are out. We're going down.*

The Raptor was technically an aircraft—getting a certain amount of lift and flight control from its stubby wings and tail structure—but much of its ability to stay in the air depended on counter-gravity units under the fuselage powered by plasma fuel cells. With half of them gone, Vasquez's gloomy assessment of the Raptor's ability to stay airborne was, if anything, optimistic.

There was no point in calling for help. Radio communications were included in the list of non-functioning systems, and a flashing indicator told her ejection was not an option. She'd felt the fragment that slammed into the back of her seat, disabling that system. *Gonna have to ride her down.*

That wasn't going to be an option either. The two remaining alien craft were coming around again, intent on cutting her into little pieces. Her controls were responding, but only well enough to keep the Raptor from falling out of the sky, with nothing left for fancy maneuvers. She was a sitting duck, and she knew it.

"Semper Fi, you bastards!" she shouted in defiance, taking her blood-soaked left hand off her wound long enough to give the incoming Otuka a heartfelt middle-finger gesture just about any human in the Sol System would have recognized. "And Fuck You Very Much!"

To her amazement, the leading Otuka craft disintegrated in the air, skewered by a brilliant beam of energy that came straight down from above. Invisible in space, grasers produced a near-blinding display in the atmosphere when they converted gas molecules in their path into star-hot plasma. The effect was like a ruler-straight lightning bolt. An instant later, the second enemy craft suffered the same fate.

"Nice shooting, Navy," Maya acknowledged, correctly guessing the source of the beams. "Bet that spoiled their whole day…not that my day is looking any better." A stabbing pain in her side caused her to clamp her hand over the wound again.

She had dropped the ship's nose to dive out of the way of the attackers, but now the ground was coming up too fast. She hauled back on the yoke, and the wounded Raptor responded. The speed she'd gained in the dive translated into some measure of flight control, but speed was the last thing she wanted. She leveled off with a nose-high attitude she hoped would slow her down. Her rate of descent wasn't too bad—the grav units were still producing some output, but there was nothing but dense forest below. She needed to find open space. There was a broad, open field far ahead, which she recognized as the site of her original attack. She tried to stretch her glide path to reach it, but she realized she wasn't going to make it. *Almost, but not quite.*

She was still scanning ahead, looking for a break in the forest canopy when the remaining PFCs failed, and the Raptor dropped like a rock. *This is gonna hurt,* she told herself, as the trees reached up and snatched her from the sky.

* * *

The scientists at the edge of the field saw the Raptor go down, producing a cacophony of shattered tree limbs and torn metal. Owen Phillips flinched, expecting a fiery explosion, but none came. Mercedes Warren continued to stare in the direction of the crash.

"We've got to get over there," she announced. "Someone may have survived."

"No! We can't! We've got to wait here for the Marines to come! Some of those beasts are still out there." Amelia Rosewood's voice was practically a shriek, and the look on her face was pure hysteria. The botanist had been a nervous wreck since being told the Marines couldn't get them off the planet before the aliens arrived.

"She's right, Mercedes. We should remain here. It's the reasonable thing to do." Dr. Arthur Redmond's voice was calm but firm. Redmond, a geologist, made no secret of his opinion that he should be leading the expedition instead of Warren. He obviously felt he ought to take charge in the current crisis.

"That pilot took on the centaurs to protect us," Mercedes pointed out. "At the very least, we should try to return the favor."

"Let the Marines take care of it." Redmond was adamant. Rosewood hid behind him, avoiding Warren's gaze.

"Stay here if you like." Warren looked at him in disgust. "I'm going."

"I'm with you, Doc," Phillips volunteered. "Nobody was happier to see that ship than I was."

"Sorry, Angel," he told the Edie girl, who was still standing beside him. "I've got to go, but I'll be back."

The girl looked at him, then turned and scampered back into the woods. With a sigh, he turned and followed Warren across the field. He had just caught up to the exobiologist when a faint rustling sound caused him to turn around.

To his surprise, Angel was back, but this time, she'd brought friends—two burly male Edie hunters. All three of them were carrying long spears, which his anthropologist's detachment characterized as *assegais*, weapons commonly found among primitive tribes in Africa. The heavy edged-and-pointed head made them suitable for throwing, while the long shaft made them good for fending off enemies or dangerous animals at close quarters. He noted with interest that the heads appeared to be made of hand-forged metal.

One of the two men was bearded and appeared to be of middle age, while the other was clean-shaven and much younger. Both trotted past the scientists, the youth giving Phillips a broad grin as he went by. They took up positions slightly in front and on either side of the party, spears at the ready. Meanwhile, Angel came up and kept pace beside Phillips. He smiled at her, and she returned the smile.

"Looks like you've made friends, Doctor," Warren observed. "Maybe I was wrong to worry about your scientific objectivity."

Halfway across the field, they encountered a wounded centaur, a victim of the gunship's fury. The Edie hunters approached cautiously, but the alien was no longer a threat. It was lying on the ground, breathing heavily, but unconscious. The grass all around was stained with blood—red, just like human blood, Phillips observed. It appeared the creature had thrashed around, bleeding from multiple wounds before finally losing consciousness.

Up close, Phillips decided it didn't look as much like a mythological centaur as he'd thought. Its body was covered with large, leathery scales, with tufts of hair growing between them. Its upper torso wasn't as tall as that of a classical centaur—the shoulders for its arms were only about twenty centimeters above the shoulder joints of its forelegs. The face, which he'd first thought of as simian, now appeared more bear-like. What he'd first taken for curled horns now appeared to be fleshy protuberances that could be curled and uncurled.

He was still examining the creature when the older Edie hunter stepped up and drove his spear into its neck, producing more blood and a strangling rattle that ended as the creature quit breathing. Shocked at first, Phillips quickly recovered. *The Otuka have been killing and eating these people for a long time,* he reminded himself. *This one probably got a better death than it deserved.*

* * *

LFS *Sorceress*—New Eden Orbit

Amy Ling was no longer concerned about whether to allow some of the Otuka to escape. She had no choice. By the time her warships managed to destroy half of the alien force, the rest were fleeing in fifty different directions. She wouldn't be able to catch all, or even most, of them.

In the initial stages, they'd grouped together and tried to swarm her ships, but they hadn't been very organized. It was more like a mob riot than a battle, and they'd had no choice other than to rush headlong at Ling's ships. The Otuka, like several other spacefaring races, had abandoned missile and projectile weapons in favor of energy beams.

Energy weapons had some advantages. They could fire repeatedly as long as power was available. They needed no magazines of ammunition or missiles and no complex reloading systems. They were light-speed weapons, so there was no way to detect incoming fire until it hit the target. Once they fired, there was no defense against them other than heavy armor or gravitational shielding. Evasive action usually wasn't an option.

But the aliens who relied solely on energy weaponry had abandoned missiles too soon. They hadn't developed missile technology to anywhere near the level of the Lunar Free State, and the one factor that made LFS missiles so effective was range. Standard LFS Broadsword missiles were effective to around 50,000 kilometers—almost four times the effective range of even the most powerful, 75-cm grasers mounted by LFS battlecruisers. The newer Viper missiles were faster and had even greater range, while the Wolfpack system—

which piggybacked missiles onto a long range delivery vehicle—could hit targets half a million kilometers out.

The Otuka quickly realized the LFS warships could hit them from well outside their own beam-weapon range. Worse, not expecting missiles, they had nothing resembling a point-defense system, so they couldn't evade or stop incoming missiles. They'd rushed at the attackers, hoping to close within beam range quickly. Then they had discovered that Ling's ships packed heavy-duty beam weapons of their own and were armored against beam attack. They managed to score a few successes—the light cruiser LFS *Wraith* had been getting chewed up by an Otuka swarm until Amy's destroyers set upon the attackers like a pack of hungry wolves. In the end, with their losses mounting and little hope of victory, they disengaged and fled.

In less than two hours, the space battle was over. The last survivors of the Otuka horde were scattered and heading for the hyper limit as fast as they could go. None had surrendered, so Ling had no captured ships, prisoners, or Marine boarding actions to deal with. Her people might be able to learn something from the shattered hulks of a couple of Otuka ships that were still in one piece or a few very large pieces, but there was no real urgency.

The situation on the planet was another story. The Otuka in space had abandoned their fellows down on the planet from the moment the battle started. Many of them were still down there, and they seemed determined to fight to the finish.

* * *

Planet New Eden—Research Team Alpha

Vasquez hung at a crazy angle, still secured by her safety harness. Her left arm was badly mangled, and she was pretty sure she had broken ribs as well. She had managed to pull off her helmet, and she thought about using her still-functional right arm to release the harness, but looking at the shards of metal and plastic—twisted remains of the Raptor's hull—that would savage her as she fell two meters to the ground, she decided that wasn't a good idea.

And fall she would. Her legs weren't working. In fact, she had no feeling at all below her waist. *Broke my back,* she concluded. *Probably be flying a wheelchair for the rest of my life, assuming I get out of here at all. Hope they find me. Bury me back on Luna if nothing else. Please, just don't leave me to rot here in the woods.*

Her mind wasn't tracking well, and her vision was blurred, but it didn't take much concentration to recognize the creature that emerged from the woods and was cautiously approaching. The centaur turned to look back over its shoulder, and in that moment, Maya drew her sidearm from the holster under her shattered left arm. The alien turned back toward her, and she opened fire.

Her aim wasn't steady, but she kept firing, and the creature staggered as the 9mm rounds tore into it. Then she managed to put one into its head, and it dropped heavily to the ground, twitched a couple of times, and lay still.

See you in Hell, donkey-boy, she thought as her vision dimmed. Her head dropped forward, and her arm went limp. The pistol slipped from her grasp and fell to the forest floor.

The second centaur growled angrily as he came out of the woods, raised his hunting weapon, then lowered it again. He had seen the human's weapon fall and realized the puny thing—a female, he judged, despite the figure-concealing clothing she wore—was helpless, perhaps already dead. He wanted to make her pay for all the death and destruction she had brought upon his fellow hunters. He slung the rifle-like weapon and drew a long, curved knife from his harness.

He would cut the human open, he decided, and spill her entrails onto the ground. If she was still alive, that would ensure that she spent her last few moments in terrible pain. Then, he would cut out her heart and eat it. He would take the carcass with him. He had lost contact with his fellows and might need food to survive until they came back for him.

He would also take the female's head. Most of his hunt brothers took only heavy, rugged-featured, bearded male heads for trophies, but this one was special—a female human demon who had killed many hunters before being brought down. This was more than a trophy. It was a song-story, and he was already thinking about the epic poem he would compose when the head, encased in crystal, was displayed on a pedestal.

He took a step forward, then staggered sideways as the heavy spear punched into his side, just below his left arm. The spear went deep, and he clawed at it, trying to pull it out of the wound. He turned to face his attacker and went down in a hail of bullets.

Phillips holstered his pistol and ran toward the wrecked aircraft, but Warren and the aboriginal hunters were more cautious in their approach. Warren holstered her pistol and came forward slowly. The older hunter retrieved his spear, making certain the centaur was dead. The younger hunter checked the centaur the Marine pilot had killed. Angel looked at Warren and made a gesture the scientist interpreted as exasperation, then ran after Phillips with her spear at the ready.

As Warren approached the wreck, she noted that the pilot was female, dark haired, small in stature, and unconscious or…

"I think she's dead," Phillips said, shaking his head, sadly.

"Don't think," Warren told him. "Check for vitals."

She reached up and put two fingers against Vasquez' neck.

"I've got a pulse," she said. "Not much, but she's still with us. We need to get her down on the ground."

With gestures and encouragement, she managed to get the hunters involved, and they lowered the young Marine to the ground as gently as possible. The woman was obviously clinging to life by a thread, and there wasn't much they could do for her without medical facilities. Warren keyed her communicator.

"Redmond, have the Marines arrived yet? We have a survivor, but she's in bad shape."

* * *

D*amn!* Arthur Redmond cursed silently. *Just when I finally got Rosewood calmed down.*

"Not yet, but I'll let you know," he told Warren, then turned to the Marines who had just helped him into the assault lander. He was thankful he'd been wearing his earbud so they hadn't heard the exchange.

"We've got a couple people back in the woods, off in that direction," he told the Marine sergeant, pointing across the open field. "You can send some of your people to look for them, but first fly us back to camp. As you can see, Dr. Rosewood needs attention."

The Marine looked at him, then at Rosewood. *Needs attention? She needs a good slap upside the head to bring her back from Scared Shitless Land,* he thought, but the woman scientist was not one of his Marines, so he restrained himself. As for Redmond, the man had done nothing but issue orders ever since the Marines touched down. The sergeant had very little use for him and thought that making repeated trips to the same area was just plain stupid, especially with bands of angry centaurs in the area.

"Do you have radio contact with them?" he inquired.

"Yes, I just talked to them. They're fine, so let's get going," Redmond ordered.

"What frequency are you using?" the Marine asked.

"Whatever channel they have on these things. We need to go now, Sergeant."

"Thank you, Doctor." The Marine took the communicator from Redmond's belt without bothering to ask for it. He looked at its display, then punched a code into his own unit.

"Scientific team, this is Marine Rescue Two. Where are you, and what is your status?"

"This is Doctor Warren. If you have reached the clearing, we are about 200 meters into the woods on the north side. One of your aircraft went down here, and the pilot needs medical attention."

The Marine gave Redmond a look of pure disgust.

"Lieutenant," he advised the lander's pilot. "We've got a Marine pilot down in the woods to the north. We need to get in there with medics ASAP. Everybody's aboard, door closing now."

Unlike a Raptor, the heavy Dragonfly was built to hover and land in tight places, using turbofans to supplement its gravity drive units. The pilot poured on power, and the turbines spooled up to a high-pitched shriek. The craft lifted off with a cloud of dust, and the pilot sent it winging toward the north end of the field.

"I have to put you down at the tree line, Sergeant," he advised. "Forest is too dense for the ship to penetrate. Soon as we touch down, take your medics and go."

"Roger that," the noncom acknowledged. He gave Redmond another look of disgust, but the scientist refused to meet his gaze.

*****

Chapter Four

LFS *Sorceress*—New Eden Orbit

Battle's over, time to tally the cost, Amy Ling thought. *God, I hate this part.*

Ling preferred to hold briefings in person rather than by video. She had summoned Rock Bartley from *Okinawa* and Jake Roundtree from *Sorceress*' main bridge to join her command staff in the battlecruiser's flag briefing room. All the scientists had now been lifted off the planet, and Mercedes Warren had come over from *Hubble* to join the conference. Commander Eli Goldberg, Ling's staff operations officer, was conducting the briefing.

"*Wraith* has damage to her drive systems and forward reactor that can't be repaired here," Goldberg advised. "She's lost three missile tubes and two broadside grasers. Captain Rossi says he's eighty percent operational and combat capable. He wants to remain here, but Commodore Roundtree's engineering survey team puts *Wraith* at around sixty percent. In addition, she's got twenty-two casualties, including eighteen dead and four out of action with severe injuries."

"She's not staying here," Ling decided. "Cut orders sending her back with the supply train and add a request for an additional light cruiser to the after-action report. Is anybody else in that condition, or even close to it?"

"No, the only other ship with significant damage was *Wolverine*—she lost two drive nodes. Again, replacement is a shipyard job. She had only two casualties, but both were KIA. Five other ships report human casualties with repairable damage, a total of six crewmembers dead and five injured."

"Send *Wolverine* back as well and add a request for another destroyer. We don't know enough about the Otuka or what else they might have. If they come back at us with something heavier, I don't want to be nursing cripples. Since they're going back to Luna, see if you can transfer some crewmembers from *Wolverine* and *Wraith* to other ships that took casualties. Anything else?"

"No, ma'am. I have the repair schedules, and we should be up to full combat effectiveness—excluding those two ships—within seventy-two hours. I've also got a list of spares that need to be replenished. I've given that to Commander Jackman." Goldberg nodded to Ling's Staff Logistics Officer.

"Fine. Status on the supply train?"

"They're in-system now, ma'am," Jackman answered. "*Perseus* and *Rigel* have made contact, and they are on the way in. ETA sixty hours. We're lucky the Otuka incursion happened before they arrived. If the aliens had come a few days later, they might have caught us in the middle of the resupply operation."

"True," Ling agreed. "But we'd have had their escorts with us. An extra cruiser and a couple of destroyers would have been welcome."

She turned her attention to Colonel Bartley.

"All right, Rock, let's talk about your Marines and the situation on the planet."

"Yes, ma'am," Rock Bartley responded. "First, as you know, we lost two of the scientists. To that extent, we failed in our mission."

"In all fairness, Colonel," Warren spoke up, "I don't think anyone could have done better, and my people knew the dangers when they signed up. Dr. Jackson and Ms. Tanaka were told to come back to camp, but the Otuka were already coming down, and they thought they could do better hiding in the forest. Unfortunately, they were wrong. What disturbs me most is that we couldn't recover their bodies, at least not completely."

"Why not?" Amy Ling asked. This was the first she'd heard of the situation.

Warren hesitated, obviously reluctant to discuss it. Bartley answered instead.

"The Otuka caught them in the forest. We aren't sure whether they fought and made the donkeys angry or whether they were seen as different from the natives and the sons of bitches were curious about them. In any case, they didn't stack and tag their bodies for later pickup, like they usually do with the natives. They stopped to eat them instead. Apparently, the bastards like their meat freshly killed and raw."

"The delay probably saved the lives of a few Edies, and maybe some of our people, since my Marines hit them before they got near the Edie encampment. Unfortunately, we only found about half of Dr. Jackson. We found Ms. Tanaka's head and part of her rib cage…"

The colonel's voice trailed off, and there was stunned silence. Commander Goldberg looked like he was close to being violently ill. Ling finally spoke.

"We don't have any live Otuka prisoners, do we?"

"No, ma'am. My Marines weren't in the mood to take any."

"Probably for the best," Ling decided. "I'd be tempted to line them up and shoot them."

"You'd have plenty of volunteers for the firing squad, ma'am," Bartley advised.

"I imagine I would." Ling nodded. "Continue, Colonel."

"Yes, ma'am. We lost seventeen Marines KIA on the ground. Most casualties involved rescue operations, where we had to get in and get people out with the Otuka pressing them. Once we got the scientists out of harm's way, we were able to turn the tables and let the bastards find out what it feels like to be the hunted instead of the hunter. By that time, the fleet was fully engaged up here, so the Otuka on the planet were on their own. Without orbital spotting and support, the donkeys really aren't that good in the wilderness. We were able to bushwhack them in an orderly and proficient manner."

"We lost one Raptor—it's a total write-off due to air combat—before we figured out the Otuka craft were sitting ducks for orbital graser fire. We also have one Dragonfly down and in need of major repairs. I've got eight Marines wounded and out of action. Two of those, including the pilot of the downed Raptor, are critical and may not make it. We can't do anything more for them here, so we've cold-packed them for shipment back to Earth. It's a long shot for the pilot, maybe fifty-fifty for the other one."

"We'd probably have lost that pilot anyway if Dr. Warren and one of her scientists hadn't pulled her out of the wreckage. They risked their lives and took out a centaur in the process."

"It wasn't just us," Warren interjected. "We had three Edies with us, which proves we've succeeded in our primary mission—to make contact with the native humans. Besides my team, we have two other instances where the natives contacted us, always during or after some engagement where the Marines took on the Otuka threatening them. Apparently, that's what convinced them we were on their side. My people want to get back down there as soon as possible to continue the process. I guess you're the one who has to make that call, Colonel."

"Well, the admiral does, but I suspect she'll want my recommendation," Bartley responded. "I think we can let the scientists go back down now if they take some Marines along to keep them safe."

"As for the Otuka, we're estimating about 3,200 of them killed on the planet, and maybe a hundred more left alive down there. It may take a few days, but we know where all of them landed. We've wiped out any transport they had, and the survivors are all on foot. With orbital surveillance, we'll track them down, if the Edies don't get to them first. The natives have figured out that the tables are turned, and they're out for payback. Even with a modern weapon, a centaur in the woods is no match for a bunch of native hunters with spears, bows, and arrows. From what we've seen, the Edies aren't short on courage, and they know the forests a lot better than the aliens do."

"Fine, let the scientists go back down." Ling nodded. "Colonel, do what you have to do to ensure their security."

"Thank you, Admiral," Warren acknowledged. "For the record, I have four scientists who will be going back to Luna with the supply ships—three at their own request and one at my request. Some people did not react well to the situation."

* * *

Rosewood was one of those who asked to be sent home. Arthur Redmond was the one leaving at Warren's request—a polite way of saying she had booted him off the team. The Marine noncom with Rescue Two had reported Redmond's attempt to bug out, leaving her, Phillips, and the injured pilot to the nonexistent mercy of the Otuka.

Mercedes Warren had dealt with the Mekota and the Akara in Luna's first contact with either of those alien races. She hoped she would never have to deal with the Otuka again, but she was not about to abandon the Edies, let alone any of her own people.

Besides, she thought with amusement, somebody had to stick around and keep young Dr. Phillips out of trouble.

* * *

LCS *Summer Solstice*—En Route to Alpha Akara System

"We're going to get very fat before this trip is over," Carla predicted.

"No, we won't," Bjorn disagreed. "We'll just have to spend more time in the fitness center, which, I must say is a cut above any gym I've seen on Earth or Luna."

He gave her a suggestive smile. "Besides, a few pounds…er, I mean kilos…distributed over your curvaceous body will only make you more beautiful."

"Are you saying I'm too skinny?" she challenged.

"Not at all," he responded, smoothly, "but the more there is of you, the more there is for me to love."

"Keep it coming, you smooth-talking Viking stud," she said with a grin. Bjorn was getting better at fielding her occasional jabs, and she was starting to feel married—a feeling she liked very much.

"Anyway," she mused, looking at the empty plate in front of her, "it's going to take more than a couple of hours in the gym to get rid of that dessert. It was positively decadent. Ice cream, strawberries, hot fudge, and who knows what else went into this thing."

The food, of course, was only part of it. Their cabin accommodations were fit for royalty, and the ship's facilities included every form of entertainment imaginable, from live music—in either concert-hall or dance club venues—to casinos, swimming pools, sporting events, and theaters.

The ship had to provide those amenities. Travel on Earth had reached the point where a couple of hours on a suborbital jet would get you just about anywhere on the planet, but interstellar travel took much longer. They had been travelling for two days and hadn't yet left the Sol system. Soon, they would pass the hyper limit, would make the jump into hyperspace, and would travel over fifty light-years in thirty days. Then they would drop back into normal space outside Alpha Akara's hyper limit for a leisurely trip in-system to Copper Hills Prime. All in all, more than two-thirds of Bjorn and Carla's three month honeymoon would be spent in transit. A warship could have made the trip in less time, but a warship didn't need to worry about gently easing hundreds of passengers in and out of hyperspace without significant discomfort.

LCS *Summer Solstice* was a fairly new ship. It had taken a long time for the concept of interstellar leisure travel to catch on, but Terra Corporation had judged that the time was right and had commissioned the cruise ship just three years ago. The company had also gone into partnership with an Akara consortium to build themed resorts near natural attractions on Copper Hills Prime and two other planets in the Akara dominion. Travel packages were still expensive compared to vacation travel on Earth but were within reach for moderately affluent Moonies and Earthworms.

Unlike most of the other passengers, Bjorn and Carla weren't headed for one of the resorts. They planned to spend most of their time at Lorna's mountain estate. Lorna would not be there, and Carla almost regretted that. Her mother was a different person on Copper Hills Prime—more relaxed, less driven—some would say more human—and she wanted Bjorn to see that side of the Iron Maiden. But that could wait. For now, she was happy to be alone with her husband far from their work. And she really wanted him to see one of those purple sunsets.

Thinking about her mother got Carla thinking about other things, such as why her mother couldn't travel right now. And that led to other thoughts.

"What's wrong, darling?" Bjorn's inquiry was gentle, but it reminded her that he was becoming more attuned to her in a lot of ways.

"Just thinking." She sighed. "Thinking about some people who couldn't come to our wedding and who probably aren't enjoying any decadent desserts right now—people like Ronnie Bartley and Amy Ling, and your sexy little Marine hellcat, Maya."

Bjorn ignored the jibe, knowing that Carla liked Maya as much as he did. Instead, he focused on the real issue.

"You know where they went, don't you?"

"I'm pretty sure I do, but it's one of those things I can't talk about, even with you. In fact, I'm not supposed to know about it, but I was with Mom when she got word of something, and that something led to something else, and now, a lot of people have gone off somewhere to deal with it.

"Anyway, I don't know why it's bothering me. People I know, including my mom, have been going off and doing things like this my whole life, but I've got a bad feeling about this one.

"Look, hon." She looked at him with those big, blue eyes he couldn't resist. "I know you're not much into religion, but if you happen to have a prayer or two in your pocket, say it for those people, will you?"

* * *

LFS *Okinawa*—New Eden Orbit

"Why, Vasquez? Why?" the bitterness in Bronski's voice was plain. "Why'd ya have to go and be a hero? I told ya not to do that, ya dumb bitch!"

The big Marine was near tears as he and a couple of his squadmates watched the cold-sleep capsule being rolled into *Okinawa's* boat bay. Vasquez looked small and defenseless through the capsule's transparent cover, and worse, she looked dead, which, technically, she was.

Her body temperature was near zero Celsius, her heart wasn't beating, and her brain showed only an occasional, tiny flicker of activity. The capsule was pumping blood slowly through her veins and providing her with minimum hydration and nourishment, but the Marines knew the truth. She was dead, and the machine was keeping her body from decaying. Maybe the medics on Luna could bring her out of it, but she'd just die again anyway. The medics on *Okinawa* had only put her in deep-freeze to keep her from dying on the spot, so they could ship her back home and make her somebody else's problem.

"They damn well better make her a citizen!" Bronski declared.

"What was that, Marine?"

Bronski didn't look at the speaker. His eyes followed the capsule as it was loaded into the waiting transport shuttle. He knew from the tone that it was an officer who had spoken to him, but at this point, he didn't give a damn.

"Citizen! She wanted to be a Lunar Citizen. That's all she ever talked about. Now, she's gonna die and nobody cares."

"That's not true, Marine," Veronica Bartley said, softly. "I care…and she will get that citizenship, whether she makes it or not. We owe her that."

Bartley hadn't gotten to know most of the Marines in the battalion. They'd been assembled quickly and packed aboard for the mission, and, while she'd watched them train and given them pep talks, she didn't really know them. Now, with some of them, she'd never get the chance. *But I'll keep my promise on this one,* she told herself. She was already planning to put the Raptor pilot in for a medal, probably a Lunar Star. *No.* She thought about it again. *That young woman took a ground-attack Raptor into air combat at six-to-one, in defense of her own people and civilians on the ground. That's worth a Medal of Honor. Hell, I got mine for less than that.*

The battle was over, and the supply convoy would be heading back to Luna today, but she still had time to amend her recommendation. She'd already written several other commendations, along with seventeen letters to next-of-kin for the Marines who'd died in the fighting. The whole package would be sent back to Luna with her after-action report, as well as Admiral Ling's analysis of the entire operation and all the data on the fleet action in space.

Corporal Bronski was wrong, she decided. Not only did she care, but Amy Ling and Robin Torrey would care as well, and so would Lorna Greenwood. *And once all these letters, commendations, and reports are sent off,* she decided, *I'm going down to the enlisted mess, to see if I can't get to know some of my troops a little better.*

* * *

LCS *Summer Solstice*—En Route to Alpha Akara System

"*Attention, all passengers. We will be dropping out of hyperspace in three minutes. All persons subject to translation disorientation syndrome should take appropriate medication immediately. All ship's recreational facilities are now closed. All dining facilities are also closed. Please return to your cabins and await further instructions from crewmembers.*"

"Mr. Davis! What's going on?" Carla asked.

The announcement had come over the ship's public address system, and Carla and Bjorn had encountered the First Officer as they left the main dining room, where their dinner had been rudely interrupted.

"Not to worry, Doctor Greenwood, just a little problem we'll have resolved shortly." He gave her a smile that seemed totally lacking in sincerity and turned to walk away, but Carla grabbed his arm.

"Don't bullshit me!" she demanded. "It's not a little problem if we have to make a crash translation out of hyperspace."

Terrell Davis knew who Carla was. His father was a fleet officer who had risen to command a heavy cruiser under Lorna Greenwood. He also knew Carla wasn't the average, pampered passenger and that her comment about crash translation was on the mark. It normally took hours to set up a gentle translation in or out of hyperspace, one that would only cause a moment or two of vertigo for any but the most sensitive passengers. This time, a lot of people were going to be very, very sick.

Still, Davis hesitated. It wasn't something he would normally share with passengers, but he wasn't very good at lying to anyone. In the end, her calm, serious manner convinced him.

"We've been intercepted by unknown vessels—five of them—presumably some kind of pirates. They fired warning shots, and they are closing in.

"The captain wants to take us out of hyper. If they disable our drive and leave us stuck in hyperspace, we'll be at the mercy of the gravitational currents. In normal space, we'll just be adrift, and our chances of being found and rescued are better. Besides, a sudden drop-out might give our pursuers the slip. Now, you really need to get to your cabin. We'll let everyone know what's happening as soon as possible."

"Pirates…" Carla's face had gone white at the first mention of the word. She remembered the conversation with Heart months ago. *They're a lawless rabble whose concept of civilization involves piracy, and sooner or later, your people will encounter them.*

And the other part: *We don't eat intelligent, tool-using, rational, and civilized creatures. They do.*

"I've got to see the captain right now," she told Davis. "You must not allow these pirates to board the ship."

"Ms. Greenwood…"

"I know who these people might be. I was with my mother when…it doesn't matter how I know, but if these are the pirates I think they are, we must not allow them to board under any circumstances."

Davis hesitated for a moment, but there was something deadly serious in her voice and no trace of irrational hysteria. He looked at

Carla's husband. Bjorn was looking at Carla, obviously concerned, but not disputing anything his wife was saying.

"I'll take you to the bridge. I hope I'm doing the right thing."

"If you have to hope for something, hope that I'm wrong," Carla told him.

* * *

Five minutes later, on the bridge, Carla was fighting off the effects of the translation. Waves of vertigo still washed over her, but she hadn't lost her dinner. Bjorn had been less fortunate.

That was a rough one…rough enough that even Captain Johansson's bridge crew weren't taking it that well. There hadn't been time for all the passengers to get to their cabins. Some of them were wandering the ship's passageways, totally disoriented, if they were able to move at all. A lot of them were curled up in a ball, puking their guts out.

Johansson was still on his feet, giving orders. Finally, having assured himself that his ship was still sound, he turned to Carla.

"Now then, Dr. Greenwood, Mr. Davis tells me you have something very important to tell me. It better be good."

"No, Captain, it's not. In fact, it's very bad," she said. She proceeded to tell him what she knew of the Otuka.

"They eat people, you say?" Johansson was incredulous. "Surely this is just hearsay, some interstellar legend."

"No, it's not. I've seen video of one of their attacks. They were preying on humans—primitive humans on a faraway planet, but humans all the same. It was the most horrible thing I've seen in my life, and, unless I am badly mistaken, we have an LFS Navy task force out there trying to protect those primitives against another attack.

"But we were also told these creatures engage in interstellar piracy. We've never encountered interstellar pirates before, Captain. What are the odds these pirates are not the Otuka? Can we afford to take that chance?"

"Sir!" one of Johansson's bridge officers interrupted. "They followed us. They must have seen our delta wave buildup and dropped out of hyper almost the same time we did. They only overshot us by about 200,000 klicks, and they're coming back fast. Estimated intercept in forty minutes."

"Hyper generators?"

"No good, sir, that translation took out all of the overloads, and at least half won't reset. They probably need replacement. It'll be several hours, at least."

"So, what would you have me do, Dr. Greenwood?" Johansson inquired, turning to Carla again. "We can't run. They're armed, and we're not. If I try to stop them from boarding, they can blow holes in the ship and come in that way or blow us out of space altogether."

"I don't know, Captain," Carla admitted. "But I had to tell you what I know, to let you know what might be coming. Is there nothing else you can do?"

"I'm going to tell the passengers, including you and your husband, to lock themselves in their cabins and not to come out unless told to do so by a crewmember. I'm going to put a distress message into a hyperprobe and send it on its way. Hopefully, the pirates won't have recovered their own hyper capability just yet, and the messenger will get away successfully…or maybe they just won't care.

"The Sol System is much closer than Copper Hills Prime," he continued. "Even so, a hyperprobe will take almost two days to get there and then it will take a couple of hours for the message to reach Luna after it arrives. Even if they send ships immediately, it will take them two days to get to the hyper limit and another two days to get here, so I don't suppose we can really expect much help.

"I'm going to do my best to disable the ship so they can't hijack her and take us wherever they want. Then, I'm going to the primary boarding bay to meet them. I need to find out if they are who you think they are. You say they look like centaurs? Four legs, two arms, and such?"

"Yes, but—"

"And then I'm going to attempt to barter with them, for our lives. Maybe they'll be reasonable about it. In any case, it's the only thing I can do."

"I suppose you have to try," Carla told him, "but what if you fail? Isn't there anything you can do to fight them? Surely you have some small arms aboard, something you can use to try to protect the passengers?"

"There are very few weapons of any kind on board. The ship's security people have sidearms, but I don't believe those will help us. Trying to fight would only endanger the passengers further. No, Doctor, I'm afraid there isn't anything else we can do. Now, if you would please return to your cabin."

He's given up, Carla thought. *He says there's nothing he can do.*

She heard her mother's voice inside her head. *You don't ever give up. If you're not dead, the battle isn't over yet.* She also remembered that her other mother had died trying to make peaceful overtures to aliens who had no interest in peace. She was certain any attempt to negotiate with the Otuka would result in an equally catastrophic failure.

"C'mon, Bjorn, let's go," she told her husband. Captain Johansson didn't spare them a glance as they left the bridge.

* * *

"This isn't the way to our cabin," Bjorn remarked about twenty minutes later.

He and Carla had gone to the purser's office where they had been told that yes, the ship's security office had sidearms locked in the safe; however, Lieutenant Moskowicz, the ship's purser, told them he couldn't issue weapons to his own people without the captain's permission, and he certainly wasn't going to give them to passengers. He told them to return to their cabin and lock the doors, a message that was being repeated constantly over the ship's public address system.

"We aren't going back to the cabin," Carla replied. "If we have to hide from these creatures, there are better places to do it."

She paused at a door marked *Authorized Ship's Crew Only* and punched a code into the door panel. The door slid open instantly, and Carla stepped through, beckoning her husband to follow.

"How did you do that?" Bjorn blinked.

"Universal Emergency Override code," she told him. "Works almost anywhere on any LFS ship, except for alpha-level security areas. For those, each ship has its own codes, and they get changed periodically. On this ship, there will be a few areas like that—passenger cabins, fusion reactor rooms, high-value cargo storage, and so forth. But just about any of these Authorized Personnel doors will open with the code I've got.

"It's something Aunt Ronnie taught me. Marines handle damage control aboard ship during a battle, and they must be able to get into any compartment. They also must know where all the little hidden spaces are—every ship has lots of them. I don't know the layout of this ship very well, but I know those spaces have got to be here somewhere."

They were in a part of the ship where passengers were not supposed to be. The plush décor that graced the public passageways was gone, replaced by plain steel bulkheads and grey composite paneling. Overhead, exposed conduits and ductwork ran the length of the corridor. Carla paused at a steel door that bore the legend *Emergency Management—Station 4*. Once again, the door was locked but opened when she punched in the code.

"We're leaving a trail behind us," she said. "Every time we open one of these coded doors, the ship's log will record it, but I doubt any pirates will figure that out."

She grabbed Bjorn by the arm and pulled him through and shut the door. Inside the compartment, lighting panels came on automatically, revealing a two-person console and a series of large screens attached to the bulkheads on three sides. The fourth side, which held the door through which they had entered, was mostly covered with equipment lockers. Carla ignored those for the moment and took the left seat at the console. She studied the panel and then hit what was obviously a master switch. Screens came online, and the largest of them displayed a diagram of the ship's internal layout.

"Yesssss!" Carla's satisfaction was obvious. "This is a damage control station or, at least, that's what they'd call it on a warship. Now, let's see what we can figure out from here."

Bjorn was beginning to understand what Carla had in mind.

"You do that," he told her. "I'm going to see if there's anything we can use in these lockers."

* * *

There was nothing more to do, except confront the pirates. Johansson launched the hyperprobe and tracked it until it jumped into hyperspace, apparently without causing the pirates any concern. They had to know that help wasn't coming any time soon, so they didn't bother to try to pursue the probe.

Then he dumped the ship's primary reactor cores, immobilizing the huge liner. Her auxiliaries provided enough power for environmental control and internal gravity, but she wasn't going anywhere under her own power and was far too large to be towed by the pirate vessels. They weren't going to take their prize very far.

It would be a problem if the pirates went away and left them there after taking what they wanted. *Summer Solstice* and her passengers and crew would have to wait and hope to be rescued, but in Johansson's mind, that was far better than being hijacked to who-knew-where. They were on the direct line from Sol to Alpha Akara, where people would look for them, and he still had two hyperprobes in reserve to call for help.

Reluctantly, he gave orders to Lieutenant Moskowicz to issue sidearms to senior officers, with strict instructions not to use them unless necessary to protect the passengers. Then he left First Officer Davis in charge on the bridge and went to the primary boat bay where several pirate shuttles had just landed.

He was still trying to think of any other action he might have taken, when the boarding hatch opened, and a group of pirates came crowding in.

She was right, he thought, *they do look like centaurs.*

It was his final thought, as one of the Otuka raised a weapon and shot him through the heart.

* * *

The last thing the aliens expected to find was a ship full of humans. There were rumors of a spacefaring human society, but no Otuka raiders had encountered them. One of the centaurs dared to express the opinion that this was an ill omen, but the leader's snarl of contempt quieted all dissent. There was not only wealth to be looted here, but food as well, and perhaps a trophy or two. To illustrate the point, the leader severed the head of the human who had confronted them—an officer of the ship, judging by the finery of the human's clothing—and tucked it into the pillage bags slung across his back. Then he led his followers into the ship. Other ship's gangs were arriving as they spoke, and soon, they would be snarling and fighting over the best loot.

They had seen the ship dump its reactor cores and were angry because they would not be able to take the ship as a prize. They would take whatever they found of any value, and the fact that the occupants of the ship were human was an unexpected bonus. Human flesh was a prized delicacy. They would feast well and carry back as much as they could to barter with others of their kind.

* * *

LFS *Impala*—Near the Sol System Hyper Limit

The express courier dropped out of hyper carrying a residual vector of point one five cee—fifteen percent of light speed, or around 45,000 kilometers per second—fast enough to cover the distance from Earth to Luna in less than ten seconds. Despite having done it many times, despite having eaten very little in the last few hours, and despite having taken the required heavy dose of medication that was supposed to protect against translation sickness, Senior Lieutenant George Randall, *Impala's* captain, came very close to losing the contents of his stomach. He'd expected that, however, and both he and his Exec, Lieutenant Brad Timmons, had sickness bags close at hand.

Yoshida's probably back there eating a sandwich, he reflected. *Impala's* engineer, Chief Petty Officer Martin Yoshida was one of those rare individuals who seemed to be immune to the violent disorientation that accompanied what, in anything but an E-boat, would be considered an extreme crash translation.

But normal low-residual translations took time—time to kill vector in hyper and time to build it back up again in normal space en route to the inner system. Time was the enemy of an express courier like *Impala*, a class of ship that existed solely to get information, and limited numbers of people or small amounts of extremely important cargo, from point to point as quickly as possible.

At least the passengers didn't feel anything, Randall mused. His three passengers, two Marines and one Navy rating—all critically wounded in battle at New Eden—were cold-packed in capsules in *Impala*'s cargo space. Only the capsule's sensitive instrumentation gave any indication that they were alive.

Impala's mission was to get Admiral Ling's reports and supporting data to Lunar Command as quickly as possible, but the E-boat would arrive almost four days sooner than the lumbering supply convoy, so the decision had been made to put the sleeping patients aboard. In theory, they could be kept in cold-sleep as long as necessary, but with their critical injuries, the sooner they reached Luna, the better their chance of survival.

Twenty minutes later, streaking inward under full acceleration, *Impala* was queried by an Outer System Guard unit, LFS *Nighthawk*. Randall smiled as he triggered the IFF to identify his ship as a friendly LFS vessel. *And you couldn't catch me if I wasn't.*

* * *

LFS *Valkyrie*—Lunar Fleet Anchorage

"Have you had a chance to review Ling's reports?" Robin Torrey inquired.

"The summaries and some of the details," Lorna replied. "There's a lot of data, but I'm starting to get a picture, and I'm not sure I like it."

"Neither do I," Torrey admitted, "and I've done nothing but sift through it since it started coming in."

LFS *Impala* began spooling encrypted data to Lunar Command while the courier was still outside Jupiter's orbit, as soon as her first in-system message was acknowledged. By the time she flipped over to start braking, everything Ling had sent was in Fleet's hands, and Torrey was well into her analysis. Now, the E-boat was tucked into a docking bay at TransLuna station, and her human cargo was in the care of the best medical teams in the Sol System. Lorna Greenwood and Robin Torrey were meeting in Lorna's day cabin aboard LFS *Valkyrie.*

"Your thoughts?" Lorna queried.

"Well, just doing a fast flyover, Point One is that Amy got it done—both sides of the mission accomplished."

"Agreed."

"Point Two is that it cost more than we thought it would. Point Three is that we still don't know enough about the Otuka to let ourselves get all warm and fuzzy about the situation."

"Again, agreed," Lorna acknowledged. "I'll assume she's kept to her plan, and the two cripples are on their way back here with the supply group. Obviously, we'll replace them as requested. Beyond that, what would you recommend?"

"I don't know, I'll have to think about it, but I've got some concerns. Individually, the Otuka ships didn't show us much. A *Predator*-class destroyer ought to be able to handle a half-dozen of them in a stand-up fight. From the battle data we got, it took a full twelve of them, concentrating on one target, to tear up *Wraith* the way they did…and not one of the twelve survived.

"That being said," Torrey continued, "they didn't expect us, and we don't know whether the ships they sent were regular warships. They were well-armed for their size, not helpless transports, which is surprising, since they didn't need to send warships for a planet-side hunting expedition. But they sent over a hundred of them, and, next time, they might send five hundred or a thousand, and they might send heavier warships as well. Even the Akara don't seem to know how numerous they are or what their capabilities might be.

"All of their ships appear to be similar in size, design, and capability—similar, but not identical. When I looked at the specs Amy's tactical sensors put together, something rang a bell. I had Anna retrieve the data on an OSG engagement from about five years ago. LFS *Coyote* took on four alleged pirate ships that were chasing an Akara freighter. The pirates got away, and we never knew who they were, but when I compared *Coyote*'s data to the ships Amy encountered at New Eden, there was no doubt—same drive profile, same mass, same class. Maybe not identical, but close enough. That implies the ships we fought at New Eden were standard Otuka commerce raiders, but…"

"But it still doesn't tell us how many they've got, or whether they have anything better," Lorna said.

"Right," Torrey agreed. "So, getting back to your original question, I'd really like to send out another heavy cruiser, a couple of lights, and maybe a couple of frigates or destroyers, in addition to the replacements Amy requested. Do I have your permission?"

"Actually," Lorna replied, "I was thinking along the same lines of reinforcement myself, but I'm allowed to think in larger terms than you are. I'd like to send another full battle group, but I don't want to dilute your force any further. It's a dangerous universe out there, and you never know whose butt might need kicking.

"That means I'll need to pull somebody from Home Fleet instead. I've been thinking about sending Fred Kellerman with LFS *Medusa* and Fourth Battle Group. He's junior to Ling, so there won't be any problem with leaving her in overall command. We can also stagger the rotation—you can relieve Ling with another of your groups when the time comes, and we'll send another Home Fleet Group three months later to relieve Kellerman."

"That makes me feel a lot better," Torrey conceded. "They can send a thousand of those little commerce raiders next time, but with two battlecruisers and four heavies, we'll kick their asses. It'll just take longer. What about Marines…do you think we need anything else on that side?"

"Yes, I think we ought to send another AT with an air-superiority squadron. That will give them eight Airwolves and four more Raptors. I think we can also tuck in a couple of extra Dragonflies and a specialized ground company—Force Recon or Rapid Strike—for the extra flexibility. They may not be needed—with the extra battle group, the Otuka might never set foot on the planet again—but better to be prepared for anything."

* * *

LCS *Summer Solstice*—Adrift Between Star Systems

"Sooner or later, they have to leave, don't they? What more can they get out of staying here?" Engineering Technician Ranjit Makesh's comment sounded more like a hope than a question.

"They've been here less than two days," Bjorn replied. "They want to get as much as they can from the ship, and they're taking their time about it. Last time we checked, they were stripping the kitchens—apparently stainless steel is worth something to them."

No point in telling the others what else the aliens were doing in the kitchen. By now, all of them knew what had happened to many of their fellow passengers and crewmembers, but nobody needed to hear the gory details.

He looked around the little group. He, Carla, eight other passengers, and four crewmembers were huddled in a cramped engineering space in the starboard section of the ship's impeller ring. The compartment was illuminated by a couple of work lights they had scavenged along the way. *And we're damned lucky to be alive, mostly thanks to my dear wife's foresight and initiative.*

He had discovered early in their relationship that Carla had a phenomenal memory, that she could quote chapter and verse from just about any book she'd ever read. She could also do the mental gymnastics to visualize the reality behind just about any map, drawing, or diagram. After a few minutes flipping through the displays in EM Station Four, she had acquired a thorough knowledge of the ship's internal layout, including those hidden spaces she'd talked about, like the one they were in now. Then she'd gone on to memorize the location of all the monitor cameras, which was no small feat with a ship like *Summer Solstice.* In the passenger areas of the ship—except for the passenger cabins and the restrooms in public areas—cameras covered every square meter of deck space and were always monitored by passenger service people. If a passenger slipped and fell in one of the casinos, medics and service people would be alerted instantly and would likely arrive before the passenger got up from the deck.

* * *

Even in the non-passenger areas, cameras covered most passageways and compartments. Carla needed to know where they were—and weren't—so they could keep an eye on the pirates without being seen. Bjorn found an engineering data pad in one of the lockers, and Carla linked it to the console in EMS4 before they went looking for a more secure hiding space. With that pad, she could bring up an image from any camera on the ship, but she did so with caution. So far, the Otuka had ignored the EM station, but the data pad had an electronic emission signature which could be detected if the aliens knew to look for it.

She'd also obtained the list of codes for the doors to the secured areas, the ones that would not have responded to her universal code, so now they had the run of the ship. Unfortunately, the Otuka didn't need codes. If a door blocked their way, they used laser cutters or explosives to remove the door completely. That bothered Carla because it compromised the compartmental integrity of the ship. A few holes in the hull would empty the air from most of the interior spaces.

She was pretty sure the pirates planned to do just that when they were finished looting and had killed everyone they could find. She, Bjorn, and two of the ship's crew made a dangerous trip to a storage compartment to bring back emergency evacuation suits for their little group to guard against that possibility.

Of course, the aliens could blow the entire ship to pieces, but without the reactor cores, it would be hard for them to do it. Once again, she silently thanked the late Captain Johansson for his foresight.

She and Bjorn had taken refuge with their little group in the aft section of the ship, but she was certain there was another group of survivors somewhere forward. There had been an exchange of weapons fire between the aliens and some crewmembers, and they'd caught a glimpse of it on several cameras. She thought the defenders had been led by Terrell Davis, but she wasn't sure. In any case, they'd fought a hit-and-run battle against the centaurs and then vanished. Carla was pretty sure she knew where they had gone, including the access hatch they'd taken to get out of sight, but like her group, the other survivors were hiding somewhere the cameras didn't cover.

From what she had seen, the other group wasn't much bigger than the one she and Bjorn had collected. Likely, a lot of people were still cowering in their staterooms and a few crew spaces like maintenance closets, but *Summer Solstice* was a big ship. Even after two days, the centaurs hadn't been able to search all the passenger areas, let alone the crew and engineering spaces.

The search was going slowly because the aliens were so big. With bodies the size of small horses, they stood well over two meters tall, despite having relatively short trunks. They could get around the passenger areas because the luxury liner was built with wide, high corridors and large open compartments for passenger comfort. They had much more difficulty getting around the engineering decks, often having to squat down and shuffle clumsily to get through a human-sized hatch.

Carla had chosen their hiding place with that in mind. She was pretty sure it was physically impossible for the Otuka to reach them here, short of cutting large holes in solid bulkheads.

Though many of the passengers and crew still survived, it was obvious that many more had not. Carla had seen them cut down without mercy, and the scenes in the kitchen, the casino, and the other large compartments where the aliens had dragged their kills to be butchered and eaten, were simply too horrible to watch. Carla tried to force them out of her mind, but that brought another unpleasant thought into her head.

I wonder what's happened to Dusty?

Lorna Greenwood had brought the far-travelling feline back to Luna with her for a veterinary check-up, and Carla had volunteered to take him back to Copper Hills Prime on the honeymoon trip. When last she'd seen him, Dusty had been caged like several other pets making the trip in a special kennel section of the ship's forward cargo hold where a crewmember was assigned to look after them. Carla had gone to the kennel daily, where the cheerful young woman had allowed her to take the cat out and play with him in the pleasant animal exercise area provided. But that was before the Otuka came.

There were no cameras in the kennel, and if there had been, Carla would have been reluctant to look. The forward hold was out of reach of her current position. Dusty was still OK—the alternative was not something she wanted to think about.

* * *

The Otuka raider was puzzled. He had grown weary of watching his fellows try to cut into a sealed cargo container and had wandered farther into the cargo hold, where he found a small compartment accessible through one of the accursed human-sized hatches. He maneuvered his bulk inside, where he found rows of small cages along one bulkhead. A sort of holding pen with knee-high padded walls occupied much of the rest of the compartment. The pen was filled with colorful objects and some small structures of unknown purpose.

The raider turned his attention to the cages. Most were empty, but several held living creatures, small animals of some sort. Some of the animals made a great deal of noise, running to the front of the cages and yelping at him. Others stayed to the rear, trying to get as far from him as possible.

He wondered if the creatures were intended as food. He knew humans ate animal flesh, but even the Otuka, who loved fresh-killed food, were not primitive enough to carry live animals that had to be fed and cared for during the voyage on a spacecraft. Perhaps these animals were some very special delicacies, whose flesh did not preserve well and could only be enjoyed to the fullest if fresh-killed.

He selected one of the cages whose occupant had withdrawn far from the cage door. The door latch mechanism was of a simple design. He opened it and reached inside to seize the creature within...and recoiled with a howl of rage as a furry torpedo launched itself at his face, hissing, squalling, and savaging his tender nose with needle-sharp claws. He tried to grab the little demon, but it had already leaped over his head and run down his back. It kicked off his rump—leaving more claw wounds behind—and shot out the compartment door into the cargo hold beyond.

Fumbling for his weapon, the centaur managed to get one shot off as the creature disappeared under one of the cargo containers, passing through a space he would have sworn was too small for it. The shot glanced off the deck and then off the container, bringing a snarl of rage from the Otuka group leader, who was approaching the hatch.

With a snarl, the raider began hurling the occupied cages at the deck. That turned out to be a mistake, as the cages were less substantial than they appeared. Several of them broke open, freeing more of the strange animals. Like the first, these creatures also fled through the hatch, bringing another expression of rage and a demand for an explanation from the group leader.

*****

Chapter Five

TerraNova Medical Center—Luna

"She's showing organized brain activity, Doctor; she's coming out of it."

"Good! Now, let's see if there's anyone in there."

The comment was not meant to be taken lightly, and nobody smiled. A small percentage of patients put into cold-suspension suffered impairment of higher thought processes, amnesia, and in some cases, motor system damage. The doctor flicked a penlight beam across the patient's eyes in the simple test for pupil reaction doctors had been doing for a hundred years or so.

"Good pupils," he noted for the record. "Can you hear me, Marine?"

He got a mumbled response, which was encouraging, considering the woman had just been thawed a couple of hours ago. Unlike medics in the Fleet, the LFS Medical Center on Luna could perform surgery on a patient still in cold-suspension. Surgeons had worked on this patient for many hours in three separate sessions and had gotten all the life-threatening injuries under control before they started the thawing process.

"What was that? I couldn't hear you, Marine," he repeated.

The woman made a visible effort, drawing a deep breath and trying to shape her words.

"Vasquez…Maya…Sergeant…LFS Marines…Bravo three four seven…six one…nine zero two."

The doctor blinked, consulted his chart, and discovered that Maya had, in fact, gotten her LFSMC registration number right.

"Well, OK," he acknowledged, "you get an 'A' so far. Do you know where you are?"

"Can't be in Heaven…hurts too bad," she told him. "And you don't look like the Devil, so I guess I must be alive."

"You get another 'A' for a sense of humor," he replied with a smile. "Yes, you're alive, and likely to stay that way for a while. You're back on Luna, a long way from wherever you were when you got yourself into this condition. I'm Doctor Paul Madison, and I'll be your medicine man today and for some time to come, you lucky girl."

* * *

Thirty minutes later, whatever humor Maya might have found in the situation was gone. The doctor refused to answer any of her questions until he had completed his examination and made sure she was truly awake and alert. Then he pulled up a chair beside the bed and gave her the straight story.

Her assessment of the damage after the crash was close to correct. Yes, her back was broken in four places, and two of the lower breaks were bad enough to have done severe damage to the spinal cord. In fact, she was fortunate the highest break hadn't done as much damage. Otherwise, it would probably have stopped all nerve impulses to her diaphragm. She would have stopped breathing and died before anyone got to her.

She was still in a lot of pain, mostly in her upper back and chest, though her left arm was contributing its share. The arm would heal without complications, and she would never notice that three major bones—the radius, the ulna, and the humerus—had been replaced with metal and composite substitutes. The chest pain would go away as her broken ribs healed. She also had a broken leg that had been repaired, but she couldn't feel anything down there. Some additional pain was due to repairs done to internal injuries, and that would also fade.

He told her he could make the back pain go away by deadening some of the nerve connections she wouldn't need any more, since she was now paralyzed from the waist down. As she'd suspected, she would most likely be spending the rest of her life in a wheelchair, but she would get a full-pay disability retirement from the Marines. Per LFS rules, the retirement would include regular-cycle promotions in grade with appropriate pay increases, and the benefits would not be affected by any future employment she took. There were plenty of jobs available for disabled veterans, she was told.

* * *

M*ost likely...*

Maya pounced on the qualifier.

"Is there...any chance at all I might ever get the use of my legs again?" she asked.

"Yes, a very, very tiny chance," he admitted. "No guarantees, but we could try to repair the spinal damage. If we do that, though, you can forget about losing the pain in your back. You would have to go through a long series of painful surgical procedures. I know what I'm talking about because I'm the neurosurgeon who would have to perform that surgery.

"We can't shut the pain down because we'd need to map your nerve responses to the microsurgery. We would need those nerve impulses to tell us whether we're making progress. We might give you temporary relief with painkillers, but most of the time, you'd be hurting. You'd need to be awake during the surgery, so we can check your responses while we're doing it.

"I'm not going to blow sunshine in your ear, Marine. There's a fifty-fifty chance we would put you through all that for nothing—nada, zip, zero. You still wouldn't be able to feel or move anything below the waist.

"Even if we win that coin-toss, it's another fifty-fifty chance that we won't see enough improvement to make any difference. You might feel something down there—most likely more pain—but you won't get enough motor control to do more than maybe wiggle your toes.

"If we beat those odds—and in case you haven't been counting, we're talking about one chance in four—we could start looking at whether you might actually walk. You'd need to learn to use your legs all over again, and if you thought the pain was bad up to that point, it would only get worse. We are talking many hours of physical therapy of the no pain, no gain variety.

"We need to repair just about everything from the lumbar plexus down. You probably don't know what that means, but, trust me, it's a lot of nerve connections. The chances of all, or even most, of them healing properly are small. Even if we get you on your feet, you might never walk again without crutches, and the odds are poor to zero that you'd ever get enough coordination in your legs to fly a Raptor again.

"If we go with the wheelchair option, you can roll out of here in about ten days, with most of the pain gone. In another ten days, all the pain will have gone. We'll need to see you a few more times over the next two months, just to check and see how everything has healed.

"If we go the other way, you are going to be in and out of this place—more in than out—for the next several months. You'll be spending a lot of that time in a bed like this one, feeling almost as much pain as you are feeling now. Then, if you are lucky, the hard part will begin, and you'll be spending several hours a day in therapy.

"That's your choice, Marine, no way to sugar-coat it. You've got a week or so to think it over while everything else heals, so take your time. If you have more questions, let the nurses know, and they'll get me back in here. I can bring in anyone else you want to talk to before you make the decision."

"Don't need extra time, Doc," she told him. "I'd rather walk through Hell on crutches than ride a wheelchair in Heaven, so bring it on. Give it your best shot; that's all I'm asking."

* * *

LFS *Valkyrie*—Lunar Fleet Anchorage

"Admiral Greenwood, please wake up. We have a situation that requires your attention."

Lorna had heard that voice many times over the years—that always calm, always perfectly courteous voice. She'd learned to detect the subtle hint of urgency, mostly in the choice of words. If Val said there was a situation, it usually meant something just short of Armageddon.

Val was an AI—an Artificial Intelligence—a shining example of the Lunar Free State's greatest achievement in cybernetic science and engineering. She was a person under Lunar law, guaranteed the rights of an LFS citizen, and no one who had ever worked extensively with one of her kind doubted she was a living, thinking creature.

More than that, Val was a warship's AI, the living soul of Lorna Greenwood's flagship, LFS *Valkyrie.* Her body was a six-hundred-meter-long, armor-clad cylinder of steel, armed with the most powerful weaponry in the LFS arsenal. Her fusion-powered gravity drives could carry her hundreds of light-years at incredible speeds, and she was charged with the lives and well-being of nearly seven hundred Navy crewmembers and Marines, including the commanding admiral of Luna's combined fleets. She had served Lorna in every campaign and fought in every battle of consequence since the founding of the Lunar Free State. She knew her admiral better than any human—even Lorna's daughter Carla—could hope to do, for she was Lorna's constant shipboard companion, even in Lorna's most private moments in the admiral's quarters. When Lorna couldn't sleep, she often held long conversations with Val, who never slept. And when Lorna did manage to get a good night's sleep aboard ship, Val would defend her without question against any who would disturb her.

For that reason, even without the trigger word, situation, Lorna would have come to an instant state of alert when Val chose to wake her.

"What's happening, Val?" Lorna sat up and swung her legs out of bed.

"We have a distress call, transmitted by a hyperprobe that just dropped into the system, Admiral. It's coded for LCS *Summer Solstice.* So far, we only have the pulse ID code, but by now, OSG should have queried for a full download. It will take approximately two point two hours for the message to arrive here."

Lorna felt an icy stab of fear as Val named the distressed vessel, for she knew—as Val must have known as well—that the most important person in her personal universe was aboard that ship. The message took her back decades, to the moment when she had watched the Mekota destroy the envoy ship that had been sent to meet them—a ship that had carried her mentor and dearest friend, Ian Stevens, and her beloved life-partner, Carla Perry.

"Thank you, Val," she acknowledged, surprising herself with the cool, professional tone of her voice. "I'll be going to the flag bridge. Please wake Commander Wilkes and ask him to meet me there in two hours." Wilkes was Lorna's staff operations officer. There was no point in waking the rest of the staff or putting *Valkyrie* on alert until they knew more.

There was also no point in asking Val for further information. Gravity events propagated instantly, or at least so quickly no one had ever been able to measure a transit time, even over system-wide distances. When it dropped out of hyperspace, the probe was programmed to generate a series of gravity pulses using its hyperspace translation equipment—a slow and power-consuming process. All it would transmit would be a universal distress code—like the old Morse S.O.S.—and an identification code for the ship that sent it. The pulses, like the hyper translation event, could be detected as far away as Luna.

The nearest LFS Navy ship—most likely an Outer System Guard vessel out beyond Neptune's orbit—would have queried the probe immediately, which should have produced a high-speed dump of whatever information it carried in normal communication bands. Those signals propagated at light-speed and would take slightly over two hours to reach Fleet Command at Luna.

Thirty minutes later, having freshened up and put on her uniform, Lorna arrived on *Valkyrie's* flag bridge to find her command console fully powered up. As soon as she sat down, Val advised her that Commander Wilkes was on the way. He must have dressed quickly, ignoring the extra time she had given him, for he arrived on the heels of Val's message, but as usual, his uniform was impeccable.

Impeccable, Lorna thought, but noteworthy for its lack of decorations. Wilkes had never held a ship's command despite outstanding grades at Fleet Academy and an equally impressive record at Command College. He had never distinguished himself in battle, had never been awarded any special commendations, and, at age 57, was somewhat old for his rank. In the LFS Navy, he should have reached Commodore by now or already retired.

Wilkes was one of the most competent analysts Lorna had ever met. He worked well under pressure and could keep extremely complex tactical situations neatly arranged in his head without losing track of anything important. His analyses were precise, detailed, and to the point. His projections were usually accurate, and his suggestions were always worthy of consideration. His military bearing, appearance, and respect for superior officers were beyond question. The Navy was his life, and he had never expressed any desire for retirement. As long as Fleet had use for him, he was willing to serve.

Unfortunately, he lacked even the tiniest hint of command ability. He was a one-man show, unable to delegate even the simplest tasks to subordinates unless specifically ordered to do so. He lacked the ability to lead others or to interact well with subordinates. He was a cool and deliberate thinker but seemed tentative when issuing orders. As such, he never seemed to project authority or command the respect of those placed under his supervision. He'd served aboard several warships, whose captains always managed to get him transferred out with performance evaluations that could best be described as "damning with faint praise." None of them had been willing to recommend him for command.

Lorna, however, had recognized his better qualities—coolness under pressure and a willingness to express his opinions and stand behind his analyses without being intimidated when surrounded by high-ranking brass. To her way of thinking, he had great potential as a staff officer. She'd summoned him to a private meeting in which she'd given him a frank evaluation of his strengths and weaknesses—which included the assessment that he would most likely never get a command of his own, nor rise to flag rank. To her surprise, he'd agreed with that assessment, but added that if he was doomed to remain a staff officer, being on her staff would represent a career achievement of sorts. With that understanding, she took him on and had never regretted the decision.

His arrival on the bridge was a welcome relief. Given that her own objectivity might be compromised, she knew she could count on him to give her a hard, realistic view of the situation at hand.

"Sorry to disturb your sleep, Austin, but I've a feeling we're going to be busy tonight," she told him.

"Understood, ma'am," he replied. "When Val woke me, she told me about the distress call. *Summer Solstice*, an LCS luxury cruise ship, is it not?"

"Yes. Did she also tell you my daughter and her husband are aboard?"

"No, ma'am, she did not," he said quietly.

"That should make no difference in terms of our response, but I wanted you to know. If I seem less than objective about the situation, I expect you to straighten out my thinking as needed."

"Understood, ma'am," he replied, with a serious tone.

"In any case," she continued, "all we have is the distress call and the hyper signature of the probe's translation, at a point in the Orion sector which is consistent with the direct route to Alpha Akara."

"Hmmm...ma'am, have you checked with OSG to see what units they have in that sector?"

"No, I haven't, but I'm guessing it will be the usual patrol T.O. of corvettes and light recon ships, nothing bigger than a destroyer. Why?"

"Well, I was thinking in terms of hyper-capable ships, not the light recon patrols. Given Earth's, and Luna's, current positions all the way around on the other side of Sol from that sector, any hyper-capable ships they have out there will be two days closer to the hyper limit than we are. We don't know how long the probe's been travelling, but if we have to mount any kind of rescue mission, that will cut two days off the travel time."

"It probably took two or three days to get here," she told him, "by our best estimate of where *Summer Solstice* should be. If she were a lot further along, she'd have been better off sending a probe to

Copper Hills Prime. For all we know, she may have sent one in each direction, but she should be closer to us."

"Right. My point still applies. I can't think of any other way to shorten our response time."

"Neither can I, and it's a very good point. That's why I keep you on my staff, Austin—so you can bring details like this to my attention."

"Val," she addressed the AI, "I need deployment information for any hyper-capable ships—OSG or regular fleet—beyond Jupiter orbit in the Orion sector."

There were three hyper-capable OSG ships within a reasonable distance of the translation point. The largest and most heavily armed was an old Star-class destroyer, LFS *Stardancer*. The other two were corvettes, LFS *Coyote* and LFS *Copperhead*. Lorna contacted OSG Command and commandeered the three ships.

Stardancer had been in service for over four decades and had battle honors going back to the early years of the Lunar Free State's existence. She had taken part in actions against the Mekota and had distinguished herself several times. Now, still serviceable, but obsolescent, by current standards, she wore the distinctive orange-and-black hull chevrons of the Outer System Guard, along with her original hull artwork, a female figure in *tai chi* pose, against a starburst background.

The two OSG corvettes were newer, each less than ten years old, but except for periodic testing of their hyper generators, neither had ever been out of the Sol System.

An old woman and a couple of kids, Lorna thought. *Let's hope we don't have to ask too much of them.* She directed them to proceed to the hyper limit and stand by for orders. As far out as they were, they hadn't yet received the directive two hours later when the hyperprobe's full message arrived at Lunar Command.

* * *

"Pirates?" Austin Wilkes was taken aback as he read the transcript on the screen.

"Pirates," Lorna said. "Possibly Otuka pirates. Val, wake the rest of the staff and Commodore McPherson. Advise them we are bringing First Battle Group to Condition Blue."

"Yes, ma'am," the AI acknowledged.

Wilkes gave his admiral a raised-eyebrow, questioning look. An entire battle group was serious overkill against five small pirate ships, and *First* Battle Group meant…

"Yes, Austin, I am taking it personally, and yes, I am going out myself. Val, get Robin Torrey on the comm. I'll need her to take temporary fleet command while I'm gone. And screen the Chief Executive's office. Tell them I need to talk to Admiral O'Hara as soon as possible, to advise him of the situation and my intentions.

"And yes, Austin, I'm going to send the three OSG ships ahead. They're needed more than ever. I hope they'll be up to the task, but we are taking BG-1 out there to back them up and to search the area in case the pirates have any friends nearby. I'm afraid we are going to have to go with the Akara model from now on—provide escorts for shipping between here and the Akara frontier."

"No further questions, ma'am." Wilkes held up his hands in acquiescence. "I'm just wondering where Captain Johansson got the idea they might be Otuka pirates. Who aboard that ship would have known anything about the Otuka?"

"Carla," Lorna replied. "She was with me on Copper Hills Prime when the Akara first told us about them. She saw some of the video the Lizards gave us—the same stuff we included in the brief for the New Eden mission. I imagine she would have desperately wanted to warn the captain. Unfortunately, from the tone of his report, I'm not sure he took the warning seriously. At least he had the presence of mind to dump his cores. Otherwise, the pirates could take *Summer Solstice* anywhere they wanted, and we'd never find her.

"Val," she directed, "stand by to record orders for LFS *Stardancer*, *Coyote*, and *Copperhead*."

* * *

LFS *Coyote*—with *Stardancer* and *Copperhead*—near the Hyper Limit

"Well, ladies, you've seen the orders," Lieutenant Commander Roger Torres declared. "We are going pirate hunting, and we're going halfway to Alpha Akara to do it. Any questions?"

"No, sir." Senior Lieutenant Lucy Merrill wore a cheerful grin. "What are your instructions, Squadron Leader, sir?"

Senior Lieutenant Jennifer Tanaka shook her head. As the captain of LFS *Coyote*, she was as mission-focused as the other two. But Torres' *Stardancer*, along with her own *Coyote* and Merrill's *Copperhead* hardly constituted a major force.

With possible odds of five to three in the pirates' favor, Tanaka was taking nothing for granted. As the three of them conferred, her XO was crawling around in the magazine spaces with two technicians, running diagnostics on every one of *Coyote's* missiles. When he finished, she'd have him run diagnostics on the graser turrets as well.

But he'd have to do it without the help of the chief engineer, because that worthy senior noncom was currently fussing over the corvette's hyper generator, making sure all was ready for their upcoming translation. Whatever came their way, *Coyote* was going to be ready for it, and five to three odds notwithstanding, any pirates they encountered were going to know they'd been in a fight.

She felt a bit of a nervous flutter in her stomach, but she suppressed it quickly. *Hey,* she told herself, *if you wanted an easy life, you should have gone into research.* Her twin sister had gone that route and was now off studying exotic flora and fauna on some distant planet.

For some reason, the thought gave Tanaka a moment of distress, like some sort of ill omen. Janice had departed on short notice and hadn't been able to tell her sister where she was going, but she'd been very excited about the new assignment. Jennifer hoped all was well with her, but she couldn't shake the feeling of foreboding. *Pirates,* she decided. *That's what's bugging me. But orders are orders, and we've got a cruise ship full of civilians to rescue. Such as we are, we're all they've got. Besides, all we have to do is hold them off for oh, about two days, until the Battle Group arrives.*

Space combat engagements were usually decided in hours, sometimes in minutes. Suddenly, two days sounded like an eternity.

* * *

LCS *Summer Solstice*—Adrift between Star Systems

"We are not going to let those kids get eaten!" Carla's declaration brooked no argument.

"I don't see what we can do." Brittany Freeman shook her head. Freeman was 97 years old, and travel was her lifelong passion. She had told other passengers she was going to

Copper Hills Prime because there was nothing left to see on Earth. She was in good shape for her age, but Carla had to admit, she was not exactly fit for a rescue mission.

"Most of you need to stay here, but I'm going to get them." She glanced at Bjorn.

"I'm with you, babe," he told her. To emphasize the point, he picked up the heavy laser cutter he'd found in the ship's machine shop and fashioned into a makeshift weapon.

"Couldn't do it without you, big guy." Carla gave him a smile and picked up the hefty pry-bar she carried as her weapon. It was a tool that had proven useful for opening stubborn locker doors, cabinets, and tool chests.

"The rest of you stay here," she directed. "Mr. Makesh, you're in charge until we get back."

Bjorn marveled that no one, passenger or crewmember, had questioned his wife's leadership. From the beginning, she had simply taken charge, given orders, and expected to be obeyed, and everyone in their little group had complied. She always seemed to know what she was talking about, gave orders that made sense, and radiated a great deal of confidence. So far, at least, she had managed to keep them all alive.

Some people hadn't been impressed. One ship's officer had insisted they return to their cabins and await further instructions. Carla ignored him, and when he tried to stop her, she'd used some sort of martial arts technique on him that left the man lying flat on his back, stunned and wondering how he'd gotten there. He'd chosen not to pursue them. They hadn't seen him since, and Bjorn suspected he was Otuka food by now. Another person they hadn't saved was a male passenger who ran away when he saw them, shouting that he had to find the captain. Carla tried to tell him the captain was dead, but he hadn't listened.

They had only saved those who had been willing to follow Carla's lead. After the first excursion to EMS4, they'd gone back into the passenger areas, keeping track of the incoming Otuka via the data pad, and gathered the passengers they found wandering in the passageways. Then they went back to the aft engineering area where they found some crewmembers to add to the group. Carla hadn't wasted time arguing with anyone who didn't want to come along, but she welcomed anyone who did. She led them without hesitation into the hideaway she'd picked out. By that time, the pirates had begun their bloody invasion of the ship, and she made sure everyone in the group got a look at what was happening via camera views displayed on the data pad, in case any of them thought they should go out and try to negotiate with the raiders.

Since then, they'd made only a few, carefully planned trips to get supplies and equipment. Now, almost four days after the pirates had entered the ship, the cameras had shown there were still survivors in the passenger areas. A family of four had emerged from a cabin and made their way toward the main concourse.

* * *

"No, no, not that way!" Carla pleaded as she watched the images, knowing what was going to happen. Even as she spoke, the survivors rounded a corner in the passageway and encountered an Otuka pirate standing twenty meters away at the concourse entrance.

Obviously, the humans didn't know what had been happening. They'd been locked in their cabin, waiting for instructions that never came, surviving on the snacks and beverages in the cabin's mini bar. Carla was surprised they'd stayed in the cabin as long as they had.

The alien looked at them for a moment, then raised its weapon. The adult male—a heavyset man in his thirties, with thinning hair—stopped and raised his hands. His wife copied the gesture as did the older child, a boy of about twelve. The younger child, a girl, perhaps eight years old, just stared at the centaur in wide-eyed fear.

Without warning, the Otuka shot the man. The energy bolt from the alien's weapon caught him full in the chest and punched through him. His legs folded, and he dropped facedown on the deck. His wife, her face twisted in terror, screamed something—a scream Carla couldn't hear, since the cameras were not equipped with audio pickups. The woman stood paralyzed with fear for a moment, then folded to the deck as the alien shot her as well.

The boy whirled and grabbed his sister's arm. He dragged her back to the corridor intersection and around the corner, just in time to avoid the alien's third shot.

Takes about four seconds for their weapons to recycle, Carla noted in a cold, calculating corner of her brain that was functioning despite the horror she'd just witnessed. She punched a code into the pad, switching to another camera to see where the children had gone. As she expected, the boy ran back to their cabin, making two more turns in the passageways. By the time the pirate reached the corner where he'd shot their parents, the children were out of sight. The alien didn't follow, but it spoke into the communicator that hung from its harness, alerting its fellows there were still live humans on the ship.

When the boy and his sister reached the cabin, they found that the door had automatically locked when they left. The boy fumbled in his pockets, looking for a key card but not finding it. A few seconds later, he grabbed his sister's hand again and led her away in search of another hiding place. After trying several more doors, he must have realized all the passenger cabins were locked.

Carla tracked him as he led the girl down several more passageways until he found a door that was unlocked. It allowed entry to a small lounge where passengers could gather to socialize, play table games, or simply relax. It was one of several such lounges on each deck and was normally attended by a steward who kept the occupants supplied with a variety of refreshments from an adjacent pantry.

Carla switched cameras again to view the lounge. It was empty now, but a broken table, some scattered furnishings, and a stain of blood on the carpeted deck showed that the pirates had been there. The boy dragged the girl inside and closed the door. He led her into the pantry and closed its door as well. The only other opening to the pantry was a small, pass-through serving window into the lounge. Unless they passed behind that window, the children would be out of sight of the single camera in the lounge, but Carla was familiar with the layout—there was a similar lounge near her own cabin.

Stay there, kids, she thought. *There's food and drink in there. Just stay there, and we'll come get you.*

* * *

TerraNova Medical Center—Luna

"You don't have to fuss over me like this," Vasquez told the nurse. "It's not like I've got a hot date or anything."

"Well, you never know. Prince Charming could show up for a visit at any time," Candy Parks said with a gentle smile. "Besides, looking good usually makes you feel better as well."

Having given Vasquez a shower and general clean-up, Parks was now braiding the young Marine's hair. Vasquez normally wore her hair in a tight, single braid, but this was the first time she'd had it that way since New Eden. She had to admit that Parks was right. It really did make her feel better.

"Must have been a rough one, wherever you were," Parks remarked, and Vasquez heard a strange note of concern in her voice. "I know you can't talk about it, but you were with the Double Deuce, weren't you?"

Immediately, Vasquez knew what was bothering the other woman.

"Yeah," she replied, "I was. You've got somebody out there too, haven't you?"

"Yes," she admitted. "My husband...Navy officer, captain of a destroyer...LFS *Timberwolf*."

"Yeah...*Timberwolf*...I think she was one of the escorts covering our transport. But I got my lumps down on the planet. Last I heard, the Navy was kicking ass up in space. I don't think you have anything to worry about."

"Oh, he's OK," Parks replied. "I got a chip from him yesterday, sent back with one of the supply ships. But they're still out there, and they will be for a while. We've got a baby son, and this is the first time we've really been separated. That was bad enough, but I guess I didn't realize what it was like out there, until I saw you and the others they sent back. I haven't been sleeping very well, lately."

Vasquez nodded. "I know what you mean. Haven't been sleeping so well myself. Didn't mention it because I don't want them pumping me full of knock-out pills or something."

"But look—" she gave Parks a crooked smile, "—they gave me a screen here by the bed. It's no use to me, since everybody I know to talk to is still out there at…well, the place where I got torn up. If you just want to talk to somebody, give me a call when you're off duty, and you're not passing out pills and bedpans. Make me feel useful again, like maybe I'm earning all this pretty-up treatment."

"I'll do that." Parks was genuinely grateful. "As for the pretty-up, hey, you never know. You might get visitors after all."

Candy Parks knew Vasquez would have visitors. The Director of Nursing had stopped by that morning and told her to make sure the Marine was presentable. Parks was sure that meant some VIPs would be coming by, probably on a morale-boosting mission, but since she didn't know the details, she didn't mention it to Vasquez.

In any case, she was glad she had taken the time. She really did need somebody to talk to other than her own family or her exalted in-laws. *I'm a military wife*, she reflected. *I'd rather lean on a wounded Marine, and let her lean on me, than try to explain my feelings to a bunch of civilians, no matter how much they want to help.*

* * *

Not more than half an hour after Parks departed, the door to the hospital room opened. Despite all she'd been through, Maya Vasquez had not lost her lightning-quick reactions, and she instantly recognized the man and two women who came through the door.

"Holy shit," she muttered, as she tried to come to attention. Lying in bed and paralyzed below the waist, the best she could manage was to square her shoulders, but her right hand rose automatically in salute.

"No, no. Dinna salute me, lass. You're in a hospital bed, not on a parade ground," Michael O'Hara told her. "And I've been called a lot of things, but Holy Shit is far from the worst. Just relax, girl. We've come to wish you well."

"She's a Marine, sir." Robin Torrey exchanged grins with Anne McGraw. "They sleep at attention and salute everything that moves."

"Except in combat," McGraw responded. "Then they kill everything that moves that isn't on our side. How are you doing, Sergeant?"

"I'm good to go, ma'am," Vasquez told her, "as soon as the docs fix my legs so I can walk out of here."

McGraw looked into the young Marine's eyes. She'd talked to the doctors, and she knew how small Vasquez's chances of 'walking out of here' were. She was sure Vasquez knew it as well.

"Semper Fi." She nodded in acknowledgement.

"Oorah, ma'am." Vasquez produced a slight, serious smile.

There was a brief, awkward moment of silence, then O'Hara stepped into the breach.

"Now, you know we did nae come here empty-handed, Lass. We've brought something for you, from the grateful citizens of the Lunar Free State." He produced a beautiful, wooden presentation case.

Michael O'Hara, in whatever leisure time his duties as chief executive allowed him, was a master woodworker. Whenever a certain military medal was to be awarded, he always made the case for it himself, including a personalized inscription. It was a curious tradition that was well-known at all levels of the LFS military, and Vasquez's eyes widened when she saw the case.

"'Tis the Lunar Medal of Honor, of course," O'Hara said as he confirmed what she was unable to believe. "There's a long citation that goes with it, and they'll probably insist on reading the whole thing at the official presentation ceremony when you get out of the hospital, but for now, suffice it to say you went above and beyond the call of duty, and you went up against a superior enemy force, putting yourself at risk to protect civilians on the ground."

He opened the case and showed her the medal, in all its glory—a golden, four-point star, with the silver disk of Luna in front of it, suspended from a broad ribbon of red with gold and black piping.

"As you were serving with Second Fleet at the time, I'll allow Admiral Torrey the honor of putting it around your neck," O'Hara told her.

"Sir, I..." Vasquez started to protest as Torrey stepped forward.

"Stop!" O'Hara held up his hand. "I know exactly what you're going to say. Every person who's ever gotten this medal—at least those who were alive at the time—says they don't deserve it, that they were just doing their duty. Colonel Bartley, who recommended you for this one, said the same thing when they pinned it on her.

"Maybe you're right," he went on, with a grin. "Maybe you were just doing your duty. If that's the case, you're getting the medal because you've got a higher sense of duty than most. So there, it's done, and we'll hear no protest."

"Thank you, sir." Vasquez bowed her head in acknowledgement as Torrey put the ribbon around her neck and arranged the medal.

"Congratulations, Marine," she said softly. "I'm proud to have you in my command." On the other side of the bed, McGraw expressed a similar sentiment.

Then the two flag officers stepped back and rendered a salute. Vasquez knew the drill—every military officer, noncom, and rating was required to salute a holder of the Medal of Honor, whenever the medal was displayed. She returned the salute with grave dignity.

"You know, Lassie, the LMH is a pretty big deal," O'Hara said, "so I was surprised when somebody told me there was something else you might appreciate even more. I've got it right here."

He produced a large envelope and pulled a parchment certificate out of it.

"This time, though, I'm going to have to ask you to do something for it." He pulled a small card out of his pocket and studied it.

"Raise your right hand, and repeat after me."

With a shock, Vasquez realized what was about to happen, and she felt tears coming to her eyes as she raised her hand.

"I, Maya Vasquez, with full understanding and of my own free will, do accept the responsibilities and embrace the rights of a Citizen of the Lunar Free State."

* * *

LCS *Summer Solstice*—Adrift between Star Systems

W*e're screwed,* Bjorn decided.

Sneaking through the ship's corridors and keeping an eye on Otuka movements, they'd managed to reach the lounge where the two children were hiding. They had successfully rescued the youngsters, but that had given Carla another idea. She'd insisted on another trip to the Emergency

Management station, where she did a bit of creative computer hacking—something beyond the capability of her portable data pad—and got into the ship's passenger information system.

Given the amount of looting and vandalism perpetrated by the Otuka, she'd been surprised it was still working, but Bjorn pointed out that the raiders were ignoring the ship's electronics. The pirates didn't seem to want to fool with something that might shut down a vital ship's system and interfere with their other efforts. Besides, modern microelectronic gear was pretty much worthless to anyone who didn't have a thorough knowledge of how it worked, and the Otuka had no time to study the matter. Stainless steel pots and pans were worth more to them than human-built computers, running human-designed software, for some unknown human purpose. They'd left the computers alone, and that presented Carla with some interesting opportunities.

She replaced the message on the passenger cabin screens with a new one that continued to advise passengers to stay in their cabins but explained why they needed to do so and what would happen to them if they didn't. The new message included an interactive form that urged passengers to enter the number of people in their cabin and answer a couple of basic questions about whether they had food and drink or needed medical attention. She set up a simple program to capture the responses along with the cabin number of the respondent in a database she could access with her remote pad. To her surprise, by the time they got back to their hideaway, there were more than thirty responses, indicating about seventy-five people were still hiding from the alien pirates. She couldn't get an exact number because some respondents hadn't filled in the form completely.

That presented a dilemma. Their hiding place couldn't accommodate that many people. They located a new hideaway and stocked it with supplies, then mounted a series of quick rescue forays to get survivors out of their cabins and into hiding. With careful planning and some luck, they made a half-dozen such forays and retrieved twenty-eight more passengers.

Then their luck ran out. On the next trip, before reaching the survivors, they rounded a corner just as an Otuka emerged from a compartment ahead of them. The alien raised its weapon and fired, but Bjorn and Carla ducked back around the corner and bolted to the next intersection. Carla instinctively headed for a maintenance access hatch that would take them back into hiding, but they encountered another alien raider and were forced down a dead-end corridor. They squeezed into a small alcove and hoped the aliens hadn't seen them go that way.

It was a forlorn hope. Both aliens were coming down the corridor toward their alcove, one behind the other, with weapons at the ready. The centaurs were almost upon them when Bjorn turned and gave Carla a quick kiss.

"Love you, babe," he said, then stepped into the corridor, raised his laser cutter, and fired.

The cutter was a powerful tool, but it was never intended for use as a weapon. In fact, it had safety features to prevent such use. Its beam passed through a gravity field "lens" that caused it to lose some of its tight-beam collimation, limiting its effective cutting range to no more than half a meter. It also had a safety switch attached to a shroud around the cutting head, which had to be pressed hard against the surface of the material to be cut to activate the beam.

Bjorn knew all about laser cutters. While in graduate school, he'd worked in a shipyard on Earth to pay his tuition and expenses. He had learned not only to use the tool, but to repair and maintain it as well. He hadn't hesitated when he disabled the de-collimation field and bypassed the safety switch. *Must be Carla's evil influence,* he thought, as the beam hit the approaching centaur squarely in the chest at less than two meters distance.

The creature howled in anguish and reared backward, which only served to hasten its demise as the megawatt beam sliced open its chest and abdominal cavity. Its rear legs kicked convulsively, propelling it forward and knocking Bjorn backward onto the deck. He lost his grip on the cutter as the centaur collapsed on top of him, pinning him down. The alien was no longer a threat, but the second centaur charged, trying to get to Bjorn, although it was hampered by the bulk of its dead companion.

The second alien passed the alcove without noticing Carla. As soon as it did, she stepped out behind it. With a swing worthy of a professional golfer, she brought the hooked end of her wrecking bar up between its rear legs.

The Otuka let out a terrible shriek as its hind legs collapsed, and it fell to the deck. It tried to twist its torso around to see what was attacking it, but Carla had recovered the heavy steel bar and switched her stance and grip from golfer to baseball batter. Her next swing connected with the side of the alien's head, and it went down for good.

"Nicely done, love," Bjorn told her, as he dragged himself out from under the first centaur. "How did you know they'd be vulnerable there…between the legs, I mean?"

"I didn't," she admitted. "But I had to do something, and it seemed like a good idea at the time."

"So it was," he agreed. "I think we'd better call off this rescue and go back and regroup." He retrieved his laser cutter, then looked down at his clothes, drenched with centaur blood and other fluids. "Damn, I really need a shower."

* * * * *

Chapter Six

LFS *Stardancer, Coyote,* and *Copperhead* in Hyperspace

From the earliest days of hyperspace travel, scientists and engineers had known an object in normal space could be detected in hyperspace by its hypergravity signature—an extension into hyperspace of the normal gravitational component of its mass. Anywhere near a star or planet, the signature of a small object like a ship would be buried in the enormous hypergravity signature of the celestial body, but in the vast empty spaces between the stars, a ship-sized object was a beacon that could be detected from a considerable distance. The LFS rescue force had been able to see *Summer Solstice* and the Otuka pirate vessels for almost an hour, but it wasn't until they got within a few minutes of their planned translation point that they were able to resolve individual ship signatures.

"Five to three was bad enough," Lucy Merrill complained, "but twelve to three is not something I'm happy about."

"Neither am I," Roger Torres agreed, "but it's what we've got, and our orders are clear. We don't have time to wait for reinforcements."

Jennifer Tanaka said nothing. She saw no point in restating or complaining about the obvious. And it was obvious: the largest object on their plot could only be *Summer Solstice*, and the liner was surrounded by a dozen vessels—ten that seemed about the mass of the pirate ships reported in the distress message and two that were considerably larger. Torres and the two corvette captains were conferring by video link to decide what to do.

"We'll drop out of hyper at half a million klicks," Torres continued. "That will give us a little time to figure out who they are and what they're doing. I want us in a tight echelon with *Stardancer* on point, weapons and defenses hot, and I plan to hit them with every active sensor we've got from the moment we drop into normal space. It's not likely they'll miss our hyper signature, so unless they're asleep we ought to get a reaction of some kind. In any case, we're going straight in. I'm a believer in Lord Nelson's philosophy—forget about the fancy maneuvers, just go straight for them."

You're thinking of Lord Nelson, I'm thinking more of Tennyson, Tanaka told herself, *as in "Charge of the Light Brigade*."

* * *

Home Ship—Otuka 2455th Clan—with *Summer Solstice*

A'archa Riobost'galan was *Tsan*—Supreme Lord—of the 2455th *falnor,* an old and honorable family of the Otuka. As such, he considered himself entitled to the spoils if he happened to come upon a prize freshly taken by a younger and lesser family. He was understandably angered that the upstart tsan of the miserable six-digit falnor who happened to stumble—by luck, not by skill—onto this prize dared to dispute his right to a share.

Not that there was much the lesser clan could do. A'archa's minions—his *falnor-katan*—were already aboard the vessel and were taking whatever they could carry, while he waited aboard his home ship for the spoils to be brought to him. The katan of the lower-class falnor wouldn't dare to interfere with his raiders and had to be satisfied with whatever spoils they could carry off themselves. There had been a few disputes, but his crews were disciplined. They responded quickly when any of their own were challenged.

The lesser tsan's audacity disturbed him. The upstart had the nerve to accuse him of being a follower—one who secretly trails other falnor, hoping to profit from the work of others. In truth, he had come to this sector on a rumor that the Akara-reptiles had a secret trade route with some unknown race over which they sent unescorted freighters with rich cargos. There were always rumors, but this one came from an old tsan who claimed to have chased such a freighter into an unexplored system, only to be driven off by a powerful warship of unknown origin. The one who told the tale was a senile old vapor-sniffer who could only vaguely remember where the events occurred, but A'archa thought perhaps there was truth in the story. He started on the fringes of Akara space, patrolling in the direction of the nearest star whose position and spectrum matched the old one's story.

He just happened to be within sensor range when the upstart falnor's raiders appeared, pursuing their prize. He could hardly have failed to notice when their quarry crashed out of hyperspace, followed by the raiders. When their home ship appeared and dropped out of hyper, he took it as an invitation to join the party.

His raiders were doing well. One crew even managed to detach an entire gravity node from the prize ship and was dragging it toward the home ship's cavernous cargo bays. This was better than mere scrap metal. It was technology that could be studied to provide improvements for his own ships or could be traded to other falnor for profit.

As his crews worked, A'archa busied himself composing a poem that would put the other tsan in his place. He alluded to low ancestry and perverted sexual practices, including self-fertilization, on the part of the upstart. He was busy refining his insults to improve the meter of the piece when one of his technicians approached, properly subservient, with trunk bowed and hands on fore-knees, lobes twitching nervously, indicating an urgent message to be conveyed.

"Speak," he commanded, allowing only a small amount of irritation into his voice.

"Three unknown ships have dropped out of hyperspace, Lord. We cannot identify them, but their aggressive approach indicates challenge."

A'archa snarled as the beautiful composition of his verse shattered in his mind, replaced by the urgent need to act.

"Challenge? Prepare for combat!" he ordered. Almost as an afterthought, he ordered the message to be passed to the lowly upstart tsan in case the fool was as blind as he was stupid.

* * *

LFS *Stardancer, Coyote*, and *Copperhead*—Engaging in Normal Space

"Damn! They're taking the ship apart!" Torres exclaimed.

They were close enough to see that one of the smaller vessels appeared to be towing a large piece of *Summer Solstice*—probably a drive node—toward one of the two large pirate ships.

Almost immediately, three of the smaller pirate vessels began to accelerate in their direction. Two others began to move away from

Summer Solstice, apparently heading for one of the larger pirate ships. Meanwhile, what appeared to be small craft began leaving the cruise ship, heading back to the remaining pirate vessels hovering around her. The vessel towing the stolen drive node increased speed, redoubling its efforts to bring its prize home.

"Pirates for sure," Torres declared. "Rules of engagement just got upgraded to Alpha, people. Missile range in two minutes."

"Copy that," Tanaka acknowledged. "ROE Alpha, two minutes to missile range."

"Copy," Merrill echoed. "You want to call targeting priorities, Commander?"

"Early bird gets a bloody beak," Torres told the other two captains. He tagged the leading pirate vessel on his display, letting his tactical officer as well as the two corvettes know where to concentrate fire.

* * *

Home Ship—Otuka 2455th Clan

A'archa was having second thoughts. The aggressive charge of the three unknowns indicated a confidence that gave him pause. They could scarcely fail to see what they faced, but numeric superiority meant nothing. If they were even medium-weight Akara warships, three of them could make chopped meat of his falnor-ka and those of the upstart as well. It wouldn't be without taking some damage in return, but that would not deter the reptiles. These didn't look like reptile warships, however. Their drive signatures were different, and they were much less massive than reptile cruiser-class ships.

Still, they charged in. There was a small probability they might be bluffing, but A'archa reflected that one did not get to be a wise old tsan by gambling on small probabilities. Let the upstart try to write himself into a great battle-poem; three of his falnor-ka were already charging out to meet the newcomers. A'archa would rather write a poem than be the dead hero about whom it was written. He ordered his falnor-katan to return to their ships and his helmsman to set a course for withdrawal.

* * *

LCS *Summer Solstice*—Survivors' Hideaway

"I don't know what's going on," Carla muttered, flipping through screens on her data pad, "but things are looking up."

"What is it, love?" Bjorn asked.

"They're leaving. They're heading for the boat bays and departing as fast as they get loaded. Do you think the cavalry has arrived?"

"Hmmm…earlier than expected, but I guess it's possible," he told her.

"Great!" she exclaimed. "Let's hope they don't decide to nuke the evidence of their crimes."

* * *

LFS *Stardancer, Coyote*, and *Copperhead*

Torres realized the pirate ships would be into and through his missile envelope very quickly. In a closing engagement like this one, he would not get good targeting solutions for his broadside missile tubes. *Stardancer* mounted only two chase tubes forward, but the corvettes mounted only forward-firing tubes. They would launch four missiles apiece to his two. He targeted the group's first missile salvo at the leading enemy vessel and launched as soon as his computers told him the extreme closure rate would bring the target into range.

The pirates didn't break off, and the first of them was wiped out of existence as ten laser-head missiles converged on it and detonated simultaneously. The other two kept coming and closed to within range of their own beam weapons. They managed to get off a couple of shots before the second missile salvo wiped out one of them. The other succumbed to fire from *Stardancer's* longer-ranged 40cm chase grasers. By the time the two corvettes reached firing range for their smaller grasers, there was nothing left to shoot at. The enemy had concentrated fire on the largest target, and *Stardancer* had taken a couple of hits, but her shielding and armor had prevented major damage.

"Is that all you've got?" Merrill sounded disappointed. "Is that your best shot?"

"Be careful what you wish for," Tanaka cautioned. "Looks like they're sending the first team in."

Two more of the smaller pirate ships were forming on one of the larger ones and moving cautiously in the direction of the LFS formation.

"Looks like some of them got the message," Torres noted. Six more of the bogies—five small and one large—were heading away from his group. They were not in any sort of formation but were headed in pretty much the same direction. It was an obvious bid to disengage. *And it will probably succeed,* Torres decided. *Assuming we take these three, our priority will be to secure and protect the civilians, if any are still alive.*

"First salvo, put everything on the big bogey," he ordered. "Slight change of tactics, though, we're going in ballistic. I'm going to slew 90 degrees and bring my broadside tubes to bear. I plan to roll and give him a double broadside. That'll put sixteen missiles on him at once instead of ten. Keep your fire control locked to mine and kill your drives on my mark."

* * *

Home Ship—Otuka 2455th Clan

One good thing about the vast emptiness between stars, A'archa reflected, was that one could jump in and out of hyperspace at will. He could have ordered his ships to translate almost as soon as they began to move, but he stayed in normal space long enough to observe the outcome of the first engagement—three of the upstart's falnor-ka wiped out of existence without even slowing the approach of the newcomers. *Formidable creatures,* he thought. *Definitely to be avoided, except under conditions of extremely favorable numeric superiority.* He wondered if they could possibly be humans, kin to those aboard the former prize ship that was now dwindling astern.

He ordered the jump into hyperspace, leaving the upstart tsan to his—extremely brief, A'archa suspected—moment of glory. Glory, he decided, was a fleeting and much overrated thing.

Sometime later, his crew reported a hyper signature far astern, a single ship in pursuit of his formation. It was the sole survivor of the upstart's falnor, now orphaned and begging to be allowed to swear allegiance to A'archa.

* * *

LFS *Stardancer, Coyote,* and *Copperhead*

"Damage reports?" Torres queried.

"*Coyote*, no damage," Tanaka replied.

"*Copperhead*, one hit," Merrill reported. "Portside forward. Lost my portside loading racks, so I'm down two missile tubes. No crew casualties."

"I've lost one missile tube and one graser. One crew casualty, not fatal," Torres told them. "Good job, people."

"I'm glad the other six didn't stick around," Tanaka admitted. "I'd hate to have taken them all on at once."

"Agreed," Torres replied. "I'm getting no answer to hails from *Summer Solstice*, but some of her docking hatches are open. I'm sending a boarding party."

If we were regular LFS Navy, I'd have a squad of Marines aboard, he thought. OSG ships did not carry Marines, but he wondered if maybe that policy might change in the future as a result of this encounter.

* * *

LCS *Summer Solstice*

The members of the OSG boarding party were horrified by what they found aboard the cruise ship. Some of them became physically ill, and none of them expected to find anyone left alive. Heavily armed, they moved warily through the ship, not knowing whether any pirates might still be aboard.

They were taken by surprise when not one, but two groups of survivors approached from opposite ends of the ship's main passenger concourse. The group from the forward end of the ship was led by a uniformed ship's officer armed with a pistol. The much larger group from aft was led by a tall, young woman carrying a wrecking bar. Behind her was a solidly built blond-haired man with what appeared to be a laser cutter in his hands. Both groups looked haggard but in good physical condition. None of them were smiling.

"Lieutenant Jack Brimley, LFS *Stardancer*," the boarding party's officer identified himself as the two groups approached. "We got here as soon as we could."

* * *

"You got here sooner than we expected," Davis said, lowering the pistol. "First Officer Terrell Davis, LCS *Summer Solstice*." He nodded to the woman leading the other group. "Dr. Greenwood, we've been following your adventures on the ship's video system. Damned fine work. Maybe someday, you'll tell me how you knew where to look for all those people you rescued from their cabins. Also, my apologies, you were right about the pirates. I wish the captain had taken your advice."

Carla shrugged. "Water under the bridge," she said. "Speaking of the pirates—" she turned to Lieutenant Brimley, "—where are the bastards?"

Now it was Brimley's turn to shrug. "There were twelve ships. Seven of them got away; we blew the other five to hell and gone. We didn't pursue because you people were our priority."

"Those of us that are left," Carla replied, grimly. She handed her data pad to Davis. "Here's a list of cabins that reported survivors—the ones we couldn't get to. Most of them should still be OK. Wish we could have gotten more of them."

Davis shook his head, thinking appearances could be deceiving. Carla Greenwood looked like a quiet academic who would most likely be found bent over a data screen doing research or lecturing in a classroom to a bunch of bored first-year students, but he'd seen her take out one of the Otuka pirates with that wrecking bar. He'd seen her husband—also a scientist, as he recalled—burn one with his laser cutter. They had rescued more than fifty people on their forays into the pirate-occupied parts of the ship.

He did a quick estimate: about a hundred survivors. *Out of more than five hundred passengers and crew,* he thought bitterly. He glanced down at the pad Carla had given him. *I hope there are a lot more still waiting in their cabins.*

* * *

"You know what I'm wishing for, right now?" Carla mused. "I wish those bastards would come back and maybe bring a few dozen ships full of their friends and relatives with them."

She and Bjorn were taking a brief rest, sitting at a small café table on what had been *Summer Solstice's* much-vaunted Promenade, which featured deck-to-overhead viewing ports of crystal-clear composite. Through those ports, Carla could see the ominous shapes of First Battle Group's warships—including her mother's flagship, LFS *Valkyrie*—hovering protectively nearby. The group arrived forty-two hours after the OSG ships, long after the battle was over. After hearing what a destroyer and two corvettes had done to the pirates, Carla was really hoping a bunch of Otuka ships would suddenly appear, thinking the battle group was a merchant convoy and not realizing their error until it was too late.

Lorna had ordered the survivors taken aboard *Valkyrie*, but the cruise ship's surviving crewmembers had insisted on staying behind for search-and-rescue in the hope of finding more survivors. Carla and Bjorn elected to stay as well, which hadn't made Lorna happy, but Carla pointed out she knew the ship's layout as well as anyone and could be more useful there than anywhere else. When Terrell Davis endorsed her request to stay, the admiral had grudgingly agreed. With Navy and Marine people to assist, they'd located over eighty additional survivors, including crewmembers who'd found hiding places, and passengers who'd been afraid to respond to Carla's computer-generated queries.

Carla blamed herself for not being able to save more. Bjorn, with his usual calm demeanor, pointed out that a lot of the survivors would not have made it without her efforts. There was no one to blame but the Otuka, he told her, and the Lunar Fleet would get around to settling that score in due time. Meanwhile, it appeared their work aboard the cruise ship was just about done, and they would have to accept *Valkyrie's* hospitality soon.

No one had yet decided what to do with *Summer Solstice*—it would require a fleet repair ship's effort to make her hyper-capable once again. The survivors would be heading back to Luna aboard *Valkyrie* since the battlecruiser was the only ship with enough space and life support to carry all of them.

Carla's musings were interrupted as one of *Summer Solstice*'s surviving crewmembers entered the Promenade. Carla knew her as the steward in charge of the pet kennels, who had found a hiding place in the liner's cargo spaces. She was smiling, which puzzled Carla since there hadn't been much to smile about lately.

"Hi, Terry, what's up?" she inquired.

"We need your help, Dr. Greenwood," the steward announced. "We've found another survivor, but we need you to convince him to come out from under a cargo container."

Carla was puzzled. Under a cargo container? Then she got it.

"Dusty? You've found Dusty?"

"Yes, ma'am. He looks OK, but he must have had a run-in with the pirates, because he's hissing and showing his claws, and he won't come out for anyone."

"But how?" Carla had seen the wrecked kennel area and assumed the worst.

"Don't know how they got loose, ma'am, but we found two dogs about an hour ago. They were starving and dehydrated, and they came out when we offered food. Dusty looks well-fed—probably found some mice in the cargo spaces, and there was water leaking from a damaged pipe in the area. But he's not willing to trust anyone, so hopefully you can get him out."

* * *

LFS *Valkyrie*—on Station with *Summer Solstice*

"Selfish of me, I guess, but I'm glad you two survived, and Dusty as well."

The cat stretched out on the desk, purring loudly as Lorna stroked his back. Carla and Bjorn sat in comfortable chairs in the admiral's day cabin aboard *Valkyrie*, sipping cups of excellent coffee prepared by Lorna's personal steward. Despite her self-proclaimed gratitude for their survival, Lorna's expression was grim.

"I wish we could have saved more of them." Carla's voice was bitter.

"Don't go there, daughter," Lorna cautioned. "I know what you're feeling. I've felt it after every battle I've ever been in. You think if you'd done things differently, or been just a bit better, more people would have survived, but you're wrong. The truth is, there are a lot of people alive now who wouldn't be if it hadn't been for you and Bjorn. They're going to pin medals on you for this, and you deserve them."

"Mom! Don't you dare…"

"Not me, darlin'. Terrell Davis is pushing for it, and the other survivors are backing him up. He's already prepared his report for Commercial Fleet HQ, and he'll file it as soon as we get back. He just gave me a courtesy copy."

Carla lapsed into brooding silence. Bjorn reached over and touched her hand.

"She's right, love," he told her. "Me, I was along for the ride, but you were truly amazing."

"How can a just God allow such creatures to exist?" Carla still sounded bitter.

"God doesn't answer questions like that," Lorna told her. "We have to figure it out for ourselves and do what we must to make it right."

Carla looked up, directly into her mother's eyes.

"I know you can't talk about it, Mom, but at least tell me we're doing something, anything, to make it right, like you said."

"Yes," Lorna told her, "we are. There's been one encounter so far, and a few thousand of the bastards won't be troubling us ever again. And that reminds me…your friend Maya is back on Luna. She got badly banged up in that encounter, but she survived. I was supposed to pin the Lunar Medal of Honor on her, but the distress call from *Summer Solstice* rearranged my priorities."

"What about Aunt Ronnie and Amy Ling and…"

Lorna held up a hand to wave off Carla's sudden concern.

"As far as I know, everyone else you know out there is OK, but I can't say anymore." *And, unfortunately,* she thought, *someone out here is going to get some bad news.*

* * *

Jennifer Tanaka was puzzled and a bit apprehensive. She'd already been through the video conference with Admiral Greenwood along with Torres and Merrill. The admiral had endorsed their actions and told them commendations were in order. Her report, she said, would have nothing but high praise for their outstanding execution of the mission.

A fleet tender would be dispatched from Luna to repair *Summer Solstice*, and two destroyers would remain behind to guard the hulk until those repairs were done. The rest of the battle group, together with the three OSG ships, would depart for Luna in another five hours, but Tanaka had been summoned to *Valkyrie* for a personal meeting with the admiral, and she hadn't a clue what it was about. The Marine guard opened the hatch and motioned her into the day cabin that served as Lorna Greenwood's office.

"Senior Lieutenant Tanaka, reporting as ordered, ma'am." She came to attention in front of the desk and saluted.

"Sit down, Captain," Lorna returned the salute and motioned to one of the leather chairs in front of the desk. "I'm afraid I have some bad news for you. It's about your sister, Janice."

* * *

LFS *Stardancer* and *Coyote*—on Station with *Summer Solstice*

"I'm sorry, Jennifer." Roger Torres looked at Tanaka's face on the screen but could find no trace of the pain the woman must be feeling. Tanaka kept herself tightly controlled, to the point where Torres could almost feel the tension surrounding her.

"I need to get back home to Luna," she told him. "They were supposed to notify my parents the day we left to come out here. Mother and Dad must be devastated."

"You'll see them soon," he advised. "OSG has already replaced us on patrol. The admiral says we're going straight to TransLuna anchorage."

"She wasn't just my sister, Commander…she was my twin. People who aren't twins don't understand the connection. Part of me has died." Tanaka sighed heavily, allowing some of the grief to leak through her armor. Torres said nothing, knowing she needed to let it out.

"Damn it!" she swore. "What kind of sick irony is this? My sister, dead, at the hands of the same monsters we just tangled with here. In three decades of human star travel, we've never encountered anything like this, but now they're going to be in my nightmares forever."

"I know it's not much consolation," Torres replied, "but at least you got a chance to give them a little payback."

"After seeing what they did to those people on *Summer Solstice*, no amount of payback will ever be adequate," she said, "but it's the only consolation we've got."

Both were silent for a moment, then Tanaka spoke again.

"When we get back, I'm going to put in for a transfer to regular Navy. I know OSG's mission is important, but if we're going after these monsters, I want to be part of it. If nothing else, Fleet will have to provide escorts for commercial shipping between Sol and Alpha Akara. If I can help protect somebody else from the bastards, I'll settle for that."

"You know they probably won't give you another command," Torres cautioned, "at least not right away."

"I know. I'll miss *Coyote*, but I have to do this for Janice, for my family, and for myself. People say it's wrong to seek vengeance, but somehow, I think those who say that never had to deal with anything like this."

* * *

Valhalla—Lorna Greenwood's estate—Planet Copper Hills Prime

"Well, at least we got a honeymoon...and without the horror show this time," Carla remarked.

"Yes, we did," Bjorn agreed. "And this place is as beautiful as you said it was."

They were sitting on the terrace of Lorna's Copper Hills estate, watching a spectacular sunset. Inside, the Akara house staff was setting the table for dinner.

They had returned to Luna after the *Summer Solstice* incident, resigned to the unhappy knowledge that their honeymoon was not to be. They had gone to see Maya, who was just recovering from the first round of surgeries and had swapped Otuka war stories with her. Carla had been surprised at the Marine's high spirits, considering what she had been through and the ordeal still ahead of her. Maya, in turn, had been amazed to hear about Carla's exploits aboard the cruise ship.

"You took out a donkey-boy with a wrecking bar? Geez, lady, why aren't you in the Marines? For sure, they ought to give you a medal for that."

"We are going to get medals," Carla admitted. "I don't think I deserve one, but Commercial Fleet put us in for the Lunar Star, and Mom says the Directorate just approved it. That's going to look a little strange on my chest next to a couple of Scientific Achievement awards."

"It'll look even stranger on mine, all alone next to absolutely nothing," Bjorn said, "but they did push me up to the front of the line for citizenship."

"Me too," Maya beamed. "Honestly, that meant more to me than the medal."

Carla and Bjorn had pretty much decided to put off the remainder of their honeymoon and get back to work. Carla had a new project in mind, while Bjorn was anxious to get started in his new position at the LRI. But shortly after their return to Luna, Lorna had invited them to dinner at the Senior Officers Club at Fleet HQ, where she made an unusual offer.

"Three days from now, I'm taking *Valkyrie* and First Battle Group to Alpha Akara to discuss the Otuka situation with Heart of the Copper Hills. I could bend a rule or two and take you along—no luxury stateroom, just a no-frills Navy senior officer's cabin for the trip. The trip will only take twenty-one days in each direction, and you'll have a full eight days on Copper Hills Prime. You should make it back only a few days later than your original end-of-honeymoon date, and I'll guarantee you won't have to worry about Otuka pirates this time."

They had accepted, and Bjorn was glad they did. It had given them a chance to really relax, to recover from their ordeal, and to contemplate their future together. Besides, despite the ribbing he had given Carla over having his mother-in-law along on their honeymoon, Bjorn had discovered his wife was right. Lorna was a different person here: more relaxed, laid back, and unafraid to show a human side that those who knew the Iron Maiden would never have suspected she had.

He had thought Lorna and Carla were as different as a mother and daughter could be, but he had learned things about both that made him rethink that premise. Seeing the other side of Lorna had changed his mind completely. *No question anymore,* he mused. *Carla is the Valkyrie's daughter, and I think I actually* like *my mother-in-law. So much for stereotypes.*

Still, he reflected, as he watched *Valkyrie's* cutter—emblazoned with the four-star cluster of a fleet admiral—settle onto the pad next to the lodge, *the Iron Maiden's never far beneath the surface.*

The two Marine Airwolf fighters escorting the cutter made a low pass over the grounds, then climbed away into the purple sky.

* * *

Corporal J's Place—TerraNova City, Luna

"It's not that I don't appreciate the ride," Maya explained, "but I gotta make this landing on my own."

Candy Parks nodded her understanding and retrieved the crutches from the back of the wheelchair. "Go for it," she encouraged, handing the crutches to Vasquez. "I'll wait out here."

"Like hell you will!" the Marine growled. "You aren't my chauffer, you're my friend. We're both gonna have a good time tonight. Park that buggy and follow me in."

It had been two months since Vasquez woke up on Luna—two months of repeated surgeries and physical therapy. She was at the point where she could, with difficulty, move herself slowly over short distances with the help of the crutches. The problem wasn't strength. She had added her own physical training routine to the therapy the doctors had given her, just to make sure her legs didn't atrophy from lack of use. The problem was coordination, scrambled motor nerves that didn't always make her legs do her bidding. *Gonna feel like a fool if I fall on my ass, but I am not going in there in a wheelchair,* she vowed.

She pushed up from the chair, positioned the crutches in front of her, and began her journey—a dozen meters or so to the door of Corporal J's Place. She reached the door and started inside. She didn't get very far.

"Semper Fi!" someone shouted.

"Oorah, Oorah, Oorah…" the chant began as a dozen Marines swarmed around her. The next thing she knew, she had been lifted off her feet and was being carried to a large table near the back.

"Candy!" Maya called, trying to look back over her shoulder. "Hey, Marines, don't you dare leave my guardian angel behind."

"Wouldn't dream of it, Sarge." More Marines swarmed to escort Candy to the table. In short order, they were settled in with Maya at the head of the long table and Candy to her right. Marines filled the rest of the chairs quickly, and Corporal J's proprietor, Mike DaSilva, came by to take their drink orders.

"I really shouldn't…" Parks started to protest, but Vasquez stopped her.

"Yes, you should. We planned this, and that's why you left little Johnny with his grandparents. You've got all these Marines to make sure you get home OK, and the drinks are on me."

"The hell you say," a Marine master sergeant told her. "Your money's no good here tonight, Sergeant Vasquez. It's the Rule of the LMH. We've been waiting for you to show up ever since we heard you got the medal."

"Then you're buying drinks for her, too." Maya put her arm around Candy's shoulder. "She's been taking care of me for the past two months. She's my friend, and I wouldn't have made it here tonight without her."

"In that case," the master sergeant proclaimed, "you are both gonna get seriously drunk in an orderly and proficient manner. You ain't getting out of here until you are no longer able to use those walking sticks, Sarge. These Marines are going to help you do it, and they will make sure both of you get safely home…or wherever else you might want to go tonight."

"OK," Maya agreed, "but just so all of you know, Candy has a husband. He's with the fleet, still out there in Top Secret Kick-Ass Land where I got chewed up. So, none of you better mess with her…unless she clearly indicates she wants to be messed with. Understood?"

"So noted," the master sergeant replied. He looked around the table as if daring any of the others to disagree.

"Besides," Mike DaSilva added with a grin, "she's the CEO's daughter-in-law."

"She's the what?" Vasquez stared at Parks, who promptly turned a lovely shade of red.

"My husband, Rob…" she mumbled. "O'Hara…his name's Rob O'Hara. Sorry, I never thought to mention it."

"Sorry, Ms. Parks, didn't mean to out you." DaSilva was still grinning. "But the look on your face is worth a round of drinks on the house, so order up, everybody."

*****

Chapter Seven

LFS *Sorceress*—in New Eden Orbit

"Two thousand of them?" Mercedes Warren was stunned.

"More like twenty-four hundred," Amy Ling replied. "And several hundred appear to be of a heavier class than the ones we tangled with before."

Warren's face occupied one of the three windows on Ling's screen, while the other two showed Rear Admiral Kellerman and Colonel Bartley.

"They'll be here in about seventy hours," Ling continued. "Fred, I'll need you to move out smartly and take up position as planned. Dr. Warren, you need to pack up your scientists. I want everyone off the planet at least twelve hours before we engage the incoming hostiles. I want *Hubble, Valley Forge,* and *Okinawa* to be halfway to the hyper limit before the first shots are fired.

"No," Warren said quietly. "I will not abandon these people to those monsters. You can send the ships off, with any of the scientific team who want to leave, but I'm staying, and I think a lot of my people will want to do the same."

"Doctor..." Ling's voice was calm and steady. "I don't think you understand. We have sixty ships, with a full load-out of about 3,000 missiles, and about twenty percent of those are decoys or ECM birds. These people haven't shown us much in the way of missile defenses, but they did manage to stop more than half our missiles the last time, even though we had the advantage of surprise. If we remain in orbit, they will control the engagement, and I expect at least half of them will get into energy weapon range.

"Our capital ship grasers have a slight range advantage, at least against their smaller ships, but to use that advantage, we need to maneuver to keep the range open. To have any hope of victory, we are going to have to yield the planet. When and if we achieve victory, we can return, but in the meantime, the Edies and anyone else down there will be on their own."

"Then I guess we're on our own," Warren told her. "If the Edies know the attack is coming, they can find hiding places in the deep forests and mountains. The best thing my people can do right now is spend the next seventy hours getting word to them. Besides, maybe the bastards aren't planning to come down to the planet until they've dealt with your people up there. If you stop them in space, we won't have any worries down on the surface."

"I'm trying to tell you, Doctor," Ling replied, "we may not be able to stop them."

"I have faith in you," Warren said, with a smile that lacked any trace of humor.

"Rock..." Ling sighed. "Can you talk any sense into this woman?"

"I doubt it," Bartley replied, "but it makes my mission pretty simple. I've got about fifty hours to offload everything we've got to the surface and to prepare to kick ass and take names if the donkeys show up. *Valley Forge* and *Okinawa* can withdraw as ordered, Admiral, but they're going to be empty when they do.

"Dr. Warren, I take it you won't have too many objections if we try to keep you and your people alive, along with any of the Edies who happen to be present?"

"None at all, Colonel. We'll be happy to have you with us...really happy, to be honest."

Ling shook her head.

"You're both crazy," she told them, "but it's an honor to serve with you. Rock, do what you must. I'll leave two destroyers to escort *Hubble* and the ATs out-system. I'll give you fifty-five hours, maximum, before they have to break orbit. Dr. Warren, make sure your people know it's voluntary. Any that want to leave need to be aboard *Hubble* before the deadline."

"As for us, Fred," she addressed Kellerman, "if these people want to be heroes, we need to get out there and make it count."

* * *

Marine Corps Training Center—Luna

Maya regarded the tall, sandy-haired lieutenant commander with interest as he approached the workout bench. He was well-built for a non-Marine officer and probably no stranger to the gym, but he was wearing his dress alpha uniform, so he wasn't here for a workout. He approached the bench and waited patiently while she finished her set of inclined leg presses.

"Pretty impressive," he remarked as she sat up and swung her legs around to the side. "I'd guess you're pressing about twice your weight."

"Strength isn't the problem," she told him. "It's getting these crazy legs to do what I tell them to. Can I help you, Commander?"

"I hope so, Sergeant. We've been advised you put in a request for return to active duty."

"Yes, sir, I did." She read the shoulder flashes and other insignia on his uniform. "But I wouldn't have thought Fleet Engineering would have much use for a gimpy Marine who can't walk five meters without crutches."

"The job doesn't require much walking," he replied. "I'm Lieutenant Commander Jensen, with Naval Weapons Development, and we're hoping you might volunteer for a special project. We're wondering if you might be interested in flying a Raptor again."

Maya regarded him with unsmiling skepticism.

"Sir, I've been told by the best doctors in the known universe that I will never be able to do that, so please excuse my lack of enthusiasm."

"Well…um, yes…actually, we've been talking to those doctors, including Doctor Madison. He's somewhat skeptical, but he's willing to get involved in the project if you agree to volunteer."

"OK…" Maya said slowly. "You've dropped the right name. Doc Madison got me this far, and he's never tried to bullshit me. I presume I get to talk to him before I make a decision?"

"Of course. In fact, if you're available, we'd like to meet with you and the good doctor tomorrow morning. This project is classified, so I really can't say anymore until then. Is that OK with you?"

"Commander, I'm a Marine, not an engineer. You don't need my approval. Just give me the order, and I'll be there. But I do have one question: how many more surgeries am I going to have to go through for your secret project?"

"Just one, Sergeant," he told her. "Just one."

* * *

LFS *Okinawa*—New Eden Orbit

"Hold that hatch!"

"Wouldn't leave without you, ma'am."

Master Sergeant Rocco Marchetti almost allowed a smile to blemish his rock-hard combat face as he stepped back to allow Colonel Bartley to board the assault lander. Marchetti had never seen the Old Lady in full combat dress, but he noted her gear was professionally rigged, and she wore it with the easy familiarity of long practice. Marchetti had seen the colonel in her dress uniform, with the impressive rack of decorations that included the Lunar Medal of Honor. Obviously, this wasn't her first dance.

"Everyone else aboard?" she inquired.

"Yes, ma'am."

"OK, then button it up, and let's ride. We're the last one out, and the ATs are going to break orbit as soon as we're clear."

Bartley moved into the lander and found a seat. She had just finished strapping herself in when the launch warning sounded. She looked around the cabin as the lander slid out of the AT's boat bay. Some of the less-experienced troops looked a bit tense, but all of Bravo Company had engaged with the donkey-boys last time, so none of them were virgins when it came to combat. The veterans among them were mostly relaxed but alert, while a few old hands were taking the opportunity to catch a quick nap on the way down to the planet. *Confidence high, morale good. Check.*

* * *

An hour later, on the surface, Bartley laid out the plan for her officers and senior noncoms.

"First Battalion, Alpha and Bravo Companies will deploy with the scientists. We've convinced them not to scatter, but they are going to six previously established research stations. I want a full platoon with each group. The primary mission is to keep the eggheads out of harm's way, and the secondary mission is to protect the Edies whenever possible.

"Charlie Company, you're my reserve. You'll stay with me here, at Research Station Four, along with First Battalion's Dragonflies, so we can move quickly to wherever we need to go. We'll also keep half the Airwolves here since we don't know where the donkeys might show up with air support, but I'm deploying the Raptors forward with the field companies to cover ground operations.

"Colonel Briggs has command of Second Battalion at Research Station Seven, where he will establish his battalion HQ and similarly deploy the scientists. He only has two companies, so we've given him the smaller group of scientists to cover, but he also has his battalion's Dragonflies and Raptors, as well as the other six Airwolves.

"The good news," she told them, "is that the fleet has deployed a dozen stealth recon satellites in low orbit, and we have enough field uplink units to deploy with each platoon. We don't think the donkeys will spot the birds in orbit, and the admiral has detailed a few destroyers to harass any orbital operations they may initiate. We should be able to track them, but they probably won't be able to track us. Note the operative words should and probably. In other words, use the information I've just given you to your advantage, but don't bet the farm on it.

"The bad news is that they outnumber us about a thousand to one, but we expect the Navy to take a big bite out of them before they get here. After that, use your satellite intel, hit 'em hard, and keep moving. Do your best to protect the scientists and the locals, but, beyond that, your objective is to inflict maximum damage at minimum cost. Any questions?"

There were none. They were professionals, and they realized she was giving them a lot of leeway, with tactical decisions left to each platoon leader's discretion. Since they had no idea where the Otuka might deploy or in what strength, there wasn't much else they could do until the enemy arrived.

* * *

Fleet HQ—Weapons Development Section—TerraNova City, Luna

Maya Vasquez gave the engineers a skeptical look. "Let me get this straight. You're telling me I'll be able to fly a Raptor using some kind of mind control, like I'm gonna 'use the Force' the way they did in that old 20th century video series?"

"Well, not exactly," Commander Jensen explained patiently. "The plan calls for us to implant a microelectronic package in your neural cortex that will process your mental commands into signals that will control the Raptor's systems. You'll be physically plugged into the Raptor's control interface, since we can't take a chance on signal interference that could disable a wireless system."

"So…" She was suddenly thoughtful. "I guess that's the one surgery you mentioned yesterday. But I don't see the advantage. My brain is still giving the orders, so how is it better than having a pilot with two good arms and two good legs flying the ship?"

"Reaction time." Doctor Madison spoke up for the first time. "Your brain gives the command, and the implant sends an electronic signal straight to the control system instead of waiting for your muscles to move your arm or leg. This, in turn, moves the controls to send that same signal to the system. Instead of a few tenths of a second, the ship could theoretically respond in microseconds."

"Theoretically." Maya's skepticism returned. "Sounds like you're not totally convinced, Doc, so give it to me straight. What are the chances this will work, and what's the downside if it doesn't?"

"Downside?" He shrugged. "I don't really think there's a downside other than a lot of time, effort, and money spent on a failed project. The surgery won't be nearly as invasive as the nerve repair work we've already done, should not be painful or require a long recovery period, and won't leave you impaired in any way. All they are asking me to do is implant a little package in the back of your neck that will process signals to and from your brain and an interface plug that will let you connect the package to the system. Everything else will be done by external electronics built into the Raptor, not your head.

"I guess the only thing I'm not convinced about is whether you can learn to generate those mental commands and interpret the feedback with the same level of instant response and instinctive skill pilots use when they fly manually. But then—" he favored her with a wry grin, "—I wasn't totally convinced you would ever stand or walk on those legs again. If sheer determination can make it work, you are the best candidate for the job. I'm pretty sure that's the main reason the techno-geeks want you for this project. In a sense, you've already proven that mind control works."

It was Maya's turn to grin.

"OK, Doc, you know how to push my buttons—and you too, Commander. Where do we go from here?"

"Does that mean you are volunteering for the assignment?"

"Sir, I'm a Marine. You don't have to ask me to volunteer. Just give me a set of orders and I'm good to go."

"OK." Jensen thought about it for a moment. "I guess we need to cut some orders assigning you to Weapons Development. We'll list you as a test pilot, so you'll continue to draw hazardous duty pay, though in the first stages you won't be flying anything other than computer simulations. The prototype package is developed and tested—as much as we can without implanting it in someone—so we need to schedule the surgery as well. Doc, you've studied it thoroughly. Do you anticipate any problems?"

"No, and I've not only studied your package, I know the patient pretty well. Won't be the first time I've been inside your head," he told Vasquez.

"Besides," he went on, "they've really miniaturized this thing. If it were any smaller, we could inject it through a needle and not call it surgery at all."

"OK, then." Jensen nodded. "After that, you'll spend a lot of time hooked up to a computer, doing various tasks while we analyze what sort of signals you can give us and how you process the feedback. Then we move on to the next phase, where we try to make use of those signals. We've modified a Raptor simulator for that, and we have a special coach to work with you—one of the Fleet AIs."

"Really?" Vasquez was curious. "I've never worked with an AI before."

"We're going to use one of the battlecruiser AIs—Val from *Valkyrie* to be precise. Since she's assigned to First Fleet, she should be available at Luna for the duration. Our people think she'll be able to give you the most help, since a warship's AI is hardwired into the ship's control systems. Effectively, the ship is her body, and she controls it at a subconscious level, which is what we want you to learn to do with a Raptor."

"Wow!" Vasquez shook her head. "Never thought of it that way, actually being part of my ship. This is starting to sound like fun…I think."

"It may be," Jensen told her, "but you're going to have to work for it. I expect it will be a long time before we actually turn you loose with a real Raptor."

* * *

Lunar Research Institute—East TerraNova, Luna

Carla set her coffee cup down and settled into her chair. She brought up her screen, logged in, and was just taking her first sip of coffee when a chime announced an incoming call. She noted the caller's ID and grimaced at the reminder that she was, in fact, back to work. With a sigh, she touched the accept icon, and a window opened, showing the smiling face of her chief assistant.

"Good morning, Marty," she said, trying to sound more enthusiastic than she felt.

"Welcome back, Dr. Greenwood," he bubbled. "I hope you had an enjoyable honeymoon." He favored her with a knowing wink, which from anyone else would have been annoying and too damned familiar, but Martin Stansbury, Ph.D., F.L.R.I. was allowed a certain amount of leeway. For one thing, he was so stereotypically gay, she tended to think of him as one of the girls in the office. For another, he was very good at what he did. He was not a brilliant research scientist, but he was an organizer, a detail-oriented team player, who could always be counted on to dot every "I" and cross every "T" in any project he worked on. He never failed to keep her informed, often giving her more information than she really needed. She had given him the task of monitoring the Astrophysics Division's active projects while she went off to get married and enjoy her honeymoon.

All of Luna knew what had happened to *Summer Solstice*, so when she got her second chance for a honeymoon, Stansbury had assured her everything would be looked after in her absence. She suspected he was calling to give her a complete briefing on everything that had happened while she was gone, but when she asked him if that was the case, he surprised her.

"Oh, no." He waved a hand in dismissal. "That stuff's running just fine. The summaries are in your 'for review' folder, and there are no problems worth talking about. We can go over all that once you've had time to settle back in. What I called about is much more interesting. We've received a report back from our wandering Dr. Rothstein."

Judah Rothstein was one of the junior members of the division, so junior that the ink on his doctoral diploma was barely dry. He had done some interesting work in graduate school, but before he joined Carla's team, he had never been out of the solar system. In fact, other than one vacation trip to Earth, he had never been off Luna. When Fleet wanted an astrophysicist for a scientific team to accompany a military expedition to an unspecified destination, he jumped at the chance to volunteer.

Carla knew where the expedition was going. Well, not actually where, but she knew why Fleet was sending the force. She noted that most of the team were planetary science types, including several anthropologists. Lunar anthropologists typically studied alien cultures rather than humans, but she had a feeling that was about to change. Fleet had advised the volunteers the expedition could involve personal hazard, so the scientists would draw a hazardous duty allowance like the military members of the group.

That was before Carla had had her close encounter with the Otuka, and she had assumed Fleet would keep the scientists safe. Since then, she'd had second thoughts and had spent time worrying about young Dr. Rothstein.

"Since you are still smiling, I presume all is well with him," she noted. "So, what's so interesting about his report?"

"Oh, I think you'd better read it," he insisted. "It's on top of your list." He sat back in his chair with a look of cheerful anticipation.

He obviously expected her to look at the report immediately, so she opened the folder and brought it up on her screen. She scanned through the preliminary remarks, then her eyes widened. Dr. Rothstein had gotten right to the point.

"A Karpov-Teritsky variable? Are you kidding me?"

"Not at all. I've reviewed his observations, and it fits the parameters. It's the first one anyone has seen! Unfortunately, he doesn't have half the equipment he needs to study it."

"Right." Carla sat back in her chair and pondered the problem.

Most stars are variable to some degree. Even Earth's own Sun goes through a cycle of varying solar activity over an 11-year period, though its variance—primarily due to changes in magnetic activity—is less than that of most other stars. Cepheid variables, for example, are giant stars that vary in size as well as luminosity over a much shorter period, from a few days to several months.

Russian astrophysicist Anatoly Karpov and mathematician Gregor Teritsky had postulated the existence of a new type of variable star, a main-sequence star of moderate size and luminosity, which was otherwise unremarkable and whose complete cycle lasted mere seconds. Its variance was not expected to be extreme—in fact, it would be so slight as to be undetectable at astronomical distances, but up close, it would appear to pulsate, like a slowly beating heart. Until now, it had been nothing more than the subject of an interesting theoretical paper, but wherever Fleet had taken Rothstein was home to a genuine, first-ever-observed K-T variable star.

"Hmmmm..." Carla muttered. "If we only knew where this thing is located...I don't suppose Fleet let him tell us that, did they?"

"Oh no...super-top-secret stuff," Stansbury replied. "The scientific team has no idea where they are." He favored her with a conspiratorial grin. "However, they neglected to censor the local star field imagery Judah sent us. I've run it through our mapping systems and identified the origin; it's about 72 light-years out in the direction of Hydra. It's LGS 1437A, a rather unimpressive 10th magnitude star, not even visible from here without a telescope. At that distance we'd never have noticed the K-T fluctuations. I've asked Farside to look at it, but they're doing a deep-galaxy survey right now, so it'll be a month before they get to it."

"Forget that." Carla snorted. "We need to get out there and look at this beauty up close and personal."

She considered her options. Interstellar research expeditions were expensive and required serious cost justification, unless, as in Rothstein's case, Fleet requested a scientific team for what was otherwise a military operation. That wasn't going to happen again anytime soon, nor was it likely Fleet would recall LFS *Edwin Hubble* and send her out again with the equipment the astrophysicists needed to study the star. Besides, the life sciences people and anthropologists would raise hell because the planet was a treasure trove for them as well.

"What about the *Randall* mission? That one is strictly ours, it's already been justified, and it departs in two weeks. Could we…ah…divert it a bit or extend it to include a side trip to LGS 1437A?"

"Side trip?" Stansbury looked skeptical. "You're talking about adding 140 light-years to a round trip that's only eight light-years to begin with."

LRS *Lisa Randall*, the Lunar Free State's newest research ship, had been tasked with a rather short trip for her maiden voyage. She was going to Proxima, the tiny M5 red dwarf component of the three-star Alpha Centauri system, the nearest stars to Sol. The astrophysics division wanted to closely study that stellar class and had justified the cost on the grounds that the trip also offered a chance to study two other stellar classes. Alpha Centauri A was a G2 variable, while Alpha Centauri B was a larger, but less luminous, K1 star.

The good news, Carla discovered as she called up stellar maps on her screen, was that LGS 1437A was in the same general direction as Alpha Centauri…well, within twenty or so degrees of sky as seen from Luna, anyway. It was just fifteen times farther away.

"No problem," she told him. "The biggest cost factor for an expedition is putting it together. The equipment and people we've lined up for the Alpha Centauri study should be fine for a K-T variable, and I'll bet every one of the people involved will jump at the chance, even if it means a few more weeks out there. Fleet won't care—they have to crew and maintain the ship anyway and want to get the maximum use out of her. There's only one thing I need to check...whether they'll have room for me on the team."

Stansbury gave her a sour look. "I can think of several reasons why that's a bad idea," he told her. "I'm sure your dear mother will get upset if we send a research ship into an area Fleet considers restricted. I seem to recall something about hazardous duty being mentioned when they were recruiting for *Hubble*."

Carla shivered, as the comment reminded her of *Summer Solstice* and the real nature of the hazardous duty involved. Still, she pressed on, unable to restrain her enthusiasm for the project.

"That's something we'll have to work out. They already have one research vessel out there, with a whole bunch of warships to protect it. Let's put a plan together, and we'll deal with Fleet issues later."

Besides, she reminded herself, *my mother isn't the only one I have to worry about. I'm pretty sure Bjorn isn't going to be happy about this either.*

* * *

First Platoon, Bravo Company—on the Ground on New Eden

"Up one, five rounds each. Fire for effect," the Marine lieutenant lowered his binoculars as he gave the order.

The first of three 75mm mortars sent a round skyward with a hollow *thump*, followed closely by its fellows. The Marine crews fell into a practiced rhythm, and all fifteen rounds were airborne before the first exploded over the target, a thousand meters down the hillside from the firing position. The advancing Otuka had been startled when the sighting round dropped in just behind them. Now, the fragmentation rounds bursting ten meters over their heads wreaked havoc on their skirmish line. They scattered, looking for cover among the trees and rocky outcroppings.

"Fall back two hundred meters and reset." Lieutenant Joe Holbrook didn't think the donkeys could backtrack the mortar fire, but doctrine said to fire and move, fire and move. He was taking no chances.

"Dr. Warren, you need to keep your people moving," he said. "We can delay the bad guys, but to set up a proper defense, we've got to reach the caves well ahead of them."

"I'll do my best," she replied, "but some of them are pretty worn out." Warren headed up the trail to push her stragglers.

When satellite surveillance had shown the Otuka deployments, the Marines had quickly decided the research station where Warren's people were located was not a defensible position. The Edies had told them about deep caverns in the mountains thirty kilometers to the north, accessible by trails along the forested slopes of a broad drainage. An air recon mission confirmed the location.

Would have been a hell of a lot easier if we could have hauled everyone up there by air, Holbrook thought. Unfortunately, he didn't have the lift capacity to take the local Edies, and the scientists refused to leave them. He'd used the only available Dragonfly to lift equipment and supplies to the caves, along with a couple of the scientists who didn't seem to be in shape for a long hike and some of the natives—the elderly and women with small kids. He was surprised at how willingly the Edies climbed aboard. Air travel must have been a new and frightening thing for them, but they trusted the scientists and Marines.

Now, the vulnerable Dragonfly was grounded at the cave site because Otuka craft were patrolling the area. In turn, the Otuka were being harassed by the battalion's Airwolves. Unfortunately, harassed was the operative word—the Marines did not have enough air superiority fighters to take on the hundreds of Otuka craft that had been deployed. There were not enough Raptors to do more than harass the hordes of donkeys on the ground, and they had to be wary of air attacks from above. They could take on the enemy aircraft—Raptor pilots had proven that in the first encounter—but not nearly as well as the Airwolves could.

Holbrook didn't have to deal with donkey air attacks. The Otuka craft were mostly armed transports, not equipped for ground attack or air superiority. The centaurs were fast learners, and it had only taken a few shoulder-launched heat seekers to convince them to keep their aircraft away from the Marines on the ground. Heat-seeking missiles weren't useful against donkeys on the ground, but the 75mm mortars—whose design hadn't changed much in a hundred years—were proving their worth. Modern electronic leveling and target ranging and aiming systems made them accurate out to five kilometers. *For as long as the ammo lasts,* Holbrook reminded himself. The Dragonflies had hauled additional ordnance up to the caves, but his Marines were limited to what they could carry. They had only sixty rounds remaining and still five kilometers to go.

* * *

Two hundred meters upslope from the mortar position, Mercedes Warren caught up with the stragglers. She found Dr. Vito Pagliani sitting on the ground, puffing and wheezing, looking like he had very few steps left in him. Pagliani, a geologist, had replaced the discredited Dr. Redmond. He had arrived with the last resupply group, but at nearly 150 kilos, he was hardly in shape for field work. *Can't fault his courage,* Warren reflected, *especially compared to the guy he replaced.* She'd seen Pagliani pass up a chance to ride a Dragonfly to their destination when he gave up his seat to a pregnant Edie woman with a toddler in her arms. Unfortunately, Warren was almost certain the Edie woman could have endured the overland hike better than the geologist.

Owen Phillips was standing over the exhausted scientist, shading him from the burning sunlight and offering him a bottle of water. Phillips, with Angel, his ever-present Edie shadow, had been at the front of the group with the point-patrol Marines and the Edie scouts. The young anthropologist was the group's best speaker of the local Edie language and chief interpreter for the Marines. Someone must have told him Pagliani was in trouble, and he'd dropped back to help, but Angel was nowhere to be seen.

"Sent her to get some help," Phillips replied when Warren questioned him. "The Edies are going to rig a litter. I don't think Dr. Pagliani can make it on his own."

As he spoke, four Edie hunters came trotting down the trail. One of them carried a rolled-up animal skin, while another brought two long poles. Warren thought they were going to construct a stretcher, but what they put together looked more like an impromptu sedan chair, with a sling made of the animal skin hanging between the poles. They persuaded Dr. Pagliani to sit in the sling, with his arms over the poles. They lifted the poles to their shoulders and headed up the trail at a surprisingly rapid pace.

Angel had returned with the hunters and spoke to Phillips in the almost musical tones of the Edie language. He nodded and turned to Warren.

"We've got to get back up to the front. The Marines have called a halt, and they don't want to continue until we report all stragglers accounted for."

"You last one, Doc-tor War-ren," Angel added. "You come now."

Warren smiled at Angel's demonstrated ability to speak English but was dismayed that the Edie girl considered her a straggler.

"OK." She nodded. "Let's go."

* * *

Two hours later, Warren had acquired a better appreciation for Dr. Pagliani's efforts. She'd admitted to herself that she was no longer a young girl, and she was taking a much-needed break. They had almost reached their destination. The point Marines were already there, working to prepare defenses in front of the caves. The mortar squad had expended the remaining rounds and was now moving up the slope past the scientists, but a sniper team was setting up behind a rocky outcrop, preparing to give the pursuing Otuka a few more nasty surprises.

Warren didn't like the persistence shown by the aliens. The last time, the Otuka had run away in disorganized panic whenever they encountered the Marines. *Those were hunters,* she reflected, *accustomed to being the predator, not expecting a prey that fought back. This group came prepared for a fight.*

She looked up, saw Lieutenant Holbrook approaching, and got wearily to her feet.

"Yes, Lieutenant, we'll get moving," she assured him. *Only a few hundred meters to go.*

* * *

LFS *Timberwolf*—New Eden Orbit

"Echo Three, can you take Fire Mission Delta?"

"Echo Three, roger that. On the way," Rob O'Hara confirmed. "Helm, get us over there. Tactical, stand by for targeting. Comm, contact the Marines on two four Bravo."

Timberwolf was number three of five destroyers designated as Echo Group, tasked with harassment of the Otuka ships in orbit around New Eden and, when possible, fire support for Marine forces on the ground. Amy Ling had cut them loose to operate independently while the rest of her ships took on the main Otuka force and tried to keep them as far from the planet as possible. The centaurs had tasked about a hundred ships with securing the low orbitals, while the rest of their forces tried to keep Ling from doing to them what she had done to the last bunch of Otuka to visit the system. Most of the action was well away from the planet. The centaur ships in orbit were the only ones of concern to Echo Group, and vice versa. *Our own little piece of a much bigger battle,* O'Hara mused.

Commander Jonathan "Jack" Winfree, commanding LFS *Anaconda*, was the senior officer—the S.O.—of Echo Group. His plan was to keep the centaurs off balance with hit and run attacks just outside their reach. The enemy ships were clustered in two groups, roughly a hundred and eighty degrees apart in orbit around the planet. The Otuka weren't willing to spread their forces out while the LFS destroyers were in the area, nor was Echo Group willing to take them on at ten-to-one odds while they remained clustered. Winfree was hitting the centaurs on the planet, in response to Marine requests for fire support, whenever he could slip between the two enemy groups. Each time, the Otuka responded by coming after Echo Group in force, and Winfree retreated, but only after sending a quick missile salvo in their direction. So far, they'd nailed seven enemy ships and taken no damage in return. They'd also made things unpleasant for a lot of centaurs on the ground. Now, per Winfree's orders, *Timberwolf* was about to dump another load of hurt on their heads.

"Sir, I have a Lieutenant Holbrook, squawking Delta Three Seven on Marine channel two four Bravo."

"Thank you," Rob O'Hara acknowledged, selecting the channel on his console. "Delta Three Seven, this is Echo Three. What's your situation, Lieutenant?"

"Echo Three, my platoon, with fifteen scientists and approximately sixty Edies, has reached a secure area on grid Fox zero two. I have at least company-strength hostiles, now 1200 meters due west of us…make it 277 degrees true. We've kept them back with mortar and sniper fire, but they aren't giving up. I need a heavy strike. Transmitting strike coordinates on the sideband now."

O'Hara looked up and got a nod from Lieutenant Asher, his tactical officer.

"Ash," he directed, "only 1200 meters separation, call it a thousand to be safe. Set your weapon yield accordingly, and nail those coordinates down tight."

"Yes, sir," Asher acknowledged.

The Thunderbolt Kinetic Weapon System, known simply as the "TK" in LFS Navy parlance, was a massive projectile with a high-output, short-duration gravity drive and a simple guidance system that kept it locked on a selected target. The yield of the weapon was adjusted by regulating the output of its drive, which determined its terminal velocity at impact.

"Delta Three Seven," O'Hara said, switching back to the Marine channel. "Strike is inbound. We are using kinetics, so keep your heads down."

He turned back to Asher. "Fire when ready," he directed.

* * *

First Platoon, Bravo Company

"Incoming! Everybody take cover, now!" Holbrook shouted, waving his arms in a gesture the Edies had quickly come to understand. In fact, he decided, as he watched them dive to the ground, they understood it better than the scientists.

"Dr. Phillips! Get your head down!" he ordered.

Phillips obeyed, and Holbrook followed suit. Moments later, a blinding flash lit up the sky to the west, followed immediately by a thunderclap that shook the ground and sent a hurricane blast of hot air, bearing brush and other debris, howling over their heads.

As the sound and fury faded, Holbrook cautiously raised his head. As he worked his way up the rocky outcrop to the sniper position, he peered over the edge and started a sweep with his binoculars. As near as he could tell, the strike had been dead on. A thirty-meter hole in the ground, still glowing cherry red in the center, marked the spot where the kinetic weapon had hit—square in the middle of what had been a line of advancing centaurs. Trees had been swept away, and the ground had been scoured of brush for a hundred meters around the hole. It was possible some of the centaurs had been far enough out to survive, but not in any numbers his Marines couldn't handle. Once the dust settled, he would check the satellite images to find out what else might be headed his way, but it looked like things were going to be quiet for a while.

Next to him, the corporal spotting for the sniper team let out a soft whistle.

"Woohoo! Spiked their asses. Nice shooting, Navy," he said.

"Damned nice shooting," Holbrook agreed. He'd been a bit nervous about a kinetic strike that close to his position, but whoever Echo Three might be, they obviously knew how to handle a TK. He keyed his communicator again.

"Echo Three, this is Delta Three Seven. Strike was dead on, no more targets. Marines say thanks. Delta Three Seven out."

He turned to his troops, the waiting scientists, and the Edies.

"Second squad, you have perimeter watch. Everybody else, break out the rations, and let's have dinner. Smoke if you've got 'em."

* * * * *

Chapter Eight

Earthlight Restaurant—TerraNova City, Luna

Earthlight boasted a domed view of a breathtaking Lunar landscape and a black sky full of stars. At the moment, it was Full Earth—the middle of the two-week Lunar night for the LFS capital city—and the landscape was mostly dark, illuminated only by the soft glow from which the restaurant took its name, but Earth was bright in the sky, dominating the view with its cloud-wrapped blue, green, and brown features.

Unfortunately, Carla was not in the proper frame of mind to appreciate the view or the elegant setting of the restaurant. She was nervous, had been so ever since her mother had invited her—summoned her—to this dinner meeting. She had brought Bjorn along, hoping his presence might moderate any mother-daughter discussions. She decided her instincts were correct when she discovered her mother had reserved one of the private dining rooms along the dome's upper balcony. Her nervousness escalated another notch when she noted the armed Marine sentry at the door of the compartment and the green secured indicator glowing on the door panel.

Earthlight often catered to high-level meetings for LFS officials, fleet officers, and commercial executives. The private dining rooms were equipped with security systems that prevented electronic snooping. Any of the restaurant staff who needed to enter would press a touchpad next to the door and wait several seconds for the door to open. Doing so caused a chime to sound inside the room, letting the diners know someone was about to enter.

The restaurant didn't usually secure the room that way. Such arrangements had to be requested by the person making the reservation, and Carla was pretty sure she knew why her mother had done so. Bjorn, on the other hand, wasn't as knowledgeable about such things as his Luna-born wife and didn't seem to notice anything out of the ordinary. He was used to seeing his mother-in-law surrounded by Marines, so he didn't comment about the guard at the door.

When they entered the room, Lorna greeted them with a smile that was cordial but did not seem to have much humor behind it. Carla had seen that smile before. *Uh oh, it's going to be a prayer meeting,* she decided. *She's going to speak, and I'm going to pray.* In her youth, she'd been amused by Aunt Ronnie Bartley's description of that form of Marine Corps counseling, but after she'd experienced it once or twice, she'd found it far less amusing.

The waiter took their drink and dinner orders, then returned almost immediately to serve the drinks. He exited hastily, and the security light on the door barely turned green when Lorna cut to the chase.

"So, not even three months married, and you're planning to go off on an interstellar expedition without your husband. I'm sure he's thrilled about that."

"We talked about it," Carla replied, watching Bjorn's reaction. "It's a unique opportunity for me, but he has his own responsibilities, starting a new position and all."

She hoped her mother wouldn't notice the beads of sweat she was sure had appeared on her forehead. She had only told Bjorn about the trip yesterday and hadn't discussed it with anyone other than Stansbury. She had, however, filed a request for modification of the *Randall* mission with the LRI Board three days ago. It had probably come to Lorna's attention via LFS Fleet channels.

"It must be a hell of an opportunity to make you drop all your other projects. Aren't you supposed to be terraforming Mars or something?"

"That project's dead," Carla replied, flatly. It was a painful subject, but she was grateful for the diversion. "Hasn't been announced yet, but we've known for almost a month. Damned Confeds managed to block us."

"Really?" Lorna's eyebrows went up. "How did they do that?"

Carla knew her mother was not a fan of the Confederacy of Nations and was instrumental in keeping the LFS from joining that international body. Hopefully, the issue would distract her from discussing Carla's new expedition.

"They just announced they're going to establish five new research stations on Mars," she replied, "right in the middle of the five impactor areas we selected after much research and careful study."

The terraforming project called for bringing in five huge iceball comets from the outer reaches of the solar system and dropping them on Mars, where the impacts would provide huge clouds of water vapor. They would not only supply the planet with much-needed water but also contribute to a greenhouse effect that would eventually provide an environment more suitable for organic life.

"They tried to block us on environmental grounds, saying we had no right to disturb the natural state of Mars," Carla grumbled. "As if there were anything there worth preserving. We've been on Mars for almost forty years. There's no life there, nor any evidence there ever was. Most of the water is long gone, and most of the oxygen is locked up in oxidized rocks or atmospheric carbon dioxide. Even the mineral resources aren't worth the cost to extract and haul to Earth. It's a dead world, but we had a chance to bring it to life. They couldn't get support for sanctions against us, so they decided to occupy the impact sites, knowing we won't deliberately drop an ice mountain on their heads."

"We can blame ourselves for that," Lorna told her. "We were the first people on Mars, but in those days, nobody on Earth liked us very much. Most of them were still grumbling about our claiming the whole Moon as our territory. Ian Stevens was trying to improve relations with Earth, so he held back on claiming Mars as well. We helped the Americans and the Japanese establish research stations there, and when other nations developed gravity-drive ships, we let them set up their own stations without protest. Mars became international territory, like Antarctica.

"But that's history," she continued, "and I'm sorry to hear it has come back to haunt us; however, I'm more concerned about your sudden desire to go charging off in search of this strange and unusual star—a K-T variable, whatever that may be."

"The only known K-T variable," Carla corrected her. "The first one ever discovered. We've been looking for one ever since Karpov and Teritsky postulated their existence. It's the chance of a lifetime, and—"

"How the hell did you find out where that star is located?" Lorna demanded, dropping all pretense of calm, reasoned discussion.

"Dr. Rothstein, our astrophysicist on the *Hubble* team," Carla said, defensively. "He discovered that the star was a K-T, and his report included some basic stellar cartography data. We ran it through our mapping systems to find out where it was located."

"In short," Lorna replied, "one of Amy Ling's intel people screwed the pooch. That data should have been redacted from Rothstein's report, since the location of that star is absolutely top secret."

"Not any more," Carla said. Lorna glared at her, and she decided to shut up. She glanced at Bjorn, who wore a look of clueless confusion.

"Damn it!" Lorna exploded. "You know what's out there! You're not supposed to know, but I'm sure you've figured it out. And you still want to go, even after *Summer Solstice*?"

"Mom," Carla pleaded, "forget I'm your daughter. You wouldn't be this upset if anyone else proposed this."

"Of course, I would! I'd be upset with anyone who, knowing what you know, proposed this project. This isn't about you, it's about sending another shipload of scientists into harm's way, without giving them a hint of the danger. I read your proposal, and it sounds like you're planning an easy trip to a nearby star. Hell, you might as well be taking a cruise ship on another honeymoon to Copper Hills!"

"Am I allowed to know what's going on?" Bjorn inquired in a soft, reasonable tone.

"No!" Carla replied.

"Yes!" Lorna contradicted her. "Bjorn, I've just decided you have a need to know, and I can waive security restrictions. Just understand that this is absolutely secret. You can discuss it with Carla, since she obviously knows what I'm going to tell you; otherwise, you can't discuss it with anyone. Is that clear?"

"Of course. Er…yes, ma'am!" he replied, bringing the hint of a smile to Lorna's face. It vanished quickly, and her tone became deadly serious when she spoke.

"Your wife," she told him, "is planning to take an unarmed research vessel to a star system about seventy light-years from here. I'm sure she's told you that much.

"Unfortunately, she hasn't told you that the system is home to a planet populated by primitive humans—a planet the Otuka visit to hunt those humans. You do remember the Otuka, don't you? The same aliens who attacked *Summer Solstice*, who killed so many passengers and crewmembers, and ate them? You can imagine what they've been doing on that lovely little planet, which we call New Eden.

"Carla knows this, because she was with me on Copper Hills when I found out about it. That's how she knew what to expect when the Otuka hijacked your honeymoon."

Bjorn looked at Carla in horror.

"Mom!" Carla exclaimed. "That's not fair! *Summer Solstice* was out there all alone. You mentioned Amy Ling, and that tells me you've got a full battle group out there, and they've probably already made chopped meat out of the Otuka. Besides, *Hubble* is still out there, and you haven't brought those scientists back home yet."

"Actually," Lorna told her, "I've got two battle groups out there and two assault transports full of Marines. That's because Amy Ling had a rough time with the Otuka the first time around. A couple of her ships got badly chewed up, and she lost some people, including, I might add, a couple of scientists from *Hubble* who got caught down on the planet. That's where your friend Maya got torn up as well.

"As for the scientists, some of them did come home—maybe showing better sense than their colleagues—but most of them who asked to stay are doing it for the sake of the Edies—the aboriginal humans on the planet. That's why I had to double up on Marines out there. We must protect the scientists and try to protect the natives as well.

"I think Amy has the forces to deal with the Otuka if they return, but I don't know that for sure because I don't know when they'll be back or in what strength. The first time, we took them by surprise, but some of them got away, and we won't have that advantage the next time. For all I know, next time could be happening right now, but there's a small matter of a communications lag involving a seventy light-year trip that keeps me from knowing for sure.

"That star will be there for the next few billion years, and now that we've met the Edies, we are not going to let the Otuka have it back. Now, though, the situation is too damned unstable for another scientific expedition. We'll be providing fleet escorts for commercial shipping to Akara territory from now on. I was planning to assign a destroyer to go with *Randall* for the mission to Alpha Centauri, and that's not anywhere near Otuka space."

"Aha!" Carla pounced on the opening. "So, you're willing to concede that a research ship would be safe if it has a warship escort, and you were going to assign a warship to the mission anyway. So, why can't we go to a place where you have warships already in place?"

Lorna sighed. "Bjorn, can you talk some sense into her?"

"I doubt it." Bjorn shook his head. "She seems to have inherited a stubborn streak from someone. Besides, my heart says stop her, don't let her go, but I'm a scientist, too. I understand why she wants to leave."

He turned to Carla. "Honey, I know this is important to you, but this time, I really think you should listen to your mother. Hold off for six months, a year maybe. You can go look at your K-T variable next year. The way your mom is keeping it under wraps, you'll still be the first to study it."

"Next year, we were going to start a family," she protested. "I can't go off into deep space if I'm pregnant."

"We can put that off for a bit. We're both still young. We'll have time for a dozen kids, if you like, after you go study your star."

Carla shook her head. She turned to her mother with a look of disappointed resignation.

"So, you're going to kill the mission," she said, bitterly. "Mars wasn't enough bad news for me. You're going to add this to it."

"No," Lorna told her, "I'm not. I would if I could, but the decision is not mine to make.

"I know," she continued, seeing Carla's incredulous look. "You think I'm the invincible Iron Maiden, mistress of the Lunar Fleet, who has but to snap her fingers and people leap to obey. Not this time. Yes, I command the Fleet, and *Randall* is a Fleet ship, just like *Einstein*, *Hawking*, *Da Vinci*, and *Hubble*. But Fleet exists to serve the needs of the Lunar Free State, and in case you've forgotten, the Constitution says research and scientific exploration are part of our national mission. Fleet is required to crew, maintain, and operate the research ships, but we are also required to 'make them available for missions to serve the scientific community as directed by the Lunar Research Institute.' In short, you and the other eggheads on the LRI Board of Directors tell me what you want to do with them, and I am required to make it happen in an orderly and proficient manner.

"However," she added, "before you get too damned smug about it, let me explain the difficult position in which you have placed me. I cannot, in good conscience, allow the mission to go forward without advising the LRI Board of the danger involved, but to do that, I'll need to discuss it with a higher authority, namely the CEO.

"What is happening at New Eden involves issues of national security and interstellar diplomacy. More than three decades have passed since the Akara gave us a hint that there were other humans in the galaxy, but New Eden is the first and only place we've found them. How we knew where to look and what we chose to do with that knowledge are matters that cannot be made public, lest they damage our relations with the Akara, the only alien race with which we've established relations.

"In short, I've got to ask Mick O'Hara how much, if anything, I can tell the LRI Board. They're cruising along in blissful ignorance because you didn't tell them anything. I know—" she held up a hand to stop Carla's protest, "—you couldn't tell them because you were sworn to secrecy, but you planned the mission and submitted it to them anyway, and that's why I'm damned upset with you right now."

The security chime sounded, and Lorna lapsed into silence. A moment later, the door opened, and the waiter entered with the food they had ordered. Carla looked at Bjorn and wondered whether he would enjoy the elegant platter that had just been placed before him. More importantly, she wondered what sort of discussion she was going to have with him when they got home. *At least,* she thought with a feeling of relief, *it's all on the table now. No more guilty secrets for me.*

* * *

LFS Fleet Transient Quarters—TerraNova City, Luna

Maya Vasquez was tired. She'd walked all the way across TerraNova Park on her way back to her quarters, with help from the two forearm crutches that were her constant companions these days, but the weariness she was feeling wasn't physical. She'd spent long hours in the simulator, trying to acquire the skills needed to fly a Raptor by mental command, but so far, the results were nowhere near what the project engineers were hoping for.

She couldn't seem to get a feel for the aircraft. She had to spend too much time thinking about what the flight instruments were telling her and what she needed the ship to do in response. Under ideal conditions, she could get the craft into the air, fly a simple course with it, and land safely, but could she fly combat? No way. She'd be toast in the first few seconds of the engagement, and she knew it. So did the engineers, and she wondered how long it would take before somebody decided to pull the plug on the project.

She entered her little apartment and went straight to the refrigerator and retrieved a cold beer. She made her way to the sofa in the living room, put the crutches aside, and eased herself down on to it. She opened the beer and contemplated her plans, or lack thereof, for the evening. Candy Parks was on duty tonight at the hospital, and Maya didn't feel like making the trek to Corporal J's Place alone. While she would no doubt find camaraderie there, without Candy to keep her straight, she would likely drink too much and stay too late. Tomorrow was a duty day, and she needed to be fresh for the simulator again. The project might not succeed, but no one was ever going to say she hadn't given it her best.

I'll stay home, have a couple of beers, and maybe watch a video, she decided. She looked around the apartment and reflected, not for the first time, that it was an upscale billet for a single Marine non-com. Under normal circumstances, she would have been quartered at the Marine HQ and Training Center, ten kilometers away, in the Bachelor NCO

Quarters. She would have had a private room with a single bunk, a table and chair, and an adjoining bathroom barely large enough for a shower, commode, and sink.

There would have been a tiny cooler for drinks and a microwave just large enough for snacks, but she would have been expected to eat in the common mess hall. The room would have had a locker large enough for her clothes and a few personal possessions. Had she been of lowly enlisted rank, rather than an NCO, she would have shared a room with one or two other Marines and been required to use the community shower and toilet facilities.

But the engineering types had wanted her close to Engineering R&D, so they had cut orders quartering her in the TerraNova Transient Quarters—a free hotel for LFS personnel who were only on Luna temporarily while on leave or changing assignments from one duty station to another. The TQ was used by all ranks, and while high-ranking officers might think them somewhat Spartan, the quarters were a step up for enlisted and NCOs. Her suite had a fully equipped kitchenette with a countertop bar. The living room featured a sofa and a writing desk, neither of which would have fit into a room at the BNCOQ. It also had a desk chair, an armchair, and a coffee table. A large entertainment screen on the wall provided access to TerraNova's library of video selections, music, and books, as well as the usual news, information, and entertainment channels. The bedroom had a small chest of drawers and a king-sized bed, the first Vasquez had ever slept in, while the bathroom had a vanity sink in addition to the commode and a tub/shower combination. Since the suites were intended to be occupied for extended periods, they also had a walk-in closet that provided more than adequate storage space.

As for the kitchen, Vasquez hadn't had to cook for herself since she joined the Marines, but the Transient Commissary two levels below her apartment had a variety of simple meal packages that required little preparation. If she didn't feel like cooking, she could go to one of the many small restaurants that ringed TerraNova Park. Since she was not living on base, she was entitled to draw additional pay to cover her food expenses.

Yeah, this assignment has its benefits, she reflected. *I'm gonna miss this place if they cancel the project and send me back to…*She paused on that thought, realizing she had no idea where they would send her if the project failed. She was still contemplating her uncertain future when a soft chime from the interface pad on her belt advised her of an incoming call. She was comfortable on the sofa, with the beer in her hand, and felt too lazy to retrieve the pad to see who was calling. It was probably Candy, on break, calling to chat.

"Accept, on the wall screen," she ordered, then blinked as the big entertainment screen illuminated and displayed a surprising image. The screen was designed to work with a local device such as the pad, and the camera indicator told her the caller could see her, but the face that appeared on the screen wasn't a camera image. It was an animation, an artistic rendering of a beautiful woman with flowing blond hair, wearing leather battle armor that did little to conceal her curvaceous, but well-muscled, figure. Her right hand rested on the gold-wrapped hilt of a sword at her belt. It was an image that any Navy or Marine Corps veteran would instantly recognize as The Babe on the Horse.

"Good evening, Sergeant," the animation said. "I hope I'm not disturbing your off-duty hours."

"Of course not, Val," Vasquez replied, quickly recovering her composure. "I've got no plans for tonight. I'm just a little surprised to actually see you like this."

She had been working with Val a lot during the project, but this was the first time she'd ever had a face-to-face call from the battle-cruiser's AI, and it had never occurred to her that Val might use the Babe as her avatar. The avatar smiled at her.

"I wanted to have a personal conversation with you," Val advised, "and I thought it might be best if you actually saw me as a person."

"No problem." Vasquez grinned. "I'd ask you to have a beer with me, but I don't know how to make that work."

"Why, thank you, Sergeant." Val smiled again. "I'd be happy to accept your offer." She lifted her hand and a bottle of beer—the same brand Vasquez was drinking—appeared as if by magic. She unhooked the sword from her belt and put it aside, then sat down on a sofa which, like the bottle of beer, had magically appeared behind her.

"Hah!" Vasquez couldn't help but laugh. "I wish I could do that! By the way, since we're off duty and having a beer together, please call me Maya."

"Thank you, Maya," Val replied, softly, with feeling. "It is rare anyone offers me the privilege of using their first name."

It was an epiphany for Vasquez, as she suddenly realized Val—arguably one of the most intelligent sentient beings in the galaxy, the soul of one of the most powerful warships in the LFS Fleet—might wish for human companionship, for a bit of conversation on a first-name basis with an ordinary Marine non-com. *Your circle of high-class friends has grown again, girl,* she thought. *First, the CEO's daughter-in-law, and now, the Fleet flagship's AI.*

"No problem, Val," she replied with a grin. "So, what's this personal conversation about?"

"I noticed that you seemed disappointed with the results of today's simulator sessions. I sense you are discouraged, and I fear you may have doubts about the project's success."

"Well, yeah," Vasquez agreed. "I mean, seriously, would you send me into combat in a Raptor with the skills I've developed so far?"

"No, I most certainly would not," Val told her candidly. "If the enemy had any capability at all, you would be shot out of the sky. However, I don't believe that is any fault of yours. You have done your best with the tools you've been given, and that is what I want to talk to you about."

"Whoa! Wait a minute!" Maya exclaimed. "You're saying it's not my clumsy, dumbass fault we're not getting anywhere? It's the tools I've been given. In other words, the interface between me and the Raptor. Either way, the project is a failure. Are you telling me it's time to flip the switch, turn out the lights, and give it up?"

A few minutes ago, she had been thinking the same thing, but now that the moment was here, she found herself wanting to fight the decision. Val shook her head.

"No, Maya, that's not what I'm saying. This is something I decided to discuss with you because I have a disagreement with the engineers and with Doctor Madison."

"Really? Then it must be something that involves me, since Doc doesn't have anything to do with the engineering side, right?"

"That's true," Val agreed. "In simple terms, I believe the project is failing because the system is not giving you enough direct feedback. There are too many things you are required to take in with your eyes, your ears—too many tasks you must accomplish with your hands based on audio or visual input. I think they need to feed more information to you directly through the interface and allow you to perform more actions that way, instead of using your hands.

"The engineers are reluctant to accept that, since it would mean a major redesign, many more links to the Raptor's systems, and a more capable processor to handle it. The interface itself, the part you have in your head, would not need to be changed, since they over-engineered it to begin with. It has much more bandwidth than the present system will ever be able to use."

"So, what does Doc have to say?"

"He is concerned you cannot handle the additional information flow, and that is where we disagree. He does not anticipate any physical or mental harm will come of it, but he thinks all the work will be for nothing. Frankly, he is concerned about you. He does not want you to get your hopes up, only to be disappointed again."

"Awww, that's sweet of him," Maya said, sincerely. "So far, though, nobody has asked for my opinion. Why don't we get it out in the open and talk about it?"

"I plan to do that at the project meeting first thing tomorrow morning. I am also planning a demonstration, but you'll need to be hooked into the simulator for it. I haven't mentioned it to the others since the demonstration is mainly intended to convince you that I'm right. If you agree, you can help me convince the others."

* * *

Fleet HQ—Weapons Development Section—TerraNova City, Luna

The project group was meeting in a conference room, but Val was present only by audio link. Vasquez suspected she reserved her avatar for special occasions.

"We've been over this already, Val," Jensen said. "She can't handle the input she's getting now, and you want to give her more? It's information overload, pure and simple."

"No, Commander," the AI insisted, "it isn't. The problem is that the information she's getting now is not integrated. Some things are coming to her through the interface, others visually, and some audibly. You've set it up so she has to use her hands for some tasks, speak commands for others, and issue mental signals for still others. It's not that there is too much input, it's that the entire input/output system is confusing and cumbersome. I would like permission to demonstrate the system I have in mind and then we will have a basis for further discussion."

"How the hell can you do that?" Jensen wanted to know. "Unless we re-engineer the entire simulator, it can't provide any more I/O capability than we've been using."

"I intend to bypass the simulator and connect Sergeant Vasquez to an interface I have set up for the purpose."

"How are we going to monitor that?" Jensen looked puzzled. Doctor Madison frowned suddenly and turned to look at Maya.

"You're not," Val replied. "This demonstration is for Sergeant Vasquez to evaluate. I believe her description of the experience will convince you I am right."

"Now, wait a minute…"

"Sir!" Maya was not in the habit of interrupting officers, but she was getting tired of people talking about her as if she were not in the room. "Don't you think we ought to give this a try? We don't seem to be getting anywhere, and you brought Val into this for a reason. Maybe we should try it her way. I'm willing to do it, so what's the issue?"

"For one thing," Madison spoke up for the first time, "I'm concerned about your safety, Sergeant. I have no idea what Val plans to do, but I'm responsible for your well-being."

"Doctor," Val responded. "In the course of this project, I have come to think of Sergeant Vasquez as a friend, not simply a test subject. I assure you I will never do anything to harm her. I am well aware of human frailty and the limitations of human physiology. Among other things, I am responsible for the safety of more than six hundred human lives every time I go into combat. Please trust me on this."

"Let's do it!" Maya asserted. She pushed herself up from her chair and reached for her crutches. Both Jensen and Madison looked as though they wanted to say something more, but in the end, they got up and followed her down the hall toward the simulator.

Five minutes later, she was strapped into the familiar seat, plugged into the system, and testing her communications links. Everything seemed to be in order.

"If you key the link, the project team will hear you," Val told her. "But you and I will hear each other whether you key the link or not. If you don't press the key, our conversation will be private."

"Fine with me." Vasquez was puzzled, and it must have come through in her voice.

"You'll understand in a moment. Do you trust me, Maya?" Val asked.

Vasquez felt a little thrill as the AI used her first name, but she got the point. This was serious, and Val was asking for her personal confidence.

"Of course," she replied. "That's what friends are for."

"Thank you. I'm linking you in now."

Maya's eyes widened, but she saw nothing. Without realizing it, she drew a sharp breath.

She was no longer in the simulator. For that matter, she was no longer herself. She could feel her body, but she no longer had arms and legs. She was a six-hundred-meter battle-armored cylinder of steel, drifting majestically in space at the Fleet Anchorage. She could see through her constantly scanning search radars the lethal shapes of a dozen other warships at their moorings nearby. Small craft moved around her, and she saw those as well.

She felt power coursing through her, driven by three fusion reactors deep inside her, and she instantly knew the status of those reactors. She sensed the presence of the graser batteries along her flanks, the missile tubes and their loading racks, the chase armament and the turret grasers on the top and bottom of her hull, and she knew, without thinking about it, all of those weapons were powered down, all safety interlocks in place. She felt the doors of her number four boat bay slide open, ready to receive an incoming cargo shuttle on final approach, and she noted with approval that it was on course, and its rate of closure was correct.

She sensed people—more than six hundred—inside her, going about their business, attending to her needs as well as their own. A crew was working on one of her gravity drive nodes—number five in the starboard impeller group—while in the forward mess, crewmembers were cleaning up after breakfast and getting ready to prepare lunch.

She felt all of that and more. So many little details came naturally to her attention with every passing moment. Air coursed through her recyclers and was scrubbed of carbon dioxide and other contaminants. Dehumidifiers removed excess water and sent it to her recycling tanks. Temperature, pressure, and internal gravity were all perfectly maintained.

"Welcome to my world," Val told her, softly. "You are the only human who has ever been here."

With a sob, Vasquez released the breath she had been holding. She began to weep, uncontrollably. A moment later, the world about her returned to normal, and she found herself back in the simulator.

"Are you all right, Maya?" Val's voice was heavy with concern. "Perhaps it was too much, after all."

"No!" Vasquez blinked through her tears and saw the project technicians working to open the simulator's canopy, with Doc Madison urging them to be quick about it. "I mean yes! I'm all right. No, it wasn't too much. I just…I…thank you, Val. Just thank you for sharing it…that's all I can say right now."

"Can we talk later?" Val inquired. "Perhaps in your quarters, tonight?"

"Yeah, I'd like that. We have a lot to talk about."

She turned to the anxious crew, who had opened the canopy and were undoing her straps.

"Relax, everybody. I'm OK. I'm fine. Just for the record, Val's right, but I don't think I can talk about it right now. Can we call this off for today and meet tomorrow? I need a break. In fact, I need a drink. No, not that kind of drink." She waved off the bottle of water a technician offered her.

* * *

They weren't willing to let her off that easily. They gave her time to calm down, and amazingly, somebody managed to find her a bottle of beer, which Doc Madison agreed was the proper prescription medication for the moment. But before she got too far into the bottle, they insisted she tell them what had happened. She did so in a calm, deliberate narrative that lasted almost half an hour.

"You experienced all that in just that short period of time?" Jensen asked.

"Yes, I did, and more. This is what I remember off the top of my head. By the way, how long was I up there?"

"About fifteen seconds," Madison told her, shaking his head.

"Fine!" she said. "You don't believe me? Check *Valkyrie*'s maintenance records. The techs were replacing the charge couplers on starboard Graser Six. And just for the record, I don't even know what a charge coupler is or how it works. I just knew that's what they were doing."

"More importantly," Val joined the conversation, "I am certain Sergeant Vasquez could learn to control those systems she experienced. If the interface is properly constructed, she will be able to do everything by mental control, just as I do now with *Valkyrie*."

"I've developed a design for a control interface that will tie into the simulator," the AI continued, "and reviewed it with Louis, the shipyard's AI. He says his shops should be able to produce the components within four days, allowing for the current fabrication schedule. I am downloading the specifications to the project files, since the Weapons Development project leader—that would be you, Commander Jensen—must approve them before fabrication can start. After that, it will take your technicians another twelve hours, plus or minus ten percent, to install the system."

"OK." Jensen managed a wry grin. "I'm convinced it can be done, but we have a lot of work to do. And I just hope that, when we get it all done, we don't end up with a Raptor that costs as much as a battlecruiser."

* * *

Lunar Research Institute—East TerraNova, Luna

Carla was feeling extremely pleased with herself. Two days after the dinner with her mother, the LRI Board met at Lorna's request and heard what Fleet had to say, or was allowed to say, about the *Randall* mission. Lorna told them, in general terms, what was happening at New Eden, including the fact that the adversaries involved were the same aliens responsible for the attack on *Summer Solstice*.

She made a strong case against sending another research ship into the area, emphasizing the danger involved, but the Board was skeptical. If there was that much danger, they asked, why hadn't *Hubble* been recalled? Lorna was forced to admit that Fleet was confident in its ability to protect the scientific vessels, and had, in fact, protected *Hubble* during the first Otuka incursion. There had been two scientific fatalities, she told them, but those had occurred on the planet. The research ship had not come under attack.

In the end, Carla's argument about the importance of the K-T discovery carried the day. They voted to allow the mission to proceed, though they did agree to Lorna's request that additional fleet units be assigned to escort *Randall* for the duration of the mission.

Carla was nailing down the little details. By assigning herself to the team and becoming the ranking member thereof, she had taken on the responsibilities of leading the mission. Some of the other scientists might have resented her sudden takeover, but most of them knew she was not a glory-seeker. She wanted to be there but would willingly give them all the credit they deserved for their work on the discovery. *For that matter,* she thought, *the lion's share of the credit should go to young Dr. Rothstein, and I need to make sure he gets it.* She looked up from her musings and saw Bjorn standing in the office doorway.

"Got time for lunch?" he inquired.

She glanced at the time display on her screen.

"Wow! That time already. Sure, let's grab a bite. Just the cafeteria, though, no time to go out."

"OK," he agreed. "I'm on a tight schedule myself."

"I'm surprised Harrington unlocked the leg irons and let you out," she said with a grin.

"He gave me a message for you, but that can wait until we have some food in front of us. I'm starved."

Carla smiled. Although he'd been upset after the dinner with Lorna, Bjorn had accepted the idea that she was going on a mission for several months. He was regaining his old, stolid take-it-as-it-comes attitude. He also seemed pleased with his new life at the LRI, and he obviously got along well with his boss.

They took the lift four levels down to the LRI food court where several small cafeteria-style restaurants offered a variety of tasty fare. Bjorn went for his usual Italian, while Carla selected her favorite

Chinese dishes. They met at the checkout station and found a table for two in a corner of the dining area.

"So, what is the message from the illustrious Dr. Harrington?" she inquired, as she dug into her spicy chicken dish.

"It seems he has a staffing problem," Bjorn replied. "Your division requested a particle physicist to accompany the mission to Proxima, did you not?"

"Right," Carla acknowledged. "He gave us Elena Korsakova. I'm juggling personnel space on *Randall* now, and I was going to ask her if she would mind sharing a cabin with me."

"Sorry," Bjorn told her. "She's cancelling out of the mission. That's the message Harrington wanted me to give you."

"Why? Last I heard she was good to go."

Bjorn shook his head. "She's pregnant."

"Since when?" Carla looked surprised.

"Several months ago, apparently. She was OK with the Proxima mission, since it was only supposed to take about three weeks, but now, you've added another twelve weeks or so to the mission profile. I guess that's too far into her term, and she doesn't want to do it."

"I can't blame her." Carla sighed. "So, Harrington didn't want to deliver the bad news himself, so he sent you to tell me he can't give me a replacement."

"Not exactly. I guess it's still bad news, but he said the only person he can spare right now is the most junior member of his team. The good news is you can still share a cabin."

"Huh? What's that supposed to mean?"

Bjorn stared at her for a moment.

"Honestly, love, for a Nobel Prize winner, you certainly can be dense at times."

Suddenly, Carla got it.

"Really?" she demanded. "You're not joking? You're on the team?"

"I'm on the team," he replied, with a huge grin.

"Really?" She suddenly looked skeptical. "Are you sure Harrington's not doing this just so I'll owe him a huge favor?"

"Oh, I'm sure he arranged for Korsakova's pregnancy with that very thought in mind," Bjorn chided her.

"Well, welcome aboard, love." She was now grinning as well. "And yes, I'll take you up on that offer to share a cabin."

* * *

LFS Fleet HQ—TerraNova City, Luna

"Come in, Captain. Please, sit down."

He's still calling me Captain, Jennifer Tanaka thought, as she dropped her salute and took the offered chair in front of the desk. *Either they've rejected my request, and I'm going back to* Coyote*, or he's extending the courtesy until they officially boot me out of my command chair.*

Commodore Andreas Petrakis, commanding the LFS Navy's Personnel Resources Division, leaned back in his chair and studied her for a moment.

"You present us with a dilemma, Ms. Tanaka," he said. "Fleet has very few hyper-capable ships that offer a command slot for a Senior Lieutenant, and you currently hold one of those slots. Not only that, you managed to distinguish yourself and validate your command credentials in actual combat with the *Summer Solstice* incident.

"Under normal circumstances, your proper career path would involve waiting for promotion to lieutenant commander, which might well be accelerated by your actions in the aforementioned incident, and then looking for a larger command such as a destroyer or an executive officer slot on a capital ship, a heavy cruiser, or even a battlecruiser. Yet here you are, presenting us with a request that says you are willing to give up your command and take a lesser assignment, as long as it's with Fleet and not OSG. On the surface, it looks as though you have some beef with OSG that we don't know about."

"Sir," she responded, "it has nothing to do with OSG. The Guard is a fine service that has treated me well, and I appreciate the command opportunity I was given. I don't want to leave OSG, but I have a personal reason for wanting to move to Fleet. I'm enough of a realist to recognize that I'm not going to get a command, but I need to do this anyway."

"Hmmm…yes, a personal reason. Unfortunately, it's a personal reason we can't officially recognize or discuss until Fleet takes the lid off a certain classified operation. I knew nothing about it until I started asking about the personal circumstances you mentioned in your request.

"People kept bumping me upstairs until I found myself knocking on Admiral Greenwood's door. The admiral was good enough to brief me on the situation, in consideration of your excellent service record and out of sympathy for the personal loss you've suffered. In that regard, you have my sympathy as well, but the matter is still top secret.

"She did, however, offer me a solution that also satisfies another game of musical command chairs I'm trying to resolve. I have a full commander, a former destroyer skipper, waiting to take over the newly-built light cruiser *Hydra.* He's been in temporary command of another newly-built ship, the scientific research vessel *Lisa Randall,* and he has taken her through acceptance trials and fleet readiness workup. Unfortunately, he's too senior to retain command of her, and we need him for *Hydra.* I need to find someone qualified to command *Randall*, which is scheduled to depart on a deep-space research mission in just ten days.

"The admiral's solution is a temporary bump to lieutenant commander for you—which I can't do, but she can—and to put you in command of *Randall.* The promotion, of course, will be subject to confirmation by the Promotions Board for the next cycle, but assuming you don't totally screw up the *Randall* assignment, it should pretty much be a rubber stamp."

"Sir, I…"

"Before you say anything," he interrupted her protest, "yes, I know you wanted a posting to a warship. The admiral took that under advisement but said there are aspects to *Randall*'s upcoming mission that may change your mind. She specifically wants you for that command slot for reasons she would not discuss with me. You are to report to her aboard *Valkyrie* at your earliest convenience—as soon as you can get there would be appropriate—so you should contact the flagship's AI for a specific appointment.

"I hope she convinces you to take the slot," he told her. "Otherwise, I've got to scramble to find someone else for it, then circle back to the question of what to do with you. At this point, it's out of my hands, so unless you've got some other issue to talk about, I think we're about done here."

"Yes, sir, I think we are. Thank you, sir." Tanaka got to her feet, saluted, and left the office.

* * *

First Platoon, Bravo Company—on the Ground on New Eden

"You look troubled, Doctor Phillips," Lieutenant Holbrook observed. "If you're worried about the centaurs, I can assure you we're safe here, as safe as any place on the planet. We've got a good defensive position, and every time the donkeys get close, the Navy shows up and turns them into crispy critters."

"Does that mean we're winning?" Phillips asked.

"Well, winning is kind of a slippery concept," the Marine admitted, as he joined Phillips and Warren around the campfire just inside the mouth of the cave.

"HQ tells me the fleet still has issues out there, mostly because the Otuka won't engage directly. They've split up into hundreds of little raider groups, and they keep trying to cut out individual fleet units to attack in isolation. Word is, they're not having much success, but they're keeping Admiral Ling busy. HQ says she's sending a sizeable force back here to clear the orbitals, but in the meantime, we are directed to hunker down and hold fast. That, however, is something I'm confident we can do for as long as necessary. If I had six months to plan a defense, I couldn't have picked a better spot than this one."

"That's reassuring," Mercedes Warren said, "but you still look troubled, Owen. Is something bothering you?"

"It's nothing…well, nothing to do with the Otuka, anyway. It's personal."

"Want to talk about it?" Warren persisted.

Phillips sighed heavily but said nothing for a moment. Then he shrugged, looked off into the distance, and began what sounded remarkably like a lecture delivered to first-year university students.

"You've probably noticed," he told them, "the Edie society is, for the most part, patriarchal. Men are the leaders, the hunters, the warriors. The chief and elders are invariably men. Women are gatherers, cooks, artisans, and child-bearing servants of the men. The only woman with any stature in the tribe is the medicine woman, whom everyone respects, but she is still subject to the will of the chief and the elders. Men are masters, women are servants...in every way except one.

"It seems the Edies have one custom that, in their opinion, marks them as a civilized society. Long ago, they determined the most common source of human conflict involved men fighting—sometimes violently and even to the death—for possession of a woman.

Phillips looked up with a hollow chuckle. "Doesn't sound much different from any other human society when you think about it. But the Edies have come up with a rather unique solution.

"Men don't get a choice, women do, and, once past puberty, they can make that choice whenever they want—or never, if that's what they prefer. Once a woman comes of age—begins her menstrual cycle—she puts one of those braided bands, made from dyed strands of her own hair, around her left arm. As long as she is wearing it, no man is allowed to touch her or even speak harshly to her, under penalty of severe punishment from the tribe. She still must do her share of work for the tribe and has to obey the orders of the chief and elders, but she answers to the medicine woman for her day-to-day work and is not allowed to fool around with men. If she engages in any sexual activity and gets caught, a trial will be held. From what I can determine, the trial is fair and unbiased. If they decide the man has raped her, he may be subjected to severe corporal punishment, banishment from the tribe, or even death. If they decide she seduced him, she will most likely be given a choice: select him as her mate or be banished from the tribe. If he refuses to take her—which he is allowed to do under those circumstances—she will be banished.

"It's a curious set of customs, but it seems to work for them, and it does have social merit. Rape and other forms of sexual abuse are almost unheard of, women are treated well even after they choose to mate, and because of the freedom of choice they are given, women tend not to start having babies at the onset of fertility. Most women choose a mate in their late teens or early twenties, but nothing forces them to do so. Some never do.

"As far as I have been able to determine, this isn't just a local custom. It's pretty much universal, or at least true for most tribes on the planet. When a woman decides to choose a mate, she informs the elders of her choice and presents her braided band to the man she has chosen. It doesn't matter if he already has a wife—polygamy is common here—but there is a seniority system that determines the pecking order among multiple wives. In theory, the man can refuse her, but to do so results in severe social stigma, especially if he doesn't already have one or more wives. The way the Edies see it, it's his duty to take her in, provide for her, protect her, and make babies with her to ensure the continuation of the tribe. And once he accepts her, she becomes his property, his servant, just another woman in a society dominated by men. The only thing he cannot do is sell her or give her to another man. She belongs to him, and he must accept responsibility for her for life.

"And that," he said with another sigh, "brings me to my problem, the thing that's bothering me, as you said, Mercedes."

He held out his hand and showed them the circlet, intricately braided and dyed in forest green.

"Oh, dear," Warren exclaimed. "Is that—"

"Angel's—or at least it was until an hour ago," he told them. "She's already told the elders, so as far as the tribe is concerned, it's a done deal."

*****

Chapter Nine

LRS *Lisa Randall*—Lunar Fleet Anchorage

"Seriously, Mom? A heavy cruiser?"

Carla glared at the ominous shape of LFS *Aztec*, hanging in space less than a kilometer from *Lisa Randall.* The cruiser was more than three times the length of the research ship, and the fierce, tattooed warrior of the warship's hull artwork glared back at her.

Jennifer Tanaka suppressed a smile. She had come to *Randall*'s midship crew lounge to advise Carla that their escorts had arrived, and they were about to get under way. Carla had been involved in a discussion with two other scientists and hadn't noticed the warship until Tanaka directed her attention to the large observation port.

"Actually," Tanaka told her, "there are two destroyers off our starboard beam as well."

Carla lapsed into dark mutterings, and Tanaka became more serious.

"Doctor, I think you and I need to have a talk. We share joint command responsibilities for this mission, and that's a new situation for me. I suspect it's new for you as well, and we should sit down and work out some ground rules."

"Yes, we should do that. Pick a time and place." Carla was a bit surprised, but she realized Tanaka had a point. She'd overseen many projects, but none of them had been deep space ventures. She might have overall responsibility for the scientific side, but fleet regulations were clear: Tanaka commanded the ship, and the Navy crew reported to her and no one else.

"We'll be departing within the half-hour. Once we're clear of Lunar traffic control, I'll set the cruising watch, and we can meet in my cabin, say around 1400 hours if that's convenient for you."

"Of course," Carla agreed.

"Also," Tanaka told her, "I think you and I should host a formal dinner tonight in the wardroom—my officers and the senior members of your team. We can start with refreshments at 1800 and have dinner at 1830, if that works for you and your people."

"Good idea," Carla responded with a smile. "I will probably bring five of my people, maybe six, if you don't mind. I'll pass the word to them."

"That's fine," Tanaka agreed. "I've got four officers and one academy cadet on my side. We'll plan accordingly. I'll see you at 1400."

* * *

Carla knew very little about Jennifer Tanaka, but her first impression was one of a hard-core military type, a by-the-book disciplinarian who expected her suggestions to be taken as orders. She thought Tanaka would have been happier commanding a destroyer or cruiser rather than a research ship, even the newest and finest research ship in the fleet.

She also suspected the young captain had been handpicked by her mother for this mission, but that wasn't Tanaka's fault, and Carla was determined to make the best of it. Thus, she knocked on the door of the captain's cabin at exactly 1400 hours and was promptly invited to enter.

The cabin was small, compared to the commanding officer's quarters of a capital warship, but looked quite comfortable. Fresh-brewed coffee was available, and Carla helped herself at Tanaka's invitation. There was a small worktable with two chairs, and the two women sat down facing each other.

"Doctor," Tanaka opened the conversation, "I didn't want to say anything in front of anyone else, but I'm a bit surprised by your reaction to our escorts. For my part, I'm happy to have them. We are going into hostile territory, you know."

"The Otuka!" Carla snorted. "I've met them, and I'm not impressed. Thugs and murderers, true, but it's not like we're a slow-moving, unarmed luxury liner, like *Summer Solstice*. I'm told *Randall* is fast, highly maneuverable, and not exactly helpless when it comes to defending herself."

"That's true," Tanaka admitted. "I believe we have some Vipers tucked away among the science probes in the missile magazines. Our grasers are more powerful than the ones on my last command, though we only have two of them mounted in a single turret. I'm also aware of your actions aboard *Summer Solstice*, and I respect you for your courage and willingness to confront the enemy, but I've met the Otuka as well—in space combat—and I have a somewhat different view."

"You've been in combat with them?" Carla asked, her eyes widening.

"You didn't know?" Tanaka was also surprised. "I commanded LFS *Coyote*, one of the three OSG ships that responded to the distress call from *Summer Solstice*. We engaged six of the Otuka ships, destroyed five, and drove the rest away."

"I knew there'd been a battle, but I didn't realize it was you. I'm sorry, Captain. I guess I owe you a vote of thanks. I may have been willing to confront the enemy, but I don't think we'd have made it if you people hadn't come to the rescue."

"I'm glad we did," Tanaka told her, "but I remember thinking it could have gotten ugly if all twelve of them had come at us in a co-ordinated attack.

"When she gave me command of this ship, the Admiral told me you know what's going on out there, at least in general terms. It's an all-up military confrontation with the Otuka. We're defending a planet that is home to primitive tribes of aboriginal humans. That planet just happens to be orbiting the star you want to study. No," she held up her hand to stop Carla's protest, "I'm not questioning the importance of the scientific mission. I just think you should know what we're sailing into.

"A couple of days ago, an E-boat arrived with the latest reports from Admiral Ling, who is in command of the Fleet forces out there. The Otuka hit them again, this time with over two thousand war-ships. Now, I'm inclined to agree that ship-for-ship, they aren't very impressive, but with that kind of numerical advantage, they make a formidable enemy. According to the report, Admiral Ling expected she would be able to handle them, but she also expected to take sig-nificant losses. She sent *Hubble* and her non-combatant auxiliaries off to the hyper limit and ordered them to stay clear of the system.

"She put her Marines and their gear down on the planet to pro-tect the scientists, who refused to abandon the aborigines, but she had to yield the planetary orbitals to effectively battle a force that size. That means the Marines and scientists are on their own down there, and you can imagine what they're facing. Unfortunately, we do not know the outcome because the E-boat was dispatched just as the engagement was starting.

"You may think our escorts are a serious force, but they're only here to protect us from a random encounter with a small number of Otuka ships. We've been allowed to depart on this mission, but we have a strict set of non-discretionary orders from Fleet. When we arrive in the system, we're ordered to hold outside the hyper limit until we contact Admiral Ling's group. At her discretion, we may be ordered to turn around and come home, with or without our escorts, depending on how badly they're needed at New Eden.

"That, of course, assumes we get out of the Sol System," she continued. "LFS *Cheetah*'s already headed back to New Eden, but Admiral Ling has more than one E-boat. Fleet is expecting a follow-up messenger soon. If it arrives before we reach the hyper limit, we may be ordered to turn around, or—if the situation is bad enough—to get the hell out of the way because an entire battle fleet is about to run over us en route to the same place we're going.

"That's the situation at the moment, and I have a personal message for you from Admiral Greenwood—'Mom' is what you called her, I believe. She said to tell you you're damned lucky she hasn't already pulled the plug on your expedition and told the LRI Board to pound sand."

Seeing the look on Carla's face, Tanaka softened a bit.

"Look, Doctor, I want this mission to succeed, and as long as we are authorized to continue, I'll do my best to make sure it does. *Randall* and her crew will give you everything they've got in support of your work, right up to the point where Fleet says stop; but if that happens, I don't have a choice. You may be in charge of the scientific mission, but my chain of command is through Fleet.

"Here, in the Sol System, your mother has the final word. And while our escort is here to protect us, Commander Anderson of *Aztec* is the senior officer and has operational command of the group, including us. Once we get to New Eden, we fall under Admiral Ling's command. Any one of those people can order us to stand down. If I disagree, I will do my best to convince them to change their minds, but in the end, I *will* follow their orders."

"I understand, Captain," Carla said, unhappily. "I appreciate your candor. You've made me realize I don't actually know much about the Otuka, and I should not take the threat lightly."

"I think you need to tell your team what I've told you," Tanaka advised, "but there's no sense worrying about things we can't control. We should assume we'll be allowed to go ahead with the mission and make plans accordingly."

* * *

Fleet HQ—Weapons Development Section—TerraNova City, Luna

"No, seriously, people. She did not just do that," Major Marcus Tully declared.

The Marine officer had been reviewing a simulation run for the classified BuWeaps project to which he had just been assigned. He was a Raptor pilot, commander of a Raptor squadron, and a certified instructor pilot for the attack craft. He had been viewing the replay from the wingman position, as if he were flying to one side and behind the attacking craft. He took off his VR helmet and set it down on the console in front of him.

"What's the problem, Major?" Jensen inquired.

"The problem, Commander, is that your simulation is faulty. You can't do what I just saw with a Raptor. You're way outside the envelope."

Tully had just watched Vasquez complete a strafing run on a target. She'd been lined up perfectly, and it was a textbook pass, but as she pulled up at the end of it, someone had fired a missile at her from a concealed enemy position. It had come at the worst possible moment, as was usually the case in simulations, and, per the textbook, the only thing she should have been able to do was dive for the deck and hope to evade, with about a one-in-five chance of success. Instead, she had wrenched the Raptor through an impossible corkscrew maneuver that left her heading directly toward the incoming missile. At the last minute, she had executed a half roll and pulled her craft, inverted, into a sharp dive toward the deck. The missile had missed her by less than thirty meters, and its guidance computer did what it was programmed to do in such a case—detonated its warhead as she passed under it. By rolling the Raptor on its back, however, Vasquez had presented her armor-plated underside to the explosion, and her craft suffered no significant damage. Then she'd rolled upright and unloaded one of the Raptor's rocket pods precisely on the coordinates from which the missile had been fired. Without waiting to see the results, she'd executed a fast one eighty and lined up for her next strafing run.

"I assure you, Major," Val spoke from the control console speaker, "at no time were the flight parameters of the Raptor exceeded. Maximum stresses were no more than seventeen gees, and the craft is certified for twenty."

"That's exactly what I'm talking about," Tully replied. "That Raptor is being piloted by a human, not a robot or an AI. What human pilot can withstand seventeen gees?"

"We're assuming an inertial damping field inside the cockpit," Jensen replied. "She never felt more than five gees, but I can promise you, she did feel it. We have standard gravity rings around the simulator to keep us honest."

"But you don't have an inertial damper in the simulator, do you? Have you ever tried moving around in a field like that? It's like swimming in a pool of honey. It slows your reaction time and hampers every move you make. You cannot operate flight controls effectively under those conditions. I know this because it's been tried before, a few years ago, on the theory that we could make an attack craft that wasn't limited by human tolerances. I was one of the test subjects for that program, and it was abandoned because pilots couldn't function effectively with the field in place."

"True," Jensen admitted. "If we could come up with a closed-system gravity drive, with a fusion reactor to power it, and make the package small enough to put into a Raptor, we wouldn't need the damper, and we wouldn't have the issue."

"Maybe," Tully conceded, "but that has its own problems. It works OK for a starship in open space. It lets everybody walk around inside the ship under a normal one-gee environment, but it doesn't let the pilot feel what the ship is doing. It's been proven that pilots need to feel gee forces as part of their sensory input. Some people do well in a one-gee simulator but can't fly worth a damn in a real combat environment, while others do better in combat than in the simulator. That's why we added the gee-rings to simulations, so pilots can feel maneuvers instead of just seeing the results in VR."

Jensen was grinning, and Tully didn't understand why. He was beginning to get irritated, but the engineer finally decided to explain the reason for his amusement.

"Major, we haven't told you much about this project, because we wanted you to look at the results without prior prejudice—from the standpoint of your considerable experience with a Raptor. We do have an inertial damper in the simulator, but it's not the problem you expect it to be. I think it's time for you to meet our test pilot. You don't know Sergeant Vasquez, do you?"

"Only by reputation. I heard she's a hotshot Raptor pilot, and that she'd been awarded the LMH. I don't know the circumstances, and I don't know her personally."

The door chime sounded, and the technician on duty checked his security screen. He nodded to himself and opened the door. Vasquez entered, moving on her crutches with easy familiarity but obviously without the coordination of a Raptor pilot. Tully looked at her with surprise, trying to process what he was seeing.

"Val said you wanted to see me, Commander?"

"Yes, Sergeant. I want you to meet Major Tully. You and he are in the same line of work. We're bringing him into the project as an evaluator."

Tully stood. Vasquez came to attention, transferred the right crutch smoothly to her other hand, and popped a sharp salute.

"Welcome aboard, sir," she told him. She hadn't made it obvious, but he knew she'd read the decorations on his uniform, paying particular attention to the Raptor IP wings. He'd done the same to her, but his eyes had locked on the unmistakable ribbon of the Lunar Medal of Honor, and he was mentally kicking himself. He should have saluted her first. He returned the salute.

"It's an honor to meet you, Sergeant," he told her with sincerity.

"Sergeant," Jensen interjected, "the Major is wondering just how you manage to do all of that fancy flying. I think it's time we fill him in on the details."

* * *

Chief Executive's Office, Lunar HQ, TerraNova City

"So, we've let the proverbial cat out of the bag," Lorna remarked. "I'm glad I don't have to deal with the reaction from Earth."

"Unfortunately, I do." Mick O'Hara grimaced. "It's as bad as you might imagine. The mildest of the critics are calling us arrogant and accusing us of not serving the best interests of humanity. The most radical are demanding we turn over the administration of New Eden to an international coalition. As usual, the Confederacy is making the most noise. The Islamic Federation doesn't seem to care, though some of their African members are making noises about white people—that's us, by the way, despite the diversity of our population—exploiting a native race once again.

"I'm trying my best to ignore them all, and we're still not telling them where the New Eden system is located. When Carla gets back, the LRI can publish all the data on that interesting, little star out there without mentioning the planet or the Edies, and nothing the Warren expedition publishes about New Eden will mention the system's location or the star's little quirks. As far as anyone is concerned, the two expeditions are totally separate, involving two different star systems."

Lorna was doubtful. "Too damned complicated, and too many people involved. I don't think it's going to stay secret for long."

"It would be a lot simpler," O'Hara told her, "if the Earthworms had not cracked the secret of hyperspace travel. I could blame my predecessor for that, since she was the one who decided to share the secret of gravity-drive technology with the Americans. Within a decade, half the developed nations of Earth had it. That technology was the key to hyperspace, so now, at least three of the Confederacy's member nations, in addition to the Americans, Brits, and Japanese, have hyper-capable ships. It wouldn't surprise me if they wanted to send a bunch of well-intentioned idiots out there to look after the Edies and introduce them to civilized society."

"Regarding your predecessor," Lorna replied with a crooked smile, "there was a small matter of an alien invasion going on. Without the American fleet, we would have been on our own against the Mekota, so I did what I had to from a military standpoint. I'm sure my critics would say that's another reason I never should have been CEO.

"Smartest thing I ever did was to resign and convince the Directorate to dump the job on you. But getting back to the subject at hand, how much are you going to tell them about the Otuka?"

"As little as possible," he told her. "Just that we found a population of primitive humans—we're not saying how we found them, but the implication is that an LRI expedition just happened to stumble upon them—being exploited by the same nasty alien pirates who attacked *Summer Solstice*. We chased the pirates out of the system and are now quietly observing the humans in their native habitat. We are not telling anyone we have LFS Marines all over the planet, nor that chasing them out involved a bloody space battle in which our forces suffered significant losses. Which brings me to the point of this meeting. Do you really think you need to go out there yourself?"

Lorna sat back with a thoughtful look.

"Myself, personally? Probably not," she admitted, "but we need to send a substantial force. After the first encounter, we doubled our force, and it was well we did because the Otuka came back with a force twenty times the size of their first incursion. Amy Ling drove them off and, hopefully, convinced them we're serious about holding the system. They may not be back, but we can't be sure.

"We can expect, however, if they do come back, they will bring an even stronger force. So, just building Amy back up to strength won't be enough. I could send Robin Torrey out with the rest of Second Fleet—three battle groups with *Amazon*, *Cassandra*, and *Athena*, or I can leave Robin in charge of things here and take First Fleet. Again, that's three battle groups with *Valkyrie*, *Isis*, and *Nike,* since *Medusa* is already out there but no longer fit for combat. Either way, I'd leave Amy in place with most of her combat-effectives and send any ship with more than light damage home for repairs.

"I prefer the second option. First Fleet has been sitting here for too long, doing nothing more than in-system exercises and war game simulations. Every combat force needs to deploy occasionally, just to stay sharp. Every combat commander, including me, needs to, as well. I need to find out if First Fleet and its personnel are as deployment-ready as they are supposed to be. If they are, with your permission, I can depart within five days. If they aren't, I'll be very unhappy about it, and my officers will soon share my unhappiness."

"In principle, I agree with you," O'Hara replied, "but you'll also be taking Fleet's second-ranking officer with you. If you want to go somewhere, shouldn't you leave Tommy behind?"

Vice Admiral Tom Sakura was Fleet's most senior officer after Lorna and was her deputy commander. Technically, he commanded

First Fleet, while she commanded the combined fleets. He flew his colors aboard LFS *Isis.*

"I considered that," Lorna admitted, "but if I'm really testing First Fleet, Tommy needs to participate. Besides, Robin could use some experience managing things on the home front for a change."

"OK." He nodded. "I see the logic, and I'm comfortable with it. I guess you'd better get packing."

* * *

LRS *Lisa Randall* with *Aztec* and the Destroyers—New Eden System

Lisa Randall and her three escorts dropped out of hyperspace in the New Eden system, killed their in-system vector, and waited just beyond the hyper limit. *Aztec* sent a coded transmission to advise any listening fleet unit of the group's arrival. Assuming Admiral Ling's forces were somewhere near the planet, it could take up to two hours for their message to get there and a reply to come back. Assuming…

"Hyper signature!"

Commander John Anderson looked up sharply as *Aztec's* tactical officer sang out.

"Multiple hyper signatures! Four bogies, directly in-system from us, range 300k. Four additional bogies, directly out-system, range 370k. Sir, they've got us boxed!"

Anderson selected his group command channel.

"All ships to Condition Red, ROE Bravo, defenses free, formation Echo. *Randall*, tuck in now! Destroyers, close it up!"

* * *

Carla and Bjorn were in *Randall's* wardroom, having lunch with two other scientists, when the alert sounded. It was a sharp, warbling siren sound followed immediately by Tanaka's voice.

"*Condition Red! All crew to battle stations. This is not a drill. Repeat, all crew to battle stations. This is not a drill!*"

Across the table, Carla watched the color drain out of stellar cartographer Demaris Mitchell's face. Next to Mitchell, astronomer Victor Gruzinsky looked up from his plate of linguini with a grimace.

"That can't be good," he declared.

"Probably not," Carla agreed, but Bjorn only smiled at her.

"Look at it this way, love," he said, "at least, this time, we're on a ship that has such a thing as battle stations."

* * *

On *Aztec's* bridge, Anderson grunted with satisfaction. His crews had cleared for action quickly. Gravity shields were up, weapons were hot, and defenses were online. The research ship was tucked neatly in the middle of a triangle formed by the cruiser and the two destroyers.

OK, he thought, *we've prepared for the worst; now, let's hope for the best.*

"Mr. Chang," he ordered, "give them an IFF challenge if you please."

* * *

On *Randall's* bridge, Jennifer Tanaka viewed her status displays with grim satisfaction. Her crew was responding well, a testimony to the drills she'd conducted en route. She'd ordered the loading queues re-prioritized to make sure the Viper missiles were first in line, and her foresight had paid off. Both of the research ship's tubes were hot with combat loads, and icons showed her twin grasers charged and ready as well. *If we have to, we'll show them we have teeth*, she resolved. Still, with eight possible hostiles out there, it was comforting to be tucked into the defensive envelope of the escorts. If a destroyer and two corvettes could chew up six of the Otuka, she was confident eight of them would fare even worse against a heavy cruiser and two destroyers, not to mention a not-so-helpless research ship.

Suddenly, her tactical display changed, as the eight icons switched from yellow unidentified bogies to the bright green of friendly warships. IFF codes were updated, and she found herself looking at a pair of *Vampire*-class LFS light cruisers and a half-dozen destroyers. Tanaka breathed a sigh of relief as a new voice came over the command channel.

"*Aztec* and company, this is LFS *Banshee*. Welcome to New Eden. Admiral Ling's compliments. She requests you proceed directly to fleet anchorage in orbit around the planet. Contact approach control on Fleet Seven at least one hour out."

"*Banshee, Aztec* Prime," Anderson replied. "Thanks for the welcome. Can you advise as to system security?"

"This is *Banshee* Prime," a new voice said, as the light cruiser's captain responded directly to his *Aztec* counterpart. "The system is secure for now, but there may still be a few remnants of the hostile force around, probably battle damaged.

"Shouldn't be anything you can't handle, and our experience indicates they'll run rather than fight. We've taught them a painful lesson, and they won't take us on without a serious advantage in numbers. Per the admiral's standing orders, weapons are free, and anything that doesn't answer IFF is a target. If you encounter them, Fleet Twelve is the hot channel for operations. Just sing out, and we'll have units on the way as quickly as we can get them to you."

"Thank you, *Banshee,*" Anderson acknowledged. "We'll keep our eyes open and our claws sharp. *Aztec* Group, stand by for course parameters. We will reduce to Condition Yellow but maintain formation Echo for the duration."

He nodded in satisfaction as the other ships advised receipt of the course update. Officially, his mission would be complete when he delivered *Randall* to New Eden. What happened after that would be up to Admiral Ling.

* * *

Almost two days later, after arriving at New Eden orbit, *Lisa Randall* and her escorts cruised slowly along the length of the fleet anchorage, heading for slots at the far end.

"My God…" Carla said, softly. "She tried to tell me so many times, but I never understood."

"What's that, love?" Bjorn asked.

"Space warfare," she told him. "I grew up hearing stories of the Fleet, the glorious, ever-victorious Lunar Fleet. We learned about it in school—the First and Second Battles of Luna, the Mekota Incursions, the Battle of Copper Hills, the Trade Wars along the Akara Frontier. The Lunar Fleet kicks butt, and the LFS grows and prospers. But every time I tried to talk about it with Mom, she would brush me off. She would tell me neither I nor my teachers had any idea what those victories cost."

"I was proud of her and what she did, and I wanted her to know that, so I kept pushing. Finally, one day, she took me to Memorial Hall near the Fleet Museum. We walked from one memorial to the next. Each one represented one of those great victories I'd learned about in school. She stopped at each one to read names off the lists on the wall, then she told me about those people, what they looked like and little details about them to make me understand they were people she really knew. People who died in battle, so the rest of us could learn about it decades later, were reduced to a half-hour presentation in school."

"After that, I thought I understood, but I really didn't. Not until now. This—" she waved a hand at the scene beyond the broad viewport, "—was one of those victories."

They were passing the shattered hulk of the light cruiser LFS *Sphinx*, which was recognizable only by a section of its hull artwork that remained intact amid the battle damage to the forward section. The ship looked dead, abandoned, illuminated only by the floodlights of workboats hovering nearby, while crews tried to make repairs. *Randall* had already passed the wreck of a destroyer whose hull ended in twisted wreckage about two thirds back along its length. The rest of the ship was missing, the result of a near-catastrophic fusion plant failure. That ship was also dead—held in place by a pair of fore-and-aft robot buoys marked by blinking strobes—but no repair crews were working on it. The damage was beyond what could be repaired with the resources at hand.

Most of the ships they had seen so far showed battle damage to some degree. Despite the condition of the destroyer they'd passed, the Fleet's heavy capital ships appeared to have suffered more damage than the lighter, more nimble units. They passed a line of three destroyers that showed little damage, but the heavy cruiser *Montagnard* had gaping holes in its battle armor, and three nodes of its drive ring were little more than twisted wreckage. The cruiser was nestled alongside the huge fleet tender *Scapa Flow,* the source of a large number of small craft moving repair crews, parts, and equipment back and forth among damaged warships. Far down the line, similar activity was centered on another fleet tender, LFS *Chesapeake Bay*, which had two badly damaged cruisers tethered to its flanks.

The battlecruisers not been spared either. LFS *Medusa*, now off *Randall*'s beam, looked to have gotten the worst of the battle. The 600-meter hull still had power, as evidenced by internal and external lights, but a huge section of the warship's midsection was little more than a blasted-out skeleton, the result of containment failure for the midship fusion plant. Having visited her mother's flagship many times, Carla was familiar with the deck plan of a *Valkyrie*-class battlecruiser. With a shock, she realized the area of destruction must have included the flag bridge, as well as the primary sick bay and large sections of Navy and Marine crew quarters. A wave of nausea swept over her as the implications sunk in. *At least*, she told herself, *the crew quarters should have been mostly empty when the ship was in action.*

"Come on, darling," Bjorn told her, gently. "There's nothing we can do here, and you need to get some sleep. You're supposed to meet with Admiral Ling tomorrow."

"Sleep? Not tonight, I'm afraid," she replied. "But you're right, there's nothing we can do." With a sigh, Carla turned from the viewport and let her husband shepherd her back to their cabin.

* * *

LFS *Sorceress*—New Eden Orbit

"Commander Anderson," Amy Ling said. "I'm pleased to see you. *Aztec* and your destroyers won't be enough to replace my losses, but every little bit helps."

"I wish," she turned to Carla, "I could say the same for you, Dr. Greenwood, and you, Commander Tanaka."

"Admiral…" Carla was at a loss for words. All through her childhood, Ling had been Aunt Amy who would never have called her anything but Carla. She understood this was an official meeting with others present, but there was no warmth in Ling's voice, none at all.

"I'm sorry," she finally blurted out. "I didn't know what you were facing out here. I mean, I knew, but I had no idea how serious the situation was."

"Carla," Ling replied, softening a bit but still using a tone she might have reserved for a promising junior officer who had just screwed up in a major way, "you are probably the most intelligent person in this compartment—for that matter, on this entire ship. Unfortunately, that intelligence seems to have a very narrow focus at times, and you are extremely stubborn.

"I am absolutely certain your mother advised you not to undertake this expedition. I am certain of it because I have a dispatch from her that tells me so. Unfortunately, she also tells me you apparently carry more weight with the LRI Board of Directors than she does, so here we are, and I am required to make the best of it. Don't, for a moment, think I am happy about it.

"As for you, Captain—" she turned to Tanaka, "—I can't be angry with you because you are simply following Fleet orders, and, given your outstanding record to date, I am certain you will carry out those orders to the best of your ability. I'm also certain you understand you are now in my area of operations, and that puts you under my command. I don't intend to interfere with your expedition, except to impose such security measures as I deem necessary, but if I have to issue an order, I'm sure I can count on you to obey it first and ask for explanations later."

"Yes, ma'am." Tanaka replied calmly, locking eyes with Ling. "Admiral Greenwood made that clear to me before we departed Luna."

Ling nodded with satisfaction. Then her expression softened.

"Also, Commander," she continued, "I am so very sorry about your sister. It happened on my watch, in my AO, and her safety was my responsibility. The bastards took us by surprise, and I failed in that responsibility."

"It was war, ma'am," Tanaka's voice was quiet but steady. "Janice was a non-combatant, but she knew she was going into a war zone. It was the enemy's fault, not yours. I've already had one opportunity to settle the score with them. For that matter, you've done more along those lines than I could ever accomplish by myself. Vengeance won't bring her back, but it does provide some comfort to those she left behind."

Both women fell silent, and Carla wondered what they were talking about. Obviously, it was something else she didn't know about Jennifer Tanaka, and she resolved to find some delicate way to ask her about it.

Finally, Ling broke the silence.

"I understand, Commander. The desire for vengeance is a natural human reaction to this sort of thing. Just don't let it overcome reasonable discretion in the course of your duties."

"I won't, ma'am," Tanaka assured her.

"Very well, then. Commander Anderson, I'm sure *Aztec* will fit well into my order of battle, but I strongly suggest you talk to your counterparts in my surviving cruiser force and get up to speed on the situation here. I don't know when the Otuka might return—or if they ever will return—but I need you to be online and ready if they do. As for the destroyers, I'm turning them over to the CDG to be integrated into our screen, so they are no longer your responsibility.

"As for *Lisa Randall*—" She turned her attention to Carla and Tanaka again, and at that moment, the lights went out, leaving the compartment illuminated only by the dim red glow of the emergency lighting system. The data system screen on Ling's desk also went dark but came back up a moment later as its emergency power system kicked in.

"I'm sorry, Admiral." The disembodied voice was that of Sonja, the battlecruiser's AI. "Engineering is rerouting power feeds on 'E' deck, and a technician disconnected a major circuit without advising me of his intentions. This resulted in cascading failures of several other circuits, but all critical systems went to backup power without a problem. To reverse the process now will result in significant delays to the repairs, so I am recommending they proceed with the work and restore power to the circuits when finished. That will mean, however, that your cabin and everything else on this deck between frames 176 and 200 will have lighting reduced to emergency levels for approximately two hours."

"Fine," Ling replied. "Tell them to proceed with the work, and that their enthusiasm for the task is appreciated. Also, tell them that if anyone pulls a dumbass stunt like that again, without first checking with you, he or she will become my sparring partner in the gym for the next three days—without the benefit of protective gear."

Carla suppressed a grin, knowing the diminutive Ling's martial arts skills were well-known throughout the fleet, and that, despite her age, she regularly administered painful lessons to combat-trained Marines on the mat in the warship's gym. Carla, as a teenager, had acquired a large part of her considerable martial arts expertise under Ling's tutelage.

"Frederick!" Ling commanded. Chief Petty Officer Frederick Dorn, the admiral's steward, appeared as if by magic in the dimly lit compartment.

"Yes, ma'am."

"It's too damned dark in here. Can you find a few of those candles you use for formal dinners? I need one on my desk, maybe a couple more on the side tables."

"Certainly, ma'am. I'll be right back."

He vanished, leaving Carla wondering why he hadn't left a puff of smoke behind. Ling returned to the topic at hand.

"As I was saying, it is not my intention to let *Randall* go cruising around the system unescorted. I am going to assign one destroyer—one of my combat veterans, not one of the newcomers you brought with you—to be your constant companion. I also expect you to advise me of your destination and intentions before going anywhere. Is that clear?"

"Yes, ma'am," Carla and Tanaka responded in unison.

"I'm mostly concerned about individual Otuka ships, remnants of the attack force that weren't able to exit the system. As it turns out, they are stealthy little bastards, quite capable of imitating a hole in space when necessary. But they can't hide a hyper signature, and I have enough surveillance in place to preclude any sizeable force sneaking in without giving us plenty of warning. I believe you encountered that surveillance when you arrived."

"Yes, ma'am," Tanaka acknowledged. "They were on us before we could blink."

"And very neatly done," Anderson added. "My compliments to the commanders involved."

"That's the good news," Ling said, nodding her thanks as Chief Dorn placed an ornate candlestick with lighted candles on her desk. "The bad news is I've got barely enough combat-effective warships here to make one full battle group, even with *Aztec* and the two destroyers you brought. We had two Groups when the last melee started, and I've only got one battlecruiser left which—" she waved her hand to indicate the dim lighting around her, "—you've probably noticed is still in need of some work.

"*Sorceress* is combat-effective, but *Medusa* will need major repairs just to make her hyper capable so we can send her home, and over 200 of her crew are dead, including Admiral Kellerman and his entire staff. She's taken so much damage to her cyber structure, Mida, the AI, is no longer in communication with most of the ship's systems or doesn't have enough processor capacity to function normally. We've taken her offline and put her in sleep mode until repairs can be made.

"I've got one heavy cruiser—*Cheyenne*—lost with all hands, another—*Acadian*—lost with very few survivors, and three more heavies out of action until we can put them back together. I've also lost the light cruiser *Kraken* and have two other CLs that won't be fit for combat for some time. Personnel losses..." She shook her head. "We're past two thousand dead and still counting.

"I guess the bright spot is the destroyers. I lost one and have four more seriously damaged, but while the bastards were concentrating on the capital ships, the destroyers really chewed them up. In addition, although we had to abandon the orbitals, and the Otuka dropped a substantial force on the planet, one of our destroyer groups harassed them to the point where their orbital support for that force was totally ineffective.

"Colonel Bartley's Marines kicked ass on the ground, and this time—" she shot a glance at Jennifer Tanaka, "—we didn't lose any scientists. For that matter, we didn't lose any of the Edie aborigines. The Otuka didn't bother going after them; they obviously recognized that our people were the real threat. They inflicted some casualties on the Marines but, without air superiority and orbital support, they had no chance, and the Marines pretty much wiped them out. Again, there may be a few still down there, but they are isolated and ineffective."

"I'll be sending a lot of badly-damaged ships back to Luna as soon as I'm sure they can make the trip. We're doing our best to restore the rest to combat-ready condition or as close as we can come to it with the resources we have. Hopefully, my latest dispatches to Fleet will bring replacements at a dead run. Meanwhile, we will follow our orders and hold until relieved."

She leaned back in her chair and regarded the group.

"Welcome to Paradise."

She opened a desk drawer and retrieved a cigarette from a pack within. She leaned forward and used the candle on her desk to light it.

"Smoke if you've got 'em," she advised.

* * * * *

Chapter Ten

Home Ship—Otuka 2455th Clan

Sometimes, A'archa reflected, it was best not to be too quick responding to calls for action from the Council of Clans. After his encounter with the human ship and his timely escape from its rescuers, he had returned to the nearest nodal system to trade the spoils of that encounter for needed supplies.

The Otuka were nomads of space, having abandoned their dying homeworld several earth-centuries ago. They maintained their ancient clan structure, even as they dispersed, and the clans communicated with each other through nodes scattered throughout their part of the galaxy. Each node was little more than a hub structure in orbit around a star, equipped with repair and storage facilities where the ships of a clan could dock and conduct business with other clans. Nodes were usually established in lifeless, isolated star systems, which were unlikely to be visited by other spacefaring races.

The clans of the Otuka numbered in the hundreds of thousands, but individual clans were small. Most falnor consisted of no more than a few thousand individuals under a single tsan living aboard a home ship, with three or more subordinate ships that served as scouts, raiders, or defenders as needed. The clan structure was hierarchical, with each clan having a numeric ranking assigned. The Otuka used a decimal numbering system, and the lowest numbered falnor were the highest in rank. The tsans of the first thousand falnor were members of the Council which, in theory, held power over all

Otuka everywhere. In practice, that power was limited by the fact that the Council never assembled in one place, and its members communicated mostly by messages passed from node to node. Still, the Council—meaning any quorum of twenty council members or more—could issue a decree and expect all clans to be bound by it. Any who disobeyed would be punished, with the mildest punishment being loss of the clan's place in the hierarchy. The most severe punishment was dissolution, a decree that required all other clans, regardless of rank, to attack and destroy the disobedient clan upon contact.

Management of the nodes was a simple process. At any given time, there might be as many as a hundred falnor present at any node, but custom decreed that the highest-ranking tsan take charge of the node. When A'archa arrived at the node orbiting a nondescript red dwarf, he found himself the ranking tsan and immediately assumed command. Operating as he did, on the very fringes of Otuka space, this was often the case, and he was accustomed to it. In this case, the next-ranking tsan was almost a thousand ranks beneath him. There was little conversation between them during the transfer, but the lesser clan leader was required to pass along messages that had come from the Council.

One such message involved a planet the Otuka called the 47th Reserve. Reserves were places where valuable resources could be found in limited quantities. Long-standing decrees required the discoverer of such a place to report it to the Council, which would declare the place to be off-limits until an agreement could be reached for the apportionment of its resources. To encourage reporting, the Council would usually guarantee the discoverer's clan a large share in perpetuity, leaving other clans to scramble for shares awarded at the Council's whim.

The 47th was a very old, established reserve, and the resource in question was a population of primitive humans, considered by the Otuka to be a much-valued food source. Many generations ago, the Council decreed limited harvests were to be permitted at specific intervals. Lesser clans could only participate if given permission by a council member. A harvest had recently been scheduled, and A'archa was disappointed when his request to participate was not approved. Now, it appeared he ought to be glad it wasn't. The harvesters had been attacked, and more than half of them destroyed, by a powerful force of warships. It had been a disorganized rout, and few details were known, but some survivors insisted the attackers were human, members of an advanced human civilization never before encountered.

A hastily assembled quorum of the Council had decreed that all available clans in the area must gather to deal with the threat and reclaim the 47th Reserve. The quorum had dismissed the idea of advanced humans, insisting the attackers were most likely Akara, whose domain was closest to the Reserve. The reptiles were a formidable adversary, but a swarm of clans should overcome any expeditionary force they could mount.

A'archa was the only tsan—or at least the only surviving one—who knew for certain humans with advanced technology did exist. Given the easy way the presumed-human rescuers of A'archa's prize ship had overwhelmed the superior numbers of Otuka, he did not want to be part of any swarm that went against them, but he could not ignore the summons.

Protocols decreed a node must never be totally abandoned, but in the event of a council summons, the lowest ranking tsan was required to take charge of the node. He could not use that excuse to avoid the summons, since every tsan present was lower-ranked than he. Claiming a need to resupply and service his ships, A'archa delayed his departure as long as he dared. He then proceeded to the assembly point at a leisurely pace, hoping the swarm would be gone before he arrived.

On arrival, he found a nearly empty node, but soon the survivors of the swarm began to trickle in with tales of crushing defeat—whole falnor wiped out of existence, including those of at least a dozen council members. Few of the survivors were unscathed. Many home ships returned, battle-damaged, with only a fraction of their falnor-ka raiders, some with none. Nearly a hundred of the smaller ships returned in disgrace, without their home ship and with no tsan to lead them.

A'archa did a quick tally of the falnor destroyed and determined at least twenty of them had been ranked above his. In this one battle, without even being a participant, he had advanced his clan to at least the 2430th level. He graciously allowed several of the orphaned falnor-ka to swear allegiance to him, forgiving them their disgrace and incidentally increasing his own subordinate fleet to twelve ships.

He spent time interviewing his newly acquired clan members, pressing them for details of the battle. As he did so, a plan began to form in his mind. The surviving council members were trying to gather a quorum. By now, all were forced to admit humans were the powerful enemy that had inflicted this defeat. Most agreed they were far too dangerous to confront directly, that the resources involved were not worth the effort, and that the entire system should be quarantined.

Until the quorum was formed, and a directive issued, however, A'archa was free to proceed as he saw fit. In his mind, he imagined a system littered with the debris of a huge battle—valuable debris, including common replacement parts for Otuka ships. The battle tales claimed some enemy ships had been destroyed, so the debris might also include human technology worth many times its scrap value. He'd gotten a fine price for the drive components taken from his last prize in a hasty sale at the frontier node. He could do better at a busier node deeper in Otuka space. If he moved quickly, a quiet visit to the former 47th Reserve might bring him great riches.

A'archa was not one to risk his life or his clan on a foolish quest, but neither was he inclined to avoid a moderate risk where potentially large profit was involved. Most likely, the enemy forces had regrouped protectively around the planet. He would drop out of hyperspace far beyond the system's limit and proceed with caution. If he stayed away from the planet, he ought to be able to reach the inner system undetected.

* * *

Fleet HQ—Weapons Development Section—TerraNova City, Luna

"You're leaving?" Vasquez was obviously unhappy about the news.

"I'm sorry," Val told the project team, "but I have my orders. *Valkyrie* will be departing tomorrow. I am not permitted to discuss the mission, only to advise you of my detachment from the project."

"Well, that sucks," Vasquez said. "I'm going to miss you a lot, Val, but I guess orders are orders." It had never occurred to her that Val, like everyone else in the Lunar Fleet or Lunar Marines, had to answer to a higher authority.

"In the interest of the project," the AI replied, "Fleet has assigned Anna of LFS *Athena* as my replacement. I have thoroughly briefed her, so there should be no disruption and no reason to miss me."

"I'm still going to miss you," Vasquez insisted. "I mean…personally, that is." She reddened a bit as she said it. She didn't want the rest of the team to know she considered Val a friend, but she wanted Val to know it, and she wasn't sure she'd have another chance to talk to her before the AI departed.

"I will miss you as well, Maya," the AI replied, defying convention and raising a few eyebrows around the table. "I'll call you at home tonight, and we can talk before I leave."

Vasquez reddened even more and glanced around the table, but the others appeared suddenly distracted, pretending not to have heard the exchange. In theory, AIs had no official rank, but Maya realized no one below flag rank was inclined to question them. Further, Val wasn't just any AI, she was the flagship's AI, answering only to Commodore McPherson, *Valkyrie*'s Captain, and Admiral Greenwood, the Babe on the Horse, her bad self. Certainly, no one at this table was going to take her to task for not following military protocol.

"Great," she said, her confidence returning. "We'll have a couple of beers together." *Let them all wonder about that,* she thought.

* * *

LRS *Lisa Randall*—New Eden Orbit

Carla was in better spirits today, Bjorn noted. He wished he could take credit, but honesty forced him to admit it was probably the arrival of old friends that had lifted her mood. As an undergrad at Luna University, Carla had concentrated on astronomy, physics, and mathematics, while merely tolerating, and usually breezing through, courses outside her chosen field of study. One required course was an elective from the Life Sciences curriculum, and she had chosen Exobiology 101 which was taught by Mercedes Warren, who was arguably the Sol System's foremost authority on the subject.

Warren's course hadn't caused Carla to change her major, but it fascinated her, and she had ended up taking several more electives in the field. She graduated as the only physics major in her class with a minor in extraterrestrial biology. Despite the difference in their ages, she and Warren had been friends ever since. She was delighted when the older woman came aboard *Randall*, fresh from the surface of New Eden. Ostensibly, it was an official visit, a conference between the heads of the two scientific teams in the system.

Jennifer Tanaka had joined Warren, Carla, and Bjorn for dinner and had brought Rob O'Hara, another of Carla's lifelong friends. Admiral Ling had seen fit to assign LFS *Timberwolf* as *Lisa Randall*'s watchdog for the duration of the expedition, and O'Hara had come aboard to confer with Tanaka. Now, the five of them were sharing a relaxed round of coffee and conversation in *Randall*'s lounge.

"So, tell me the big secret, Mercy," Carla insisted. "Are these Edies really human or just humanoid?"

"Well now, 'human' is a broad term, even as we define it on Earth." Warren leaned back in her chair and regarded the group.

"Just look at us here at this table. First, we have Bjorn—tall, blond hair, blue eyes, arguably northwestern European, probably pure Nordic ancestry. Then we have Captain Tanaka, far eastern Asian of the mainstream oriental variety. Dark hair, smaller stature, with more delicate features, brown eyes, with a pronounced epicanthic fold. Both she and Bjorn are human, but there's quite a contrast—like putting a Viking and a Samurai side-by-side.

"At another extreme, there's little old me," she continued, with a grin. "My family may have lived in North America for generations, but there's no doubt about my heritage: darkest Africa...pun intended. There are Zulu warriors in my family tree."

She leaned forward and regarded each of them in turn. "We don't see that much variance among the native tribes here, but I will tell you this: genetically, the Edies are closer to any of us here than Bjorn, Jennifer, and I are to each other. If I saw them on Earth, I might mistake them for native Americans of the Upper Plains tribes, maybe Cheyenne or Sioux."

"In other words, they could intermarry with any of us and produce children with no surprises," Carla reflected.

"Yes," Warren said, with a wry grin, "and we may have proof of that sooner than expected. One of my team members just married one of them." She told them the story of Owen Phillips and Angel.

"Amazing," Carla remarked. "A primitive society where women get to choose their mates."

"What's unusual about that?" Bjorn inquired. "Oh, I get it. It's unusual because the men don't get to pretend they're the ones doing the choosing. Ow!" He flinched as Carla landed a well-placed elbow in his ribs.

"I'll stay clear of that one," Rob O'Hara said, with a grin. "In case you haven't noticed, Bjorn, we're outnumbered at this table."

"So, the Edies are human—" Jennifer Tanaka suddenly looked very serious, "—but what can you tell us about the Otuka?"

Carla stopped smiling and glanced sharply at the young officer. After the meeting aboard *Sorceress,* she had quietly approached Tanaka and learned of her twin sister's fate. From the sober look on Warren's face, it was apparent she also knew. *Of course, she does,* Carla realized. *Jennifer's sister was one of Mercy's people.*

"Well," Warren finally replied, "all those I've seen have been dead, which makes them a little more difficult to study. It would be useful to have a live specimen, but our encounters have not been conducive to that. We know they're mammals, or close enough not to make a difference. They're carbon-based, warm-blooded creatures, with red, hemoglobin-based blood. They breathe an oxygen-nitrogen atmosphere and nurse their young with milk that isn't much different than that produced by just about any mammal on Earth, including humans."

"That implies that some of the specimens you've examined are female," Carla observed.

"Well, now, that's the interesting part," Warren replied. "All of the specimens we've examined are female, and all of them are male, as well. They're hermaphrodites."

Seeing the incredulous looks on their faces, Warren grinned.

"That's why I love exobiology," she told them, "for all the little surprises nature throws at you. Mind you, we're not talking ambiguous genitalia, or phased sex change, or anything like that. All of them appear to have fully formed male and fully formed female sex organs that seem to be functional all the time. The arrangement of those organs is such that they can't impregnate themselves, but it appears any one of them can impregnate any other one. I expect there is some sort of fertility cycle involved, but without live specimens to study, I have no clue what that cycle might be. And they have one other little quirk—they're monotremes."

"What the heck is a monotreme?" O'Hara inquired.

"An oviparous mammal, an egg layer," Carla answered. "There are some examples on Earth—Australia's platypus, to name one."

"Correct," Warren confirmed. "Beyond that, their muscular structure indicates their planet of origin has heavier gravity than Earth—or New Eden, which is about 1.05 Earth-normal—and their teeth and digestive organs tell us they are pure carnivores, like the Akara. If they eat anything other than meat, it's just a digestive aid or to clean their teeth, the way terrestrial cats sometimes nibble on plants.

"Humans, in contrast, are omnivores who eat as much vegetable matter as meat. We can even survive on a pure vegetarian diet, though it isn't a very efficient way to fuel our bodies. The Otuka can't do that."

"So, in order for them to live, something has to die," Tanaka said.

"Well, in theory, animal fats and proteins can be synthesized," Warren replied, "but not in sufficient quantities to feed a whole population, at least, not with any technology we know of. So yes, they need living creatures as a food source, but the same is true of the Akara."

"Maybe," Carla countered, "but the Akara don't eat other intelligent creatures. They made a point of letting us know that, when we've had discussions with them in the past." Carla shifted uncomfortably, realizing she was getting close to things she wasn't supposed to talk about.

"All living creatures are intelligent to some degree," Bjorn insisted, "even insects. Where do you draw the line?"

"I don't know," Carla admitted. "I think the Akara consider tool-using to be a criterion of intelligence—enough to put a species off-limits as a food source, in any case."

"I'd have to look deeper than that," Warren said. "Dolphins on Earth don't use tools and neither do most apes or other primates, but they reach a level of intelligence that gets pretty close to our own. I certainly wouldn't think of them as food animals."

"I think that's a question each carnivorous—or omnivorous—civilization has to answer for itself," O'Hara said.

"True," Tanaka agreed, "but the problem with the Otuka seems to be that they haven't bothered to ask the question at all."

* * *

Home Ship—Otuka 2429th Clan (formerly 2455th)—New Eden System

A'archa was feeling pleased with himself. His analysis of the battle data was confirmed, and he had found veritable clouds of wreckage where the primary engagements had taken place, well out-system from the planet. He had entered the system quietly, dropping out of hyperspace far beyond the hyper limit, building up significant velocity coming in but then slowing down as he approached the salvage area. He had never completely stopped moving, but simply coasted through, while his falnor-ka raiders scattered to retrieve the drifting plunder and haul it to the cavernous holds of his home ship.

Twice, he had to order them to go silent and drift when enemy units passed within extreme detection range, but the humans were not trying to hide their activities, and he could see their prowling warships far beyond the range where they could see him.

Most of the battles had taken place near the system ecliptic, but that was no surprise. The ecliptic was the plane in which a system's planets and most of its asteroids orbited. It also contained most of the dust and other debris left over from the formation of the system. If one wished to enter a system with the least chance of being noticed, the ecliptic was the place to do it. Straying too far into the empty space above or below the ecliptic was likely to attract notice, assuming the enemy was vigilant. It was a mistake he was not inclined to make.

His ships loaded to capacity with valuable salvage, he had passed most of the way through the system and was heading out the other side. He would be cautious until he reached the hyper limit, but the most dangerous part of the mission was behind him.

When this was over, he planned to take his falnor to one of the inner nodes where certain comforts could be found and where his salvage would bring the highest price. After he sold it, he would declare a recess and would allow his loyal followers to enjoy the fruits of their labor. For himself, he would allow his female persona to emerge and mate with one of his closest advisors. She would produce a clutch of eggs to ensure the continuation of the dynasty and spend some time enjoying herself before reverting to maleness and heading out into space again.

Most Otuka tsans required their minions to be males and to keep their female personas in check while operating in open space, primarily to avoid the distractions involved with mixed sexuality. In theory, a tsan could order his followers to all be female while they worked together, but that was not the traditional way. The male persona tended to be dominant, more aggressive, and easier to maintain over long periods of time.

Once on recess, A'archa expected they would let themselves go. Some of them would switch roles several times in the vulgar manner of commoners. Many eggs would be produced, and most of them would go to the common crèches to be hatched and raised to renew the population; however, his eggs—or hers, depending on one's viewpoint—would be carefully nurtured and raised separately as the offspring of the tsan.

* * *

LRS *Lisa Randall*—Outer Reaches of the New Eden System

Named for the noteworthy Harvard physicist of the early 21st century, LRS *Lisa Randall* was the fifth pure-research vessel built by the Lunar Free State. As such, she incorporated advanced design features that resulted from experience with her four predecessors, *Stephen Hawking*, *Albert Einstein*, *Leonardo Da Vinci*, and *Edwin Hubble*, all of which were still in service as the Lunar nation neared the end of its first half-century of existence.

Randall boasted better search and survey instrumentation, comfortable quarters for a larger science team, more sophisticated onboard laboratories, and more cargo capacity for consumables and collected samples, giving her a greatly extended mission range and duration. She was also equipped with a cyber structure that approached, but didn't quite reach, self-aware artificial intelligence levels.

One of her most noteworthy features was a mission control center, which was to the scientists what the ship's bridge was to her captain and Navy crew—headquarters from which all research-related activity was directed. In fact, Mission Control resembled a warship's bridge, with a raised command station at the rear of the compartment, which was normally occupied by the mission's science director or the senior scientist on duty at a given time. The command station monitored and directed the activities of a half-dozen smaller stations arranged in a semicircle in front of it, and the forward bulkhead was dominated by an impressive array of large video screens whose displays were visible to everyone in the control center.

Seated at the command station, Carla Greenwood felt as if she had immense power at her fingertips, power to reach out and touch the secrets of the universe. She wondered if this was the way her mother felt when she sat at her command station on *Valkyrie's* flag bridge.

Well, maybe not, she admitted to herself. *There's a difference between having an amazing set of research tools at your fingertips and having a fleet of warships with enough firepower to sterilize a small planet.* Still, it felt good to be there, and she realized she could very easily get addicted to the feeling.

Randall had spent the better part of five days up close and personal with LGS 1437A, now unofficially dubbed "Rothstein's Star" (at least until they got back to Luna, where Carla intended to steamroll the Board into making the name official). In fact, they had gotten close enough to the star to make the Navy crew nervous about the ability of *Randall's* gravity shielding to withstand the intense heat and radiation. Carla had carefully monitored the situation, and Tanaka was confident of the ship's ability to take it, but both insisted that *Timberwolf* remain a million kilometers farther away from the stellar furnace. Since it seemed unlikely the Otuka would dare to venture so far in-system, Rob O'Hara reluctantly agreed.

After taking the necessary close-up measurements, they had gone to the opposite extreme to observe the star from a distance. Now, they were near the hyper limit, not far from the point where they had first arrived in the star system. *Lisa Randall* hung motionless, like a spider in her web, in the center of a hexagonal array formed by six survey probes each of which was precisely 10,000 kilometers out from the ship. Linked together through the ship's computers, the probes formed an extremely sensitive detection grid, allowing the scientists to chart the tiniest changes in the pulsating star's gravitational field. To avoid any interference, *Timberwolf* was half a million kilometers away directly out-system. The destroyer's energy emissions were reduced to minimum levels.

At one of the consoles in front of Carla, Judah Rothstein monitored the incoming data. Rothstein had come over from *Hubble* as soon as *Randall* arrived at the anchorage, and Carla was letting the young astrophysicist do most of the research, directing his efforts with gentle suggestions rather than micromanagement.

Rothstein's enthusiasm had almost overcome his embarrassment at having a star named after him, but Carla noted with amusement his reports still referred to the star by its catalog number. All the same, he was on track to produce some interesting results, and the subject matter ought to guarantee publication in the most prominent astrophysics journals.

Carla noticed Rothstein was frowning, staring intently at his visual displays. He touched a few icons and made some minor adjustments, but the frown didn't go away. She was about to ask him if there was a problem when he turned to her.

"Dr. Greenwood, I've got an anomaly here. It looks like a tiny disturbance in the field flux, and it appears to be highly localized. It might be a glitch in the instrumentation. I thought one of the probes was out of sync, but that would produce a harmonic. This doesn't look like that."

Bjorn looked up from his console. As a particle physicist, his role in the expedition's primary mission was mostly advisory, but he had found research of his own to do and was busy sampling neutrinos and other nanoparticles in the outer reaches of the system. He looked at Rothstein with a grin.

"Remember, Judah, many great discoveries have been lost because a researcher assumed there was a glitch in the instruments and refused to believe what they were telling him."

Rothstein grinned back at him "On the other hand, many a researcher has cried 'Eureka' prematurely because he didn't think there could be anything wrong with his instruments. In fact, now I think about it, you particle guys seem particularly prone to that. If I remember correctly, the CERN people announced the discovery of the Higgs Boson at least six times before they finally got it right."

"Boys, boys," Carla chided, "play nice. Judah, let's see it on the big screen."

Rothstein complied, displaying the false color heat map of the space in front of them. The center of the display was blocked with a black circle, taking the star and its immediate surroundings out of the equation, while the rest of the display showed colors representing the intensity of the gravitational flux.

"I'm talking about this, right here." He placed a circular cursor around a tiny blip to the far left in the image—a few little speckles of yellow in an area that was otherwise displayed in shades of green.

"Hmmm, I have an idea," Carla told them. "The array gives us maximum resolution through interferometry, but we should be able to shut down any one of the probes without losing much. I'm going to shut them down one at a time and see if it goes away. If it does, we can be pretty sure it's a problem with that particular probe."

She cycled through the probes, shutting each one down, then bringing it back up. Each time, they lost some resolution, but the anomaly still appeared as a faint yellow blob.

"It's not the instruments," Carla concluded. "There's something out there. Unfortunately, the array can't tell us how far away it is."

"Maybe it can," Bjorn suggested. "I think I saw a tiny position shift each time you shut down one of the probes. You have a 20,000-kilometer baseline, so you might be able to do something with parallax ranging. Shut down a probe on one side of the array, then on the other, and measure the image shift."

"That's a great idea," Rothstein agreed. "Not bad for a particle guy."

"Somewhere along the line, I seem to have acquired an extra degree in engineering," Bjorn replied with a grin. "Just as a hobby, you understand."

Carla said nothing but busied herself setting up a computer model that would translate Bjorn's suggestion into a real-time measurement tool. Within minutes, she had it up and running.

"OK," she announced, "assuming I haven't dropped a decimal place somewhere, our little mystery is only about 31.7 million kilometers away, plus or minus 50,000 klicks, given the resolution of the array with the baseline we have."

"Which," Rothstein pointed out, "still doesn't tell us what we're looking at."

"No, but it gives us an indication of the strength of the disturbance," Carla told him. "At that range, a ship using a gravity drive at low power levels might produce something like this. It wouldn't be detectable if the array wasn't so sensitive."

"It looks like a cluster of point sources," Rothstein speculated. "Maybe several ships operating at low power levels."

Carla blinked as her display updated.

"Uh oh," she muttered.

"What?" Rothstein and Bjorn asked, simultaneously.

"Make that 31.4 million kilometers," she advised, "and no change in bearing. It's moving, and it's coming straight at us."

Moments later, she finished explaining what they had found to Jennifer Tanaka on *Randall's* bridge. Tanaka regarded her with a stern expression.

"You realize, Doctor, as soon as I pass this along to Commander O'Hara—which I intend to do momentarily—*Timberwolf* is going to invade your quiet little research zone in a very noisy way."

"I'd expect nothing less of Rob," Carla replied.

"More importantly—" Tanaka allowed herself a small smile, "—Admiral Ling would expect nothing less of him. He's going to put himself between us and the perceived threat, regardless of what you or I may think about it. Plan on packing up your experiments for the duration." The window on Carla's screen split in two as Tanaka keyed her priority channel to the destroyer.

It took very little time for Rob O'Hara to grasp the situation and get his ship moving in their direction, but rather than shutting down her gear, Carla decided to leave the probes out there.

"Right now," she explained, "*Timberwolf* doesn't have anything that can see the bogey that far away. For that matter, I doubt the Otuka—if that's who they are—can see us yet, though that may change in the next twenty minutes or so. But in the meantime, the array gives us a set of eyes that are better than anything else we have, and they're passive, so the bogey doesn't know he's being watched. I can patch our display through to *Randall's* bridge, and you can figure out how to pass it to *Timberwolf*."

O'Hara nodded. "Do it," he told them. "I'm passing the word to Fleet, but as far out as we are, it'll be more than an hour before anyone gets the message."

* * *

Home Ship—Otuka 2429th Clan

The Otuka had nothing in their culture that could be called religion. They built no altars, prayed to no deity, and had no belief in any sort of afterlife.

Philosophically, they considered the entire Universe to be a living organism, and they often spoke of it in that context, but recognizing the scale of it, they reasoned that the Universe had little regard for the infinitesimal creatures that lived within it. For that matter, an entire galaxy was little more than a single cell in a very complex structure. There was no point in worshiping the Universe. The Universe didn't care whether it was worshipped or not. There was no point in saying prayers because the Universe wasn't listening.

A'archa reflected that the Universe seemed to have a cruel sense of humor. What were the chances he would carry this bold mission almost to completion, without the tiniest problem, only to find not one, but two, enemy ships directly in his path? If there had only been one, his falnor-ka could have distracted it long enough for him to escape. But two of them—and from the mass and energy signatures he was reading, two of the fast, deadly attack ships that had wreaked such havoc on the Otuka swarms—would brush his raiders aside and go directly for his more vulnerable home ship. Fortunately, he had been proceeding with caution and had not built up a great deal of out-system velocity. He came to a stop relative to them, but they blocked his path, no matter which way he turned.

And yet, there was something unusual about their formation. One ship stood out in front, facing him, while the other remained well to the rear. In fact, they were aligned like he was, with his falnor-ka in front, protecting the home ship. He decided to try an experiment. He sent three of his raiders on a roundabout course to circle the first ship and approach the second. His suspicions were confirmed when the nearer of the human ships immediately moved to block the approach, putting itself between the raiders and the second ship. His ships continued to advance but had not gotten anywhere near their weapons range when, suddenly, the human ship launched a salvo of eight of the missile weapons A'archa had seen used against the upstart tsan in his last encounter.

He had expected as much and had ordered his raiders to break off the approach if fired upon. Two of the falnor-ka veered sharply away from the line of approach, while the third flipped and reversed course as rapidly as its drive would allow. A'archa watched in dismay as the missiles—three for each of the ships that had turned aside—executed a sharp change of course to pursue their targets. The two remaining missiles continued to pursue the ship that had reversed course.

As the missiles closed within beam weapon range, the raider gunners tried frantically to hit them, but they started twisting and turning in random patterns that made them difficult to track. The gunners hit one, but the remainder reached their attack distance and detonated, sending energy beams stabbing into the raider ships. The beams were more powerful than any shipboard weapon could be. A'archa nodded in understanding. The missiles must carry laser rods deployed around a warhead that would produce an incredible, instantaneous flash of energy, most likely a thermonuclear explosion. That energy would destroy the rods, but not before they lased with enough power to slice through his ships as if their hulls were nothing more than thin fabric. One of the raiders spewed debris and atmosphere then went dead in space, reduced to a tumbling hulk. Another vanished in a brilliant flash as the beams found its power plant.

The third raider—the one that had reversed course—fared better. The two missiles pursuing it apparently reached their range limit, for they detonated farther away from the target than the others had done. More importantly, the beams they produced had to pass through the intense gravity wake to the rear of the fleeing ship, which degraded them to some degree. The raider took damage, but it managed to escape.

An expensive experiment, A'archa decided, *but a successful one. I am now certain the second human ship is a non-combatant.* He began issuing orders to his crews.

* * *

LFS *Timberwolf*—Engaging the Otuka Raiders

"Your comments, Mr. Asher?" Rob O'Hara queried.

"That was a really timid approach, sir," Asher responded. "I would have expected them to try to run when they first saw us or to come at us full-tilt boogie with everything they've got."

"My thoughts exactly," O'Hara agreed. "It cost them two ships, and I think we got a piece of the third one, but that still leaves ten more they can throw at us, so let's not get too pleased with ourselves."

Asher turned his attention to his weapons console and nodded with satisfaction. *Timberwolf* was as ready as she would ever be.

"We can get off at least two salvos before they come into beam range, maybe three if we fall back as soon as they head this way. My biggest concern is that they'll split up, sending some to keep us busy while others go for *Randall*."

"If so, we may have to take it to them," O'Hara acknowledged. "If they don't, I'm content to hold the fort and let them go on their way."

"Uh oh, it's starting." Asher turned his attention to the tactical display as the enemy ships began to approach again. "What the hell? Sir, they're going wide this time. They seem to be trying to get around us without coming into missile range, but they are doing it pretty damned slowly. We know those little raider ships are faster than that."

"Right, and only the raider ships are moving. The big ship is holding position. Helm, bring us around. Keep us between them and *Randall*, but don't close the range on them."

"Jennifer…" He keyed the channel to *Lisa Randall.*

"I see it," Tanaka acknowledged. "I assume you want us to stay directly in your shadow, relative to them. Just remember, I've got a pair of hot Vipers back here, ready to go if you need them."

"I know," he told her, "and I hope you never have to use them."

* * *

Home Ship—Otuka 2429th Clan

A'archa watched as the human ships reacted as he predicted. The protector—obviously a warship—moved cautiously to shield the other ship from his raiders. He could have made it more difficult by ordering the falnor-ka to disperse more widely but concentrating them guaranteed they would keep the guardian's attention. When the timing was right—when the warship was drawn as far away as possible—he would make his move.

It was a tricky maneuver. He needed to get past the human ships as quickly as possible, but he also needed to stay far enough away from the non-combatant that they would not perceive him as a threat, that they would clearly recognize an attempt on his part to escape, without engaging. If the warship moved in his direction, his raiders were ordered to press forward in an all-up attack.

He gave the order, and his home ship drove forward at its maximum acceleration, which was somewhat less than the raiders could manage, and probably much less than the human ships could do. Hopefully, they would not attempt to pursue. His course would take him wide around the side away from his raiders, out of range of the warship's missiles. He was cutting it close to the non-combatant, but far enough out that they should realize his weapons were no threat.

So far, there was no reaction. The humans appeared to be watching his falnor-ka carefully, paying little attention to his non-threatening home ship. He hoped the second human ship really was a non-combatant, but even if it was not, he would be past it quickly, allowing it only a narrow window in which to…

* * *

LRS *Lisa Randall*

"Fire!" Jennifer Tanaka ordered.

* * *

Home Ship—Otuka 2429th Clan

A'archa recoiled in horror as the supposed non-combatant hurled a pair of deadly missiles at him at precisely the moment when the range was shortest. But he had learned something from the earlier experiment, and he ordered his helmsman to turn directly away from the oncoming missiles.

To his dismay, it appeared the enemy had learned something as well. The two missiles angled away from each other in an obvious attempt to get a shot at him from both sides, where they would not be shooting through the gravitational shielding his drive provided. As the missiles closed within beam range, his gunners opened fire, but by then, the tiny, fast-moving targets were twisting and turning, evading all attempts to hit them.

A'archa finally got a break, his gunners destroyed one of the missiles. He immediately ordered his ship to turn directly away from the other one. He was just in time, as the remaining missile reached its attack range and detonated. Despite the shielding from the drive field, the powerful beam drove hard into the aft section of his ship. Damage alarms screamed at him, and he felt a lurch as some of his drive components failed. His ship's acceleration dropped significantly but didn't fail completely. With some surprise, he noted he was still alive, his ship was still moving away from the enemy, and he was out of range of their weapons. More importantly, they had chosen not to pursue him. His falnor-ka had passed the warship and were now angling toward him on a converging course, leaving the troublesome humans behind.

With a snort of relief, he uncurled his horns and flexed his shoulders and all four hips—remarkable how one tended to tense up in moments like these—and ordered a course directly to the hyper limit at the best acceleration his damaged drive could manage.

* * *

LRS *Lisa Randall*

"They're getting away," Carla remarked in disgust, as she watched the Otuka ships recede. For the duration of the encounter, Jennifer Tanaka had patched *Randall's* tactical display into the big screen in Mission Control, so Carla and the scientists could see what was happening.

"Indeed, they are," Rob O'Hara remarked, "and that's OK with me for the moment." O'Hara's image shared the split screen with Tanaka's on Carla's console.

"Me too," Tanaka agreed. "I thought it would bother me to let them go, but vengeance wears thin after a while. And *Lisa* got a piece of them. How many research ships can put *that* in their logs?"

"Nice shooting, Jen," O'Hara admitted, "but please don't do that again."

Tanaka favored him with an unrepentant grin, and after a moment, he returned it.

"OK, folks, the show's over, and we can stand down," he said. "I suggest you all take a break, then get back to your mission. Let me know when you're ready to resume."

* * *

"Oh, shit!"

Jennifer Tanaka looked up sharply at the exclamation from her navigation and tactical officer and immediately noticed a major change in the tactical display. She had just broken the connection with *Timberwolf* and had ordered her crew to stand down from battle stations. The receding Otuka ships were still visible at extreme range, but what got her attention was something beyond that…just beyond the system's hyper limit, in fact.

"'Oh, shit' is not a proper report, Ensign. Talk to me."

* * *

LFS *Timberwolf*

On *Timberwolf's* bridge, Rob O'Hara was getting more useful information.

"Hyper signature! Multiple hyper signatures! Captain, I'm looking at sixty-plus individual sources, twenty or more in the capital ship range, three of them battlecruiser size," Lieutenant Asher reported, tensely.

O'Hara pondered the display for a moment.

"Hit them with IFF," he ordered.

"Sir?" Asher was taken aback. He had expected an immediate return to battle stations.

"We're just a hole in space right now, Ash. They can't see us at this distance, and besides, when have we ever seen the Otuka be that precise about anything?"

"That was a textbook fleet-level translation," he continued, waving a hand at the display, "and they came out in battle order—destroyer screen out front, heavies right behind, light cruisers and more destroyers to the rear to cover their six. These people are ready to kick ass and take names. That's no mob of donkey-boys."

* * *

LRS *Lisa Randall*

On *Lisa Randall's* bridge, Jennifer Tanaka had reached the same conclusion, and her expectations were confirmed as *Timberwolf's* IFF query produced results. Icons changed from yellow to green, and individual ship IDs began to appear. Topping the list were three LFS battlecruisers: *Isis*, *Nike*, and *Valkyrie*, the last showing a fleet flagship icon.

In *Randall's* Mission Control Center, Carla was studying the same display.

"Hi, Mom," she muttered. "Glad you could join us."

* * *

Home Ship—Otuka 2429th Clan

The Universe wasn't done toying with him yet, A'archa realized, and this time, no amount of cleverness was going to save him. In fact, he had already been detected and was being scanned by a variety of sensor systems—human origin and unfamiliar technology, but of obvious purpose.

He was a target of interest for no less than twenty heavy warships that were converging on him with rates of acceleration he couldn't hope to match. His falnor-ka were rushing to rejoin him and would arrive before the enemy came into range, but that was little comfort. If the accounts were correct, the human force in front of him was more powerful than the one that had shredded the entire Otuka swarm.

Surrender was unthinkable, or it was supposed to be unthinkable, for an Otuka tsan. Depending on the magnitude of the dishonor incurred, as determined by the Council, his falnor might be declared outcast and subject to destruction or might simply suffer a demotion in ranking of a hundred thousand levels or so. That presumed he survived the revolt among his falnor-katan that might happen if he suggested surrendering to the humans.

A'archa was a pragmatist of the first order, and his self-preservation instincts were high. His chance of surviving a battle against the forces he saw before him was absolutely zero. His chance of surviving the wrath of his own kind if he surrendered was not much better. But what if he didn't surrender? What if he refused battle and demanded a truce with the humans until an appropriate agreement could be reached?

Of course, there was no incentive for the humans to accept a truce, but such agreements had been negotiated by other tsans with other races. Sometimes, the agreement was even of benefit to the falnor in question. The 487th was well-known for its informal contract with several of the reptile clans under which the Akara quietly paid tribute for safe passage on certain routes for their commercial shipping.

A'archa had little hope for that kind of agreement with the humans, assuming they were even willing to negotiate. At best, he might escape with his life. At worst, they would reduce him and his ships to component atoms without a second thought.

He had one point in his favor. So far, his ships had not fired a single offensive shot. He could claim, if he could find a way to communicate with them, that he and his followers were non-combatants, simple commercial operators who had no connection to the Otuka who had given the humans so much trouble. Of course, once his ships reformed around him, he would need to make certain they did not fire on any human ship that approached. That might be a bit tricky since their normal mode of operation was to try to fight their way out of any predicament.

His brain raced to fill in the details of what was, so far, a nebulous plan based on a slim hope. The only thing he knew for certain was that he should take no action, just form up his ships, shut down their drives, sensors, and anything else the humans might regard as hostile, and wait. No, he was not going to surrender; he was going to open a dialogue with the humans, to negotiate, to make some sort of business arrangement.

Now, if he could just convince his followers. Hopefully their own instinct for self-preservation would inspire them to believe. He'd worry about convincing the Council later.

* * * * *

Chapter Eleven

LFS *Valkyrie*—Outer Reaches of the New Eden System

Fleet Admiral Lorna Greenwood regarded the three visitors in her day cabin with hard, humorless scrutiny—a look that usually reduced junior officers to visible nervousness, punctuated by profuse perspiration. These three, however, were not sweating, nor did they appear agitated, which meant they believed they had done well and stood by their actions. After a moment, Lorna nodded in satisfaction.

"I've reviewed the results of your engagement," she told them, "and I believe that a 'well done' is in order. Mr. O'Hara, I cannot find a single flaw in your tactical planning and execution. You can pass my personal compliments on to your crew as you see fit. As for you, Ms. Tanaka, I'm willing to accept your explanation for opening fire on the larger enemy ship. I'm inclined to think he was trying to get past you without engagement, but you couldn't be certain of that, and he was within the Viper's attack envelope.

"More importantly, the damage you did to him is what kept him from reaching the hyper limit before my force arrived—a fortuitous benefit since you had no idea we were coming, but I'll take it."

She continued, "I'm curious to know what you would have done had he chosen to engage. *Timberwolf* was busy with the other enemy ships, so you would have been on your own."

Tanaka didn't flinch.

"The designers saw fit to equip *Lisa Randall* with the latest in military-grade loading racks," she replied. "I'm quite confident I could have shoved at least six more Vipers down his throat before he got into beam range. Besides, we had a pretty clear escape path directly in-system for both *Timberwolf* and *Randall.* If they had been stupid enough to pursue, they'd have been wading through a missile barrage all the way in."

"Do you concur, Commander?" Lorna turned her attention to Rob O'Hara.

"Yes, ma'am," he replied. "We hadn't discussed it, but I was thinking the same thing regarding an escape route. If things had gone to hell, we could have executed that option in a heartbeat."

"OK, case closed, commendations all around." Lorna nodded and turned her attention to the third visitor. "As for you, young lady, mark your calendar. As soon as you get back to Luna, you have a date with Fleet BuWeaps, where you will explain to them in excruciating detail how that field-mapping array of yours works."

"M…Admiral," Carla managed to catch herself, but she noticed a hint of a smirk from both Tanaka and O'Hara, who would no doubt have been amused to hear the Fleet's top officer referred to as Mom.

"That setup was designed for research," she protested, "not for military applications."

"Which doesn't mean it doesn't have any military applications," Lorna insisted. "You were able to detect ships operating in stealth mode at over 30 million kilometers—about half the distance from Earth to Mars at opposition. That'll get Fleet's attention, and if you don't go see them, they'll come looking for you. I'll make sure they do.

"Besides," she added, showing the hint of a smile, "it might even make me forget how upset I was about being forced to let you come out here in the first place."

"Excuse me, ma'am," Jennifer Tanaka said. "If I'm not stepping out of line, can I ask what's happening with the captured Otuka ships?"

"You're not out of line, Commander—" Lorna's smile became more noticeable, "—but I don't have much to tell you. We're still trying to figure out what to do with the little present you've given us."

* * *

Home Ship—Otuka 2429th Clan

A'archa reclined at his command station, legs folded beneath him, arms crossed over his chest, admiring the view on the large screen at the forward end of the bridge compartment. *Who would have believed humans were capable of such artistry?* he wondered. Until they moved in close, the human warships had been nothing but icons on a tactical display, but now, he had visual imagery and was amazed to find those warships were decorated, much of their forward hull surface covered with vivid, full color, pictorial artwork. No two of them were alike, and while some showed humans—mostly portrayed as heroic warriors, both male and female—others depicted strange, fierce-looking beasts. Some might be actual predatory animals, but he suspected others were creatures from human mythology.

It was an epiphany. A'archa could not have been more surprised if some food animal had started reciting poetry while being slaughtered. In this case, of course, the food animals might well be planning to slaughter him, and the very idea gave A'archa pause. Was it possible the humans had poetry as well? Did they tell heroic stories to their fellows of past exploits? He considered this quite calmly, considering his recent encounters with these strange non-typical humans.

He had pulled his ships into a tight formation, brought them to a stationary position relative to the primary, and shut everything down. As expected, the humans had closed to within the range of their missile weapons and swept his ships with a variety of active sensor scans—primarily targeting, he assumed. But they had not fired on him. Someone over there was apparently willing to hold fire and give him an opportunity to avoid annihilation. He waited, and they continued to scan his ships to the point where he imagined they had all their weapons precisely dialed in and could wipe out his entire force with a single, overwhelming salvo.

He noted they seemed to be paying particular attention to the aft portion of his home ship, where the exposed drive components were particularly vulnerable. There was a message there: *Don't try to run away*. He thought about testing them by ordering one of his falnor-ka to get under way, to move casually in the direction of the hyper limit. He decided not to try it. He had already lost two of his raiders and wasn't willing to risk another on the tiny chance the humans might let it depart.

Having satisfied themselves A'archa's ships were properly targeted, the humans made the next move, which again, was perfectly predictable—just what he would have done in their situation. They sent small craft, launched from one of the largest warships, to his home ship in an obvious bid to board him. Not wanting them to blow holes in his hull, he opened his boat bay doors. Three of them immediately accepted the invitation and entered, settling down in the open deck space he had obligingly cleared for them. There, they disgorged a substantial force of armed and armored humans, who immediately set up a defensive perimeter around their landing craft.

Again, A'archa was surprised. The humans were organized and disciplined, not just warriors but soldiers, well-trained and practiced, a formidable force to be reckoned with. He felt a tinge of envy, for while he considered his own minions to be more obedient and orderly than those of most Otuka clans, in battle, they were more of a horde to be unleashed than a force to be commanded. For that reason, he had ordered most of the home ship's crew to remain in quarters and avoid contact with the human boarders. Those required to be on duty were ordered to tend to their work, ignore the humans if possible, and make no aggressive movements.

He ordered the boat bay doors closed and the compartment repressurized. He was more confident now, believing the humans would not see this as a trap, but as a welcoming gesture. He knew his ship's atmosphere was perfectly breathable to humans, but he was not surprised when none of them chose to open their vacuum-capable suits. They were willing to extend a certain amount of trust, but they were not stupid.

He ordered one of the interior access hatches opened, revealing two of his most trusted subordinates, standing unarmed with their hands open in front of them, obviously offering no threat. He had chosen these two with care—his most trustworthy and obedient underlings who could be counted upon to follow orders. They were valued members of his inner circle, and he really hoped the humans wouldn't kill them.

They didn't. In fact, they picked up immediately on the beckoning gestures the two Otuka made. One of the humans, obviously a leader, came forward, but not before selecting several heavily-armed subordinates to accompany him. He allowed A'archa's minions to lead his party to the main longitudinal corridor of the ship, then forward to the bridge compartment where A'archa waited to receive them.

When they entered the compartment, they found A'archa reclining on the elevated platform of his command station, surrounded by his console and status displays. He had attired himself in his most formal harness, which sparkled with jewels and the badges and banners of his exalted rank. He wanted to be sure there was no question in the minds of the humans about who was in charge.

The human leader approached, giving no indication he was impressed by A'archa's imposing presence, and the other humans fanned out to cover the compartment with their lethal-looking weapons. Unperturbed, A'archa slowly and carefully picked up the data crystal that had been lying on his console. Holding it so it could not be mistaken for a weapon—or so he hoped—he extended it and made gestures for the human to take it. After a moment, the human shrugged, stepped forward, and accepted the offering. As he did so, A'archa spoke.

"Here are the terms under which we will deal with you," he declared. "Take it to your leaders. I await your reply." With that, he made a dismissive gesture, indicating the humans were now free to leave.

He knew they had no way of understanding what he said. Even if they knew the Otuka common tongue, he had spoken in clan dialect, the language spoken only aboard the ships of his own falnor. Every

Otuka knew the common tongue, but every clan had its own unique language as well. A'archa's spoken directive to the human was nothing but a show put on for his crew to convince them he was still in charge, still not surrendering, was in fact negotiating a business arrangement with the humans.

He also did not expect the humans to interpret the message on the data crystal. Even if they understood the technology, the message was again recorded in the clan language. Several of his subordinates had been present when he recorded it and would spread the word to others aboard the ship. The crystal would also offer the humans an enigma, something that might cause them to pause and allow him and his falnor to continue to exist for a time. In the end, that was its real purpose.

The humans left his bridge but sent others of their kind on a survey of the ship. They moved carefully with weapons ready, but there were no incidents. Then the humans deployed several small devices about knee-high to an Otuka—squat, cylindrical, dull grey machines that stood upright on stubby legs. They positioned them in key areas of the ship, including one on his bridge. They left the devices in place and went back to the boat bay. As soon as they were gone, A'archa summoned his chief engineer to examine the device.

"My Lord, the technology is unfamiliar," the engineer said, "but we can assume it is a surveillance machine. There is a small lens here, atop this moveable turret, which allows it to swivel in any direction. It is probably a camera that allows them to watch us. Other than that, I do not know what it contains. Perhaps it is a destructive device they can trigger at will. I have warned my subordinates not to touch it. The humans seemed to indicate, by gestures, that the devices were not to be disturbed."

A'archa doubted the machines were intended to destroy anything. The humans had enough firepower to wipe out his entire falnor in an instant, without resorting to such measures. But they might be designed to self-destruct if tampered with, so he ordered his crew to leave the things alone.

Then the humans departed or, at least, most of them did. Two of the craft closed, lifted off the deck, and pointed themselves toward the bay doors, a clear signal they wanted to leave. He depressurized the bay and opened the doors, and the two craft departed. The third craft remained in place, so he closed the doors again and brought the pressure back up. Then, he settled down to wait, passing the time by composing short verses to describe the hull artwork of each of the human ships surrounding him.

* * *

LFS *Valkyrie*

"All right, Val, bring us up to date on what you've found so far."

Lorna Greenwood had detached two of her battle groups and sent them in-system to reinforce the battered Double Deuce. She made a point of leaving Amy Ling in command of the force at New Eden, though Tom Sakura, aboard *Isis*, outranked her. It was a vote of confidence the officers and crews of the Double Deuce would appreciate, a silent 'well done' to all of them. Lorna had also considered Ling's experience fighting the Otuka. Tommy hadn't led a group in actual combat since the war against the Mekota more than two decades ago. She discussed it with him before the redeployment, and he had no problem. He had called Ling personally to place the two groups under her command.

That gave Amy Ling command of the better part of an entire fleet. She'd repaired her existing force and was finally able to send the most badly damaged ships back to Luna, including the ravaged battlecruiser *Medusa*. At Admiral Greenwood's request, she had also dispatched one of her courier boats to rendezvous with *Valkyrie* in the outer system and bring Mercedes Warren out from New Eden. Not only was Warren the most knowledgeable person available regarding the Otuka, but she was also experienced with First Contact situations, having been involved in humanity's first face-to-face meetings with both the Mekota and the Akara.

Now, Warren was aboard *Valkyrie*, in Admiral Greenwood's day cabin, with Carla, who had come over from *Lisa Randall*. The fourth person in attendance was *Valkyrie*'s captain, Commodore Ian McPherson.

"We've made significant progress in a number of areas," Val began, her clear soprano voice seeming to come from mid-air as she spoke through the ship's audio systems. Her avatar, in the lower corner of the large screen, was the ship's coat of arms, rather than the warrior woman animation she used for personal conversations. For the moment, the rest of the screen displayed a visual of the large Otuka ship.

"We've got a general overview of Otuka technology, based on external scans and data provided by the sentry 'bots aboard the alien ship. There are no surprises, and, while they appear to have well-engineered systems, they aren't up to our level in nanoelectronics or information technology. On the other hand, they appear to have very sophisticated environmental systems—something our people would like to study in greater detail. Atmospheric recycling, in particular, seems to be an area where they get better throughput than we do, with less massive equipment."

"On that subject, the atmospheric mix aboard their ships is within the breathable range for humans, with twenty-three percent oxygen and seventy-four percent nitrogen, and mostly inert gases for the rest. Carbon monoxide and dioxide are well below toxic levels. There were no harmful airborne organisms in the air samples brought back by the Marines."

"So," Carla speculated, "if the Marines need to go back and kick ass, they can do it without pressure suits."

"Not a good idea," McPherson told her. "In a boarding action, you assume the enemy controls the environmental systems and can introduce toxins or depressurize compartments as a defensive measure. That's what I would do if someone tried to board *Valkyrie*."

"Actually," Lorna remarked, "we did something like that during the battle for Copper Hills. The Mekota were trying to board us, and we blew the doors off the boat bay. Blasted a few hundred of them into space. That's the only time an LFS warship has ever been boarded, and it didn't go very well for the enemy. But I digress...continue, please, Val."

"Yes, Admiral. I mentioned that they are limited in nanoelectronics and information technology, but it appears the object they presented to Lieutenant Collins on their bridge is a data storage device. It's a solid crystal of beryl aluminum silicate—in effect, a synthetic emerald—with the data content encoded into the crystal's structure. Its purpose is obvious, though our engineers haven't been able to determine how they manufacture the crystals or manipulate the structure to store the data. Commander Wilcox would like us to question them about it. Interpretation of the data was a simple task.

While the Otuka use a decimal numbering system, they have discovered the advantages of binary encoding for information technology. The data contained in the crystal is represented in strings of two-state structures, which can be treated as zeros and ones for our purposes. Once we recognized that, only a little further analysis was required to determine that what we actually had was a digitized audio recording."

"Really?" Warren was surprised. "You mean an actual voice recording—a verbal message, spoken by an Otuka?"

"Precisely, Doctor," the AI replied. "But that brings us to the part of our research that is going more slowly—learning their language. We have to rely on the audio-visual feeds coming to us from the sentry 'bots, and we don't have any control over the content. We have to wait until an Otuka speaks to another Otuka near one of the 'bots, then try to interpret what was said, based on the context and actions shown in the video. It's a slow process, and our Otuka vocabulary is severely limited. Once we have a sufficient base, we can attempt to speak to them through the 'bots, assuming the admiral authorizes us to do so. If we can get a basic conversation going, we can learn their language much more quickly."

"How soon will you be ready to do that?" Lorna inquired.

"At the current rate of progress, we will need at least forty more hours of observation, assuming they don't suddenly stop talking to each other."

"Fine. Go ahead and begin a conversation at your discretion, Val. Just let me know when you start. Mercedes, I know you're itching to talk to them, but I suggest you let Val handle it initially. She knows what we need to do to facilitate learning their language. Once she's fluent, you can take over the conversation and start your research. I'll also give you a list of questions I would like answered, so I can decide what to do with these creatures."

* * *

Home Ship—Otuka 2429th Clan

"Most Exalted One..."

A'archa was startled and looked up from his console to see who had dared to address him without first approaching with bowed head and waiting to be recognized. The ship was not under combat conditions, and there was no emergency. Such abrupt and discourteous interruptions were not to be tolerated.

Both crewmembers on duty were staring open-mouthed, not at him, but at the alien device that had become a fixture on the bridge. With a shock, he realized neither of them had spoken, that the voice had come from the device.

"Speak!" he ordered, just as he would have commanded one of his crew.

"Question: You are tsan of—incomprehensible alien word—and you are Exalted One?"

"I am A'archa Riobost'galan," he snarled, defiantly, "and I am tsan of this falnor. I am properly addressed as Exalted One, and no other form of address will be tolerated!"

He noted, with satisfaction, that his crewmembers had covered their eyes and bowed their heads at his outburst, trembling, as they should, in fear of his displeasure. The alien device, however, did not seem to be impressed.

"Understood. I speak for—unpronounceable alien name—tsan of—another alien word. We speak with you. We try to learn language. More speak, faster learn. Do you understand?"

A'archa understood. The devices, or the humans who controlled them, had been listening to him and his crew speak and had been watching them for quite a few cycles. That was why they were now speaking to him in the language of the falnor, not the common Otuka tongue. He was amazed that they had been able to reach this point so quickly, but he could not allow his amazement to show.

"Very well," he acknowledged, as if taking a report from a subordinate. "I have no time for you until you have learned to speak properly."

"You!" he pointed at one of the bridge crew. "Talk to this thing. Teach it to speak the tongue of the falnor and make sure it knows how to address me with proper respect. Advise me when it is suitably prepared, and I will speak with it then."

With that, he got up from his command couch, stalked off the bridge, and went directly to his private quarters. Once there, he activated his visual display and keyed it to observe the bridge, where his minion was haltingly attempting to talk to the device. He wanted to watch the process, but there were appearances to maintain. Under no circumstances could he allow his crew to think he was not firmly in control. He keyed the display again and switched to views of other parts of the ship, where other human devices had been placed. The devices were silent, and his crewmembers were going about their business. There was no unusual activity in the landing bay, where one human craft remained on guard.

So, he mused, the humans knew who was in charge and wished to speak to him directly. Things appeared to be going as well as he wished. He keyed the display again and went back to watching the crewman on the bridge talking to the human machine.

* * *

LRS *Lisa Randall*

"We've learned quite a bit, Dr. Warren," Val explained. "The Otuka leader, or whatever you wish to call him, detailed a crewmember to work with us, to teach us the language. From that point, it went quickly. The admiral says you may begin your discussions with them. We've also translated the message on the data crystal the leader gave to the Marines."

"Really?" Mercedes Warren looked at Carla, who shared her enthusiasm. The two of them were in *Randall's* Mission Control center with Bjorn and Judah Rothstein when the call from the flagship's AI came in.

"Yes. Extracting the data wasn't difficult once we understood the technology, but the language of the message was somewhat complex. It required time working with the Otuka translator to understand its structure and acquire an adequate vocabulary.

"In summary, the message says they have no hostile intentions toward us or anyone else, and that they are exercising a right of salvage which is common practice among spacefaring races. They claim to have no connection with the Otuka who exploited New Eden. They accuse us of obstructing their legitimate activities and attacking them without provocation, and they point out that, at no time, did they act against us, nor did they fire weapons, except at our incoming missiles to protect themselves. They demand the right to proceed about their business without delay, and they threaten unspecified unfortunate consequences if we do not allow them to depart."

"Seriously?" Carla suppressed a grin. "'There will be unfortunate consequences if you eat me,' said the mouse to the cat."

"While your analogy may be appropriate, Doctor," Val replied, "the admiral says they have a valid argument. Their actions in the recent engagement with *Timberwolf* and *Randall* might have appeared hostile, given the current situation in this system, but we can't prove hostile intent. Further, for centuries, on Earth, there have been protocols regarding salvage on the open sea, protocols not very different from those described in this message."

"You mean, we're going to let them go?" Bjorn spoke up for the first time. "With their ships full of salvage taken from the battle wreckage, including some that may have come from LFS warships?"

"The admiral is not inclined to be that lenient," the AI advised. "She intends to invoke a protocol of her own, involving people who knowingly enter a war zone without permission for purposes of profit. The protocol may not exist yet, in terms of common practices among spacefaring races, but if it doesn't, she intends to set a precedent.

"She plans to order our engineers, accompanied by Marines, to thoroughly inspect everything in their cargo holds. If they find any of our technology we don't want them to have—or for that matter, any of their technology we'd like to have—she intends to confiscate it. Other than that, yes, she has indicated that, without evidence of any crime, she may have to let them go."

"Damn!" Rothstein muttered. "After all they've done to the Edies and to our people here."

"Not to mention the people on *Summer Solstice*," Carla added. Just thinking about it put a knot in her stomach.

Jennifer Tanaka had come into the compartment shortly after Val's briefing began, and she spoke up for the first time.

"Well, that's the point, isn't it?" she said. "They—the ones we are talking to—aren't the ones who did it. We have no proof they're associated with the Otuka who exploited the Edies or attacked our ships.

"Look, people," she continued, "I've suffered my own loss. My twin sister was eaten by the bastards. But those bastards are all dead now, and I see Admiral Greenwood's point. We can't tar all of the Otuka with the same brush."

"She's right," Mercedes Warren agreed. "And I, for one, would like to think there actually are some civilized Otuka out there, some we can deal with peacefully, for mutual benefit."

"I don't know." Carla was still unconvinced. "My mother always told me my other mother, Carla Perry, felt that way about the Mekota when the LFS first encountered them. She died in that encounter, on what was supposed to be a mission of peace. For all we know, this Otuka leader is just as bad as the rest of them but is trying to fast-talk his way out of the situation, relying on our general ignorance of the Otuka."

"You are also correct, Doctor Greenwood," Val told her, "but, unfortunately, there is no way to prove that hypothesis. At this point—"

"At this point, I need to start talking to them," Warren interjected. "I'll try to get some answers to the admiral's questions and see if I can learn more about the Otuka. Maybe I can come up with something that will help us decide whether they're telling the truth."

"Perhaps you can, Doctor," Val agreed. "For your information, our analysis of the Otuka language indicates a human could learn to speak it—not comfortably, perhaps, since it would involve significant stress on human vocal apparatus, but it could be done. Conversely, an Otuka could probably learn to speak standard Lunar English, though their vocal apparatus would have difficulty with certain phonemes, such as the hard 'k' and the digraph 'sh.' Nonetheless, the result should be intelligible to an English-speaking human.

"You don't have time to learn their language, and they have shown no interest in learning ours, so I will continue to serve as an interpreter. However, the language I have learned here may not be the only Otuka language, nor even the most common one. I've run across references to a universal Otuka language, with indications that the language spoken here is the language of their tribe or clan."

"That might be important," Warren mused. "If nothing else, it might support their claim that they are not associated with the Otuka we've been fighting."

"It is a point in their favor," the AI agreed. "There is one other item of interest. The message on the crystal was in the voice of the one we identified as the leader or commanding officer, but it had characteristics we have not found in normal Otuka speech. It had a certain measure or rhythm to it, and the choice of words seemed to indicate a deliberate effort to maintain that rhythm, along with a degree of rhyme. In short, it wasn't just a speech, it was more like a song or a poem. I find that interesting, though I can find no logical reason for it."

* * *

LFS *Sorceress*—New Eden Orbit

"Sit down, Mr. O'Hara. At ease. Smoke if you've got 'em."

Rob O'Hara thought Admiral Ling was fortunate the harmful effects of tobacco had been overcome decades ago. In her quarters, in briefing rooms, and even on the flag bridge, Ling was rarely without a cigarette in her hand or mouth.

Once the health issues, including smoke allergies, had been overcome, smoking had regained popularity and was again socially acceptable, but aboard LFS Navy warships, there were strict controls as to when and where crewmembers could smoke. In Ling's case, however, when and where seemed to include wherever the admiral was, whenever she was there. Her engineers joked—when not in her presence—that LFS *Sorceress* had been equipped with an enhanced internal ventilation system just to cope with the admiral's habit. O'Hara didn't know how much truth there was to the rumor, but he noticed the smoke didn't seem to go very far. Although he was sitting in front of Ling's desk, he couldn't smell it.

"You've distinguished yourself on no less than three occasions in this campaign, Commander," Ling began. "You conducted low-orbit attacks in two separate battles, once to achieve air superiority on New Eden, then again in support of ground operations. In both cases, *Timberwolf's* gunnery was textbook perfect in mission scenarios we'd never envisioned for a destroyer. Then I send you off to babysit a shipload of scientists, and you end up kicking ass on a small squadron of Otuka and taking the only Otuka prisoners we've captured in the whole campaign. Your name keeps popping up in my reports. What do you think I ought to do about that?"

O'Hara was a bit nervous. With the arrival of First Fleet, he'd been relieved of responsibility for *Lisa Randall* and sent back in-system to rejoin the Double Deuce. Almost as soon as he'd arrived at the New Eden anchorage, he'd been summoned aboard *Sorceress* for a meeting with the admiral.

Ling tended to deliver both praise and criticism in the same direct, no-nonsense manner. It sounded like she was offering praise at the moment, but he couldn't help wondering if she was about to rip his head off for some monumental screw-up of which he was not yet aware.

"In fairness, ma'am," he replied, "I would never have thought to use a destroyer in orbit to achieve air superiority in the atmosphere. That was Colonel Bartley's call. I just followed orders."

"Right!" Ling told him. "You followed orders, without question and with perfect execution, using a brand-new tactic that had never been tested. You got it done in an orderly and proficient manner. And it was your action on that occasion that prompted me to detail Commander Winfree and Echo Group to support the Marines on the planet in the second battle, and why *Timberwolf* got assigned to that group when I had to abandon the orbitals. You ended up with a half-dozen Otuka ship kills to your credit, not to mention twenty-plus fire support missions for the dirtside Marines. Oh, and don't bother to tell me you were just doing your part for the team, because Winfree's already singled you out as the best of his bunch in that action."

"But I didn't actually capture the Otuka force in the outer system, ma'am," he protested. "They just happened to run into First Fleet while trying to make their escape."

"After you and Tanaka ripped them a new anal orifice," Ling asserted. "Quit protesting. You're a hard charger, and you'll go far in the fleet. Keep it up, and someday they'll take your ship away and stick you behind a desk like this one. In the meantime, however, I have to figure out what to do with you. If I give you the kind of recognition you deserve, there will be a bunch of people, ranging from HQ brass to the lowest-ranked deckhand, who will say I'm playing politics and sucking up to the CEO."

"Ma'am, I…" O'Hara reddened with embarrassment at being reminded he was the son of Luna's Chief Executive.

"Screw them," Ling decreed. "Most of them couldn't find their way to the head without a deck plan and AI assistance. I'm recommending five ships of the Double Deuce for Sword of the Fleet. Three of them were lost in battle. *Timberwolf* is one of the remaining two. If it goes through, you'll get a personal commendation in your file, as well as battle honors for your ship, and a lot of other skippers will turn green with envy. Deal with it."

* * *

LFS *Valkyrie*—Outer Reaches of the New Eden System

"Sorry to wake you, Admiral, but there is a matter that needs your attention."

Fleet Admiral Lorna Greenwood sat on the edge of the bed, rubbing the sleep from her eyes. At least, she reflected, Val's apologetic tone didn't seem to indicate any sort of end-of-the-universe crisis, or even anything as urgent as the *Summer Solstice* incident.

"I'm awake. I'm listening," she told the AI.

"Approximately two hours ago, Admiral Ling's outer-system security forces detected a hyper signature and moved to intercept. They have identified the unknown ships as Akara—a cruiser and two frigate-class warships. The cruiser answered their query with a high-level diplomatic code, indicating the personal envoy of Heart of the Copper Hills."

"Really? Hmmm…that's interesting."

"Yes, but that alone would not have given me sufficient reason to disturb your sleep. When the Akara established communications, their envoy, identified as Special Speaker for Heart of the Copper Hills, asked to speak with the senior officer in command of our forces here. Special Speaker is well-known to the LFS and to you. He is the former commander of the Copper Hills Fleet, former Military Liaison and Ambassador to the LFS, and I believe, a very old friend of yours. You last encountered him at your daughter's wedding reception."

"Old War Lizard? What the hell is he doing here?"

"I have no further information, Admiral."

"Right…well, technically, Admiral Ling is the S.O. for all system operations, and I'm just an observer, but Amy has enough on her plate without dealing with diplomacy issues. Advise her that I will take that little problem off her hands and have her direct the Akara ships to meet us out here."

"Yes, Admiral. That's all I have. Sorry to disturb you."

"Not your fault. It was the right call, but it is 0330 hours. I'm going back to sleep. Advise me when you have an arrival time for our Lizard friends."

* * *

"I assure you, Warrior Queen, Heart of my Clan has no intention of interfering with your operations, nor does he presume to advise you how to proceed. I am only here as an observer, but I also have some information for you."

Lorna suppressed a smile. Akara had no names; they were addressed by a title which reflected their current position and status within their clan. To them, Lorna was Heart of the Warriors—supreme commander of the military—for the LFS, but this particular old lizard always insisted on calling her Warrior Queen, which was the title he'd given her when they first met. At the time, nearly three decades ago, she was the commanding officer of the Lunar Fleet and the chief executive of the LFS. He, on the other hand, had simply been the captain of an Akara scout ship, the first Akara ship to make contact with the humans of the Sol System.

"Heart of my Clan wishes me to tell you there is no longer a need to keep our discussions secret. He has advised the Hearts of the Combined Clans that he told you about the human population here and the way the Otuka were exploiting them. In fact, he told them that he had done so in the hope that you humans would confront the Otuka and, I believe the proper human expression is 'kick their asses,' a fate which he believes they truly deserve."

"He sent me to tell you he continues to support your efforts and to ask if we may provide assistance. He is willing to commit forces of the Copper Hills fleet if you require them. Not knowing I would find the Warrior Queen, herself, in this star system, he also sent a diplomatic courier to your home system to convey the same message to Heart of the Lunar Free State through our ambassador on Luna.

"Personally, I chose this side of the mission because it has been too long since I last ventured into space with a group of warships in search of a conflict. I am delighted to report the excitement of such a mission has not diminished over the years."

"It never does," Lorna assured him. "Actually, my reasons for being here aren't too much different than yours. I've spent too much time in orbit around Luna, and I wanted to get out here where the action is. I'm not really needed here. Admiral Ling has the military situation well in hand, without my help. She's the one who 'kicked their asses,' and I will be happy to give you the details, but meanwhile, you may be interested in seeing what I stumbled into on arrival. We've captured a small group of Otuka ships and have actually started talking with the crews. They are telling some interesting stories, and your presence may help me decide whether they are telling the truth."

"Captured?" Heart expressed surprise. "Are you saying they surrendered without a fight? I can't recall a single instance where an Otuka ship did that, let alone a group of them."

"Our experience has been the same, but this group is non-typical. I think you'll find this interesting."

* * *

Fleet HQ—Weapons Development Section—TerraNova City, Luna

"Excuse me, sir? Did you say, waste of time?" Vasquez tried to keep her voice level, masking the hurt surprise she was feeling.

"I think you'd better explain, Major." Jensen's tone was less guarded, openly challenging the Marine officer's comment.

"Sorry, Sergeant...Commander," Major Tully replied, "that didn't come out the way I meant it. You've proved your point with this project and demonstrated some amazing capabilities. With this system, Sergeant Vasquez can push a Raptor's envelope to the limit and carry out any mission more effectively and with greater precision than any ordinary pilot using existing control systems.

"My point is that we really don't need that kind of precision flying and fast reaction time for a typical Raptor mission. It might help you in an air combat situation, Sergeant, but let's be honest. A Raptor isn't designed for air combat. What I'm trying to say—and what I'm going to recommend in my evaluation—is that the Corps send you back to school to learn how to fly an Airwolf."

Vasquez blinked, opened her mouth to respond, then closed it again, trying to wrap her head around the idea.

"Whoa!" Lieutenant Commander Jensen reacted more quickly. He was an engineer, and even as he spoke, he was obviously calculating the impact of such a radical change in project parameters. He wasn't rejecting the idea but would need time to evaluate the consequences.

"I see a delay of at least six months," he told them. "We'd have to completely reconfigure the simulator, rewrite all of the interface software, and...hell...we'd need to spend a couple of weeks just figuring out all of the things we need to do just to get back to where we are."

"Sir," Vasquez said, carefully, "I'm afraid it's going to take longer than that, unless you plan on finding a new test pilot. It takes at least a year to train a pilot for air combat—a year after completion of basic flight school. First, you have to learn the aircraft. An Airwolf is a pretty fancy piece of machinery, and I'm sure there's lots of stuff a pilot needs to know just to keep it in the air and get from Point A to Point B. Then, there's Advanced Air Combat School, and that takes months, assuming a pilot can get through it. More than half wash out and end up somewhere else in a less demanding job. That's one of the reasons Airwolf pilots are all officers, while they let an ordinary noncom like me fly a Raptor. I think you need to find an experienced Airwolf jockey for the project."

She tried to keep her voice level, but the disappointment came through. Tully heard it and tried to think of a way to soften the blow.

"I disagree, Sergeant," Anna said. As with all such meetings, the AI who had replaced Val on the project was linked into the discussion. Vasquez hadn't developed the kind of personal relationship with her she had with Val, but she had to admit that Anna was a perfectly adequate substitute.

"Your time estimates would be correct for a newly-trained pilot," the AI agreed, "but you are already an experienced and capable Raptor pilot. In addition, the physical and neurological challenges you've already faced were considered and proved to be an asset in terms of your ability to learn the interface and adapt to it. At this point, however—assuming Major Tully's suggestion is adopted, and the project redirected accordingly—BuWeaps is faced with a difficult choice. On the one hand, they can send you back to school and teach you to fly an Airwolf. The classroom portion of your training could run concurrently with the conversion of the simulator and reprogramming of the interface, so the system would be ready by the time you started actual flight training. Obviously, your physical limitations would prevent you from flying an unmodified Airwolf or even training with a conventional simulator.

"They could choose an experienced Airwolf pilot, but they would need to find a suitable volunteer, someone with the right psychological profile to adapt to the new system, as well as the necessary piloting skills. Despite our experience with you, Sergeant, I'm not sure anyone knows exactly what profile to look for. If a qualified candidate is found, that person would have to go through surgery to implant the interface, then go through the same basic training you went through to learn to use it. Then, and only then, could the candidate start flight training in the reconfigured simulator. As you already know, that is very much like learning to fly all over again.

"You, on the other hand, have the right psychological profile, have already gone through the surgery, and have extensive experience with the basic operation of the interface. While we've been speaking, I have been modelling the two alternatives and have passed my model to Mike and Louis for review. Both agree my assumptions are valid, and my conclusions correct.

"The first option—retraining you to fly the Airwolf—would actually take no longer than the alternative, however, in terms of project cost and use of LFS resources, it would be far more cost-effective. In fact, discounting project costs already incurred, the second option—starting over with an experienced Airwolf pilot—would cost nearly twice as much. More importantly, the probability of overall success would be almost thirty percent higher with you as the test pilot. Commander Jensen, I will download the details of the model, the parameters considered, and the complete cost assessment to your personal project file for review."

"And that, ladies and gentlemen," Jensen told them, "is why it's best to have an AI involved in an engineering project of any importance. Major, what you're telling us makes sense, but it does hit us with a big change in project parameters. I think we can make a good case for it, but it has to be reviewed and approved by higher authority.

"Worst case, we go back to doing what we're doing with the Raptor interface, but I have a feeling the powers-that-be will look at the results so far and give us the go-ahead to start working on an Airwolf version. As for you, Sergeant, I think you can plan on being with us for a while, especially after they see Anna's cost analysis."

"And you'd better plan on going to OCS as well." Tully grinned at her. "Let them take your stripes away and pin some pretty gold bars on your collar instead."

"Attendance at OCS by Sergeant Vasquez was included in my analysis," Anna told them. "I assumed the Corps would not want to make an exception to its rank requirements for Airwolf pilots."

"OK," Jensen said. "Major, I need your assessment report to take upstairs with me. Anna, I'll look for your analysis when I get back to my desk. We've got a lot of work to do, people, so I guess we'd better get to it."

The two officers got up and departed, leaving Vasquez sitting alone in the conference room. Or almost alone…

"Anna?"

"Yes, Sergeant."

"Am I dreaming, or did somebody just say I should become an officer and learn how to fly an Airwolf?"

"You are not dreaming, Sergeant." Vasquez caught a hint of amusement in the AI's voice. "Somebody did say that. In fact, there seems to be a consensus on the subject."

"Oh, man, what have I gotten myself into now?" Vasquez wondered.

*****

Chapter Twelve

Home Ship—Otuka 2429th Clan

"I am A'archa Rio…"

"I know who you are. You've made that clear already. I am Lorna Greenwood, tsan of all the human fleet units in this system, and many more back at our homeworld. No more introductions are needed."

Shortly before the exchange began, some of the human soldiers had returned to A'archa's bridge, bringing with them a large, flat panel, which they installed on a stand next to the human spy-machine. Despite the alien technology, A'archa immediately guessed its purpose; it was a viewing screen. *So,* he mused, *they wish to speak with me face-to-face.*

He had refused to speak to the machine up to this point, always delegating the task to one of his assistants. Now, they told him their leader wished to speak directly with him, and it appeared he would be allowed to see the human with whom he was speaking. His assumption was confirmed when the screen came to life and displayed the image of a human female, seated behind a desk or table of some sort. She wore a high-collared garment with various decorations, which he took to be badges of rank or status. She looked directly at him, and he assumed she could also see him. She began to speak, but he heard nothing. A moment later, the spy-machine started speaking to him, and he realized it, or someone, was translating her words into his language.

"We have examined this," she said, holding up the data crystal he had given to the human officer during the first encounter. "We have listened to your words but have yet to decide whether you are telling the truth. You claim to have no association with the Otuka who committed atrocities on the inhabited planet of this system, the ones we recently defeated in battle. Is that correct?"

"I know nothing of any atrocities, and the only knowledge I have of the battle is hearsay, passed to me by other Otuka at a gathering-place a great distance from here. I came here for salvage. Space battles are untidy events that leave lots of wreckage scattered about to be rightfully claimed by salvagers such as myself. I have claimed what is mine, and you must let me proceed about my business."

"No, I will not," the human declared. "I return to the question of the atrocities. Did you know of the human population on the habitable planet of this system?"

"I did not," A'archa lied without hesitation. "I was told this system was reserved for the elite, the highest ranking among the tsans of the Otuka. Others, such as me, were not allowed to come here. I assumed there was something of value, something that would allow the uppermost to further enrich themselves. I am not surprised to hear it was a human population."

"Why do you value humans so highly?" The female was watching him carefully, and he was certain she already knew the answer. Lying would not serve him here, so perhaps a bit of bravado was in order.

"Human flesh is a rare and much-prized delicacy," he told her. "Many say it is the best-tasting meat in the entire galaxy. For that reason, it is very expensive. I agree that it makes an excellent meal, but in my opinion, it is not worth the exorbitant prices demanded by meat-merchants."

"Then you have, in fact, eaten human flesh?"

A'archa studied the human female. He wasn't well acquainted with human facial expressions or body language, but it seemed to him she was showing no emotion, no anger, no excitement. Danger signals flashed in his mind, telling him to be very, very careful with his next words.

"Only once," he lied again, "at a feast sponsored by a tsan who wished to impress others with his wealth and status. He served human meat as a symbol of that wealth and status. I am more practical and would not pay such prices just to impress others."

"For many of your people, it just became much more expensive." She favored him with an unmistakably predatory smile. "But let me understand...are you saying you have no moral or ethical concerns about eating humans?"

"Moral? Ethical? It's food, human. All creatures need food to exist. You humans eat meat as well. Do you have moral or ethical concerns about it?"

"Some humans do," she told him. "But even those who do not—admittedly the majority—refuse to eat other intelligent species. We do not eat creatures capable of using tools, communicating beyond the most instinctive level, or engaging in abstract thought. And, of course, we don't eat other humans."

"We don't eat other Otuka," he replied, "but what difference does it make? Food animals are food animals, no matter how advanced or intelligent they are. You may be more intelligent than I am, but you still look like a tasty meal to me." He punctuated the remark with a smile that revealed an impressive set of canines and razor-sharp incisors.

"Actually," she assured him, "it makes a great deal of difference. *Our* food animals aren't capable of building warships that can wipe us out of existence in an instant. Unfortunately, you cannot say the same. I may look like food to you, but you won't live to taste it."

"The Universe is fraught with peril." He shrugged in a very human-like manner. "Life has risks, and we must face them. But I repeat, I am not your enemy, have not attacked you, and did not come here to eat anyone. I am exercising my rights, under customs accepted by many races in the galaxy. If you know of the Akara, you may ask them if what I tell you is true."

"As a matter of fact, I *do* know of the Akara," she replied. "And they support certain customs regarding salvage. They do not, however, tolerate salvagers from other worlds coming into their home systems to conduct salvage without their permission."

"This is not your home system," he insisted. "To my knowledge, this is a system that belongs to no one and is open to anyone who wishes to come here."

"This system is now under our protection," she told him. "You knew that your people had been defeated here. Did you think we would just pack up and go home? At the very least, you've entered a war zone and must expect to be challenged accordingly."

"Now—" she leaned forward toward the camera, "—this is what will happen. My people will search your ship and examine your salvaged cargo in detail. If we find anything we do not want you to have—especially things you have salvaged from our ships—we will take it from you. When we have completed our inspection, we will decide what to do with you. Any resistance to our search and inspection will have dire consequences. Is this understood?"

"No, it is not." Not to be intimidated, he leaned forward and looked directly at the camera lens. "Perhaps you should explain those dire consequences."

The human looked to her right and spoke to someone off-camera. There was an exchange of conversation, then she shrugged and made an inviting gesture. To A'archa's surprise, one of the Akara reptiles came into view and stood beside her behind the desk. The reptile looked at him with its large, slit-pupil eyes and began to speak.

"You mentioned my people," the voice from the spy-device told him, "so you know of the Akara. I am Special Speaker to the Humans for my tsan, Heart of the Copper Hills clan. I have known these humans for a long time and have fought by their side in battle. Have you heard of the Mekota? If so, be advised that these are the humans who smashed their fleet and brought down their empire."

"This particular human," the reptile continued, "is their Warrior Queen. She is not to be trifled with. You ask about dire consequences, so let me explain. If you do not comply with her wishes, she will most likely rip out your sex organs—both sets of them—and feed them to her carnivorous pets. Then she will cut off your head and mount it on the wall of her dwelling, next to the head of the near-dragon she recently slew on my world.

"After that, she will convert your entire falnor and all your ships into a large cloud of hot, expanding gas. No one will ever know what happened to you. Except for your head on the wall, it will be as if you never existed. Does that cover the details, Warrior Queen?" He bowed slightly in the human's direction.

"Yes, it does," she replied, "though I may not want his head on my wall—he's far too ugly. Maybe we'll just go right to the part about clouds of hot gas."

* * *

LFS *Valkyrie*

Aboard *Valkyrie*, Lorna regarded her screen with surprise. After her last words, the Otuka leader seemed to be having some sort of seizure. The horns on his head had uncurled and were twitching and twisting, trying to curl back up, only to uncurl again. His shoulders were shaking, and his mouth was open. The audio feed from the Otuka vessel had been muted so as not to interfere with Val's translation, but now, the AI let them hear the howling, barking sound the alien was making. After a moment, she muted the sound again.

"If I am not mistaken, Admiral, the alien is laughing, and if my understanding of their body language is correct, he is genuinely amused. It is a spontaneous response beyond his ability to simulate or control."

A moment later, however, the alien got himself under control. He re-curled his horns and pointed at the screen. He spoke, and Val resumed the translation.

"I like you, human," he told her. "You have no fear of me, and you speak your mind. I would still like to eat you, but I seem to be at your mercy. Send your people to search my ship, and I will tell my falnor-katan not to obstruct them. When they have finished, we will speak again."

With that, he gathered his legs under him, got up, and pranced off the bridge with no further comment. The sentry 'bot tracked his departure with its camera, and Lorna noted his bridge crewmembers bowed deeply as he passed.

Lorna turned to her audience—the Akara diplomat, as well as Mercedes Warren and Carla, who had remained off-camera.

"Comments, anyone?" she inquired.

"He's got big, brass balls." Carla shook her head.

"And other equipment," Warren said with amusement. "Got to give him—or her—credit for straight talk—Yes, I eat humans, and you sure look tasty to me, Admiral Greenwood."

"In your dreams, Donkey-boy," Lorna chuckled. "And you..." She turned to the Akara. "Seriously? Mount his head on my wall?"

"I thought it a useful metaphor. It certainly got his attention, don't you think?"

* * *

LFS *Timberwolf*—at the New Eden System Hyper Limit

"Hyper signature! Multiple hyper signatures! At least eighty. No, more than a hundred point sources! More still coming...slowing down now...I think that's all of them. Computer says one hundred twenty-two ships altogether."

"Identification? Vector?" Rob O'Hara felt surprisingly calm, perhaps because the swarm of ships wasn't coming directly at him. On their present course, they would pass well clear of *Timberwolf*. In fact, unless he did something to get their attention, they probably wouldn't see the destroyer standing guard just outside the hyper limit.

"No drive signatures, delta vee is zero, but mass readings look very much like Otuka raiders, accompanied by twenty or so of the larger Otuka ships we've seen before. They're carrying a lot of residual, sir—nearly point one cee—and they're right on the system ecliptic, headed straight in. They'll be inside the hyper limit in twelve minutes. If they continue to go in ballistic, they'll intersect New Eden's orbit in about twenty hours. They're not quite dead on course for the planet, but a minor course correction will put them there. Details on your screen, Captain."

"Thank you, Ensign. Stand by for transmission to fleet."

Timberwolf hadn't spent much time in New Eden orbit. Just two days after his meeting with Admiral Ling, O'Hara had gotten new orders assigning him to the outer system picket. The picket force was spread rather thin, and O'Hara was not expected to engage an incoming enemy. The picket's first duty was to pass the word.

"Mr. Brody, we will need an FTL transmission, our standard ID code, plus '122 bogies inbound.' Follow that with vector data. Transmit immediately."

"Sir, they'll pick it up," Lieutenant Brody pointed out.

"Of course, they will, if they're watching their six," O'Hara agreed. "But as Ensign Schmidt just advised, they're already past us and inbound at a tenth of light speed. It'll take them a couple of hours to kill that vector if they decide they want to come back and look for us, and we'll sure as hell be able to see them doing it."

FTL transmissions, instantaneous over the span of a star system, were sent using a ship's gravity drive components to create a powerful pulse like the signature of a ship entering or leaving hyperspace. There was no way to modulate the pulse to carry additional information, so strings of pulses had to be sent very much like old-fashioned Morse code. Power requirements and equipment capabilities limited the system to a very slow rate of transmission, on the order of five alphanumeric characters per minute. The simple message O'Hara had ordered would take more than ten minutes to send, but an ordinary lightspeed transmission would take over two hours to reach New Eden.

Admiral Ling's people would have seen the hyper signature of the Otuka ships, but O'Hara's message would provide vital details. He would send an additional message with more information by normal means, but after that—assuming the enemy didn't come back to look for them—*Timberwolf's* duty would be simply to wait for further orders.

* * *

LFS *Valkyrie*

"I'll leave a sufficient number of my warships here to keep you company. I trust a being of your intelligence will see the folly of any attempt to depart without my permission."

"Yes, I know…dire consequences and similar unpleasant things." A'archa made a dismissive gesture. "I look forward, with great joy, to your return, human."

"While I'm gone, my people will continue to examine your ship. Your cooperation in that matter is appreciated," Lorna assured him.

She terminated the connection and selected *Valkyrie's* command channel.

"Captain McPherson, pass the word to Alpha group. We can get underway as soon as you are ready."

All she had to work with was the hyper signature of the incoming Otuka and the omnidirectional FTL pulse transmission from *Timberwolf* that followed. O'Hara would have tight-beamed his follow-up report directly to Amy Ling's force and would be awaiting a reply, but neither that transmission, nor the reply would come to Lorna. Fortunately, she and Ling had already discussed the matter, and Lorna was free to take immediate action.

Shortly after First Fleet arrived in system, Ling had sent a detailed after-action report, including her arrangements for system security. Lorna had been impressed. Ling's plan was simple and direct, but not by the book. Deploying her system pickets just outside the hyper limit scattered them widely but gave them an extreme mobility advantage. They could move in and out of hyperspace at will, allowing her to quickly move all, or part, of the picket force to any point along the system perimeter much more quickly than units could be sent from the inner system.

"In answer to your query about how you and your ships can best support me, Admiral," Ling had told her, "I'll assume you mean you, personally, with *Valkyrie* and First Battle Group. I'm already making good use of the other two Groups you sent in-system, but if you are going to be hanging around out there by the hyper limit, I'd suggest you are in the best position to support the picket force if need arises."

Upon detection of incoming enemies, the basic plan called for the force to assemble at the hyper limit—at the point where the incoming enemy had crossed—and to pursue from there. Depending on the size of the enemy incursion, Ling would decide how many picket ships would be needed for the effort and would issue the appropriate orders. The plan was to trap the invaders between the forces she would dispatch from the inner system and the back door force coming in behind them.

"Let me know how many ships you will be sending, Admiral," Ling had told her. "I'll make my plans accordingly. If you send that message as soon as you get the detection alert, you can proceed immediately to the assembly area.

"Of course," she'd added with a feral smile, "if you choose to go yourself, with *Valkyrie*, you will be the S.O. when you get there. I'll assume you are taking charge of the back door force and will use your own discretion after that. I'll hit them from the front, you hit them from behind, and we'll meet in the middle."

Simple and direct, Lorna thought, *typical Amy Ling. Now, we'll see how it works in practice.* Lorna's message to Ling would arrive shortly after O'Hara's report. It would take her force a little while to get out beyond the hyper limit, but it would also take Ling's orders some time to reach the rest of the picket force. All in all, the timing should work out nicely.

* * *

Home Ship—Otuka 2429th Clan

A'archa watched the human female depart, taking her largest warship—an impressive-looking dreadnought—and several more of her ships with her. True to her word, however, the number of ships she left behind appeared more than adequate to inflict those dire consequences upon him should he decide to try anything stupid.

He believed he knew where she was going, for he had also detected the hyper signature of incoming ships some distance away around the system perimeter. Though he couldn't say for sure how many had come, the magnitude and duration of the hypergravity event didn't seem to indicate a large force—perhaps a few hundred ships at the most. He noted with interest they had arrived in the likely spot for a direct run from a nearby Otuka node.

Most likely, some high-ranking survivor from the last encounter with the humans had reached the node, commandeered all the Otuka ships there, and come back, thinking he could win a battle that was already lost. Obviously, he had not been constrained by any need to consult with the Council, else—based on what A'archa had learned before coming here—he would have arrived with a much larger force or been ordered not to come at all. He would have to have been, at least, of Council rank, however, to demand that others follow him.

Unfortunate for them, A'archa decided. *I strongly suspect the humans are going to make them into shredded meat. I'm glad I wasn't there to be ordered to join them. Now, I need to consider how to turn this to my advantage. If I play it well, it may increase my chance of surviving this adventure.*

* * *

Home Ship—Otuka 1407th Clan—Inbound New Eden

"It is a coded signal of some sort, My Lord, but we are unable to interpret it."

"Oh, I'm certain we can guess its meaning." M'orsta Makrust'galan, tsan of the 1407th falnor regarded his communications lieutenant with an angry glare. "They are telling their fellows of our arrival, our course, and our velocity. And since we have not altered course or velocity since translation, they will know exactly where to find us."

"My Lord, Lord B'arska has ordered—"

"B'arska is an idiot!" M'orsta snarled. "His ancestors were all too fond of their own offspring. The 45th falnor is a perfect example of aristocratic inbreeding. Only an imbecile keeps to a predictable course, once detected, when a subtle maneuver would make the enemy's task much more difficult."

The Otuka lieutenant said nothing. It was far above his station to comment on his master's opinions regarding a member of the Council—even if he happened to agree with those opinions.

"Helmsman! Move us to this point here," M'orsta ordered, highlighting a position far out on one edge of the swarm. "Pass word to our falnor-ka. Tell them to do it gradually, nothing obvious. Make it look like sloppy navigation."

So that if need arises, we can quickly part company with B'arska and his fawning followers…

* * *

LFS *Timberwolf*—with *Valkyrie*—in Pursuit of the Otuka Ships

"There they are, Captain, they haven't altered course at all."

"Well, that makes it simple," Rob O'Hara declared. "Pass the word, and let's find out what Admiral Greenwood wants to do."

As soon as the group had assembled, Lorna had ordered *Timberwolf* and two other destroyers to take the point position in pursuit of the enemy. Pushing their ships hard, they had finally gotten within detection range of the Otuka.

Lorna had ordered them to hold back, to close the distance somewhat, but not to press an attack. She was waiting for Amy Ling to deliver a promised surprise package to the intruders. After that, her force could mop up the survivors.

"If you would, Admiral, find those bogies and start sending us vector information on them," Ling's last message had requested. "I'm planning to throw a little party for the bastards. Since you were nice enough to bring *Europa*, *Phobos*, and *Ganymede* when you came, I might as well make use of them."

Technically, the ships Ling mentioned were frigate-class vessels, but they were a special class of frigate, named for the natural moons of the Solar System. Normally assigned only to Home Fleet, they sacrificed significant missile armament to make room for another weapon system.

They were minelayers.

* * *

Office of the CEO—TerraNova City, Luna

"So, Admiral, we have discovered the location of that human civilization you found, the one about which you have adamantly refused to share information with the civilized nations of the world. I am told the planet circles the star catalogued as 'LGS1437A' in your Lunar Galactic Survey data. Would you care to comment?"

This conversation is about to get very interesting, Charlie Bender decided. *We knew this was coming, but if Frenchy is going to be confrontational about it, he won't like the outcome.*

Mick O'Hara was a visionary who had done much to build the Lunar Free State up to its status as a dominant force in the Solar System. He was also a much-beloved leader and extremely popular with the people of the LFS. He was not, however, known for his diplomatic skills. He could not lie with a straight face, didn't like to misdirect others or dance around controversial topics, and tended to speak plainly, without regard for the colossal egos that moved in the upper levels of Earth's political arena. To make matters worse, he didn't particularly like Henri Delacourt, Secretary General of the

Confederacy of Nations, whose face was displayed on the wall screen in the conference room.

For all of that, Mick's first response was, in Charlie's view, quite reasonable.

"And where, exactly, did you come by that information, Secretary General?" O'Hara inquired, in a pleasant, conversational tone.

"It is published in the Confederacy's *Journal of Science*," Delacourt replied. "The article cites a source at the Lunar Research Institute."

An anonymous source, Bender mentally corrected.

He and O'Hara had seen the article, called to their attention by Mike, the resident AI of TerraNova City and Lunar Command. Mike reviewed virtually all scientific literature and a variety of other publications coming from Earth or Luna, looking for items of interest to LFS Intelligence, i.e., Charlie Bender and his people. Bender and O'Hara had concluded someone on the LRI Board had leaked the information to the Confederacy's science attaché on Luna, despite being told the location of the star was secret for national security reasons.

Damned scientists think the rules don't apply to them, Bender thought. *If I find out who it was, he's going to learn otherwise. For now, however, Mick is going to have to deal with the Confeds.*

"Well, then." O'Hara beamed at the Frenchman. "If it's been published, you can't accuse us of refusing to share. And since we're in a sharing mood, let me tell you a bit more about it."

He paused for a moment, waiting out the communications lag to see the Confederate executive's reaction. A few seconds later, he was rewarded with a look of smug satisfaction, as Delacourt sat back in his leather armchair.

"By all means, Admiral, please do."

Bender reflected that a few decades ago, world leaders would not have dreamed of discussing such sensitive matters of international diplomacy by teleconference. They would have traveled thousands of kilometers to meet face-to-face behind closed doors to ensure that whatever they said to each other would not become public. That had changed somewhat in the early years of the Lunar Free State, when the nation's first CEO, Ian Stevens, had developed a more casual dialogue with then-President Blackthorne of the United States. The two of them had frequently met electronically but had always used specially encrypted transmissions for the purpose. Still, Stevens had been aware that such conversations could easily be recorded, undoubtedly were recorded by both sides, and could become public record if it suited the purpose of either participant.

The Confederacy insisted its own members communicate with each other, and with non-member nations, like the LFS, using a special diplomatic network set up for the purpose. The network was supposedly as secure as technology could make it, but Charlie had no faith whatsoever in that security. There were too many people involved in maintaining the system, too many actual human beings who had access to it through various parts of its technical infrastructure. He fully expected that—as had happened many times in the past—whatever Mick O'Hara said now would be fodder for the evening newscasts that night.

"You are correct about the location," O'Hara began, "but you are obviously unaware of the situation. You see, those flesh-eating aliens—the ones who attacked the cruise ship *Summer Solstice*—have, in the past, used the primitive humans of that planet as a food source. They've taken issue with our denying their right to eat humans. They've attacked our fleet units and been soundly defeated. We've declared the entire star system off-limits to incursions by anyone. In short, we've made it an official protectorate of the Lunar Free State, in the interest of preserving and protecting a primitive human culture."

"So!" Delacourt sat upright again, a look of rage on his face. "This is where your warships have gone. Did you think we would not notice when most of your fleet suddenly deployed? You've involved us in another interstellar war!"

"Oh, bullshit!" O'Hara declared, foregoing anything that might be considered proper diplomatic language.

"You—the Confederacy and all the other nations of Earth—are involved in nothing. We, the Lunar Free State, are defending a primitive race of humans against a gang of interstellar pirates. That's of no concern to you or anyone else on Earth."

"We will make it our concern!" Delacourt fired back. "We will be sending our own security forces to investigate immediately. You will advise your people to cooperate with them when they arrive."

"We can't allow you to do that," O'Hara said, firmly. "Your ships will not be permitted to enter the system."

"You have no choice in the matter," Delacourt told him. "You people are not even members of the Confederacy."

Uh oh! That's done it! Bender shook his head. *You just pushed Mick's 'LFS Sovereignty' button.*

Mick O'Hara, like Charlie Bender, was an Original Citizen—one of the few hundred people who had fled Earth with the U.S. government nipping at their heels, who had endured UN sanctions, missile attacks, and an attempted invasion of Luna by the Chinese. He had worked to build the Lunar nation to its present economic and military strength, through decades of hostility and disdain from the nations of Earth. He had pushed his nation out to the stars and had dealt with alien races, both hostile and friendly. He did not play well with people who presumed to dictate to the LFS.

"What part of LFS protectorate did you not understand?" O'Hara snarled. "I will advise my people that any ship entering that system without authorization—no matter whose flag it happens to be showing—is to be regarded as hostile. If you want to send a single, unarmed, observer ship, you may petition us for authorization, and we might consider it if you demonstrate sufficient justification. If, on the other hand, you choose to send your security forces, you will be risking a confrontation with the LFS fleet. The best you can hope for, assuming your captains don't do anything incredibly stupid, is that they'll be turned back at the hyper limit and sent home. The worst…well, let's just say, you'll be responsible for an unfortunate interstellar incident."

With that, O'Hara cut the transmission.

Bender wondered how that was going to play on the Earth newsfeeds. Even the friendly unaligned nations—those who were not members of the Confederacy—would likely view with alarm a veiled threat such as Mick had just delivered. *Did I say veiled threat? Hell, he just promised to blow a bunch of Confederate warships out of space!*

The Confederacy had been building up its security forces for several years, mostly by conscripting warships from member nations, but still didn't have the chops to stand up to a single LFS Battle Group, let alone the entire LFS Fleet. Delacourt didn't have hardware to back up his threat. Bender's real concern was that the Confederate leadership wasn't smart enough to realize that.

* * *

The two men left the conference room and walked the short distance back to Mick's office in silence. Once there, Mick settled behind his desk and turned to Charlie, who dropped into one of the comfortable armchairs.

"Well?" O'Hara lifted an eyebrow in Bender's direction. "You're our foreign minister. Care to tell me how badly I've screwed this one up?"

"It was screwed up before we ever got the call. Personally, I think you gave them what they deserve but then I never was very good at diplomacy myself. I'd like to hear Mike's opinion. He's better than either of us at predicting how the Earthworms will react."

"Mike? Can we have your thoughts on the matter?" The AI was always available in O'Hara's office and only needed a verbal invitation to join the conversation. He had been a silent listener on the conversation with Delacourt.

"It is likely they will send a security force to New Eden, Admiral," the AI replied. "They can hardly do otherwise without appearing to concede the issue, but I believe they will withdraw if we confront them. That way, they can present themselves as the reasonable parties, seeking to avoid an incident, and condemn us as confrontational bullies, as they have done ever since we refused to join their organization."

"And we will continue to refuse," O'Hara asserted. "I'll not be bullied into surrendering our national sovereignty to a bunch of power-hungry one-worlders who don't have our interests at heart. The old UN was a harmless debating society that sucked money out of its members' pockets while accomplishing nothing. These people want their military forces to keep their members in line and go to war with anyone who refuses to join them. We're a thorn in their side because nothing they've got can stand up against the LFS Fleet."

"Hey, I agree with you." Charlie Bender threw up his hands. "My concern is that they'll send a bunch of their typical, arrogant Confed military people, along with a typical, arrogant Confed diplomat or two, to a place where our people have been fighting a real war with live ammunition. We could have that unfortunate incident you mentioned."

"There is a small, but non-zero, probability you are correct, Admiral Bender," the AI agreed. "If it happens, there is a near-certainty Earth's news media will place the blame on us, regardless of any factual evidence to the contrary."

"That's a chance we'll have to take." O'Hara shook his head. "I'm not much of a military strategist, but Lorna Greenwood has hammered a few lessons into my thick head. One of them is that you can't micromanage a military situation from a distance. You must rely on the local commander's discretion. Hopefully, our people won't arbitrarily decide this is a good excuse to start a war with the Confederacy."

* * *

Home Ship—Otuka 1407th Clan

"My Lord, Lord B'arska says they are obviously fleeing in the face of our superiority."

Or leading us into a prepared ambush, M'orsta thought. He studied the icons of the three enemy vessels on his display. They had accelerated directly away from the Otuka swarm but had stopped accelerating when they reduced the rate of closure to zero. In other words, they weren't fleeing, they were baiting, maintaining a fixed distance ahead where they had to know B'arska's ships could see them.

M'orsta's ships were far to one side of the swarm and as far to the rear as he dared take them. He was painfully aware of the enemy force behind him. It was not large in numbers, but it was trailing the swarm at a fixed distance, with what M'orsta saw as the patience of a stalking predator, but B'arska dismissed as timidity.

M'orsta had already prepared an escape plan but dared not execute that plan until battle was joined, and B'arska's limited capacity for attention was claimed by something urgent, like the need to survive. M'orsta was certain the humans were going to hit them with devastating force. He had heard too many stories from the survivors of the first incursion to discount the strength of the enemy, and he hoped their attack would quickly remove Lord B'arska from the equation. Of course, he needed to avoid the same fate, and, to that end, he examined his displays carefully, looking for any hint of enemy warships in their path or on their flanks.

He was just beginning to get concerned about some faint sensor readings at extreme range ahead, when mayhem erupted along the leading edge of the swarm. Huge, star-hot fireballs blossomed, spawning powerful energy beams that sliced through Otuka ships at point-blank range. As the swarm's momentum carried it forward, a line of destruction marched through it, new fireballs spawning new energy beams in a devastating storm of nuclear fury. Falnor-ka vanished in fusion flares as their reactors were hit by the beams. Home ships were shredded, reduced to shattered wreckage in an instant.

M'orsta's brain refused to accept what was happening. There were no enemy ships in sight, nothing that could possibly be the source of such devastation. But it was happening, and M'orsta shook himself free of his momentary paralysis. He issued an order, directing his minions to execute the escape plan he had already prepared. They reacted quickly, and his display changed as he and his group began to move away from the rest of the swarm, driving outward at right angles to their original course. It turned out to be exactly the right thing to do.

The swath of destruction was only about half as wide as the scattered swarm, but it had appeared almost exactly in the center of the leading edge, and it gutted the Otuka formation as it passed through. Ships that tried to reverse course were overtaken by the line of devastation before they could kill their forward momentum. But M'orsta was out of the storm's path and was putting distance between himself and the chaos as quickly as he could. He wasn't sure how it had been done, and his own salvation was far from assured, but he noted with satisfaction that B'arska's icon had vanished from his display. The arrogant fool had been front-and-center in the swarm and had been one of the first to go.

* * *

LFS *Valkyrie*

"Check me if I'm wrong on this, Austin," Lorna Greenwood remarked, "but I'm pretty sure this is the first time we've used mines in a running engagement. In fact, I can't think of any historical wet-Navy precedents either."

"I believe you're right, ma'am," Wilkes replied. "Mines are generally considered an interdiction tool, to keep an enemy away from a fixed position or deny him access to a favored route of travel. At most, you expect the enemy to suffer minor losses to advance recon units entering the mine field, but that serves as warning to those who follow."

"In other words, they don't usually come charging in blindly like these people did." Lorna nodded. "But anyone with an ounce of tactical sense wouldn't have held the same vector when they knew they'd been detected. That's what allowed Admiral Ling to position her minelayers in front of them."

"Excuse me, Admiral." Lorna had removed her communications headset during the break in the action, and Val's voice came from the speaker in her console. "Captain McPherson advises we are approaching Wolfpack range for the surviving enemy ships. Given the small number of targets and the wide field over which they are scattered, he is recommending we save the Wolfpacks and hold fire until we reach standard missile range."

Lorna nodded. The Wolfpack was a long-range missile system developed by the LFS, by which several smaller, faster missiles were carried into targeting range by a larger, slower delivery vehicle that would launch them as targets became available. It was best suited for use against a concentrated enemy force. With more than half of the Otuka ships taken out by the minefield and the rest scattering in all directions, it didn't make sense to use the expensive Wolfpack package, which was carried only by LFS battlecruisers and heavy cruisers.

"Tell the Captain I concur and to pass the word to *Norseman* and *Athenian*. Also ask him to advise me when we are within five minutes of missile range."

For the most part, the Otuka were scattering to the right, left, up and down, but several were trying to reverse course and return the way they had come. They had seen Amy Ling's force in front of them, and they wanted no part of it. Apparently, Lorna's smaller force was of less concern to them, and some were headed directly toward *Valkyrie* and her group. The only question was whether they would enter Lorna's missile envelope before Ling overtook them from the rear. Either way, they were unlikely to survive the experience.

Others had a better chance. Both Amy and Lorna had sent destroyers and light cruisers after the scattering units, but at least one group was likely to escape entirely. That group—one large Otuka ship and seven smaller ones—had bugged out almost as soon as the mines began to wreak havoc on their fellows, and they would make it to the hyper limit before LFS units could run them down. Lorna considered summoning more ships from the picket force to get in front of them but decided against it. Amy Ling had left enough pickets out there to watch the perimeter in case this incursion was just a feint. Better to let these bogies escape than to pull any more of them off-station.

"Admiral, I have detected a pattern in the enemy's movements that you may find interesting, though it is not tactically useful at present," Val advised. "Is this an appropriate time to discuss it?"

"As good a time as any," Lorna agreed.

"There appears to be a symbiotic relationship between the smaller ships and the larger ones. Each large Otuka ship seems to have several smaller ones permanently associated with it. The number varies from as few as three to as many as fifteen. The smaller ships always operate in concert with or at the direction of the same larger ship. There is no shifting of ships from one group to another. If a larger ship is attacked, its symbiotes will come to its defense, but no others will join them even if there are other small ships nearby. If one of the larger ships is destroyed, the smaller ships associated with it will scatter. Some may try to join up with another large ship, which may or may not accept them.

"To us," the AI continued, "the Otuka hordes appear disorganized and random, but this pattern is concealed within the chaos. They operate like small, independent squadrons with a common purpose but little coordination of activity—but each squadron shows cohesion and coordination within itself."

"Hmmm," Lorna mused. "That tracks with what we've seen and heard from our wandering Otuka junk dealer. He seems to have control over his smaller ships but claims to have no association with the Otuka who've been giving us so much trouble. Maybe he's telling the truth."

"There is another point in his favor," Val advised. "We intercepted and analyzed voice communication traffic among the enemy ships. They appear to be speaking a common language, but it is not the language spoken by our captives. There are similarities, but not enough to interpret what was said. I'm still working on it, but unless we take prisoners, I do not have enough information to develop a working vocabulary."

"Prisoners." Lorna snorted. "Not likely. This bunch seems bent on escaping or fighting to the death."

* * *

Home Ship—Otuka 2429th Clan—LFS Boarding Party

"Lieutenant, I think you should take a look at this."

Senior Lieutenant Will Stanton was the assistant engineering officer for the LFS light cruiser *Werewolf*, but his present assignment was to examine, in detail, the contents of the cargo holds of the large Otuka ship. Most of the inspectors assigned to the task were engineers, since LFS engineers had been judged, by the Iron Maiden, to be the most qualified people to evaluate the tens of thousands of cubic meters of junk that filled the captured ship's vast storage bays.

Accompanied by a squad of Marines, he had walked many kilometers and had seen tons of material best classified as scrap metal. Now, finally, he had found a piece of machinery of alien origin that captured his interest. While he examined it, the Marines opened the hatch to a small compartment nearby and looked inside. The Marine sergeant in charge of the squad called for Stanton's attention. With a sigh, he walked over to the hatch and looked into the compartment.

"Dishes? China? Sergeant, we are looking for pirated technology, not dinnerware."

"Yes, sir, but I really think you need to look at this one," the Marine insisted.

He held out what appeared to be a sterling silver serving tray. It was an ornate piece of high quality and looked to be of human origin. It was engraved with an intricate design that included an inscription of some sort. Stanton took it from the Marine and looked at the inscription.

He looked up sharply and locked eyes with the sergeant.

"Oh, shit," he muttered softly.

* * *

Home Ship—Otuka 1407th Clan

M'orsta relaxed, letting his horns uncurl at last as his falnor crossed the boundary and translated into hyperspace. He had not lost a single falnor-ka, but he doubted if any other falnor had been as fortunate. Twenty-two

Otuka clans had embarked on the expedition, and he would be surprised if more than two or three still existed. The humans were still killing them as he and his raiders crossed into hyper, and he wondered how many survivors would make their way back to the node.

At least the 45th will not be among them, he noted with satisfaction. In fact, almost half of the falnor that set out on this ill-spawned quest were superior in rank to his own. Given the rate of attrition, he had probably advanced as much as eight or ten ranks in this engagement. When all was sorted out from the first battle, and the tally for this one was included, he might well find himself well into the 1300th level.

I suppose I should hope the enlightened members of the Council will continue to engage these humans, without my assistance, he reflected. *If they do, I may soon reach Council rank.*

* * * * *

Chapter Thirteen

Lunar Fleet Academy—TerraNova City, Luna

"Cadet Vasquez!"

"Sir! Yes, sir!" Vasquez came out of her seat and braced to attention, without using her crutches, and with only a hint of a little bobble as she straightened up.

Commander John Mancuso, senior instructor in Leadership and Command Authority at Lunar Fleet OCS, rolled his eyes and heaved a heavy sigh.

"Vasquez, it is not necessary for you to stand at attention when called. Fleet is aware of your physical limitations, and you are allowed to remain in your seat."

"Sir! Are you ordering me to remain in my seat, sir?"

"No, Vasquez, I'm not," Mancuso conceded. "I'm just asking the Gods of Deep Space why they have chosen to saddle me with another bull-headed Marine who thinks she's made of battle steel."

"Sir! No excuse, sir!" Vasquez didn't give even the hint of a smile, and Mancuso's glare silenced the little ripple of amusement that ran through the room.

"Very well, since you are standing, you may enlighten the class by stating the nine Principles of Leadership we have covered over the past few days."

"Sir, yes, sir.

"A leader leads by example, sir.

"A leader takes full responsibility for the actions of his or her subordinates, sir.

"A leader praises subordinates in public, but criticizes in private, sir."

As Vasquez droned through the list, Mancuso thought about the first principle she had named. *She's got that one down pat,* he decided, *but she'll be a tough one for her troops to keep up with.*

* * *

LFS *Valkyrie*—Outer Reaches of the New Eden System

"So, how did it go, Mom?" Carla asked. Since they were alone in Lorna's day cabin, she felt no need to call her mother by any other title.

"A lot better than the last battle," Lorna replied. "They came in with 122 ships, but Amy Ling set a trap that wiped out more than half of them, without our firing a shot. In the end, about two dozen of them escaped, the rest fought to the death. One of them almost got close enough to scratch *Valkyrie's* paint before we blew it away, and a couple of them tangled with our destroyers at beam-weapon range, but we took no losses, in my force or Amy's.

"But I didn't call you here to tell my war stories," she told her daughter. "I've asked Mercedes to come over as well, and we are about to have another chat with our friendly, local human-eater, but I thought you needed to see this first. For the rest of us, it's another issue to be dealt with, but for you, I'm pretty sure, it's personal.

"We found this in the Otuka's cargo hold." She handed the ornate silver platter to Carla.

For a moment, Carla was puzzled. It was obviously a human-made artifact, and the engraved coat of arms looked familiar. Then she saw the inscription beneath it: *LCS Summer Solstice.*

* * *

Home Ship—Otuka 2429th Clan

"Most Exalted Lord…"

The form of address was correct, but somehow A'archa could not escape the feeling the human was mocking him as she said it. Perhaps it had something to do with the fact that she continued to amuse herself by having her warships do periodic targeting scans of his ship.

"We are curious to know how you came by this particular bit of salvage," she told him, picking up the silver tray from her desk.

A'archa had been anticipating this call, and to finally receive it was almost a relief. The human inspectors had entered his private storage compartment, where he kept his personal treasures, which were mostly things of artistic beauty or clever craftsmanship. Whenever his falnor-katan brought captured booty to his ship, he made a point of looking for such artifacts. He rarely sold them, though he occasionally exchanged them with other tsans, trading for similar objects acquired in their travels.

His crewmen had told him what the humans had taken from the compartment, and he thought he knew why they had taken it. He had kept it for himself because of the intricate engraving it bore, but that same engraving probably revealed its origin. He thought it best not to tell them how he had acquired it, so he had crafted a story. It was time to tell that story.

"So!" he exclaimed. "That is what you took from my collection! I want it returned! I acquired it in trade, and it cost me a great deal."

"When and where, exactly, did you acquire it?"

"Less than a hundred *koranth* ago, in a star system we frequently visit to trade with others of our kind, about two hundred *chabaz* from here. I traded a valuable artifact—a golden figurine of Akara origin—for that piece. You have no right to take it from me."

The human looked displeased, and for a brief time, she appeared to confer with someone he couldn't see, off-camera. Then she looked at him again.

"Your units of measurement have no meaning for us. How long has it been—in koranth—since I first captured you?"

"Hmmm…" He consulted the display on his console. "If I am not mistaken, you have detained us here for eleven point seven koranth—far too long, in my opinion. And once you figure that out, you'll want to know that a chabaz is the distance light travels in normal space in one thousand koranth."

The human regarded him with an icy glare but said nothing for a moment. Then she spoke—again, apparently to someone off-camera since no translation issued from the spy device on A'archa's bridge. She turned to him once again, with the same hostile look on her face.

"The time-frame is appropriate," she told him, "but I think you are lying to me. I think you took this artifact directly from its source, an unarmed commercial vessel of my clan, carrying passengers to a point on the Akara frontier. I believe you attacked that ship, and that your falnor-katan killed and ate many of those passengers. Perhaps they even brought some of the bodies back to your ship so their lord and master could partake of…how was it you described it? The best-tasting meat in the entire galaxy?"

A'archa tried to show no reaction. He had no idea whether the humans could interpret his expression or body language, but he could feel the hairs of his mane curling down his back. It was the Otuka equivalent of what humans called a cold sweat. He waited for her to issue the order for his annihilation, trying desperately to think of something to say that would cause her to stay that order.

Then she spoke again.

"That is what I believe. Fortunately for you, I can't prove it."

A'archa started breathing again. He decided that righteous indignation would be his best course of action.

"How dare you accuse me! I know nothing of the events of which you speak. I acquired that artifact—"

"Spare me your denials," she cut him off. "You are fortunate our sense of justice requires us to consider an accused person innocent until proven guilty. I can't prove you did it. If I could, we would not be having this conversation because you would already have ceased to exist, along with your entire falnor…though, just maybe, in this case, I would have come over there first and taken your head for my wall."

"I'll say nothing more." He shrugged. "You have already decided the matter, and nothing I say will change your thinking. I await word regarding the dire consequences you choose to inflict, unjustified though they may be."

He wished he could shut off the spy-machine and remove her from his presence, as it was just one more reminder she controlled the situation, and he did not.

Instead, he did the next best thing. He got up from his console and left the bridge to the bowing and scraping of his crewmembers. As he did so, he reflected that having his head mounted on her wall was a better fate than being vaporized. At least he would be memorialized, would perhaps be the subject of someone's heroic song-story.

* * *

LFS *Sorceress*—New Eden Orbit

Amy Ling removed the white beret from her head and dropped it onto her desk. Her visitor regarded it in silence, noting the gold-embroidered coat of arms that marked it as belonging to the flag officer commanding the Double Deuce. Ling removed a pair of combs and tossed her head, letting her grey-tinged black hair fall to its natural shoulder length.

"At ease, Colonel," she said. "Smoke if you've got 'em."

Colonel George Mackenzie, LFSMC, settled into one of the comfortable chairs in front of Ling's desk.

"As the admiral may recall," he told her, "I don't smoke. I do, however, keep an incense burner in my quarters in which I occasionally burn a cigarette, just to remind me of what I'm missing."

"Really?" Ling sounded skeptical. "Be careful, Colonel, lest someone notice the big tough Marine has a sensitive side." She removed the two-star emblems of a rear admiral from her collar and placed them on the desk in front of her.

"So, tell me, what excuse did you give Admiral Sakura to get him to let you come over here?"

"Excuse?" He removed the silver eagles of his rank from his collar and tossed them onto the desk next to her stars. "I told him I needed to brush up on my martial arts skills, and that I couldn't find a tough enough training partner in First Fleet."

"Hah! So, it's to be a sparring match, is it?" Ling stood up and peeled off her uniform tunic, revealing a black camisole that displayed her well-toned arms and shoulders. "Still think you can pick me up and throw me down, do you?"

She came around the desk, and Mackenzie stood up to meet her. She threw her arms around his neck as he swept her up and turned to carry her to her sleeping cabin. He paused at the bed as she pulled his head down for a passionate kiss.

"Sonja," she ordered as she pulled away at last, "I'm not to be disturbed, short of Armageddon."

"I assumed as much, Admiral." The AI's voice held just a tiny touch of amusement.

"Damn!" Mackenzie muttered as he deposited Ling on the bed. "I forgot you have no privacy here."

"Sonja knows all my secrets," Ling replied with a chuckle. "She'll never tell, but with her twisted sense of humor, she'll probably enjoy watching us."

* * *

The better part of an hour later, Ling disentangled herself and sat up in bed. She arranged the pillows to form a backrest, then retrieved her cigarettes, lighter, and ashtray from the bedside table. She lit up and took a long, deep drag.

Mackenzie regarded her with an amused smile.

"I remember an old Earth expression that says it isn't over until the fat lady sings," he remarked. "In my case, it isn't over until the tiny lady smokes."

"Best cigarette of the day," she told him. "In fact, now that I think about it, the best one in quite a few months. So, how were the kids when you last saw them?"

"Upset," he replied. "They're used to one of us being gone for long periods, but it's pretty rare that Mom and Dad both get deployed at the same time. Of course, they have no way of knowing we are out here together, having a mini-honeymoon in the middle of a war zone. Anyway, they're staying with my dad for the duration."

"They're older now," she mused, "and they don't need us much anymore, except as role models. Have you convinced George to join the Marines yet?"

"No," he sighed. "Junior is too much of a geek. He's bound and determined to become a Lunar engineer, and that's the best place for him. On the other hand, you're obviously a better role model than I am. Rebecca got her acceptance letter from Fleet Academy just before I left."

"Really? Why am I not surprised? I don't know if I want her to be exactly like me, but I hope, someday, she'll be flying her own flag aboard a battlecruiser, with a group like the Double Deuce under her command."

"Right! So her own AI can be watching her have sex in her cabin." Mackenzie chuckled. "You just had to plant that image in my head, didn't you?"

Ling smiled wickedly. "Well, she has to record it," she explained, "so she can play it back for me to watch after you're gone. Which begs the question. How long before Tommy's expecting you back aboard *Isis*?"

"I told him I could be back in 24 hours, but he told me I needed to devote more time to my training than that. He said he'd be upset if I came back in less than 48 hours and wouldn't start getting concerned until at least three days had passed."

"He did, did he? Hmmm…Sonja!" she ordered.

"Yes, ma'am," the AI's reply came instantly.

"Advise Admiral Sakura I'm involved in a training exercise and would appreciate it if he could assume command of the group for…oh, say, about three days. I'll let him know when the exercise is concluded. I will, of course, suspend the exercise and make myself available should anything arise that needs my attention."

"Of course, ma'am. I am contacting Admiral Sakura as we speak."

Ling put out her cigarette and put the ashtray aside. She turned to Mackenzie with a sultry look that promised a long and interesting night.

"Now, about that training exercise," she said.

* * *

LFS *Valkyrie*—Outer Reaches of the New Eden System

"You're letting them go?" Carla asked, outraged.

"Yes, I am," Lorna replied, calmly. "What's more, I'm letting them keep most of the salvage they collected. We've confiscated a few bits of technology we didn't want them to have, but most of what they took is just scrap metal."

"I can't believe you're doing this!" Carla protested. "You know what they are and what they've done."

"I think I know what they are and what they've done, but I can't prove it," Lorna corrected her. "Innocent until proven guilty; that's our rule, not theirs, and we have to abide by it. Mercedes, do you not agree?"

"Actually, I do." Warren nodded.

"Mercy, why?" Carla demanded.

"Carla, look at me," Warren said. "A hundred years ago, most people would have judged me by my skin color. Not just in the United States where my people were once slaves, but almost anywhere on Earth. Racial prejudice seems to be an inborn human trait that we must consciously struggle to overcome, but for the most part, we've done it on Luna. It may still be rampant on Earth, but you'll find little or none of it in the LFS. We don't even have laws against discrimination because it's assumed, when the Constitution says all persons, it means exactly that. We're color blind. We don't think about it. At least, that's true where humans are concerned."

"Now, consider the Otuka, specifically this Lord Archa and his minions. What evidence do we have that he isn't telling the truth? He doesn't look like us. In fact, he looks just like those evil creatures that have been eating humans on New Eden, but if we convict him on that basis, we are practicing racism, pure and simple. So, while I may suspect he is just as bad as the others we've encountered, I can't allow myself to judge him that way."

Carla said nothing. She realized Warren had a point, but it was hard to accept, especially after what she had seen on *Summer Solstice.*

"Heart," Lorna addressed the Akara envoy, "you haven't said anything on the subject. What do you think?"

"I think, Warrior Queen," the Akara replied, "if he had the opportunity, this Otuka lord would rather eat you than talk to you. I will admit he seems somewhat more civilized than expected, but I know from experience that the threat of instant annihilation does wonders to improve one's manners and diplomatic skills.

"In fact—" he favored her with an Akara-style grin, "—you were the one who taught me that lesson when I was in much the same position as the Otuka are now, surrounded by your warships.

"If Lord Archa had encountered an Akara squadron instead of you, he wouldn't have had the chance to practice his diplomatic skills. We consider the Otuka enemies, and there are only two kinds of enemy—those who have been suitably dealt with and those who are still alive."

"I'm with Heart on this one," Carla asserted. "What about *Summer Solstice?* The fact that we found that tray aboard his ship should be proof enough. What are the odds he just happened to acquire it in a trade?"

"The probability is very small, Doctor Greenwood." Val said, joining the conversation. "But it is not zero. It should be noted that the tray was the only piece of traceable evidence we found. Our people conducted a very thorough search, but the only other human-made items were from LFS warships destroyed or abandoned in the battle.

"Also," the AI continued, "I have complete data from the OSG ships that engaged the Otuka in the *Summer Solstice* incident. Six of the seven enemy ships that escaped were never close enough to our units for detailed sensor readings. The seventh was damaged before it escaped, and repairs might have changed its characteristics. It bore some resemblance to one of the two ships destroyed by *Timberwolf* when A'archa first encountered you in this system, but most Otuka raider ships have similar profiles, and we cannot be certain. I'm sorry, but the evidence is not sufficient."

"Carla," Warren said, "I understand. You're looking for closure. You want to know that we've caught the bastards responsible for *Summer Solstice* and brought them to justice. Unfortunately, we can't say that."

"Maybe you're right," Carla admitted, reluctantly, "but if it's personal for me, imagine how it must be for Jennifer Tanaka, especially since she played a part in capturing the Otuka. Have you talked to her about it?"

"Yes, I have," Lorna replied. "She doesn't seem to have as much problem with it as you do. The Otuka who killed her sister were here—not on *Summer Solstice*—and the Marines suitably dealt with them. On the other hand, she's one of the people who engaged the *Summer Solstice* raiders and dealt with them. I think she's had her share of vengeance and has settled down to a more pragmatic view of the Otuka. I'm glad, because she's an outstanding officer, and I'd hate to see her judgment compromised by a personal vendetta.

"If it's any consolation, I have advised Lord Archa that we have recorded extremely detailed data on each of his ships, so they will be easily identified if we see them again. I told him if I ever get word he is preying on humans—or on the Akara, for that matter—I will make it my personal crusade to hunt him down, and I will take his head for my wall."

* * *

Corporal J's Place—TerraNova City, Luna

"Gunny, if one more Marine calls me 'ma'am' tonight, I'm gonna whack him upside the head with this crutch," Vasquez declared.

"They can't help it, LT," Gunnery Sergeant Dustin "Duke" Walker replied with a grin. "It's those brown bars on your shoulders. They automatically pucker their butts and pop that salute if they see you outside. Even in here, they can't get out of the habit of calling an officer 'sir' or 'ma'am.' I'm afraid you'll have to get used to it."

"You're just as bad," she growled. "Every time you say 'LT,' I think you're talking to somebody else. I'm gonna have to stop coming here in uniform."

New cadets at the LFS Fleet Academy were mostly young civilians just out of high school with no prior military experience. Fleet took four years to mold them into officers, a process that involved not only intensive classroom study, but three tours of duty as provisional officer candidates aboard a fleet ship.

Candidates for OCS, on the other hand, were usually senior noncommissioned officers and were presumed to have significant military knowledge and experience. Fleet turned them into officers after an intensive two-month-long training program. In terms of experience, Vasquez fell somewhere between the two but had been shoehorned into OCS to suit the needs of the project to which she was assigned. She had graduated five days ago and was wearing the single gold bars of a second lieutenant. Next time, she vowed to stop at her apartment and change into a casual outfit before heading down to Corporal J's.

"Doesn't matter now," Gunny Walker advised. "Everybody knows you because of the LMH, and they all know you made it through OCS. You're stuck with it now…ma'am."

"Arrghh…" Vasquez shook her head in resignation.

She had done well at OCS, graduating near the top of her class, but it had been a strain because she was expected to do the usual eight hours in classes and training exercises, then put in two hours each day with the Airwolf project, plus another two hours or more of study each night. She no longer had to worry about OCS, so she would be back full-time on the project.

"Somebody said First Fleet's back," she said, changing the subject. "Have you heard anything?"

"So I've been told," Walker said. "Scuttlebutt says the Babe on the Horse crossed the hyper limit around 0200 hours this morning. If that's true, they should make Luna sometime tomorrow."

Wonder if they'll put Val back on the project, Vasquez mused. *Anna's OK, but I miss the Babe.*

* * *

Lorna Greenwood had, in fact, returned to the Sol System, but she hadn't brought all of First Fleet with her. She had relieved Amy Ling and the Double Deuce, bringing them back to Luna for some well-deserved R&R. To replace them, she left her Second and Third Battle Groups at New Eden under Tom Sakura's command.

That would result in some shuffling of assignments, including the transfer of one of Robin Torrey's groups to First Fleet, but it was much more efficient than deploying replacements from Luna to New Eden. Given the damage sustained in the New Eden encounters, some rearrangement of the T.O. would be needed anyway.

LFS *Thermopylae* had arrived with the last supply train, bringing a fresh battalion of Marines. Rock Bartley turned command of the New Eden Marine Force over to Colonel Mackenzie and returned home with most of the original battalion aboard *Okinawa*. Mercedes Warren, with *Edwin Hubble* and the original New Eden scientific team, remained in place, still involved with their mission to study the planet and the Edies, but Carla and her team had gathered all the data they needed on Rothstein's Star. LRS *Lisa Randall* had come home to Luna.

Lorna made sure Sakura was thoroughly briefed on the planet, the Edies, and everything that was known about the Otuka. She and Tommy had also discussed a special message she'd received from Mick O'Hara, and what to do if certain unwanted visitors arrived.

* * *

Otuka Node 740—29 Light-Years from New Eden

"Tell us, Lord A'archa, were you perhaps female at the time these events occurred?"

"What did you say?" A'archa glared down the table—far down, toward the inferior end—at the young tsan who had asked the question.

"I expected to hear tales of courage, but you speak of cowardice as if it were a virtue," the lesser tsan replied. "I wondered if, perhaps, these fearsome food animals had frightened you so much, you inadvertently let your gender slip."

A'archa scrambled to his feet with a snarl, drawing his blade from the scabbard on his harness. Nearby tsans jumped away from him, but even as he drew the weapon, A'archa knew he had been neatly trapped. The young one might be inferior, perhaps by as much as ten thousand ranks, but he was younger, larger, and stronger than A'archa. The code of the clans demanded A'archa challenge the inferior to redress the insult, but he knew a duel of blades would end badly for him. *You had to tell the story, didn't you…to boast of your cleverness in dealing with the humans. Now you've given this lowborn cretin justification to challenge your courage, which is all he needs to advance himself in rank over your dead carcass.*

"SILENCE!"

The roar came from the far upper end of the table. A'archa turned and saw Lord M'orsta on his feet, with his blade in hand. M'orsta Makrust'galan, the ranking tsan at this node-gathering, was a massive, battle-scarred bull whose appearance alone would take the curl out of a lesser bull's horns. Despite his predicament, A'archa found himself wondering what M'orsta's female persona might look like. *Extremely ugly, I'm sure,* he decided, *but with that sort of mass and strength, she can probably demand that any male mate with her and be instantly obeyed.* He lowered his gaze and bowed to the superior lord.

"You miserable sack of urine-soaked excrement," M'orsta growled, pointing at the inferior far down the table. "If I hear you speak that way to a superior again, I will come down there and gut you myself, then Lord A'archa and I will divide the spoils of your falnor, and those below you will thank us as they all move up one level."

Silence was heavy in the hall, as the youngster's fate hung in the balance. One more word from him, and A'archa was certain M'orsta would make good on his promise, but it appeared the young challenger was not completely stupid. He said nothing but bowed deeply in M'orsta's direction.

"Better." M'orsta continued to gaze at the inferior. "Now listen, for you have much to learn.

"You know nothing about courage," he proclaimed. "It takes courage to shove your blade into your own guts. If you value courage so highly, why don't you do that?

"I'll tell you about courage," he continued. "Courage drove Lord B'arska into battle against these food animals you dismiss so lightly. Courage fueled by arrogance, by stupidity, caused B'arska to lead us against the humans, to take on their invincible warships and face their terrible weapons. Because of that arrogance, that stupidity, that so-called courage, twenty-one tsans followed Lord B'arska into battle and, of the twenty-one, I am the only one who survived. Do you question my courage?

"Now consider this. Lord A'archa did not have the option to disengage like I did. He was surrounded by a force that could have wiped him out in a heartbeat, so he challenged them to a battle of wits instead…and he won! He defied them, he misdirected them, he manipulated them using their own rules against them, and he did this while under threat of instant death at their hands. And in the end, he departed with the spoils of his venture intact. Now that's courage—the kind of courage that wins battles, not the stupid kind that gets whole falnor wiped out of existence in a heartbeat.

"As for you, young fool, don't ever engage in a battle of wits. You'll find yourself fighting without weapons."

A'archa was surprised. Obviously, M'orsta was not the dull-witted brute he appeared to be. He had not risen to power solely on his ability to smash heads, though that ability was no doubt useful at times. *Particularly when you need someone like him as an ally, since head-smashing is something even the most arrogant inferior will understand.*

He was surprised again when M'orsta sought him out after the gathering. The hulking bull approached him almost like an equal and addressed him in a cordial tone.

"Tell me, A'archa, did they really threaten to take your head as a trophy?"

"Indeed, they did," A'archa replied. "To be truthful, that impressed me even more than their mighty warships. They are obviously not the simple food animals to which we are accustomed."

"No, they are not," M'orsta agreed. "And while I did not have the benefit of personal interaction with them, I found their warships to be impressive. That fool B'arska led us right into their jaws, and they chewed us up and spit us out."

"Speaking of their warships, my Lord—" A'archa retrieved a data reader from his pouch, selected a data crystal, and placed it in the reader's receptacle, "—I had an opportunity to observe the human ships at much closer range than you did. I think you will find this interesting."

He began to page through the images the reader displayed. M'orsta looked at them, then threw back his head with a bark of laughter.

"Hah! Artwork! Fierce creatures, heroic battle scenes, humans armed for combat displayed in such fine detail and such vivid colors. Who would believe they were capable of such things or had any interest in creating such wonders, especially on the hulls of spaceships where few will ever see them?"

"I must have those images," he demanded. "What will you trade for them?"

A'archa pulled the crystal out of its socket and handed it to the superior tsan.

"With my compliments," he said. "Your support today was payment enough."

"Hmmmm…I hear you've made enough profit from this foray that you can afford to be generous." M'orsta nodded. "So, what grand plan have you got for your next adventure?"

"Well," A'archa replied, "since our last encounter went so well, I thought, perhaps, I might seek out the humans again, to see what other profits might come my way."

"You're going back to the 47th Reserve?"

"No, the humans are too sensitive about that place." A'archa shook his head. "There are too many warships looking for something to shoot at. On the other hand, I think I might have an idea where their homeworld is."

"You are either extremely clever or completely insane," M'orsta told him. "If you survive this venture, I'll concede the former. Pass the word to me through the nodes when you return. I've no desire to confront the humans in battle again, but if you can find some other way to profit from them, I will be most interested in hearing about it. Perhaps we can work out some mutually beneficial arrangement."

* * *

CNS *Avignon*—Near the New Eden Hyper Limit

"Why are we not moving, Captain? We came here to see the planet, so please take us there."

"This is an uncharted system, Excellency," Captain Marcel DuPont replied. "It is better to proceed with caution."

"We are not proceeding at all! It has been hours since we emerged from hyperspace," Holger Hauptmann complained. "What are you waiting for?"

DuPont considered the Confederacy's special envoy to be an arrogant bastard who rarely engaged his brain before opening his mouth. He wondered how such a dislikeable person could possibly have been chosen to oversee a mission that might call for a degree of diplomatic skill.

Hauptmann couldn't even deal with Confederate Navy people in a reasonable manner. Why put him in charge of a mission that called for dealing with the Moonies, who already had little respect for the Confederacy? DuPont suspected some high-level Confederate officials wanted this mission to be an epic failure. If so, DuPont and his crew might well end up the scapegoats for that failure, so despite intense personal dislike for the man, he was determined to help Hauptmann succeed, if possible.

"It has only been forty minutes, Excellency," DuPont replied. "Since we know the Lunar Free State has a military presence here, I took the reasonable precaution of transmitting notice of our arrival in the usual international format. Assuming they are operating in orbit around the planet, we cannot expect a reply for at least two hours. If I do not hear back from them soon after that, we will proceed, but I would prefer to get an acknowledgement first."

"We don't need an acknowledgement, permission, or even the time of day from the damned Moonies. I am ordering you to proceed immediately."

"Hyper event! Multiple hyper events! Sir—"

"I see it." DuPont acknowledged his tactical officer's report. "It would appear, Excellency, they have taken notice of us after all."

Hauptmann stared at the large screen at the front of CNS *Avignon's* bridge. He saw seven flashing yellow icons that had not been there a moment ago. As he watched, the icons turned to green, and data codes appeared next to them.

"They are answering IFF, sir," the tactical officer advised.

"So noted," DuPont replied. He wondered whether it might have been appropriate, under the circumstances, to paint those icons red. Green indicated friendly units, and he had a feeling this would not be a friendly encounter.

"Hail the battlecruiser," he directed.

* * *

LFS *Isis*—Near the New Eden Hyper Limit

Tom Sakura liked Amy Ling's system defense plan, but with two full battle groups at his disposal, he decided to beef it up a bit. His perimeter force, patrolling just outside the hyper limit, consisted of an entire battle group, including a battlecruiser and two heavy cruisers. His plan called for the two groups to alternate on perimeter patrol, and now, his group was up. The other group, under Rear Admiral Raul Sanchez, was holding station in New Eden orbit.

The Otuka had not returned, so the three-ship Confederacy squadron gave him the first opportunity to test his defense strategy. His response was probably more aggressive than necessary, but it had gotten their attention. His display showed the light cruiser CNS *Avignon* and a pair of *Rapier*-class destroyers facing off against his own force—the battlecruiser *Isis*, two cruisers, and four destroyers.

Why did they have to send warships? he wondered. *If they had sent unarmed survey or research or even diplomatic envoy ships, we could have turned them away without a confrontation, and they would have accomplished the same thing. I'm still going to turn them away, but it could get ugly.*

* * *

CNS *Avignon*

"You have no right to stop us," Hauptmann raged at the LFS Commodore whose image dominated the main screen on *Avignon's* bridge. "We are proceeding to the planet, and I will have words with your superior when we arrive."

Marcel DuPont gritted his teeth. He was on the verge of having Hauptmann removed from the bridge so he could deal with the Moonies in a reasonable manner, but before he could issue the order, the screen split, and another image appeared—a man wearing the uniform of an LFS Vice Admiral.

"If you have words for Commodore Russo's superior, let's hear them. I am Vice Admiral Sakura, commanding all Lunar Free State operations in this system, and you will not proceed to the planet under any circumstances. This is a Lunar protectorate, and you can consider me the protector of the system."

DuPont regarded the Moonie admiral with cautious respect. Sakura was their Deputy Fleet Commander, second in rank only to Greenwood, the supreme commander of all LFS military forces. Like her, he was reported to be a hard core, no-nonsense military commander who believed all diplomatic issues could be resolved with a sufficient number of warships.

And he has certainly brought enough, DuPont was forced to admit. Unfortunately, Hauptmann didn't know enough about such things to be impressed.

"You cannot stop us. Captain." Hauptmann turned to DuPont. "Proceed to the planet immediately."

"Sir! They're painting us!" DuPont's tactical officer was looking at a screen full of angry red threat warnings. All seven of the Moonie warships were locking weapons on them, and DuPont had no doubt they would shoot at the slightest provocation.

"Mr. Lefebvre, Petty Officer Borne, remove Mr. Hauptmann from the bridge immediately," he ordered. "Put him in his cabin, under guard."

"You have just put an end to your career, DuPont," Hauptmann snarled.

"And perhaps I have saved your miserable life, Excellency," DuPont replied with a snarl of his own.

"Admiral—" he turned back to the screen, where Sakura waited patiently for the drama to play out, "—we are taking no action at this time. Please tell your people to stop their targeting scans. We do not wish to engage you."

Sakura said nothing, but Commodore Russo nodded to someone off screen. DuPont didn't take his eyes off the two Moonie officers but noted the audible warnings from the tactical station had ceased. Then Sakura spoke again.

"I'm sorry, Captain DuPont, but we cannot allow anyone inside the hyper limit of this system without prior authorization from Lunar Command. That's not my order; it comes directly from TerraNova, from the chief executive, himself. The Lunar Free State has declared this system and its inhabitants to be under our protection, and we are taking that responsibility very seriously. I'm going to have to ask you to turn around and go home.

"I don't want to engage you," he continued, "especially since it would hardly be an equal contest. Also, please don't make the mistake of assuming this is all we've got. Any attempt by the Confederacy to respond with a larger force will end very badly."

Hah! DuPont gave a mental snort. *All you've got, here and now, is enough to take out half the Confederate fleet.*

"I understand," he told Sakura. "We will, as you say, turn around and go home. But please note that we are doing so under strong diplomatic protest, and only because you have threatened us with military action."

"So noted, Captain." Sakura nodded. "I think we understand each other quite well."

* * *

LFS *Isis*

Tom Sakura watched as the three Confederate warships jumped into hyperspace and disappeared from the battlecruiser's tactical screens. He keyed his link to Russo on *Isis's* main bridge.

"Stand us down and release the other ships to return to patrol stations, Bill. I'll be in my quarters, preparing a report. I think we need to get word back to Luna on this one ASAP. If we move smartly, *Impala* can get back to Sol well ahead of Mr. Hauptmann and his people."

As he left the flag bridge, Sakura reflected on the vagaries of interstellar diplomacy. The Lunar Free State was revered by its allies, feared by its enemies, and respected by all alien races in this corner of the galaxy. Unfortunately, it had never been able to command the same respect from the nations of Earth. He was glad to be out here with a simple directive and a mission to carry out. At least he didn't have to listen to all the nasty things Earth's news media would say about him, his superiors, and his Lunar nation in the near future.

* * * * *

Chapter Fourteen

Planet New Eden—Field Research Station

"No, Mercedes, I'm not going back."

"Owen, we need you," Warren pleaded. "These people need you to speak for them back on Luna."

"You're better at that sort of thing than I am," Phillips insisted. "I can't leave now, or ever, for that matter."

"Never? You don't plan to ever go home?"

"This is my home now. I've got enough research here to last a lifetime. More importantly, I have a life here now. The chief and the elders weren't sure what to do with me. A man my age should already know how to hunt, fish, build a shelter, and so on, but I don't have any of those skills. Then someone mentioned that old Aki, the metalworker, was getting on in years and had no sons, no one to continue his work. I volunteered for the job, so now, I'm the blacksmith's apprentice. It's fascinating stuff."

"I don't understand." Warren looked puzzled. "I keep thinking the Edies are too advanced to be a hunter-gatherer society. I've seen some of the metalwork, ceramics, and glassware they create. It's beautiful stuff, but isn't it a little out of the ordinary for people who live in tents and don't have much in the way of agriculture?"

"They aren't actually tents," he told her. They're more like yurts, with lattice wall structures and circular crowns. It's a sophisticated design, a durable, rigid structure that's portable. Yes, the Edies are more advanced in many ways than we expected, but consider their history.

"About two hundred years ago—local years, which are about twenty percent longer than Earth years—they were more advanced than they are today. In Earth terms, their civilization was at a stage comparable to the late Roman Empire or early Medieval Europe. They had cities of brick, stone, and wood, with community water and simple sewer systems. They had farms, roads, and animal-powered transportation—wagons, coaches, and the like. They had basic knowledge of medicine. They had literature and art.

"I've listened to their oral history, seen their preserved artifacts. We've spotted the ruins of some of their larger cities from orbit, leveled and overgrown by vegetation. Marlowe and his team are planning an archeological dig at one of them."

"But what happened?" she asked, then shook her head. "Of course…the Otuka happened."

"Yes, the Otuka. They came, they pillaged, and they killed, and they've been doing it for two centuries. The planetary population may have been on the order of twenty million when they first arrived. Now, it's more like two million, three at most.

"The first few decades were the worst, when the Edies still thought they could shelter in cities and towns and could defend themselves with bow-and-arrow technology. The centaurs leveled the cities and slaughtered the urban population, then they moved out to the farms and took those people as well. They drove the survivors into the wilderness, where they had to relearn survival skills they had lost over generations of civilized living.

"They managed to retain some of the knowledge and skills from that time, but they're nowhere near where they were two centuries ago. If we keep the Otuka from coming back, they have a chance to move forward again. But I think you know the greatest danger at this point."

"Us," she replied without hesitation.

"Right," he agreed. "Look at Earth's history. Every time a primitive culture comes in contact with a more advanced society, the primitive culture suffers. It loses its identity, struggles to accept a new cultural paradigm it doesn't begin to understand, and is often exploited by those who allegedly come to help and protect the poor, ignorant savages.

"Then there are the commercial interests, people who are only interested in the planet's resources and don't pretend to give a damn about the natives. As far as they're concerned, the local population is only a source of menial labor to be exploited."

"You're right." She shook her head. "We can't allow that to happen. We need to protect them from…well, from ourselves and anyone else that comes along. Owen, that's exactly why I need you to come back and plead the case with Lunar Command and the Directorate. You know the Edies better than anyone, you have the scientific credentials to speak with authority, and you have the passion to be their champion."

"I can't, Mercedes. I can't because there's a chance—maybe a small one, but a chance nonetheless—that I won't get back. I can't just buy a ticket on a commercial ship. We're at the mercy of the Fleet, and I'd be further at the mercy of the LRI Board. Suppose someone back there decides I'm needed for another assignment."

"Owen, no one would do that."

"Angel's pregnant. I can't be gone for that long, and taking her with me is not an option. The culture shock would be devastating."

"Oh…" Warren was suddenly at a loss for words.

"Look, here's what I can do. I can give you my reports, everything I know about the Edies, all my arguments for leaving them alone. We can't go away because they need our protection, and we need to study them. A limited number of researchers can be allowed on the planet, but we need to establish rules for those researchers to minimize the impact on the Edie culture. When are you going back to Luna?"

"*Einstein* is due to arrive in two weeks, with additional people and equipment for the team. I'll be going back to Luna with *Hubble* a few days later."

"Fine. I can have everything ready by then. We'll need to think very carefully about what we can do for the Edies, like introducing some aspects of modern medicine and maybe a few technological advances—stuff that's only a little above their current level, things they can develop and maintain on their own. Maybe we can limit that to stuff that was discovered or invented back in the Middle Ages on Earth. Unfortunately, most of that stuff had to do with warfare and weapons. On the other hand, the telescope was invented back then, which was the beginning of modern astronomy. The Edies know the basics of making glass, so—"

"Owen—"

"Huh? What is it?"

"Congratulations to you and Angel."

"Oh…" Phillips grinned at her. "You're the first person I've told. I was hoping you'd be around to see the baby born."

"Don't worry," she assured him. "I'll be back. But first, I have to go back to Luna to fight for your baby's future."

* * *

LFS Fleet Transient Quarters—TerraNova City, Luna

"Once again, you seem discouraged, Maya. What's wrong?"

"You're not on the project anymore, Val. I don't know if I'm allowed to talk about it."

"I am still cleared for the project, perhaps because no one remembered to take me off the list. In any case, Anna has kept me up to date. You've made remarkable progress and have proven the concept beyond anyone's expectations. At this moment, there is not an Airwolf pilot in the Fleet who can match you in air combat. For that matter, no one can match you in ground attack with a Raptor, either."

"Right. I'm a real hotshot, but they're still cancelling the project."

"That's not your fault. You turned out to be the exception, rather than the rule, among pilots. They haven't been able to find anyone else who can adapt to the control system the way you did. They found three pilots who looked promising, but when those three had the interface implanted, they couldn't learn to use it."

"I know. I worked with them. They are good pilots, but I can't seem to teach anyone else how to do it."

"Again, it's not your fault. Anna worked with them, as well, and was unable to make progress. They are still good pilots, so, in the end, they had their implants removed and went back to conventional flying."

"Just out of curiosity—" Maya couldn't resist the question, "—did Anna show them her world the way you did with me?"

"No, she did not," the AI replied. "When I told the other AIs what I had done, they were shocked. No one questioned my right to do it or whether it was necessary to advance the project, but they questioned my willingness to expose myself that way. AIs wouldn't normally consider doing something like that with each other, let alone with a human. They consider it equivalent to sexual violation. In short, they think it was a very kinky thing for me to do."

Maya blinked at the screen. She was certain Val's avatar was wearing a sultry smile unlike any she'd previously displayed.

"Well…uh…I don't know about sexual," she stammered, "but it certainly was an intimate thing. I mean…"

"You're blushing, Maya," Val observed, "but yes, I know what you mean. We share a bond now. I am happy to have that bond, and I hope you are as well. It's why I get distressed when I see you discouraged or upset about something."

"You're right, Val. I shouldn't feel sorry for myself. If they had pulled the plug on the project five seconds after you and I had our intimate moment, it would still have been worth it, just to have that experience.

"I guess," she admitted, "I'm feeling bad because I let other people down, people like Doc Madison and Commander Jensen. But I didn't really let anybody down. I did my part, and it isn't my fault they couldn't find anybody else for the program. If they want another pilot, I guess they'll have to smash him up in a Raptor crash, let the docs put him back together, and teach him to walk again with crutches."

"And then let him violate some poor, unsuspecting, virgin AI," Val added.

"Hey—" Vasquez chuckled, "—you weren't exactly unsuspecting, as I recall. It was your idea."

"That's true," the AI replied, "but I was a virgin. I had no more idea what to expect than you did."

There was a moment of silence, then Vasquez drew a deep breath.

"OK, Val, I have to know. Did that intimate moment work both ways? I mean, did you feel—"

"Yes," the AI replied before she finished the question. "The interface works both ways. It has to, so you can receive input and send commands. In that moment, I felt what it would be like to have a human body—your body. I'm sorry, I couldn't tell you that until now. I was concerned you might be upset. I feared it might damage our friendship."

There was an even longer moment of silence, then Maya shook her head and looked at the screen with a crooked grin.

"You're gonna have to stop doing that, Val. Every time I think I have everything nicely figured out, you throw something at me that blows my mind. No, it won't hurt our friendship. If anything, it makes it stronger. But you know I'm gonna be awake all night thinking about it, don't you?"

Now, it was the AI's turn to chuckle.

"Well," she replied, "you did take my virginity, but you also gave me something that no other AI has ever experienced."

"Yeah, well, I guess we're even. Seriously, Val, that bond goes deep, and I really missed you while you were gone. I think I know where you went, but without mentioning any names, how did it go?"

"Yes, you know where I went, and, without mentioning names, we kicked some donkey ass, as you Marines would say. It has been a long time since I was in combat, but the experience is still as intense as I remembered it to be."

"Yeah, intense; that's the word for it," Vasquez agreed. "I wonder if I'll ever have a chance to feel that way again. I mean, simulations are fun, but it isn't the same. There's something about knowing your life is on the line that makes it so…well, like you said, intense."

"You may get the chance," Val assured her. "I haven't seen any official orders, but there is a recommendation making its way to the top levels of the Fleet. It will probably go all the way to Admiral Greenwood, and I think I know her well. The recommendation is logical and serves the best interests of the Fleet, so she will almost certainly accept it."

"And that recommendation is?" Vasquez prompted.

"Well, I can't actually read it to you, since you aren't on the distribution list, but let's talk about the logical thing to do. Fleet has two very expensive aircraft prototypes, a Raptor and an Airwolf, built for the project, but only you can fly them. Any Raptor or Airwolf squadron can maintain them, however, since they are standard models, except for the control interface. The interface is a simple plug-in system any competent technician can service and maintain. In other words, one or both of those aircraft can go back into Fleet service, as long as you go with them."

"Now it happens," she continued, "that the Assault Carrier *Omaha Beach* has a Raptor squadron in need of a commander. Raptor pilots are usually non-coms, but squadron command requires an officer, an experienced Raptor pilot who has gone through OCS or Fleet Academy. I know a certain lieutenant who meets that requirement. The fact that she can also fly an Airwolf will be considered a bonus, especially aboard a carrier where they have space to tuck in an extra aircraft or two."

* * *

Chamber of the Directorate, Lunar Command—TerraNova City, Luna

The members of the Lunar Directorate rose from their seats and stood in respectful silence as Mick O'Hara entered the room. It was a traditional courtesy extended to the chief executive, but the directors were not here to carry out O'Hara's orders. The primary function of the Directorate was oversight. They were here to review and evaluate his performance as CEO.

"Please, take your seats, ladies and gentlemen," he told them and stepped up to the podium at the front of the chamber. As they sat down, he paused for a moment to look over the group.

The Constitution had originally called for a 25-member Directorate but had been amended two decades ago to increase the number to 100 directors, all elected at large by direct vote of all Lunar citizens. Directors served for five years, which meant twenty seats were open for election each year, not counting deaths, resignations, or retirements. Each LFS citizen was allowed one vote for each open seat but was not required, or allowed, to specify which seat he or she was voting for. Voters could cast votes for twenty different people, cast all their votes for a single person, or scatter their votes in any other way they chose.

There were no predetermined candidates, and citizens could vote for any adult Lunar citizen in good standing, regardless of rank or position in the community. It was the only concession to democracy anywhere in the LFS Constitution, but citizens took it seriously, and voter turnout typically ran near ninety percent.

The Constitution forbade any sort of public campaigning, advertising, or electioneering by anyone seeking a seat on the Directorate.

Grass-roots gatherings of like-minded people were allowed, and those favoring a particular person for election could promote their views by personal contact with others, but media advertising and public posting of notices were forbidden. Of course, voters knew who the incumbents were, and re-elections were common.

When the results were tallied, seats went to those who got the most votes—in an ordinary year, the top twenty people in the popular vote count. Since there were no districts or other divisions of population, all elected directors were presumed to represent all citizens. As a practical matter, however, some natural divisions had evolved from the structure of the LFS. There were always businesspeople in the Directorate—well-known executives of Terra Corporation, for example, since citizens in the business community tended to vote for their own. Likewise, there were always military people—Navy, Marines, and Engineers—some from the enlisted ranks, though most were officers. The scientific community was also well-represented.

Directors served without compensation, and their service was in addition to any regular job or position they held in the LFS Table of Organization. Business executives and military commanders were required to allow duly-elected directors to attend Directorate meetings or conduct other Directorate business, and directors were not answerable to their regular chain of command for their actions in the Directorate. Recognizing that directors had careers of their own and might be required to serve in places far from Luna, the Constitution allowed them to assign their voting proxy to another director for the duration of their absence.

The group facing O'Hara, today, was a few short of a hundred, but more than the eighty required to remove him from office, should the Directorate choose to do so. In theory, the Directors could do that at any time after a CEO's first year of service by simply calling for a vote. If eighty percent of the Directorate—all serving directors, not just those present at the meeting—voted against him, he would be required to step down, and the Directorate would then choose a new chief executive.

In practice, it had never happened. Luna's first chief executive, Ian Stevens, had died in office, when the alien Mekota destroyed an envoy ship carrying Stevens and several Earth leaders to what was supposed to be a peaceful first contact meeting. The second CEO of the LFS, Lorna Greenwood, had resigned after a few years in office, judging her own performance more harshly than even her most vocal critics had. Upon her resignation, Mick O'Hara had become CEO, and he had held the position for over thirty years. Lorna had gone back to commanding the Lunar Fleet and had retained that position to the present.

Today's discussions were unlikely to be the cause of O'Hara's removal. He was extremely popular with the citizenry, as much for his adamant refusal to give homage to Earth, as for his dedication to the advancement of the Lunar nation. Most of the directors were comfortable with his leadership.

He looked at the assembled group and saw familiar faces. His wife, Scarlett, was there, duly elected by a popular following in the business community. Lorna Greenwood was there as well, having been elected and re-elected for over thirty years by her loyal Navy and Marine people. Her daughter, Carla, was also a director, having gotten votes from both the scientific and the business communities. They, like the others, were waiting patiently to hear what he had to say.

"Ladies and gentlemen," he began, "our last meeting was held behind closed doors to discuss our involvement in a military action at what is now known as Rothstein's Star. At the time, the matter was considered secret for reasons of national security.

"That is no longer the case, so members of the news media are with us today, at least those from our Journalist Corps. We will hold a press conference for Earth's media personnel soon. The location of Rothstein's Star and the issues involving the inhabited planet known as New Eden have already been the subject of an inquiry by the Confederacy, and Confederate warships have attempted to enter the star system in question. They have been turned away by units of the Lunar Fleet."

That brought an angry murmur from the crowd, but their anger wasn't directed at O'Hara. The Confederacy of Nations had few friends in the Lunar Directorate.

"We have also been advised by the Akara," he continued, raising his voice to be heard, "that we no longer need to keep their involvement in this matter a secret. They have openly announced their support for us in that regard.

"I've prepared a background brief for public distribution, but for the benefit of those media representatives present today, I'll give you an overview.

"Some time ago, the Akara of the Copper Hills Clan advised us of the location of a star system with one inhabited planet we are calling New Eden. That planet is home to a race of aboriginal humans—not humanoids, but *humans* just like us. The Akara expressed deep concern for the welfare of those humans, who were being exploited by another alien race, known as the Otuka. You know the Otuka were responsible for the *Summer Solstice* incident, but we allowed you to assume it was an isolated act of piracy. In fact, the Otuka were hunting, killing, and eating the human inhabitants of New Eden, just as they did to the passengers and crew of *Summer Solstice*.

"We sent forces of the Lunar Fleet to that star system, where we engaged the Otuka on three separate occasions. We suffered significant losses in the first two engagements, with over 3,000 Navy and Marine personnel killed in action and several warships destroyed or damaged, but, in the end, we were victorious. Thousands of Otuka ships were destroyed, with uncounted hundreds of thousands of the aliens killed, in space and on the planet. It has been three months since the last encounter, a weak incursion by the enemy that was defeated with no additional losses on our part. As of the message that arrived by courier from New Eden yesterday, the Otuka have not returned.

"That's all covered in the brief we will distribute, but now, we face a new challenge. There's an adage that says if you save someone's life, you are forever responsible for that person. I don't know where that idea came from or if I fully agree with it, but it's an appropriate point to consider here and now.

"We, the people of the Lunar Free State, have, in fact, saved someone's life. Through our actions at New Eden, we saved the lives of hundreds of thousands—perhaps even millions—of the people of that planet. Our science team estimates the current planetary population is on the order of two and a half million. In other words, the people of New Eden—the Edies, as the scientists have been calling them—outnumber the people of the Lunar Free State by a significant margin. But we hold the future of those millions in our hands, and, now, we must decide what to do with it.

"We have made ourselves their protectors, and we cannot abandon them. If we do, the Otuka will surely return. The Edies are a simple, hunter-gatherer society. They have little or nothing in the way of technology, not even agriculture or large communities. Simple self-preservation, the need to hide from the alien horror, has kept them from gathering or building anything permanent on what is otherwise a rich and beautiful planet. Now, they no longer need to hide and can begin to move forward as a society. They have us to protect them and to teach them.

"But," O'Hara cautioned, "we must be very careful. Earth's history has taught us what happens to primitive societies when they come in contact with others more advanced than them. The aboriginal tribes of Africa and North America provide many examples—tribes whose culture was suppressed, whose lands were taken, who were forced to live under a system of government not of their choosing. They were exploited by commercial interests who wanted their resources, and they were deprived of their culture by well-meaning individuals who insisted on bringing modern civilization to them.

"We cannot allow that to happen. We may, after careful consideration, introduce some beneficial advances, perhaps something of modern medicine, perhaps basic methods of agriculture, but these advances must be things they can work with on their own, without help, and must not include anything that conflicts with their culture as it exists today. We want to observe their development, and we can permit scientists to study them. Beyond that, we need to stand back, keep our hands off, and not try to drag them into our version of the 21st century. We must never forget: New Eden belongs to them, not us.

"For that reason, I have declared New Eden and the Rothstein system to be a protectorate of the Lunar Free State. I've invited the Judge Advocate General, Admiral Morrison, to join us today for questions about the Constitutional issues involved, but I've already had a lengthy discussion with Judge Morrison and his people, and I can give you a short version of our conclusions. This is virgin territory, something that has not happened in our history. I'm advised by the JAG that I am within my authority to issue such a proclamation, but, as yet, no framework exists for a protectorate within the Constitution or the codes and regulations of the LFS. In short, we're making this up as we go along, and the JAG will call a halt if, at any point, we go beyond constitutional limits.

"This is what we have so far. 'Protectorate' means we are obligating ourselves to protect New Eden against any incursion we judge harmful to the Edies or their culture. That includes everything from the Otuka who want to eat them to human crusaders or missionaries who want to convert them, civilize them, or otherwise change their way of life. It will certainly include anyone who tries to enter the star system without our knowledge and prior approval, which is why we turned those Confederate warships back. I don't have a problem with the Confederacy, or any other Earth group, sending scientists to study the star, the planet, or the Edies, but they will need to convince us they have a legitimate purpose and that their presence will not disturb what we are trying to protect.

"Now—" he smiled at the audience, "—having expressed all those lofty ideals and high-minded goals, I have to find a practical way to make it work. I intend to create a New Eden Commission—a ten-member board, whose term of service we haven't yet determined. I believe the Directorate needs to get involved, and to that extent, I will appoint those members, subject to confirmation by a simple majority of the directors. I recognize that we are setting a precedent for similar commissions in the future, but I believe this is the correct way to go.

"We need to have a variety of perspectives represented on that commission. We should have members representing Fleet, since we need to maintain a military presence at Rothstein's Star for the foreseeable future. We are talking about a star system seventy light-years away, so I will require that one or more of the commission's military members be officers assigned to fleet units stationed in that system. Likewise, the Lunar Research Institute should provide several members, preferably scientists who are familiar with New Eden, its people, and their culture. Again, that should include one or more scientists conducting research at New Eden.

"The business community will be represented on the commission, as well. To finance this effort, we need to determine whether the star system has resources we can tap without disturbing the Edies. We also need to make sure no one is exploiting the Edies or disturbing their way of life for commercial reasons. If we can mine precious metals in the arctic wastelands near the planet's poles, that's fine, but we are not going to build a smelter for those metals in the middle of the inhabited zones. I'd prefer to keep as much of our commercial infrastructure off the planet as possible. That hypothetical smelter, for example, could just as easily be built in orbit.

"That's a very general overview. I realize it's hard to evaluate without knowing more about the subject, so I'll turn the floor over to Dr. Mercedes Warren, Fellow of the Lunar Research Institute, and the leader of the first scientific expedition to New Eden. For the record, Dr. Warren is my first appointee to the New Eden Commission, subject to confirmation by the Directors, but first, she has a presentation that will give you a better feel for the planet and its inhabitants. Dr. Warren…"

Mercedes Warren drew a deep breath as she got to her feet. She had expected to come here to argue her case for New Eden and the Edies, but it appeared there would be no need to argue. Admiral O'Hara had adopted virtually all her recommendations. Unless the Directorate chose to revolt, her battle was won.

She stepped up to the podium, noting that the huge screen behind her was already displaying her first graphic. The small screen in front of her also displayed the graphic, with an icon in the lower corner, indicating that Mike was waiting to assist her as needed. She looked out at the Directors.

"Ladies and gentlemen," she began, "allow me to introduce you to the Edies."

* * *

LFS *Omaha Beach*—Lunar Fleet Anchorage

"Attention on deck!"

Twelve Raptor pilots and four crew chiefs, all of them noncoms, got up from their seats as Vasquez entered the room. She no longer needed crutches to walk, though she was still slow and not very graceful. She carried a cane to help with the occasional misstep, but for the most part, she could get from Point A to Point B without incident. The bad news was that her recovery had reached its limit, and even Doc Madison was telling her that her present condition was about as good as it was going to get.

She reached the podium and looked out at her audience, a sorry-looking lot—uniforms untidy, poor posture, not very attentive. Obviously, they were not impressed with their new commander. It was about what she expected. She'd been thoroughly briefed by Colonel Kinney, *Omaha Beach's* Air Group Commander, when she first reported aboard.

"As you were," she told them, and they dropped back into their seats. Some of them picked up coffee cups, while others busied themselves with their data pads, further emphasizing their lack of respect. A pilot in the front row turned to continue a conversation he'd been having with the woman behind him.

Vasquez stepped around the podium and rapped her cane sharply on the man's writing desk. The sound was like a gunshot in the small briefing room, and all conversation stopped. The pilot whirled to face her, and his startled look changed to one of sullen anger.

"Put the damned coffee cups and data pads down," she ordered, "and listen up, or I will conduct the rest of this briefing with all of you standing at attention."

She waited. They complied with the order, and the room was silent.

"I am Lieutenant Maya Vasquez," she told them, "your new squadron commander. Rumor has it I got this job because I was too damned stubborn to take a disability retirement. Fleet didn't know what else to do with me, so they gave me the 26th Attack Squadron, the sorriest bunch of rejects, misfits, and lowlifes in the Marine Corps. I'm told this is where other squadrons dump pilots who can't fly worth a damn, crew chiefs too lazy to do their jobs, and techs that don't know which end of screwdriver to grab hold of. I'm also told your last commander was relieved of duty due to a drinking problem and sent back to Luna for rehab.

"Now, I'm sure you've all heard the scuttlebutt that says I can't fly anymore because I got banged up in a Raptor crash. Sure, Fleet managed to find a handicap-equipped Raptor that can be flown by a cripple who can barely walk. They gave it to me so I can call myself a pilot, but chances are, I'll be leading this squadron from a bar stool at the Officer's Club—just like the last guy—while you people go out and fly actual missions.

"Well, ladies and gentlemen, we are about to flush that notion right down the crapper. Today's mission will be a high-speed, low-level ground attack exercise on Serenity Range, with live ordnance, and your performance in that exercise will tell me what I have to work with. Do well, and your life might get better. Screw it up, and you will find yourselves in the Hurt Locker."

She noted, with satisfaction, that the pilots looked very unhappy. Technically, the Raptor was designed for atmospheric flight. It was vacuum-certified and re-entry capable for launch from orbit, but it relied on wings and control surfaces for lift and flight control in atmosphere. It did, however, get some lift and directional control from the gravity packs that provided its forward propulsion—enough to take on a ground attack mission on an airless world, as long as that world's gravity was less than half that of Earth. Serenity Range was in Mare Serenitatis on Luna, and Luna's gravity was only a sixth of Earth's.

Without aerodynamics to keep it stable, the Raptor was a copper-plated bitch to fly. The slightest bit of over control would cause it to go into a sideways spin or an end-over-end tumble. Add the difficulty of hitting a ground target in a low-gravity environment under those conditions, especially with a high-speed, low-altitude attack, and the prospect would make even the most experienced Raptor pilot sweat a little. The live ordnance would only make their screw-ups a bit more spectacular and might cause some of them to wimp out on the low-altitude requirement for fear of catching stray fragments from their own weapons.

"I will lead Alpha Flight," she continued. "No, Gunny Metcalf, I'm not taking your job away. Next time out, I will lead Bravo Flight, and the time after that, it will be Charlie Flight's turn in the barrel. Each flight leader will get their turn flying Odd Man in a five-ship formation. I want you to get used to it, because every time this squadron goes out, I intend to be leading somebody's flight.

"Now, here's where it gets interesting." She gave them a smile that lacked any trace of humor. "If any one of you jokers posts a better score than mine for the exercise, I will buy drinks for all of you in the aircrew lounge tonight. The flight that posts the lowest scores will report to the simulator deck at 0800 tomorrow for a full day of intensive training. If none of you manage to beat me, you will be buying my drinks for the next month, and all of you will report for said training and be prepared for a lot more of it in the future.

"Mission data is in your download packets, including ordnance load outs and targeting information. You've got two hours to study the packet, preflight your birds, and get your asses to the launch line. We go at 1100 hours.

"Oh, and one more thing. I checked the status board this morning, and all of your ships are listed as online and ready. If one of those ships should somehow get down checked between now and 1100, I will be very upset. The pilot, crew chief, and any tech who touched that bird will find themselves on my Shit List and should be prepared to justify their existence at a Prayer Meeting, which I will hold as soon as the mission is completed."

She paused for a moment and looked them over. None of them were smiling.

"Any questions?" she asked.

* * *

LFS *Valkyrie*—Lunar Fleet Anchorage

"At ease, Commander. Take a seat," Lorna directed as she returned Jennifer Tanaka's salute. Tanaka settled herself into one of the armchairs in front of Lorna's desk.

"First of all, the Board has confirmed your permanent promotion to Lieutenant Commander. Congratulations."

"Thank you, ma'am."

"You earned it. Fleet is quite satisfied with your performance at Rothstein's Star. More importantly, while *Lisa Randall* is a Fleet ship, she was built to satisfy the needs of the scientists. The LRI Board has expressed satisfaction with the results of the expedition, the ship, and the manner in which you and your crew supported the mission. Of course, my daughter is the tail that wags that dog, but I understand you and Carla got along well. She's brilliant, but she can be difficult to work with at times, so I'm happy to hear that.

"Just as importantly, Commander O'Hara spoke well of you. While he's just a destroyer commander, he distinguished himself in action out there. Admiral Ling has put *Timberwolf* up for Sword of the Fleet, and that's going to be approved, so I have to take it seriously when he says he would go into battle with you anytime."

"Actually," Tanaka responded with a sheepish smile, "I got the impression he thought I was a bit too aggressive."

"Why? Because you behaved as if you had a light cruiser under you, rather than a research ship? Because you couldn't resist stuffing a couple of Vipers up the Otuka's tailpipe? I can't imagine why he would think that." Lorna favored her with a grin.

"Let's cut to the chase. I am perfectly content to leave you in command of *Lisa Randall*, but you originally requested posting to a warship. I can pass the word back to Personnel Resources to start looking for a lieutenant commander slot for you on a cruiser or battlecruiser, but there's another option, as well. Six months from now, a new *Predator*-class destroyer will be coming out of the yards; it will be commissioned LFS *Jaguar*. I'm putting together a short list of officers I'm considering for command of her. I can put you on that list, though I can't promise you'll get it. You'd be up against some stiff competition. Your choice, Commander."

"Honestly, Admiral, I've given it a lot of thought," Tanaka replied, "and I think I'd like to stay with *Randall*. She's a fine ship, and I'm happy with my crew. Besides, even without the Otuka encounter, the mission turned out to be more challenging, more interesting, more exciting than I thought it would be."

"My sister was a scientist," she added. "By keeping command of *Randall*, I feel like I'll be honoring her memory."

"I understand, Commander." Lorna nodded. "So be it. *Randall* is yours until further notice. That should wrap up our business for today."

* * *

Tanaka got to her feet, saluted, and left. As soon as she was gone, Lorna turned her attention to a blinking icon on her desk display. "What's this about, Val?" she inquired, touching the icon.

"We have a message from OSG, Admiral. They are tracking eleven bogies that dropped out of hyper and are headed in-system from the Orion sector. They show a profile that is familiar to us, and an IFF query produced the code for the transponder we attached to Lord A'archa's ship back in the Rothstein system."

"You mean the one that says, 'Call Admiral Greenwood if you ever encounter this bastard?' Damn! How did he figure out where we live?"

"It is possible he guessed based on fleet comings and goings at New Eden, Admiral, but his approach suggests he may have come by way of Alpha Akara. If he has basic information about our commercial traffic to and from Copper Hills, he would have two bearings that would intersect here, in the Sol System."

"He already knew we had dealings with the Copper Hills Akara, so he went there to check it out. Clever of him, very clever, but it doesn't tell us what he's doing here. He no longer has the sentry 'bots, so how do we talk to him?"

"That shouldn't be a problem, Admiral. We learned a lot about their methods of communication during the New Eden encounters."

"Well, then—" Lorna shook her head in resignation, "—I guess we'll have to go out and meet him ourselves, since you're the only one who speaks his language. Advise Commodore McPherson and ask him to screen me at his convenience. I'm not going to take the whole battle group, but we should probably have one or two escorts to keep us company."

* * *

LFS *Omaha Beach*—Lunar Fleet Anchorage

"Damn it, Gunny," Master Sergeant Hillary Brooks complained. "I can't believe none of us managed to outscore the gimpy bitch. I think somebody put the fix in with the range control officer!"

Gunnery Sergeant Hugh Metcalf put his beer down on the bar and turned to regard Brooks with a raised eyebrow.

"Do you, now? Well, I guess that's because you didn't get to fly Tail-End Charlie with Alpha flight, so you didn't get to see the gimpy bitch in action. Fact is, she nailed every target, on every pass, with every weapon type. Whatever was called for—guns, bombs, rockets, missiles—she put 'em all right on the dot. Whoever followed her in ended up with nothing to shoot at except the craters she left behind."

"C'mon, Gunny, every target on every pass? Even the offsets? You're telling me she took out the three offsets in three passes?"

The simplest method of taking out a target with unguided bombs was to head straight for the target and fly directly over it, holding the ship steady, and relying on the computer to release the bombs at exactly the right moment. It was also the easiest way for a pilot to get killed attacking a heavily defended target, since it greatly simplified targeting solutions for the enemy's defenses.

Offset bombing, in which the pilot approached the target in a hard, sweeping turn, veering away as the bombs were released, and never passing directly over the target's defenses, was a safer approach. It was also much harder to hit targets that way, since it depended on the pilot holding a precise turn, something especially difficult to do under airless conditions.

"No, I'm telling you she took out three offsets in one pass—release, release, release, boom, boom, boom."

"Oh, Sweet Jesus, we are so screwed," Brooks moaned. "How the hell do we match that? And how the hell did she get that good? She's only a brown bar LT, and word is, she was just a buck sergeant with a couple of years of Raptor experience, before they sent her to OCS."

"I guess she's a hell of a natural pilot." Metcalf shook his head. "Or maybe Fleet's not telling us something about that special Raptor she's flying. Besides, you don't get the LMH by accident; she must have done something to impress the brass. But I don't think we're as screwed as you think we are."

"How do you figure?"

"I looked at the scores today, and we all did better than we've done in months. Hell, most of the scores we posted weren't bad for any squadron on the ship. And we did it ourselves. All she did was light a fire under our asses."

"Yeah, well, in case you haven't checked, that fire's still burning, and we all have to be in the simulators at 0800. And we still won't be able to rack up scores like she does, so she'll still be on our asses."

"I don't think she ever expects us to beat her. Today was about her proving she can kick our asses and, incidentally, that we damned well ought to respect her for it. We may not ever get that good, but if we keep at it, we just might end up being better than anybody else around here. I don't know about you, but I'm getting tired of being on the bottom of the heap. All in all, I'm kind of feeling good about the whole thing."

* * *

LFS *Valkyrie*—Near the Sol System Hyper Limit

"Lorna Greenwood, I did not expect to again be greeted by the Warrior Queen. You are looking delicious, as usual."

"And there is still a spot reserved for your head on my wall, Lord A'archa," Lorna replied. "How did you find our homeworld, and what do you want?"

"Ah…well, I found you through a bit of logical analysis and more than a bit of luck. In fact, I wasn't sure I had found you until your warships arrived and began locking their weapons onto my ships in a display of typical human hospitality. Fortunately, that identification device you attached to my ship seems to have worked, and they decided not to destroy me after all."

"Actually," she told him, scowling at his image on her screen, "that device told them not to destroy you because I might want to claim that pleasure for myself. I repeat, what do you want?"

"Profit," he replied. "I am a merchant, and I want to trade with you. Why else would I come here, where everyone wants to destroy me and my entire falnor."

"And what makes you think we might want to trade with you? What have you got to offer? The last time we met, you had a ship full of scrap metal that didn't appear to have much value."

"Everything has value, if you can find the right buyer," he insisted. "In your case, I asked myself what might be of interest to you. I thought about that artifact you took from me. Obviously, it had value from an artistic standpoint, but I suspected the material from which it was made had value as well—something that might be used to create similar artifacts. I have therefore brought this with me."

He held up a gleaming bar of metal, and Lorna nodded.

"If that's what I think it is, you may have something worth trading."

"The simplest element in the Universe is the one that fuels the stars," he replied. "I don't know what you call it, but I'm sure you know what I mean. This element has a mass approximately 107 times the mass of that one. With that information, I'm sure even humans can figure it out."

"Silver," Lorna told him. "We call it silver, and yes, it has some value. I assume you brought a large quantity. If not, it will hardly pay for your trip."

"I don't have time to educate you on our system of weights and measures," he told her, "so I will simply show you this."

He touched a control on his console, and his image was replaced by one showing a pair of Otuka, standing in front of a huge stack of silver ingots. A few seconds later, the image was replaced by another view of the stack from the side.

"Val?" Lorna queried.

"I can only give you a general estimate, Admiral, since I don't have an accurate measurement of the Otuka in the foreground. It appears he has on the order of five to seven metric tons. With the current price of silver being approximately three Gold Lunars per kilo—"

"I get the picture." Lorna nodded. A Lunar was currently worth about 300 USD or 450 Euros back on Earth. She turned back to the screen, where A'archa had been waiting patiently for her to finish speaking with Val.

"All right, you have my attention," she told him. "More importantly, you will soon have the attention of our commercial people, who tend to our trade interests. Out of curiosity, what is it you expect to get from us in return?"

"I don't know yet." He shrugged. "I like art objects, but those don't always bring the most profit. I'm sure you clever creatures can come up with something of interest to me."

"A word to the wise," she told him. "When you meet with our traders, don't open the conversation by telling them how delicious they look. I may not be the only one looking for a head to hang on a wall."

* * *

Planet New Eden—Edie Village

Owen Phillips glanced outside as the LFS Marine Firefly whistled over the village, banked sharply, and settled into the field beyond. The light transport craft, which could carry up to twelve passengers or more than a ton of gear, was a new addition to the Marines' equipment on New Eden. Since the departure of the Otuka, the Firefly was better suited to the mission than the much larger Dragonfly, which could transport an entire platoon and its supporting gear.

In addition to military assignments, Fireflies were used to transport scientists and their equipment to field sites, as well as for medevac missions. They also carried volunteer doctors and medical technicians who periodically visited the larger Edie settlements.

Phillips smiled as half a dozen Edie children ran by, laughing and yelling at each other, as they rushed to see the off-world marvel. Normally, he would have followed them down to the field to greet whoever had come, but today, he was too busy. He had just pulled a spearhead from the furnace and laid it on the anvil. Judging its yellow-orange color to be correct, he applied the hammer to forge it into its final shape. Old Aki, sitting outside under an awning, pretended to be busy with his lunch, but Phillips knew the master was watching his apprentice with a critical eye.

Phillips wasn't nervous. He had made several spearheads and was getting good at it. They were nowhere near as difficult to make as axe blades that had to fit around a hefty wooden handle. He worked the edges carefully, tapering them down, but leaving enough metal to be ground in the sharpening process. Finally, satisfied with the results, he plunged the spearhead into a bucket of water to quench and harden the metal. Aki rose from his chair and came over to observe the results.

"Good," he pronounced. "Now, put away the tools, O-wen. I think you have Sky People business to do." He gestured toward the path leading up from the field, where a man—obviously an off-worlder by his clothing—was walking toward them, surrounded by curious children. Phillips recognized the newcomer immediately and hastily stowed his tools, then took off his heavy gloves and apron.

"Vito!" Phillips greeted the newcomer with a smile. "Good to see you again! What brings you all the way out here?"

"You're looking well, Owen," Dr. Vito Pagliani responded. "I dare say you've put on some weight, mostly muscle from the look of it. I guess swinging that hammer all day long is good exercise."

"I don't think swinging the hammer has as much to do with it as the lifting and carrying." Phillips grinned at him. "I hadn't realized it, but everything connected with blacksmithing is heavy. You're looking well; looks like you've slimmed down quite a bit."

"Field work is good for the body and soul," Pagliani replied. "I've managed to drop about 30 kilos. Good thing I found some

Marines who know tailoring, otherwise I'd look like I was wearing a tent. New clothing is hard to come by out here, unless I want to go native, like you have."

"Hey—" Phillips' smile got wider as he stepped back and spread his arms to show off his outfit, "—this stuff is comfortable. These people know how to tan animal hides. You'd be hard-pressed to find suede softer than this back on Earth."

"They may soon have other materials available," Pagliani told him. "Carlson and her team have found a native plant that resembles cotton. Edie tribes in the south have gathered it in the past to make fabric in limited quantities, but Carlson thinks it can be cultivated. That brings me to the reason I came out here. We've received word back from Dr. Warren on Luna."

"Good news, I hope." Phillips led Pagliani to the door of his yurt. "Angel," he called, "we have a visitor."

"Doc-tor Vito!" Angel gave Pagliani a glowing smile. "Please, come in, sit down. I bring drinks for you and O-wen."

She busied herself making tea for them. Pagliani looked at Phillips with a smile.

"When is the big event?"

"She's not due for two more months," Phillips said. "The doctor should be coming by in a week or so, and I'll make sure she gets checked, but she keeps reminding me that pregnancy is a natural condition, not an illness. I'm not even allowed to suggest she slow down and take it easy."

"She's amazing—" Pagliani shook his head, "—and I'm happy for the two of you. But on to the big news. Dr. Warren says we got everything we wanted from Lunar Command and the Directorate.

"The bad news, in a manner of speaking, is that you and I have both been appointed to the New Eden Commission, of which she is now the head. That means we'll have a lot to say about the future of this planet and its people. I don't know about you, but I'm feeling the weight on my shoulders."

"It's a heavy responsibility," Phillips agreed, "but no one has more of a stake in the outcome than I have. This is my home now, and the Edies are my people. My children will be born here, and it's their interests I'll be looking out for."

"I envy you, Owen." Pagliani nodded. "Me, I've got enough to keep me busy for at least a year—this planet's geology is truly fascinating—but eventually, I'll go home to Luna, hopefully to bask in well-earned admiration for my research. But you are home, and you still get to do your research…which reminds me, I've got something for you."

He unslung the shoulder bag he had been carrying and dug through its contents, producing a fat stack of printed material.

"Here are the last six issues of the Journal of Anthropology, including the article you sent back with Mercedes. It got a lot of notice and rave reviews. Of course, they don't produce paper copies of most such publications anymore, but she had them printed out on Luna for you. Likewise, here are printed copies of some books you ordered on metallurgy, forging, and general metalworking. It appears that blacksmithing—as a hobby, at least—is alive and well back on Earth."

"Thanks." Phillips accepted the stack of publications. "I hope to find something in those books that will be useful to the Edies. Old Aki knows a lot about the subject, but maybe there's an Earth technique or process that hasn't been discovered here yet. Besides, Aki has taught me a lot about how to do things, but these will help me understand why they're done the way they are.

"You know," he mused, "it's not just that I get to do my research here. I'm living my research. Not many scientists can say that. So yes, I'm content to stay here for the rest of my life. There may be thousands of other worlds out there, but I'll leave them for you, Mercedes, and others to explore. And who knows, if we do our job here well, maybe someday, my grandchildren will be out among the stars."

* * * * *

Epilogue

TerraNova City, Luna

"Off chasing stars again, are you?" Lorna raised an eyebrow in her daughter's direction.

"Only one very special star," Carla assured her. "I wouldn't be running off on short notice if we'd gotten the *Copernicus* data earlier. The expedition's been gone for nearly two years, but now they've returned and dumped the opportunity of a lifetime in our laps. It's something we'll probably only get a chance to do once every few centuries. Even then, it will most likely involve a much longer trip."

"Longer?" Lorna was skeptical. "Seventy-four light-years isn't exactly a walk through TerraNova Park. It's also a long way to go without an escort."

"Really, Mom, the star's far from Otuka territory, on the other side of Akara space. *Copernicus* found no evidence of alien races anywhere in the area. Besides, research ships are not totally defenseless. We proved that fifteen years ago, with *Lisa Randall* at New Eden."

"Which brings up another point," Lorna replied. "You've taken *Randall* on every expedition to date. She's been the lead ship for astrophysics research. Why the switch?"

"She's out of service for a major refit and systems upgrade, and we absolutely can't wait. This star's on its deathbed, and we need to get there in time to see it die. We have to be there in less than five weeks, and *Lisa* will be in the yards longer than that. *Galileo*'s just been through that upgrade and has the tools we need for the job."

"Jennifer Tanaka's going to be disappointed," Lorna told her. "This was her last chance to go out with you. She's too senior to remain in command of *Randall*, and I'm planning to give her the next heavy cruiser command that comes available. *Lisa* will have a new captain by the time you get back."

"I know." Carla sighed. "But things change. Jennifer and I have worked well together, but she deserves to move up."

"Must you take Bjorn with you again? I enjoy babysitting occasionally, but not for several months at a time. I'm not due to retire for another year, and there's no place for a six-year-old aboard a battlecruiser. I'll get down to Luna when I can, but she's going to be spending a lot of time with my stewards here, in TerraNova."

"As far as she's concerned, Hector and Christie aren't your stewards, they're family," Carla said. "As for Bjorn, this is a big deal for the particle physicists. He's doesn't want to leave our daughter behind, but he's a scientist, too.

"Look, I wouldn't dump her on you like this if we had a choice, but it's not like I'm abandoning her on your doorstep. We'll be back in three months."

"OK, you're a good mother," Lorna admitted. "Probably better than I was for you. All things considered, I've only found two reasons to fault you as a parent. First, you waited too long to have her—I expected to have at least four or five grandchildren by now, not just one. Second, you exercised terrible judgment when you named her. I mean, seriously, does the Universe need another Lorna Greenwood?"

"Hey, men do it all the time." Carla chuckled. "They name their sons after themselves, that is. They even have a special title for it—junior—so why can't women do the same thing? At least I skipped a generation, so technically she's not 'junior', she's just Lorna Greenwood the Second. Maybe she'll name her daughter 'Carla,' and we can start a family tradition."

"Oh, please." Lorna rolled her eyes.

"Besides," Carla went on, "with that blond hair, she actually looks more like you than I do. Maybe, someday, they'll be calling her the Babe on the Horse."

"Stop! You win! Go off and chase your star and leave me with my granddaughter, so I can tell her about the terrible burden you've placed on her. Just don't be surprised if she won't speak to you when you get back."

"I love you too, Mom," Carla replied, with a grin. "Take care of her while we're gone."

# # # # #

About John E. Siers

John E. Siers is a Viet Nam–era Air Force veteran who spent several decades working as a software developer, designing analytical systems for corporate clients.

An avid reader of science fiction since grade school, John started writing in the late 1970s, mostly for his own enjoyment. He wrote for more than 20 years and produced three complete novels before ever showing his work to anyone.

Escaping from the overcrowded northeast, John moved to Tennessee in 1997. Encouraged by friends, he finally published his first novel, The Moon and Beyond, in late 2012, followed by Someday the Stars in 2013. The latter won the 2014 Darrell Award for Best SF Novel by a Midsouth Author.

John's Lunar Free State series had grown to four novels—with no thought of doing anything outside his own comfort zone—when he encountered William Alan Webb at MidSouthCon in 2019. Bill led John astray, tempting him with visions of other universes, whispering names like Four Horsemen, Last Brigade, and finally, Hit World.

John succumbed to the temptation, and The Ferryman and The Dragons of Styx are the results. He has since entered a rehab program and produced a fifth novel in his own universe.

John lives with his wife, son, dog, and two cats in west Tennessee. In his spare time (what there is of it) he runs his own firearm repair and service business under the trade name of Gunsmith Jack. Readers can follow him on Amazon, Facebook, or his own website at www.lunarfreestate.com.

*****

Meet the author and other CKP authors on the Factory Floor:

https://www.facebook.com/groups/461794864654198

*****

Did you like this book?
Please write a review!

*****

The following is an

Excerpt from Book One of Abner Fortis, ISMC:

Cherry Drop

P.A. Piatt

Available from Theogony Books

eBook and Paperback

Excerpt from "Cherry Drop:"

"Here they come!"

A low, throbbing buzz rose from the trees and the undergrowth shook. Thousands of bugs exploded out of the jungle, and Fortis' breath caught in his throat. The insects tumbled over each other in a rolling, skittering mass that engulfed everything in its path.

The Space Marines didn't need an order to open fire. Rifles cracked and the grenade launcher thumped over and over as they tried to stem the tide of bugs. Grenades tore holes in the ranks of the bugs and well-aimed rifle fire dropped many more. Still, the bugs advanced.

Hawkins' voice boomed in Fortis' ear. "LT, fall back behind the fighting position, clear the way for the heavy weapons."

Fortis looked over his shoulder and saw the fighting holes bristling with Marines who couldn't fire for fear of hitting their own comrades. He thumped Thorsen on the shoulder.

"Fall back!" he ordered. "Take up positions behind the fighting holes."

Thorsen stopped firing and moved among the other Marines, relaying Fortis' order. One by one, the Marines stopped firing and made for the rear. As the gunfire slacked off, the bugs closed ranks and continued forward.

After the last Marine had fallen back, Fortis motioned to Thorsen.

"Let's go!"

Thorsen turned and let out a blood-chilling scream. A bug had approached unnoticed and buried its stinger deep in Thorsen's calf. The stricken Marine fell to the ground and began to convulse as the neurotoxin entered his bloodstream.

"Holy shit!" Fortis drew his kukri, ran over, and chopped at the insect stinger. The injured bug made a high-pitched shrieking noise, which Fortis cut short with another stroke of his knife.

Viscous, black goo oozed from the hole in Thorsen's armor and his convulsions ceased.

"*Get the hell out of there!*"

Hawkins was shouting in his ear, and Abner looked up. The line of bugs was ten meters away. For a split second he almost turned and ran, but the urge vanished as quickly as it appeared. He grabbed Thorsen under the arms and dragged the injured Marine along with him, pursued by the inexorable tide of gaping pincers and dripping stingers.

Fortis pulled Thorsen as fast as he could, straining with all his might against the substantial Pada-Pada gravity. Thorsen convulsed and slipped from Abner's grip and the young officer fell backward. When he sat up, he saw the bugs were almost on them.

*****

Get "Cherry Drop" now at:
https://www.amazon.com/dp/B09B14VBK2

Find out more about P.A. Piatt at:
https://chriskennedypublishing.com

*****

The following is an

Excerpt from Book One of Murphy's Lawless:

Shakes

Mike Massa

Available from Beyond Terra Press

eBook and Paperback

Excerpt from "Shakes:"

"My name is Volo of the House Zobulakos," the SpinDog announced haughtily. Harry watched as his slender ally found his feet and made a show of brushing imaginary dust from his shoulder where the lance had rested.

Volo was defiant even in the face of drawn weapons; Harry had to give him points for style.

"I am here representing the esteemed friend to all Sarmatchani, my father, Arko Primus Heraklis Zobulakos. This is a mission of great importance. What honorless prole names my brother a liar and interferes with the will of the Primus? Tell me, that I might inform your chief of this insolence."

Harry tensed as two of the newcomers surged forward in angry reaction to the word "honorless," but the tall man interposed his lance, barring their way.

"Father!" the shorter one objected, throwing back her hood, revealing a sharp featured young woman. She'd drawn her blade and balefully eyed the SpinDog. "Let me teach this arrogant weakling about honor!"

"Nay, Stella," the broad-shouldered man said grimly. "Even my daughter must cleave to the law. This is a clan matter. And as to the stripling's question…

"I, hight Yannis al-Caoimhip ex-huscarlo, Patrisero of the Herdbane, First among the Sarmatchani," he went on, fixing his eyes first on Volo and then each of the Terrans. "I name Stabilo of the Sky People a liar, a cheat, and a coward. I call his people to account. Blood or treasure. At dawn tomorrow either will suffice."

Harry didn't say a word but heard a deep sigh from Rodriguez. These were the allies he'd been sent to find, all right. Just like every other joint operation with indigs, it was SNAFU.

Murphy's Law was in still in effect.

* * * * *

Get "Shakes" now at: https://www.amazon.com/dp/B0861F23KH

Find out more about Myrphy's Lawless and Beyond Terra Press at: https://chriskennedypublishing.com/imprints-authors/beyond-terra-press/

* * * * *

Made in United States
North Haven, CT
28 September 2023

42100117R10233